AF147348

Wives And Widows
Or, The Broken Life

by

Ann S. Stephens

Double 9
BOOKS

Wives And Widows
Or, The Broken Life
by Ann S. Stephens

Copyright © 2024

All Rights reserved.

No part of this publication may be reproduced,
stored in a retrieval system, or transmitted in any
form or by any means, electronic, mechanical,
photocopying or Otherwise, without the written
permission of the publisher.
The author/editor asserts the moral right to
be identified as the author/editor of this work.

ISBN: 978-93-64284-75-2

Published by

DOUBLE 9 BOOKS

2/13-B, Ansari Road
Daryaganj, New Delhi – 110002
info@double9books.com
www.double9books.com
Tel. 011-40042856

This book is under public domain

ABOUT THE AUTHOR

Ann Sophia Stephens (1810-1886) was an American novelist and magazine editor who is credited as the progenitor of the dime novel genre. She began her writing career in Portland, Maine, where she co-founded and edited the Portland Magazine. Later, in New York, she served as the editor of The Ladies Companion and adopted the pseudonym Jonathan Slick. Stephens wrote over twenty-five serial novels, along with short stories and poems for well-known periodicals. Her novel "Malaeska, the Indian Wife of the White Hunter" is considered the first dime novel and was highly influential. Stephens also published her own magazine, Mrs Stephens' Illustrated New Monthly. Her works include "High Life in New York," "The Old Homestead," and "A Noble Woman."

CONTENTS

CHAPTER I
LEAVING MY HOME

At ten years of age I was the unconscious mistress of a heavy stone farm-house and extensive lands in the interior of Pennsylvania, with railroad-bonds and bank-stock enough to secure me a moderate independence. I shall never, never forget the loneliness of that old house the day my mother was carried out of it and laid down by her husband in the churchyard behind the village. The most intense suffering of life often comes in childhood. My mother was dead; I could almost feel her last cold kisses on my lip as I sat down in that desolate parlor, waiting for the guardian who was expected to take me from my dear old home to his. The window opened into a field of white clover, where some cows and lambs were pasturing drowsily, as I had seen them a hundred times; but now their very tranquillity grieved me. It seemed strange that they would stand there so content, with the white clover dropping from their mouths, and I going away forever. My mother's canary-bird, which hung in the window, began to sing joyously over my head, as if no funeral had passed from that room, leaving its shadows behind, and, more grievous still, as if it did not care that I might never sit and listen to it again.

One of the neighbors had kindly volunteered to take charge of the gloomy old house till my guardian came, but her presence disturbed me more than funeral stillness would have done. I had a family of dolls up stairs, and any amount of tiny household furniture, which I would have given the world to take with me; but this thrifty neighbor protested against it. She said that I was almost a young lady and must forget such childish things, now that I was going into the world to be properly educated.

To a shy, sensitive child, this was enough. So, with a double sense of bereavement, I saw my pretty dolls and delicate toys swept into a basket and carried off to the woman's house, between two stout Irish girls, who seemed to be taking my heart off with them.

In less than half an hour one of this woman's children came down the road with my prettiest doll under her arm. Its flaxen curls were all disordered, and its tiny feet, with their slippers of rose-colored kid, had evidently been in the mud, where she had probably insisted on making the doll walk. While I sat by the window, waiting and watching, this bare-headed little girl sat down by a fragment of stone that had fallen from the wall close by, and began pounding the head of my doll upon it with all her might. A cry broke from me that made the little wretch start and run away, leaving my poor mutilated doll by the stone.

I ran out, seized upon my ruined doll, and came back to the house, crying over it in bitter grief. With trembling hands I unlocked my trunk, which was ready packed for travelling, and laid my broken treasure down among the most precious of my belongings. Just then Mrs. Pierce, our neighbor, came in, and in a half jeering, half kind way, expostulated with me for being such a little goose as to cry over a doll. This woman did not mean to be hard with me; far from it. Persons exist who are really kind-hearted, and seem cruel only because they cannot comprehend feelings utterly unknown to themselves. To me that doll was a type of my wrecked home; to her it was a combination of wax, sawdust, and leather, which a few dollars could at any time replace; besides that, she was put a little on the defensive by the fault of her child.

While she reasoned with me in her coarse kindness, which only wounded me deeper, a carriage had driven up, and two persons entered through the outer door, which had been left open by the little girl when she ran into the house to claim her mother's protection. I was sitting on the floor by my trunk, with both hands pressed to my face, sobbing piteously, when a sweet, strange voice checked the force of that woman's harangue; some one sank down to the floor by me, and I was all at once drawn into a close embrace.

"Don't cry, dear; it is all very sad, no doubt, but you are going with us, and to-morrow will be brighter."

I looked through a mist of tears that half blinded me, and saw the kindest, sweetest face that my eyes ever dwelt upon. It was that of a young woman, perhaps twenty or twenty-two years of age. "You must not feel yourself alone, dear child," she said, smoothing my hair with one hand, from which she had drawn off the glove.

"Oh," said Mrs. Pierce, pushing her daughter behind her, "you will never believe, marm, what she is crying about,—leaving home, you think it is? Oh, no; Miss is just taking on about a snip of a doll which my little girl here smashed a trifle, not meaning any harm, for children will be children, you know."

Here Mrs. Pierce patted her child's head, who cast sidelong glances at me and attempted to hide herself behind her mother's dress.

I looked up at the young lady, blushing red, and begging her in my heart not to think me so very ridiculous.

She smiled encouragingly, and turning upon Mrs. Pierce, said, very gravely,—

"I am surprised, madam, that you should think this a slight cause of grief. The smallest thing connected with the child's home must be dear to her."

Mrs. Pierce gave her head a fling, and muttered that she meant no harm. Miss was welcome to all her things back again; her children did not want them, not they.

"You are right," said the young lady, quite seriously; "have everything she has owned or loved packed up at once."

Mrs. Pierce went out muttering; the child followed her with a finger in her mouth.

"Now," said the young lady, "is there anything else you would like to take away,—a bird, a little dog, or the cat you have loved; we can find room for them?"

My heart leaped. I had the dear old canary-bird; and lying upon the crimson cushions of my mother's easy-chair was "Fanny," a pretty chestnut-colored dog, that had all the grace of an Italian greyhound, and the brightness of a terrier.

"May I take her with me?" I cried, springing up and falling on my knees before my mother's arm-chair, and hugging Fanny to my bosom. "I am so glad, so grateful, so—"

Here I broke down, and burying my face in Fanny's fur, cried and laughed out my thankfulness. When I looked up, one of the handsomest men I ever saw stood by the young lady, who was smiling upon him, though I saw bright tears in her eyes.

"So this is your father's ward," said the gentleman, reaching out his hand as if he had known me all his life.

I put my hand in his, and felt my heart grow warm, as if it had found shelter from its loneliness. He exchanged glances with the lady, and I felt sure that they were pleased with me.

"Now," said the gentleman, "we have a little time, if you want to take leave of anything."

"Oh, I have been taking leave ever since she died," I answered, saddened by his words. "I couldn't do it again."

"Perhaps that is best," said the gentleman; "so get on your things; we have a long ride before us."

I started to obey him, but all at once a doubt seized upon me. Who were these people? I did not know them. Mr. Olmsly, my guardian, I had been informed, was an old man. What right had these people to take me away from my home?

I stole back to the gentleman, trembling, and filled with sudden apprehension.

"Please tell me who you are," I said; "Mr. Olmsly! I thought he was an old man."

"And so he is," answered the gentleman, smiling pleasantly, "but he is not very well, and so his daughter came after you in his place. This is Miss Olmsly."

The young lady stooped down and kissed me. My arms stole around her neck unawares, and from that moment I loved her dearly. When I turned away from the young lady's caresses, her companion said,—

"Now you would like to know who I am; isn't that so?"

I nodded my head, feeling that I could tell at once who he was.

"Her brother, I am sure of that, you are both so—so—pleasant."

I was about to say "handsome," but changed it to the less flattering word.

They both laughed, and the gentleman glanced at Miss Olmsly's face, which, I was surprised to see, turned red as a wild rose.

"No, I am not her brother," he said, flushing up himself; "but I shall be a great deal at your guardian's, and I shall think that you are almost my sister. Will you like that?"

"So much!" I replied, with a light heart, for all my anxieties were put to rest. "Now I will get my things."

I went up-stairs and entered my own little room for the last time. How homelike and familiar everything looked: the little bed in the corner, with its draperies of white net; the muslin window-curtains, through which I could see great clusters of old-fashioned white roses, still wet with morning dew, and lying like snow among the vivid green of the thick leaves; my little walnut-wood desk, where I had got my first lessons,—all appealed to me with a force that swept away the dawning cheerfulness which the conversation down-stairs had inspired. I sat down by the window and looked sadly out. The sash was open, and a sweet fragrance came up from the white clover-field, mingling with that of the great rose-bush, which had reached the second-story windows, ever since I could remember. I could not bear to leave all these things. Yet the house had been so lonely that I had no clear wish to stay. To me there was something terrible in leaving that safe home-shelter. I grew cold, and began to cry again. Afar off I could see the graveyard where my mother was lying. Her presence was close to me then. How could I go away and leave her resting there within sight of the old house? But she had herself arranged that I should live with my guardian. Why should these bitter regrets depress me, while obeying her? It was that strong home feeling which has never left me during my life,—the feeling which prompted me to gather a handful of those white roses, and keep them till they crumbled into nothing but the ashes of a flower. Oh, how my heart ached when we drove away from that old stone house! the picture is even yet burned in on my brain. That tall hickory-tree at one end—the willow in front. Those fine old lilac-bushes, and the clustering roses reaching luxuriantly to the upper windows, in the full rich blossoming of early June. Many a time since, when in sadness and sorrow this picture has come back to my mind, I have wondered if it might not have been better had I stayed in that quiet old home.

CHAPTER II
MY NEW HOME

Mr. Olmsly was a very wealthy man. His property stretched far into an iron and coal district of Pennsylvania, and every day increased its value. It lay in and around a fine inland town, situated among some of the most picturesque scenery to be found in the State. His residence was about five miles from this town, and a most beautiful spot it was. The house was built on the last spur of a range of hills, which ran for some distance down the valley of the Delaware. Around this tall ridge the noble river made a bold sweep, turned an old stone mill on its outer curve, and went careering down one of the richest and most beautiful valleys that the eye ever dwelt upon. The whole of this mountain spur, the mill and the land down to the river, which swept around it like an ox-bow, was the property of Mr. Olmsly. His house of heavy stone was built half-way up the side of the ridge, in the form of the letter T, which ran lengthwise along the face of the hill, presenting a pointed roof, and one sharp gable in the front view. The walls were stuccoed like many houses to be found in European countries, and were settled back on the hill by three curving terraces, two of them blooming with rare flowers. These terraces cut the hill as with a girdle of blossoms about half-way up from its base. The first was a carriage-road, which was connected with the house by a long flight of steps leading across the first flower-terrace to the front door.

In front, the house was three stories high. The basement story opened on the first broad terrace, with its wreathing vines, and glowing blossoms. An oriel window curved out from the gable, and a square balcony surrounded by an arabesque railing, formed a pleasant lounging-place over the front entrance. At the back of the house the entrance was from the third terrace, directly to the second story, which was half occupied by a broad hall, ending in the square balcony; a noble drawing-room, whose latticed windows opened on every side save the front, from which the oriel jutted, opened upon a platform some ten feet wide, which formed a promenade around one end of the second story, and along the back of the building, surrounded by a low balustrade, to which a hundred rare plants and vines were clinging; beyond this was a labyrinth of flower-beds, through which a broad gravel-path wound gracefully, separating the green turf of the hill-side from the third and last terrace, which was most beautiful of all.

These terraces threw broad belts of flowers half across the face of the hill, and ended in pleasant footpaths which led through the turf and under some sheltering trees to the top of the ridge. There everything was wild as nature left to herself can be. At noonday the sunshine was darkened by the woven branches of pines, hemlocks, beech, and oak trees, with a tangle of blossoming laurel among the dusky undergrowth. From this eminence, you commanded a glorious sight of two magnificent valleys, — one stretching off toward the Blue Ridge and overlooking the town, the other opening in rich luxuriance down the banks of the Delaware, mile after mile, league after league, till villages in the distance seemed scarcely more than a handful of snow-flakes.

Half-way down you saw the house I have been describing, the carriage-road that wound beneath it, and below that, the hill sloping downward in a broad, rolling lawn, which lost itself with gentle undulations in the green bosom of the valley.

This was the home to which I was brought, and this beautiful view lay before me as I stood upon the terrace-steps, wondering that the earth could be so lovely. Miss Olmsly paused by my side, enjoying my surprise.

"You like it," she said; "we shall be very happy here, for I know how it will be with my father when he sees your demure little face."

"Happy," I said, looking at the flowers which bloomed around me everywhere. "I did not know that there was any place in the world so lovely as this."

"I am glad you are pleased, young lady."

I started, turned toward the speaker, and saw a fine old gentleman, with soft brown eyes, and hair as white as snow, standing on the step above me.

"It is my father, dear," said Miss Olmsly, mounting a step higher and offering the old man a kiss; "she is a dear, good child, papa, and we love her already."

"I am glad of that," he said, stooping down and kissing me on the forehead. "Your father was my friend, child, and I will be yours. Come into the house; you must be tired and hungry."

We entered the house which was henceforth to be my home. Miss Olmsly took me directly to a pretty chamber, that had been evidently prepared for my coming. Everything was simple, neat, and pure as snow. As if they had known how I loved flowers, they were placed in the deep window-seats, on the white marble of the mantelpiece, and the principal window opened on the loveliest portion of the third terrace, where a world of flowers were in bloom from May till November.

There I hung up the bird-cage which I had brought from home in the carriage, and the little inmate began to sing joyously, as if he understood all the beauties of our new home and rejoiced over them.

Fanny, too, put her paws on the window-seat, and looked out demurely, as if taking a survey of the landscape. She dropped down with what seemed a little bark of approval, and curling herself up on my travelling-shawl, which had dropped to the floor, watched me as I unlocked my trunk and prepared for dinner.

Miss Olmsly was right. I had a demure little face, but it looked upon me from the glass less sorrowfully than I had seen it since my mother's death. The sombre blackness of my dress threw it all into shadow and made the deep blue-gray of my eyes darker, by far, than was natural. This, contrasting with the slightness of my form, made me look like a little woman who had known suffering, rather than the sensitive child that I really was.

The dinner filled me with awe; the bright silver, the cut-glass, and delicate china impressed me greatly, and I was half afraid to tell the waiter what I wanted, he seemed so great a gentleman. Everybody was kind, the conversation was bright and cheerful; I understood it all, and felt myself brightening under it. Once or twice I caught myself laughing at the pleasant things the old gentleman was saying.

After dinner, when Mr. Olmsly was asleep in his great easy-chair, Mr. Lee and Miss Olmsly went out on the platform, lifted a little from the third terrace, and walked up and down, now and then looking in through one of the open French windows, and saying a kind word to me. I remember thinking what a splendid couple they were, and how happy they seemed to be in each other's company. No wonder; she was a lovely creature, slender, graceful, and caressing in all her ways, while he was like a demigod to my imagination, grand as a monarch, and good as he was kingly. Even then, young as I was, the smile with which he occasionally bent to her, made my heart yearn with a strange desire that I, too, might be so smiled upon.

Still, I was neither lonely nor home-sick, for my whole heart had gone out toward those young people, and I had begun to connect the old gentleman lovingly with my own father, whose face and kind ways I could just remember.

After a while I stole up to my own room again, unpacked my trunk, hung up my mourning dresses, and lingered regretfully over my doll a few moments, ashamed of having loved it so; for the sneers of Mrs. Pierce had made a deep impression on me, and I began to feel that I ought to be something more than a child. Still I could not put the poor, broken thing entirely away, but a sight of it always gave me a heart-ache. It is a terrible thing when one's childhood is broken up with harsh words and coarse jeers.

Where refinement is, illusions remain beautiful far beyond childhood. They belong to innocence, and seldom dwell long with the worldly and the bad.

Mrs. Pierce had swept away one joy from my life, but a beautiful compensation had been sent me in my new home and my new friends. It all seemed like paradise to me when I went to bed that night.

CHAPTER III
A NEW LIFE

The next morning, Miss Olmsly came into my room and helped me arrange my little mementos in a homelike fashion. My work-box was brought forth and placed on the little table provided for it. My pretty writing-desk was unlocked and placed convenient for use. Brackets were ready for the ornaments that had been so dear that I could not leave them behind. From that hour, this room became in fact my home; the old stone farm-house receded into the shadows of the past. I thought of it sometimes sadly, as I thought of the graves where my parents lay. The sight of an old-fashioned damask-rose has still power to bring tears into my eyes, and my heart would thrill if I passed a white clover-patch, years and years after that I left at home had been ploughed out of existence. But after all, the brightest sunshine of my life fell through the latticed windows of my room on the Ridge.

No humming-bird ever loved flowers as I did;—no artist ever gave himself up to the enjoyment of a fine landscape more completely than it was in my nature to do. I have no doubt that the beauty that surrounded me was one great cause of the tranquil happiness which settled upon my whole being as I became accustomed to the place. I loved to spend whole mornings alone on the Ridge, collecting mosses and searching for birds'-nests, which were abundant in the pines and the drooping hemlock boughs. Among Miss Olmsly's old school-books I found one that gave me an elementary knowledge of botany; I did not consider it a dry study, but loved to sit upon a rock carpeted with moss, and look into the fragrant hearts of the wild-flowers, searching out their sweet secrets with a feeling of profound sympathy in their loveliness and in the races to which they belonged. Child as I was, these things satisfied me, and I wanted no other companionship.

Mr. Olmsly's land covered extensive woods beside those on the Ridge. There was nothing likely to harm me anywhere in the grounds, and I was allowed to run wild out of doors wherever I pleased. Thus I made acquaintance with many things beside the flowers; gray squirrels and pretty striped chipmunks, with bushy tails curled over their backs, would sit upon the tree-boughs just over my head and look at me with shy friendliness.

Now and then, I saw a rabbit peeping at me through the ferns. These pretty creatures were not afraid, for no sportsman was ever allowed to bring his gun into those woods, and I think they knew how far I was from wishing to harm them.

My mother had been a timid woman, and her love for me always rendered her unduly careful. She had a terror of allowing me out of her sight, and being feeble herself, kept me mostly indoors, where I had learned to content myself in a passionate love of my dolls, that really seemed to me like living creatures capable of loving me as I worshipped them.

But at the Ridge I really did enjoy living companionship. Nature lay all before me, wild as the first creation; or so blended with art that its richest beauties were enhanced threefold. There was also vitality and intelligence in these living creatures that stirred my heart with a strange sympathy.

My dog Fanny sometimes troubled me a little: she would insist upon routing the ground-birds from their nests, and in an effort to become friendly with the rabbits, would send them scampering wildly into the underbrush. I loved Fanny dearly, but it was not pleasant to see my pets driven off by her frolicsome way of making herself agreeable.

One day I had gone farther than usual into the woods, and come out upon the outer verge of Mr. Olmsly's estate. Here the trees grew thin and scattered off into a pasture, where a flock of sheep was grazing; beyond that, some fine meadow sloped down toward the valley, cut in two by the highway, on which a large stone house was visible through the trees growing thickly around it.

A flat rock, half in sunshine, half in shadow, lay hidden in the grass close by the footpath I had been pursuing, and I sat down upon it, somewhat tired from my long walk in the woods. Fanny was with me and sprang with a leap to my side, but kept moving restlessly about, as if she did not quite like the position, or saw something that displeased her.

I had gathered some spotted leaves of the adder's-tongue, with a few of its golden flowers, and had found some lovely specimens of cup-moss on an old stump, which nature was embellishing like a fairy palace, and sat admiring them in the pleasant sunshine, when Fanny gave a sudden yelp, and bounded from the rock, barking furiously.

I dropped the flowers into my lap, half frightened by her sudden outburst; but as she continued wheeling around the rock, darting off and back again, yelping like a fury, I ordered her to be quiet, and fell to arranging my treasures once more.

All at once Fanny ceased barking, but crept close to me, seized upon my dress with her teeth and began to pull backward, almost tearing the fabric. Just then I heard a rustling sound on the rock behind me; forcing my dress from the dog's teeth, I sprang up, and saw quivering upon the moss what seemed to be a dusky shimmer of jewels all in motion. In an instant the glitter left my eyes. I felt myself turning into marble. There, coiled up ready for a spring, its head flattened, its eyes glittering venomously, was a checkered adder preparing to lance out upon me.

I could not move, I could not scream; my strained eyes refused to turn from the reptile, who, quivering with its own poison, seemed to draw me toward him. For my life I could not have moved; my lips seemed frozen, — a fearful fascination possessed me utterly. It was broken by the rush of a fragment of rock, under which I saw the reptile writhing fiercely. Then my faculties were unchained, and a shriek broke from my cold lips. I sprang from the rock and was running madly away, when Mr. Lee caught me in his arms, and I shuddered into insensibility there.

When I came to, the crushed adder lay dead upon the rock, from a crevice of which he had crept forth upon me. Fanny was barking furiously around it, and Mr. Lee had carried me to a spring close by, where he was bathing my face with water.

I looked around in terror. "Is it gone? is it dead?" I questioned, shuddering.

He pointed out the adder, which hung supine and dead over the edge of the rock, and attempted to soothe my fears, but I trembled still, and could hardly force myself to take a second look at my dead foe.

How kind Mr. Lee was then; how tenderly he compassionated my terror, and assured me of safety. Fanny, too, forgot her rage, and came leaping around me. Oh, how grateful I was to that man. My heart yearned to say all it felt, but found no language. I could only lift my eyes to him now and then in dumb thankfulness, wondering if he cared that I was so grateful, or dreamed how much a girl of my years could feel.

How foolish all these thoughts were; of course, he only thought of me as a frightened child. From that day I never knelt to God, morning or evening, without asking some blessing on the head of Mr. Lee. Gratitude had deepened my reverence for that man into such worship as only a sensitive child can feel. Yes, worship is the word, for this young man in the grandeur of his fine person, gentle manners, and superior age, seemed as far above me as the clouds of heaven are above the daisies in a meadow. Even now I cannot comprehend the feelings with which I regarded him.

Have I said that Mr. Lee was a partner in the Olmsly Iron Works, and though he boarded in town, half his time was of necessity spent at the Ridge? My guardian only attended to business through him, and expected a report at least twice a week.

Many and many a time, when I knew that he was coming, have I wandered down the carriage-road to the grove where it curved off from the highway, and was closed into our private ground by a gate. There, sheltered by the spruce-trees and hidden by the laurel-bushes, I have waited hours, listening for the tread of his horse, and feeling supremely rewarded by a brief glimpse of his manly figure, as it dashed up the road, unconscious alike of my presence and my worship.

I never mentioned these feelings, or all the secret sources of happiness to which my soul awoke, not even to Miss Olmsly. I would have died rather than breathe them to any human being; they were sacred to me as my prayers. Sometimes I would be days together without speaking to Mr. Lee, but I was seldom out of the sound of his voice when he visited the Ridge, and would follow him and Miss Olmsly like a pet dog about the garden, glad to see her brighten and smile when he looked upon her, and loving them both with my whole heart.

Sometimes other company came from the town. We frequently drove over there and brought Mr. Lee home with us; indeed, he was one of the family in every respect, save that he did not sleep at the Ridge, and called himself a visitor. One thing is very certain—on the days he did not come Miss Olmsly was sure to grow serious, almost sad; only there never was any real sadness at our house in those days.

CHAPTER IV
THREATENED WITH SEPARATION

This beautiful life must have an end. Even childhood has its duties, and mine could no longer be evaded.

One day Miss Olmsly came into my room, and looking around, sighed; but there was a smile on her lip and an expression in her face that made me wonder at the sigh; for I had not learned that superabundant joy has sometimes the same expression as grief; but oh, how different the feeling.

She sat down by the window, and drawing me close to her, kissed my forehead two or three times with so much feeling that I began to tremble.

"Is anything the matter?" I said, winding my arms around her neck; "have I done wrong?"

"Wrong, my sweet child, no; who ever accused you of being anything but the best girl in the world? I was only thinking how lonesome you would be without us."

"Without you?" I faltered,—"without you?"

I felt myself growing pale, my arms fell away from that white neck, and I looked piteously in her kind face, afraid to ask the meaning of these words.

"Don't look so frightened, dear," said Miss Olmsly, drawing me fondly to her side. "Even if we were not going, you must have been sent to school. No young lady can get along without education, you know; still, I shall feel very anxious about you."

"Are you going away; am I to be left?"

I could ask no more; the very idea of parting with them choked me.

Miss Olmsly drew my face to hers as if she wanted to keep me from looking at her so earnestly. My cheek was wet with tears, but hers was red as it touched mine, and I could feel that it was burning.

"I am about to tell you something that I hope you will be glad to hear, darling," she said, almost in a whisper. "In two weeks Mr. Lee and I are going to be married. Why, how you shiver, child! I should have told you of this first; the very thought of a school terrifies you."

I heard this and no more. Another death seemed upon me; I fell upon my knees and caught at her dress with both hands.

"Oh, do not leave me—I shall die! I shall die!" She lifted me from the floor and attempted to soothe me, but I was not to be pacified. To live without him—never to see him! There would be nothing worth loving in my life after that.

"Is it so hard to part with us," she said, smoothing my hair with both hands.

I flung my arms around her neck in passionate grief.

"Let me go too; oh, take me, take me!"

"But we are going to Europe."

"Over the sea? I know, I know, take me!"

She kissed me again, and seemed thoughtful. My heart rose: I began to plead with hope. She listened tenderly; told me not to cry, and left me in a state of suspense hard to bear. An hour after this I saw her walking in the garden with Mr. Lee. She was addressing him with sweet earnestness. He looked smilingly down into her face and seemed to expostulate against something that she was urging. At last he appeared to give way, but shook his head and threatened her with his finger, which she answered by tossing the ripe leaves of an autumn rose in his face. As he shook them laughingly away, his eyes fell on me where I leaned from the window, and he made a sign for me to come down.

Breathless, and wild with anxiety, I ran down to the garden and stood beside him, panting for breath, eager to speak, and yet afraid.

"Well, little lady," he said, holding out a hand; "you are determined that we shall not leave you behind."

"It would kill me," I murmured, striving to read my fate in his eyes.

"But we shall be gone from home a long time."

"My home is where—where she is," I answered.

Why did I hesitate to include him. I think he noticed it, for he said, laughing, "Then you care everything for her, nothing for me?"

I burst into tears and cried out in my trouble, "Oh, you are cruel to me; you laugh when I am so unhappy."

"But no one shall be made so unhappy when—when—" Here Miss Olmsly broke off what she had begun to say, and flushed like the rose she had just torn to pieces.

"When we are married; that is what she will not say, sweetheart," broke in Mr. Lee, blushing a little himself; "and if it really will make you unhappy to stay behind, why, there must be some way found by which you can go with us."

I caught a deep breath and felt a glow of keen happiness rush up to my face, but no word would leave my lips.

"Now, this will make you happy?" questioned Miss Olmsly, looking into my eyes,—I think as much to avoid his, as from a wish to read my joy there.

"So happy," I answered.

"But we shall be gone a long time and shall travel a great deal, while you must be put to school."

This dampened my spirits a little, but I answered, bravely, that I did not mind, so long as there was no ocean between us.

Then they informed me that Mr. Olmsly had consented that I should go with them to Paris and remain in school while they travelled. Then he would join us and make new arrangements for the future.

After explaining all this to me, the young people walked off together, satisfied that I was made happy as themselves; and so I ought to have been; but my poor heart would not rest, and I went off into the woods like a wild bird, wondering why it was that a flutter of pain still kept stirring in my bosom.

They were married just two weeks from that day. All the principal families of the place were invited, and the entertainment proved a grand affair. All the grounds were illuminated for the occasion. The house was one blaze of lights. Every tree on the hill-side or the sloping lawn seemed blossoming with fire, or drooping with translucent fruit, so numerous were the colored lamps and gorgeous lanterns that hung amid their foliage.

It was like fairy-land to me. The moon was at its golden fulness, and never before had the purple skies seemed so full of stars; but, spite of this, I was sad and restless. Miss Olmsly insisted upon it that my mourning should be laid aside, and I felt strange in the cloudy whiteness of my dress, simple and plain as it was. Indeed, the whole thing seemed to me like a dream which must pass away on the morrow. Perhaps it was this abrupt change in my dress which made me feel so lonely when all the world was gay and brilliant beyond anything my short life had witnessed. Perhaps I felt sad at the thought of leaving my native land. Be this as it may, I can look back upon few nights of my life more dreary than that upon which the two best friends I ever had, or ever shall have, were married.

Memory is full of pictures; events fade away, feelings die out, but so long as the heart keeps a sentiment or the brain holds an image, groups will start up from the past and bring back scenes which no effort of the mind can displace. It is strange, but such pictures are burned, as it were, upon the soul unawares, and often without any remarkable event which can be said to have impressed them there. You may have known a person all your life, yet remember him only as he was presented to you at some given moment. Whole years may pass in which you scarcely seem to have observed him; but at some one moment he comes out upon your recollection with all his features perfect and clearly cut as a cameo.

Of all the pictures burned in upon my life, that of Mr. Lee and his bride, as they stood up in that long drawing-room to be married, will be the last to die out from my mind. No bridesmaids were in attendance; no ushers coming and going drew attention from that noble couple. This was the picture,—a woman standing at the left hand of a tall, stately man. He was upright, firm, and self-poised as the pillar of some old Grecian temple. She drooped gently forward, her hands unconsciously clasped, the long black lashes sweeping her cheeks; a soft tremor, as of red rose-leaves stirred by the wind, passing over her lips; draperies of satin, glossy and white as crusted snow, fell around her; a garland of blush-roses crowned the braids of purplish-black hair thickly coiled around a most queenly head. Draperies of rich, warm crimson fell from the windows just behind them, and swept around the foot of a noble vase of Oriental alabaster, from which a tall crimson and purple fuchsia-tree dropped its profuse bells. Directly the clergyman, with a book in his hand, broke into the picture; but my mind rejects him and falls back upon the man, and the woman who stood with lovelight in her eyes and prayers at her heart, waiting to become his wife.

There was great rejoicing after the picture was lost in a crowd of congratulating friends; music sent its soft reverberations out among the flowers, that gave back rich odors in return; for it was a lovely autumnal night, and the whole platform to which the windows opened was garlanded in with hot-house plants. I remember seeing groups of persons wandering about in the illuminated grounds. Their laughter reached me as I sat solitary and alone in the oriel window, over which lace curtains fell, and were kindled up like snow by the lights from without.

I was very sad that night, and felt the tears stealing slowly into my eyes. Every one was happy, but joy had forgotten to find me out. All at once the lace curtains were lifted softly and fell rustling down again. *She* had thought of me even in her happiest moments. Her arms were folded around me; her lips, warm with smiles, were pressed to my face.

"All alone and looking so sad! why will you not enjoy yourself like the rest?" she said.

"I am so young and so wicked," I answered, wiping the tears from my eyes.

"Wicked! oh, not that, only there is no one of your own age here; come out a little while; he has been asking for you."

"For me?"

"Of course; who else should he think of? Why, child, you will never know how dearly we both love you."

"And you always will?" I asked, holding my breath in expectation of her answer.

"And always will, be sure of that. Ah! here he comes to promise for himself."

Yes; there he stood holding back the curtains, proud, smiling, and strong, as I shall always remember him.

"Ah! you have found her, silly thing, hiding away by herself," he exclaimed, kindly.

"I have just made a promise for you," answered the bride with gentle seriousness.

"Which I will keep; for henceforth, fair lady, am I not your slave."

"I have promised to love this girl so long as I shall live, and that you will be her very best friend, and love her dearly."

"Dearly, you say?"

"Most dearly."

"Next to yourself?"

"Next to myself; and after me, best of all."

"Ah, it is easy to promise that, for, next to yourself, sweet wife, she is the dearest creature in existence." She held my hand in hers while he was speaking. When he uttered the word wife, I felt her finger quiver as if some strange thrill had flashed down from her heart, and the broad white lids drooped suddenly, veiling the radiance of her eyes.

"Now that I have promised, let us seal the compact," he said, with touching seriousness; and lifting me for a moment in his arms, he pressed a kiss upon my lips.

"Why, how she trembles; don't be afraid, you sensitive little thing; come, come go with us and see how the people are making themselves happy."

The bride took his arm, and leading me with his disengaged hand, he crossed the drawing-room and went out on the flower-wreathed platform, where a band of music was filling the night with harmonies.

Here an ecstasy of feeling came upon me; I remembered all that both these persons had promised, and that it would be a solemn compact which they would never think of breaking. I should be with them, not for a time only, but so long as I lived. Remember, I was an imaginative girl, and knew but little of the mutability of human affairs. I only felt in my soul that these two persons whom I loved so entirely, would be faithful to the promise they had made that night, and this certainly filled me with exultation that was, for the time, something better than happiness. After a while, Mr. Lee dropped my hand, but it crept back to his, and I made a signal that he should bend his head.

"It is a promise," I whispered; "you will never, never send me away from you?"

"It is a promise," he answered, smiling down upon me.

"Good night," I said, longing to be alone in my room where I could feel of a certainty that the few words spoken that night had anchored me for life. "Good night; I shall never leave you or her while I live."

It seemed a rash promise, but I made it to God in my prayers that night. The reader shall see how I kept it.

CHAPTER V
AFTER THE WEDDING

Our Jessie was born in Paris, a little more than a year after her parents were married, and a lovelier child never drew breath. I was in school then, and she was two months old before I saw her, but she had learned to smile, and was a beautiful, bright little creature even then. How I worshipped the child! no elder sister ever rendered her heart more completely up to an infant of her own blood, than I gave mine. All the affection I had ever felt for the parents was intensified and softened into infinite tenderness for their little girl. In her I resolved to repay some of the kindness which had been so lavishly bestowed on me. How this was to be done, I could not tell, but I had dreams of great sacrifices, unlimited devotion, and such care as one human being never took of another. Thus the first existence of this child was woven into my own better life and became a part of it.

Our Jessie was two years old when Mr. Olmsly joined us in Europe, and for the first time saw his little grandchild; before she had counted another year, the good old man was dead and buried in a strange country. He left a will contrary to all expectation, written after he had seen and loved little Jessie. All his vast property was left to Mr. Lee and his wife, but on the death of Mrs. Lee, even though the husband was still living, one half the estate was to revert, unrestricted and uncontrolled, to her daughter.

This was all, and with it the persons in interest were satisfied; indeed, the property was large enough to have been pided half a dozen times, and still have been sufficient for the ambition of any reasonable person.

Mr. Lee did not return to the United States at the death of his father-in-law; there was, in reality, nothing to call him home. He had retired from active business soon after his marriage, and the old world had so many resources of knowledge and pleasure, for persons of their fine cultivation, that they lingered on, year after year, without a wish for change, sometimes travelling from country to country, but making Paris their head-quarters so long as I remained in school.

After that, we spent a year in Italy, and some months in Germany and Spain, where I became perfect mistress of the languages, and found happiness in imparting them to "Our Jessie," who became more lovely and lovable every year of her life.

At last we went to the Holy Land, and lingered a while in Egypt, where Mrs. Lee was taken ill, almost for the first time in her life, and then came the only real sorrow that we had known since Mr. Olmsly's death.

The moment it was possible, we returned to Paris, in order to get the best medical advice. It came all too soon; Mrs. Lee was pronounced a confirmed invalid, some disease of the nerves, in which the spine was implicated, threatened a tedious, if not incurable illness.

At this time Jessie was ten years old, and I had entered the first stages of womanhood; as her mother became more and more frail, the dear child was almost entirely given up to me, and my love for her became absolute idolatry. The child had always been taught to call me aunt, and for her sake I was ready to give up all the bright social prospects that opened to me just then. Indeed, there never was a time in my life that I could not have found pleasure in sacrificing anything to the parents or the child.

One thing troubled Mrs. Lee at this time,—a craving desire to go home seized upon her. With an invalid's incessant longing, she wearied of the objects that had so pleasantly amused her, and sighed for rest. But it had been arranged that Jessie should be educated at the same school which I had left, and the gentle mother could not find it in her heart to be separated from that dear one.

Now came the time for my dream to be realized. Why should "Our Jessie" be given up to the hard routine of a school, when I could make her studies easy and her life pleasant. It was in my power to keep the mother and child in one home.

I found Mr. Lee and his wife together one day, and made my proposition. I would become Jessie's governess.

My generous friends protested against this. It was, they said, the opening of my life. In order to do this, I must give up the society which I had but just entered, and perhaps injure my own prospects in the future. No, no, they could not permit a sacrifice like this.

But if they were generous, I was resolute. To have Jessie always with me, had been the brightest dream of my girlhood. I could not be persuaded to give it up. What did I care for society, if she was to suffer the dreary routine of the school-life from which I had but just been emancipated? I really think it would have broken my heart had the dear child been left behind. But great love always prevails. We sailed for America a united family, happy even with the drawback of Mrs. Lee's illness, which in itself was seldom painful, and her untiring cheerfulness was never broken.

The valley of the Delaware had become highly cultivated in our long absence. A railroad ran up the banks of the river, from which our house could be seen standing on the hill-side miles and miles away. I started with surprise when it first met our view. A square stone tower, three stories high, loomed up behind the pointed gables and balconied front, giving a castellated air to the whole building.

This had been done by Mr. Lee's orders. He had drawn the plans, and his architect had carried them out splendidly. Our first view of the house was accompanied with exclamations of pleasure which delighted Mr. Lee, who had kept all his improvements a secret, that he might enjoy our surprise. Indeed, the site of the house was so finely uplifted from the valley, that the effect was that of many lordly mansions we had seen on the Continent, though I do not remember one more picturesque in itself, or that could command a landscape to compare with this in extent or varied beauty.

It was a lovely June day when we reached the Ridge; everything had been prepared for our reception. In the years of our absence nothing had been permitted to go to decay, but many improvements presented themselves as we turned up the carriage-road. A young peach-orchard had grown into bearing trees; grape trellices were tangled thickly with vines; choice fruit-trees of every kind had just lost their blossoms. A range of hot-houses glittered through the trees. All this made the Ridge more beautiful by far than it had been years before when it seemed a paradise to me. On entering the house, we were still more pleasantly surprised. Everything rich and rare that a long residence abroad had enabled Mr. Lee to collect, was arranged through the rooms,—bronzes, statuettes of marble, old china carvings, pictures, ornaments of malachite, and Lapes lazula, met us on every hand. All this might have seemed out of place in a country house of almost any ordinary description, where the occupant was likely to spend half the year in town; but Mr. Lee had fitted up this place as his principal and permanent residence. The health of his wife demanded quiet; her tastes required beautiful objects, and all these rare articles had been carefully selected for her pleasure. Here she found many a precious gem of art which she had seen in her travels, admired, but never thought to possess. But he had remembered her faintest preference, and the proofs of his unbounded devotion met her at every turn, as we entered, what was, in fact, the blending of an old and new home.

Not one article of the old furniture was missing, every sweet association had been preserved with religious care; but affection had grafted the new life she had been leading on the reminiscences of her girlhood, and, spite of her infirmity and fatigue, Mrs. Lee was supremely happy as she entered her home. The square tower was entirely modern, and everything it contained had been sent from abroad. The lower room was a library, with pointed windows, a black-walnut floor, and a small Gobeline carpet in the centre of the room, upon which a heavily carved table was placed. From floor to ceiling the walls were lined with books, richly bound, and carefully selected; the book-cases were each surmounted with a bas-relief in bronze, representing some classical subject, while the glass that shut in the books was pure as crystal. Easy-chairs of every conceivable pattern stood about this room, and between each book-case a bronze statuette reminded you of some classic name, or hero known to history.

The second story of the tower opened into the main building; thus the large square chamber fitted up for Mrs. Lee was connected with two smaller rooms, one intended for her personal attendant, the other a dressing-room.

The principal window of this room opened upon a balcony, which overlooked the brightest portion of the terraces; near this window a couch was drawn, from which even an invalid might attain lovely glimpses of the clustering flowers, without changing her position. A carpet, thick and soft as a meadow in spring, covered the floor, and in the back part of the room stood a bed, surmounted by a canopy carved from some rare dark-hued wood, from which curtains of lace that a countess might have worn, swept to the floor, and clouded the bed, without in any degree obstructing the air. In this room everything invited to repose. The pictures were all dreamily beautiful. On one side of the large window a marble child lay sleeping, with a smile on its lips. On the other, just within the frost-like shadow of the curtains, an angel, of the same size, knelt, with downcast face, and hands pressed softly together, praying. This was the room into which Mr. Lee carried his wife, after she had rested a few minutes in the drawing-room. He laid her upon the couch with gentle care, but she rose at once, and leaning upon her elbow, looked around. Everything was new and strange; but, oh, how beautiful! tears came into her eyes; she leaned back upon the cushions, and held out both hands.

"And you have done all this," she said. "Was ever a woman so blessed?"

Then she turned her eyes upon the window and saw the flowers gleaming through.

"The garden is as he left it," she murmured. "I am glad of that—I am glad of that."

Mr. Lee sat down by her couch, smiling, and evidently rejoiced that he had given her so much pleasure. Jessie was moving about the room, happy as a bird; to her everything was new and charming, and the restlessness of childhood was upon her.

CHAPTER VI
TELLING HOW LOTTIE INTRODUCED HERSELF

As we were settling down to a quiet admiration of all these things, a strange little girl appeared at the door, where she hesitated, and peeped in as if half afraid. Thinking that she wished to speak with some of us, I went toward her, but she waved me off with an air, saying,—

"It's no use your coming, you're not the madam, I'll bet."

With these words she walked into the room and took a general survey of our party. First she cast a sharp glance at Mr. Lee, but withdrew it directly; passed a careless look over my person, broke into a broad smile as Jessie came under her observation, and having thus disposed of us, came up to Mrs. Lee, who opened her eyes wide, and was for a moment astonished by the sudden appearance of the girl.

"Perhaps you don't want me here, now that so many other folks are coming," said the girl, clasping and unclasping her hands, which at last fell loosely before her. "They tell me down-stairs that I don't belong here nohow, and hadn't ought to put myself forward. But I haven't got no one to speak up for me, being an orphan, so here I am; do you want me, or must I up and go."

"Who are you, my girl?" asked Mrs. Lee, in her gentle way.

"My father was the gardener here, marm, but he's dead; so is my mother, long ago. My name is Lottie, and I've stayed on here doing things about, because I hadn't anywhere else to go. That's pretty much all about it."

"And you wish to stay?"

"Do I wish to stay, is it? Yes, I do, awfully. I can earn my board and more, too, in the kitchen, cleaning silver and scouring knives and feeding chickens, but since I catched sight of you being carried up them steps, marm, my ideas have ris a notch. I should like to tend on you dreadfully. You could tell me how, you know, and I'm cute to learn; ask 'em down below, if you don't believe me."

Mrs. Lee broke into a faint laugh; the manners and abrupt speech of the girl struck her as comical in the extreme. As for myself, I have seldom seen a creature so awkward, so brusque, and yet so interesting. She was, I should fancy, about eight years of age, square, angular, restless, but no lily was ever more pure than her complexion, and her hair, thick and soft, was of that delicate golden tint we find in new silk, before it is reeled from the cocoon. Altogether, she was a strange creature, full of vivid feeling and dreadfully in earnest. Mrs. Lee liked her, I could make sure of that, from the serene pleasure which came to her face as she looked into the girl's large gray eyes, which were shaded with lashes much darker than her hair.

"And you would like to make yourself useful up here," she said, smiling at the girl's intense eagerness.

"Goodness—wouldn't I?"

"But, can you be quiet?"

"As a bird on its nest."

"And cheerful?"

"Why, marm, I'm the cheerfullest creature on these premises. You may count in the squirrels, rabbits, and robins, and after that, I can say it."

Mrs. Lee turned her eyes on her husband, who sat near her couch, greatly amused by the dialogue.

"What do you think? She seems bright, and I dare say will try her best."

"At any rate, she promises to be amusing," answered Mr. Lee, and a good-natured smile quivered about his lips.

"And kind-hearted, I will answer for that, don't you think so, Martha?"

"I am sure of it."

As the words left my lips, Lottie made a pe at me, took my hand in both hers, and kissed it with a wild outgush of feeling. "You're good as gold, silver, and diamonds," she said. "I was sure that you would be on my side, though you do look as if butter wouldn't melt in your mouth. Tell me just what to do about the lady, and see if I don't come up to the mark. It's in me, I know that."

Mrs. Lee closed her eyes wearily; even this short conversation was too much for her weak nerves.

"Go down-stairs now," I said to the girl in a low voice; "by-and-by you shall be told about your duties. The first and greatest is quietness."

She nodded her head, put a finger to her lips, and went out of the room on tiptoe.

Mrs. Lee opened her eyes as the girl went out, and beckoned to Jessie.

"Do you like that strange little orphan?" she questioned.

"Like her? indeed I do, mamma," said the kind-hearted girl. "She is so warm, so earnest, and uses such queer words. But Aunt Martha will cure her of that. I was just thinking how pleasant it would be to teach her."

"That is a good idea, child; who knows what we may do for her?"

Here Mrs. Lee turned upon her cushions a little wearily, and from that time, Lottie became her attendant.

Now our domestic life began in earnest. Mrs. Lee's disease was not often painful, nor immediately dangerous. Contented with the love that surrounded her, she fell gently into the invalid habits, which had something pleasant in them when incited by a home like that.

For my part, I knew no more attractive spot than her room. There Jessie took her lessons in the morning, and in the afternoon, Mr. Lee always sat with us, reading to her while we worked or studied. Never in this world, I do think, was a family more closely united, or that seemed so completely uplifted from care or trouble as ours.

Sometimes Mrs. Lee would regret what she called the waste of my youth in her daughter's behalf, but I had no such feeling. Society was nothing to me, while those I loved so dearly were part of my every-day life. Of course I had seen my share of social life in Europe, had met many agreeable people, and knew what it was to be admired,—perhaps loved,—but my heart had never, for one moment, swerved from its old affections. Ardently as in my childhood, I loved those two first and last friends. As for "Our Jessie," I cannot trust myself to speak of her. If ever one human being adored another, I adored that bright, beautiful girl. They talked of sacrifices; why, it would have broken my heart had Jessie been taken from me and sent to school. Of course, we had plenty of society, the best people from the town visited us often, and sometimes an old friend whom we had met on our travels would find us out. But Mrs. Lee's state of health precluded much hospitality, and so we were left almost entirely to the quiet home-life which all of us loved so well.

Thus months and years rolled on, stealing the freshness and bloom from me, and giving them tenfold to my darling.

If I have dwelt somewhat at length on my early life, it is not because I am attempting to give prominence to my own feelings or actions, but that the reader may understand how intense and all-absorbing a feeling of affectionate gratitude may become,—how it may color and pervade a whole existence.

In my helpless orphanage, two noble young people had found me lonely, despondent, and almost friendless. At once, without question or reservation, they took me into their hearts and gave me a permanent home. Now that my benefactress had fallen into entire dependence upon those she loved for happiness, was it strange that I stood ready to give up my youth for her and her beautiful child?

This generous woman was forever speaking of my action as a noble sacrifice. But to my thinking it was happiness in itself. I loved to watch what might have been my own life, dawning brightly in the youth of Jessie Lee; and when her first lover appeared, I was almost as much interested as the girl herself, who was, in fact, quite unconscious, for a long time, that the young man loved her at all.

He was a splendid young fellow, though, and even "Our Jessie" might have been proud of the conquest she had unconsciously made.

Young Bosworth was the grandson of a fine old lady, born in England, I think, who inhabited the large stone house I have spoken of as forming a picturesque feature in the landscape, on the day I was rescued from the adder. He was interested in an iron company near the town, financially, and was about to enter into active business in the partnership, having just completed his minority. His business brought him frequently to our house, for Mr. Lee was considered a safe adviser in such matters; thus an intimacy sprung up between the young man and "Our Jessie" just when the first bloom of her girlhood was deepening into the rare beauty for which she was so remarkable in after-years.

But Jessie was all unconscious of the love that I could detect in every glance of those fine eyes, and in every tone of the voice that grew tender and musical whenever it addressed her. Indeed, the young man took no pains to conceal the feelings that seemed to possess him entirely. No one but a person utterly innocent and unconscious of her own attractions could have remained an hour ignorant of such devotion.

I think Jessie liked this man, and if nothing had happened to intervene, that liking would have ripened gently into love, as fruit exposed to the sweet dews of night and the warm noonday sun, ripens and grows crimson so gradually that we mark the result without observing the progress.

But something did happen, which not only interrupted the pleasant relations which had been established between this young man and our family, but which broke up all the quiet and happiness of our domestic life.

Hitherto our lives had been so tranquil that there was little to describe. We had, to an extent, isolated ourselves from the general world, and so surrounded ourselves with blessings, that the one misfortune of our lives had proved almost a beneficence, for Mrs. Lee's illness had only drawn us closer together. But all was to be changed now.

CHAPTER VII
OUT IN THE WORLD

When Jessie reached her eighteenth year, Mrs. Lee became more languid than usual, and early in the season her physician suggested a few weeks at the sea-side.

I think the dear lady was induced to follow his advice from a desire to give our girl a glimpse of the life which should have been opened to her about that time, rather than from any hopes of benefit from sea-bathing. She entered into the project at once, and brightened visibly under the influence of Jessie's openly expressed enthusiasm. The dear girl had in reality seen nothing of life, and she was happy as a bird at the prospect of entering what seemed to her like an enchanted land.

Late in June, that year, we went to Long Branch upon the Jersey shore, and there among the crowd of fashionables from Philadelphia and New York, a new life opened to our Jessie, whose wealth and exceeding beauty soon made her an object of general admiration.

I cannot tell you how we first became acquainted with Mrs. Dennison. She was a Southern woman, about whom there was a vague reputation of wealth inherited from an old man, whom she had married in his dotage, and of a very luxurious life which had commenced so soon after the funeral as to create some scandal. She was certainly a very beautiful woman, tall, exquisitely formed, lithe and graceful as a leopardess. Her manners were caressing, her voice sweetly modulated, and her powers of conversation wonderfully varied. At first I was fascinated by the woman. She occupied rooms that opened on the same veranda with ours, and had stolen so completely into our companionship by a thousand little attentions to Mrs. Lee, before we really knew anything about her, that afterward it seemed unnecessary to make further inquiry. It would have proved of little avail had our research been ever so rigid, for no one seemed really to have any positive knowledge about her. Even the gossip I have mentioned could always be traced back to a remarkably bright mulatto lady's-maid, who was generally in attendance upon her, and who conversed freely with every one who chose to question her. But all the intelligence so gathered was sure to add to the power and wealth of a mistress whom the mulatto pronounced to be one of the most distinguished and beautiful women of the South. All this rather interested Mr. Lee, who found this lady so often bestowing little attentions upon his wife, that he came to recognize her as a friend, and, after a time, seemed to take great pleasure in her conversation. All this troubled me a little. Why? surely the feeling which turned my heart from that woman was not jealousy. Had I indeed so completely identified myself with my friends, that the approach to confidential relations with another person gave me pain? I could not understand the feeling, but, struggle against it as I would, the presence of that woman made me restless. She never touched Mrs. Lee that I did not long to dash her hand away.

Jessie, like the rest, was fascinated with her new friend. They would walk together for hours on the shore, where a crowd of admirers was sure to gather around them, while I sat upon the veranda with my benefactress, anxious and disturbed.

After a time, another person was introduced into our party. He first became acquainted with Mrs. Lee, and seemed to drop into our companionship in that way without any connection with Mrs. Dennison; but I learned afterward that Mr. Lawrence had been very attentive to her from her first appearance at the Branch, and that a rumor had for a time prevailed that they were engaged.

All this might not have interested me much but for something that I observed in Jessie, who was evidently far better acquainted with the man than any of us; for it seems he had been in the habit of joining her and Mrs. Dennison in their walks long before he attained an introduction to Mrs. Lee. Lawrence was a tall, powerful man, very distinguished and elegant in his bearing, wonderfully brilliant in conversation, and one who always would be a leader for good or evil among his fellow-men. He had been a good deal connected with the politics of the country, and at one time was considered a power in Wall Street, from which he had withdrawn, it was impossible to say whether penniless, or with a large fortune.

This man was soon on terms of cordial intimacy with our family, but I watched him with distrust. He was just the person to dazzle and fascinate an ardent, inexperienced girl like our Jessie, and I saw with pain that her color would rise and fade beneath his glances, and that a look of triumph lighted up his eyes when he remarked it.

Here was another source of anxiety. This man of the world, who had spent half his life in the struggles of Wall Street and a tangle of politics, was no match for a creature so pure and true as our Jessie. Yet I greatly feared that her heart was turning to him at the expense of that brave, honorable young man whose very existence seemed to have been forgotten among us.

But young Bosworth came at last, and I was more at rest. Jessie was certainly glad to see him, and, much to my surprise, he dropped at once into intimate relations with Lawrence, and recognized him as an old friend whom he had met during the few months that he had spent abroad.

I have not said that Lottie was one of the attendants whom we brought from the Ridge. This girl had grown somewhat in stature, but was still very small. Her light-yellow hair was wonderfully abundant, and she had a dozen fantastic ways of dressing it, which added to the singularity of her appearance. At times, her eyes were clear and steady in their glances; but, if a feeling of distrust came over her, both eyes would cross ominously, and she seemed to be glancing inward with the sharp vigilance of a fox.

There always had been a remarkable sympathy between me and this strange girl. From the day I first saw her, she seemed to pine my feelings, conceal them as I would, and to share all my dislikes almost before they were formed. At first, she had kept aloof from the servants of the hotel. This was not strange, for Lottie was, in fact, better educated than some of their mistresses. She had managed to pick up a great deal of knowledge as she sat by while Jessie took her lessons, and I had found pleasure in teaching her such English branches as befitted her station in life. In fact, Lottie had become more like a companion than a servant with us all.

To my surprise, after keeping aloof for a whole week, Lottie fell into the closest intimacy with Cora, Mrs. Dennison's maid, and I could see that she lost no opportunity of watching the mistress and Mr. Lawrence.

What all this might have ended in I cannot tell, for just as our intimacy became closest, the strong sea-air began to have an unfavorable effect on our patient.

A sudden longing for home seized upon her one day, after Lottie had been with her talking about the Ridge, and it was decided that we should leave the Branch at once, though the season was at its height, and Jessie had entered into its gayeties with all the zest of her ardent nature.

I think Mr. Lee was rather reluctant to go away so suddenly. He had been so long excluded from this form of social life that it had all the charm of novelty to him; but the least wish of his wife was enough to change all this, and he became only anxious to get her safely home again.

I do not know how it happened, or who really gave the invitation, but on the night before I left we learned from Mrs. Dennison herself, that she had promised to make us an early visit; and half an hour later, as I sat alone in the lower veranda, young Bosworth and Mr. Lawrence passed me, talking earnestly. "Of course, my dear fellow, I shall come if a careless person like me will be acceptable to that fine old lady, your grandmother. That promise of partridge-shooting is beyond my powers of resistance."

It was Mr. Lawrence who spoke, and I knew by this fragment of conversation that he too was coming into our neighborhood.

CHAPTER VIII
OUR GUEST

I stood in the oriel window that curved out from one end of the large parlor and looked toward the east; that is, it commanded a broad view from all points, save the direct west. The heavenly glimpses of scenery that you caught at every turn through the small diamond panes were enough to drive an artist mad, that so much unpainted poetry could exist, and not glow warm and fresh on his canvas. I am an artist, at soul, and have a gallery of the most superb brain-pictures stowed away in my thoughts, but among them all there is nothing to equal the scene, or rather scenes, I was gazing upon.

The window was deep, and when that rich volume of curtains shut it out from the parlor, it was the most cosy little spot in the world. A deep easy-chair, and a tiny marble stand, filled it luxuriously. On the outside, white jasmines, passion-flowers, and choice roses, crept up to the edge of the glass in abundance, encircling you with massive wreaths of foliage and blossoms.

This window had always been my favorite retreat, when sadness or care oppressed me, as it had begun to do seriously of late, for a degree of estrangement had arisen between Jessie and myself, after our return from the sea-side. I could not share her enthusiasm regarding some of the persons we had met there, and for the first time in her life she was half offended with me.

I can hardly express the pain this gave me. All her life she had come to me in her troubles; and her bright, innocent joys I always shared; for, like a flower-garden, she sent back the sunshine that passed over her, enriched and more golden from a contact with her loveliness. I can hardly tell you what a thing of beauty she was; yet, I doubt if you would have thought her so very lovely as I did, for my admiration was almost idolatry. Of late I had remarked a certain reserve about her, the reticence which kept a sanctuary of feeling and thought quite away from the world, and alas, from me also. Yet she was frank and truthful, as the flower which always folds the choicest perfume close in its own heart. What secret feeling was it that kept her from me, her oldest and best friend.

I was thinking of Jessie while I sat in the easy-chair, looking down the carriage-road that led through our private grounds from the highway; for ours was an isolated dwelling, and no carriage that was not destined for the house ever came up that sweep of road. I looked down upon it with a sad, heavy feeling, though my eyes passed over a terrace crowned with a wilderness of flowers, reached by a flight of steps. The gleam of these flowers, and the green slope beyond, were a part of the scenery on which I gazed, yet I saw nothing of them.

We expected Mrs. Dennison. The carriage had gone over to the country town which lay behind the hills piled up at my left, and I was listening for the sound of its wheels on the gravel with a strange thrill of anxiety. Why was this? What did I care about the young widow who had been invited to spend a few days with our Jessie? She was only a watering-place acquaintance—a clever, beautiful woman of the world, who, having a little time on her hands, had condescended to remember Mrs. Lee's half-extorted invitation, and was expected accordingly.

Jessie was rather excited with the idea of a guest, for it so chanced that we had been alone for a week or two; and though I never saw a family more independent of society than Mrs. Lee's, guests always bring expectation and cheerfulness with them in a well-appointed country house.

"I wonder what keeps them?" said my darling, softly lifting one side of the silken curtains, and unconsciously dropping them into the background of as lovely a picture as you ever saw. "Here are some flowers for the stand, Aunt Matty. She'll catch their bloom through the window, and know it is my welcome."

I took the crystal vase from her hand, and set it on the little table before me.

"Hush!" she said, lifting the drapery higher, and bending forward to listen. "Hush! Isn't that the carriage coming through the pine grove?"

I turned in my chair, for Jessie was well worth looking at, even by a person who loved her less fondly than I did. Standing there, draped to artistic perfection in her pretty white dress, gathered in surplice folds over her bosom, and fastened there with an antique head, cut in coral, with its loose sleeves falling back from the uplifted arm, till its beautiful contour could be seen almost to the shoulder, she was a subject for Sir Joshua Reynolds. I am sure that great master would not have changed the grouping in a single point.

"No," I said, listening; "it is the gardener's rake on the gravel walk, I think."

She bent her head sideways, listening, and incredulous of my explanation. Some gleams of sunshine fell through the glass, and lay richly on the heavy braid of hair that crowned her head in a raven coronal.

We always remember those we love in some peculiar moment which lifts itself out of ordinary life by important associations; or, as in this case, by the singular combinations of grace that render them attractive. To my last breath, I shall never forget Jessie Lee, as she stood before me that morning.

"Well," she said, with an impatient movement that left the curtains falling between us like the entrance of a tent, "watched rose-buds never open. I'll go back to the piano, and let her take me by surprise. I'm glad you're looking so nice, aunt. She'll be sure to like you now in spite of herself, though you were so cold and stiff with her at the Branch, and I defy you to help liking her in the end."

As Jessie said this, her hand fell on the keys of the piano, and instantly a gush of music burst through the room, so joyous that the birds that haunted the old forest-trees around the house burst into a riot of rival melody. Amid this delicious serenade the carriage drove up.

I saw Mr. Lee alight, in his usual stately way; then Mrs. Dennison sprang upon the lowest step of the broad stairs that led up to the terrace, scarcely touching Mr. Lee's offered hand. There she stood a moment, her silk flounces fluttering in the sunlight, and her neatly gloved hands playing with the clasp of her travelling satchel, as the servant took a scarlet shawl and some books from the carriage. Then she gave a rapid glance over the grounds, and looked up to the house, smiling pleasantly, and doubtless paying Mr. Lee some compliment, for his usually sedate face brightened pleasantly, and he took the lady's satchel, with a gallant bow, which few young men of his time could have equalled.

Certainly our guest was a beautiful woman: tall, queenly, and conscious of it all; but I did not like her. One of those warnings, or antipathies, if you please, which makes the heart take shelter in distrust, seized upon me again that moment, and I felt like flying to my darling, who sat amid the sweet harmonies she was herself creating, to shield her from some unknown danger.

I left my seat and passed through the curtains, thinking to warn Jessie of her friend's arrival; but when I was half across the room, our visitor came smiling and rustling through the door. She motioned me to be still, and, darting across the carpet, seized Jessie's head between both hands, bent it back, and, stooping with the grace of a Juno, kissed her two or three times, while her clear, ringing laugh mingled with the notes which had broken into sudden discords under Jessie's fingers.

"So I have chased my bird to its nest, at last," she said, releasing her captive with a movement that struck even me—who disliked her from the beginning—as one of exquisite grace. "Hunted it to the mountains, and find it in full song, while I searched every window in the house, as we drove up, and fancied all sorts of things: a cold welcome among the least."

"That you will never have," cried Jessie, and the smile with which she greeted her guest was enough of welcome for any one. "The truth is, I got out of patience, and so played to quiet myself while Aunt Matty watched."

"And how is the dear Aunt Matty?" said the guest, coming toward me with both hands extended. "Ah! Jessie Lee, you are a fortunate girl to have so sweet a friend."

"I am fortunate in everything," said Jessie, turning her large, earnest eyes on my face with a look of tenderness that went to my heart, "and most of all here."

"And I," said Mrs. Dennison, with a suppressed breath, and a look of graceful sadness. "Well, well, one can't expect everything."

Jessie laughed. This bit of sentiment in her guest rather amused her.

"Ah, you never will believe in sorrow of any kind, until it comes in earnest," said the widow, with an entire change in her countenance; "but I, who have seen it in so many forms, cannot always forget."

"But," said Jessie, with one of her caressing movements, "you must forget it now. We are to be happy as the day is long while you are here. Isn't that so, aunt? We have laid out such walks, and rides, and pleasant evenings—of course, you have brought your habit."

"Of course. What would one be in the country without riding?"

"And your guitar? I want Aunt Matty to hear you sing. She never was with us when you had an instrument."

"Oh! Aunt Matty shall have enough of that, I promise her; the man who follows with my luggage has the guitar somewhere among his plunder."

"I'm very glad," said Jessie, smiling archly. "Now everything is provided for except—"

"Except what, lady-bird?"

"Except that we have no gentlemen to admire you."

"No gentlemen!"

"Not a soul but papa."

The widow certainly looked a little disappointed for the first instant, but she rallied before any eye less keen than mine could have observed it, and laughed joyously.

"Thank heaven, we sha'n't be bothered with compliments, nor tormented with adoration. Oh! Jessie Lee, Jessie Lee! I am so glad of a little rest from all that sort of thing: a'n't you?"

"I never was persecuted with it like you, fair lady, remember that," replied Jessie, demurely.

"Hypocrite! don't attempt to deceive me; I had eyes at the sea-side."

"And very beautiful ones they were—everybody agreed in that."

"There it is!" cried the widow, lifting her hands in affected horror; "when gentlemen are absent, ladies will flatter each other. Pray, put a stop to this, Miss,——"

"Miss Hyde," I said, rather tired of these trivialities; "but Jessie, in the eagerness of her welcome, forgets that our guest has scarcely time to prepare for dinner."

"Ah! is it so late?" said Mrs. Dennison.

"Shall I show the way to your chamber?"

"We will all go," said Jessie, circling her friend's waist with her arm and moving off.

We crossed the hall, a broad, open passage, furnished with easy-chairs and sofas, for it was a favorite resort for the whole family, and opened into a square balcony at one end, which commanded one of the heavenly views I have spoken of. The widow stopped to admire it an instant, and then we entered the room I had been careful to arrange pleasantly for her reception.

It was a square, pleasant chamber, which commanded a splendid prospect from the east; curtains like frostwork, and a bed like snow, harmonized pleasantly with walls hung with satin paper of a delicate blue, and fine India matting with which the floor was covered. We had placed vases and baskets of flowers on the deep window-sills, those of the richest fragrance we could find, which a soft, pure wind wafted through the room; the couch, the easy-chair, and the low dressing-chair were draped with delicate blue chintz, with a pattern of wild roses running over it.

Mrs. Dennison made a pretty exclamation of surprise as she entered the room. She was full of these graceful flatteries, that proved the more effective because of their seeming spontaneousness. She took off her bonnet, and, sitting down before the toilet which stood beneath the dressing-glass, a cloud of lace and embroidery, began to smooth her hair between both hands, laughing at its disorder, and wondered if anybody on earth ever looked so hideous as she did.

"This woman," I said, in uncharitable haste, — "this woman is insatiable. She is not content with the flattery of one sex, but challenges it from all." Yet, spite of myself, I could not resist the influence of her sweet voice and graceful ways; she interested me far more than I wished.

"Now," said Jessie, coming into the hall with her eyes sparkling pleasantly, — "now what do you think? Have I praised her too much? Are you beginning to like her yet?"

I kissed her, but gave no other answer. A vague desire to shield her from that woman's influence possessed me, but the feeling was misty, and had no reasonable foundation. I could not have explained why this impulse of protection sprung up in my heart, or how Jessie, the dear girl, guessed at its existence.

But she was perfectly content with the approval which my kiss implied, and went into the parlor to await the coming of her guest. That moment Mrs. Lee's maid came down with a message from her mistress, and I went up-stairs at once.

CHAPTER IX
FANCIES AND PREMONITIONS

It seemed a wonder that Mrs. Lee ever could have been a beautiful woman like her daughter, for she had faded sadly during her illness. Her hair was still thick and long, but the mountain snow was not whiter. Her face, too, was of opaque paleness; while her delicate eyebrows were black as jet; and the large eyes beneath them had lost nothing of their penetrating brightness.

Mrs. Lee was lying on the couch, in the light of a broad window which opened to the south; the balcony was as usual filled with plants, and every morning her couch was moved, and the window drapery put back that she might command some feature in the landscape over which her eye had not wearied the day before. It was a harmless enjoyment, and one which the whole family loved to encourage. Indeed, there was not a fancy or caprice of hers which was ever questioned in that house.

"Ah, Martha, it is you; I am glad of it. For when I am ill at ease, you always do me good."

She held out her little thin hand while speaking, and pressed mine almost imperceptibly.

"What has happened, Martha? During the last half hour something oppresses me, as if the atmosphere were disturbed; yet it is a clear day, and the roses on the terrace look brighter than usual."

"Nothing has happened, dear lady. Mr. Lee has come back from town, bringing the lady we all expected."

"Mrs. Dennison?"

"Yes, Mrs. Dennison. She has just gone to her room."

Mrs. Lee closed her eyes a moment and opened them with a faint smile, which seemed to ask pardon for some weakness.

"Have you seen her?"

"Yes. I was in the parlor when she came, and went with her to her room."

"And you like her better than at first, I hope?"

I hesitated.

"She is beautiful!"

"Yes, in a certain way," I answered; "but when one has got used to our Jessie's style, nothing else seems to equal it."

The mother smiled and held out her hand again.

"You love Jessie?"

I felt the tears filling my eyes. There was something so tender and sweet in this question that it made a child of me. The mother turned upon her couch, bent her lips to my hand, and dropped it gently from her hold.

"Martha Hyde, what is this which troubles me?"

"Indeed, I cannot tell."

"Does Jessie seem happy with her friend?"

"Very happy; I have seldom seen her so animated."

"But you have not told me plainly. Do you like this lady?"

"I—I cannot tell. She is beautiful; at least most people would think her so;—rich, I believe?"

I rather put this as a question.

"I think so. She had splendid rooms at the hotel, you know, and spent money freely, so Mr. Lee was told; but that is of little consequence; we want nothing of her riches if she has them."

"Certainly not; but if she has expensive habits without the means of gratifying them within herself, it is an important proof of character," I said. "May I ask, dear lady, who really recommended Mrs. Dennison to you or your daughter?"

"Oh! a good many people spoke highly of her; she was a general favorite!"

"Yes; but did you meet any person who had known her long?—who had been acquainted with her husband, for instance?"

"No, I cannot remember any such person."

"And you invited her? she said so."

"That is it. I cannot quite call to mind that I did invite her. Something was said about our house being among pleasant scenery, and she expressed a desire to see it. I may have said that I really hoped she would see it some time; and then she thanked me as if I had urged her to come. Still Jessie liked her so much that I was rather pleased than otherwise, and so it rested."

"Well," I said, "if Jessie is pleased, that is everything, you know, madam. I sometimes think the dear girl ought to have the company of younger persons about her."

"Yes, certainly; but with a girl like my Jessie, so sensitive, so proud, for she is very proud, Martha."

"I know it," was my answer. "I have never seen more sensitive pride in any person of her age."

"Well, with a disposition like that, the kind of young person she is intimate with is very important. This is the reason I wished to see you and learn if your opinion has not changed regarding our guests; my own feelings are strangely disturbed."

"You are not as well as usual this morning," I replied. "Let me draw the couch nearer and open a leaf of the window."

She assented, and I drew the couch so close to the window that with a sash open she could command a view of the richest corner of the flower-garden and a slope of the lawn. The wind swept pleasantly over the balcony, in which pots of rose geraniums and heliotrope had been placed. Mrs. Lee loved the breath of these flowers, and sighed faintly as it floated over her with the fresh morning air.

She lay some time in this pleasant position without speaking. When she was disposed to be thoughtful, we seldom disturbed her, for so sensitive had disease rendered her nerves, that the sudden sound of a voice would make her start and tremble like a criminal. So I kept my place behind the couch, looking down into the garden, and thinking of many things.

All at once, sweet, dear voices rose from among the flowers, and I saw our Jessie and the widow Dennison turning a corner of the house, each with an arm around the other's waist, laughing and chatting together. Jessie had not changed her dress, but a cluster of crimson roses glowed in her hair, and coral bracelets tinted the transparency of her sleeves. The sun touched the black braid which surrounded her head as she came out of the shadow, and no raven's plumage was ever more glossy.

Mrs. Dennison was strangely attired. The period of which I speak was about the time the Zouave jacket took its brief picturesque reign. This woman was, in a degree, her own inventor of fashions, and something very similar to this jacket fell over the loose habit-skirt that draped her bosom and arms. This garment of black silk, richly braided, matched the rustling skirt of her dress, and the Oriental design of the whole was completed by a net of blue and gold, which shaded half her rich brown hair, and fell in tassels to her left shoulder.

In my whole life I never saw a more striking contrast than these two persons presented. I cannot tell you where it lay. Not in the superiority which the widow possessed in height—not in her elaborate grace. Jessie was a little above the medium height herself, and a more elegant creature did not live. But there was something which struck you at once. It is of no use attempting to define it. The difference was to be imagined, not explained. The mother felt it, I am certain, for her eyes took a strange, anxious lustre as they fell on those two young persons, and she began to breathe irregularly, as if something oppressed her.

She looked up to me at last to see if I was watching them. I smiled and said, "At any rate, she is a splendid creature."

"No one can dispute that! But our Jessie! Do you know, as I was looking at them, something came across me. Through the hazy light which settled around me, I saw a bird with its wings outspread flitting in the folds of a serpent? The picture passed through my brain one instant, and was gone— gone before Jessie, who had stooped to gather something, regained her position. This has happened before in my life—what can it be?"

"You are anxious and nervous, dear lady, that is all. Since your visit to the sea-side, these strange visions have become more common."

"I hope they will pass off," she murmured, pressing a pale hand over her eyes. "But there was another in the group; behind Jessie's frightened face, I saw that of Mr. Lee."

While she was speaking, I saw Mr. Lee come out of the hall-door, and cross the platform which led to the garden, where his daughter and her guest were walking. He was a handsome man, still in the very prime of life, one of the most distinguished persons that I ever saw. It was from him that our Jessie had inherited her queenly pride, which the exquisite sensibility of the mother's nature had softened into grace.

Mrs. Lee closed her eyes, and I saw her lips turn pale; but she repulsed my approach with a motion of the hand. I have no idea what she had seen which escaped me. But when I looked again, Mr. Lee was talking with his daughter; while the widow stood by, grouping some flowers which she held coquettishly in her hand. I saw Mr. Lee look at her, indifferently at first, then with smiling interest. They were evidently talking of her graceful work, for she held it up for both father and daughter to admire.

As Jessie lifted her eyes, she saw us near the window, and, forgetting the bouquet, waved a kiss to her mother. That instant I saw the widow press the bouquet lightly to her lips.

Mr. Lee reached forth his hand; but she shook her head, laughed, and placed the flowers in her bosom.

Mrs. Lee was not in a position to see this. I stood up and had a better view; but she instantly complained of dizziness, and faint spasms of pain contracted her forehead.

I had seen nothing, absolutely nothing. Yet the glances of that woman, as she looked at Mr. Lee over the cluster of flowers, seemed absolutely like wafting kisses with her eyes. Jessie saw nothing, save that the little cluster of blossoms somehow found its way into her friend's bosom. So, in her sweet unconsciousness, she passed on, and was lost on the other side of the tower.

CHAPTER X
NEW VISITORS

Mrs. Lee never went down to dinner, or, if she did, it was so rarely that we looked upon her presence as a sort of holiday. She was very dainty in her appetite, and on ordinary occasions was served by her own maid, or of late by Lottie. I think she had rather intended to come down that day in honor of our guest, but the illness that seized upon her drove this idea from her mind; so, leaving her with Lottie, I went away restless and unaccountably unhappy.

How bright and blooming they came in from the garden, bringing its fragrance with them to the dinner-table! What a joyous, piquant conversation it was, that commenced with the soup and sparkled with the wine! There is no disputing it, our guest was a wonderful creature, her graceful wit sparkled, her sentiment fascinated. She was calculated to keep the man her beauty should win,—no doubt of that. Her conversation charmed even me.

Jessie was constantly challenging admiration for her friend—interrogating me with her eyes, and looking at her father to be sure that he fully appreciated the brilliancy which filled her own heart with a sort of adoration. But the widow seemed quite unconscious that she was an object of special admiration to any one. Nothing could be more natural than her manner. At times she was really child-like.

Still I did not like her. Why, it is useless to ask. Perhaps Mrs. Lee had left an impression of her strange fancies on my mind,—perhaps the atmosphere which surrounded her mingled with the subtile vitality of my intelligence and gave me the truth.

We had music in the evening. Our Jessie possessed the purest of soprano voices. Many a celebrated prima donna has won laurels from inferior capacity. As in all other things, her musical education had been perfect. Mrs. Dennison was her inferior in this. She performed splendidly, and her rich contralto voice possessed many fine qualities; but our birdie swept far above her, and soared away upon an ocean of harmonies that seemed born of heaven.

The windows were open, and we knew that this heaven of sweet sounds would float to the invalid's chamber. Indeed, when I went out upon the platform, back of the house, I saw Mrs. Lee lying in her white, loose dress, on the couch, as if the music had lulled her to sleep.

I think Mrs. Dennison was not quite satisfied with herself. The glorious voice of our Jessie seemed to take her by surprise, for after the first trial she refused to sing again, but still kept the piano, and dashed through some fine opera music with spirit. Was she exhausting her ill-humor in those stormy sounds?

On the next day, our young ladies rode on horseback. Both were superb equestrians; and Mr. Lee's stately management of his coal-black horse was something worth looking at. As they dashed round a curve of the road, Jessie turned on her saddle and waved me a kiss, where I stood on the square balcony watching them. What a happy, bright creature she looked!

It took me by surprise; but when the equestrians came back, two gentlemen had joined the party. One was young Bosworth, who had returned to the old country place, a mile down the valley, directly after we left Long Branch, and since then had managed to join our Jessie in her rides oftener than any supposition of mere accident could warrant. The dear girl seemed a little annoyed when these meetings became more frequent; but she bore our joking on the subject pleasantly, and up to that morning had, I fancy, given little thought to his movements. The other man I recognized at once. It was Mr. Lawrence.

This gentleman rode up with Mr. Lee and Mrs. Dennison, who was evidently piding her fascinations very equally between the two gentlemen. Jessie followed them with her cavalier, and I observed, as they dismounted, that her cheeks were flushed, and her lips lightly curved, as if something had disturbed her.

The gentlemen did not dismount, for Jessie left Mrs. Dennison on the foot of the terrace-steps, and, without pausing to give an invitation, ran into the house.

I left the balcony and went up to her chamber. She was walking to and fro in the room, with a quick, proud step, the tears sparkling in her eyes.

"What is it?" I said, going up to where she stood, and kissing her. "Who has wounded you?"

"No one," she answered, and the proud tears flashed down to her cheek, and lay there like rain-drops hanging on the leaves of the wild rose,—"no one. Only, only—"

"Well, dear?"

"You were right, Aunt Matty. That man really had just the feelings you suspected; I could hardly prevent him from expressing them broadly. Keep as close to papa as I would, he found means to say things that made my blood burn. What right has any man to talk of love to a girl, until she has given him some sort of encouragement, I should like to know?"

"But perhaps he fancies that you have given him a little encouragement."

"Encouragement! I? Indeed, Aunt Matty, I never dreamed of this until now!"

"I am sure of it; but then you allowed him to join your rides, and seemed rather pleased."

"Why, the idea that he meant anything never entered my mind. Ah! Aunt Matty, haven't we said a thousand times that there must be some blame, some coquetry on the lady's part, before a man, whom she is sure to reject, could presume to offer himself?"

"But has he gone so far as that?" I asked.

"Let me think. Alas! I was so confused, so angry, that it is impossible to remember just what he did say."

"But your answer?"

"Why, as to that," she cried, with a little nervous laugh, "I gave Flash a cut with the whip and dashed on after the rest. Aunt Matty, upon my word, I doubt if I spoke at all."

"My dear child, he may half imagine himself accepted then."

"Accepted! What can you mean?" she exclaimed, grasping her whip with both hands and bending it double. "I shall go wild if you say that."

"Why, do you dislike him so much?"

"Dislike! no. What is there to dislike about him?"

"Well, then," I said, a little mischievously, "he is rather good-looking, well educated, of irreproachable family, and rich."

"Don't, don't, Aunt Matty, or I shall hate you."

"Not quite so bad as that," I cried, kissing her hot cheek. "Now, let us be serious. All young ladies must expect offers of this kind."

"But I don't want them. It distresses me."

I saw that she was in earnest, and that young Bosworth's attentions had really distressed her. So, drawing her to a sofa, we sat down and talked the matter over more quietly.

I told her that it was useless annoying herself; that, until the young gentleman spoke out more definitely, she had nothing to torment herself about; and when he did, a few quiet words would settle the whole matter.

"But can't we prevent him saying anything more? Or, if he does, will you just tell him how it is?" she said, anxiously.

I could not help smiling; there was no affectation here. I knew very well that Jessie would give the world to avoid this refusal; but in such cases young ladies must take their own responsibilities: the interference of third parties can only produce mischief.

She began to see the thing in its true light after a little, and talked it over more calmly. Many a girl would have been delighted with this homage to her charms; but Jessie was no common person, and she felt a sort of degradation in inspiring a passion she could not return. Besides, it placed upon her the necessity of giving pain where it was in every way undeserved; and that she had never done in her life.

While we were talking, a light knock at the door heralded Mrs. Dennison. There was nothing to call her to that part of the house, and her first words conveyed an apology for the intrusion, for we both probably looked a little surprised.

"I beg ten thousand pardons for rushing in upon you; but the gentlemen are waiting in the road to know if they can join us to-morrow. I could only answer for myself, you know."

"Let them join you," I whispered; "the sooner it is over with the better."

Jessie stood up, gathered the long riding-skirt in one hand, while she walked past her guest with the air of a princess, and stepped out on the balcony, from which she made a gesture of invitation, which the two gentlemen acknowledged with profound bows, and rode away.

"That's an angel!" exclaimed Mrs. Dennison, laying her hand on Jessie's shoulder. "I almost thought something had gone wrong, by the way you left us. Poor Mr. Bosworth was quite crestfallen."

Jessie made a little gesture of annoyance, which the widow was quick to observe, and instantly changed the subject.

CHAPTER XI
THE BASKET OF FRUIT

"I should not have thought, by the way you parted, that you and Mr. Bosworth were old friends."

Jessie seemed annoyed, and replied, with a flush on her cheek, "that it was rather difficult to be demonstrative on horseback."

"At any rate, he's a splendid man," said the widow. "Rich or poor? Bond or free? Tell us all about him. I never thought to inquire before, but this looks serious."

"What strange questions you ask!" answered Jessie, and the color deepened in her cheek.

"Well, well, but the answer?"

Here I interposed: "Mr. Bosworth is not very rich. At least I never heard that he was."

"What a pity!" whispered the widow. "But the other questions?"

"If having no wife is to be free, you can hardly call him a bondman. Yes."

"What has he ever done to distinguish himself, then? Can you tell me that, Miss Hyde?"

"He is considered a man of brilliant parts, certainly," I answered; "but at his age few men have won permanent distinction, I fancy."

"At his age! Why, the man must be over eight-and-twenty, and half the great men that ever lived had made their mark in the world before they reached that age."

"Well, that may be," I replied; "but in these times greatness is not so easily won. The level of general intelligence, in our country at least, is raised, and it requires great genius, indeed, to lift a man suddenly above his fellows. In a dead sea of ignorance, superior ability looms up with imposing conspicuousness. This is why the great men of past times have cast the reflection of their minds on history;—not entirely because they excelled men of the present age, but from the low grade of popular intelligence that existed around them."

"Why, you talk like a statesman," said the widow, laughing. "I had no idea that anything so near politics existed in the ladies of this house."

"What is history but the politics of the past?" said Jessie. "What is politics but a history of the present?"

"Perhaps you are right," said the widow, flinging off her careless manner, and sitting down on one of the rustic chairs, where she began to dust her skirt with the fanciful whip fastened to her wrist. "I have often wondered why it should be considered unfeminine for an educated woman to understand the institutions of her own or any other country."

Mrs. Dennison looked at me as she spoke. Was the woman playing with my weakness? Or, did she really speak from her heart? If the former, she must have been amused at my credulity, for I answered in honest frankness:

"Nor I, either; except in evil, which is always better unknown. I can fancy no case where ignorance is a merit. Imagine Queen Victoria pluming herself on lady-like ignorance of the political state of her kingdom, when she opens Parliament in person."

Mrs. Dennison laughed, and chimed in with, "Or the Empress of France being appointed Regent of a realm, the position of which it was deemed unwomanly to understand; yet, on the face of the earth, there are not two females more womanly than Victoria of England, and Eugenie of France."

"What true ideas this woman possesses!" I said to myself. "How could I dislike her so? Really, the most charming person in the world is a woman who, under the light, graceful talk of conventional society, cultivates serious thought." While these reflections passed through my mind, the widow was looking at me from under her eyelashes, as if she expected me to speak again; so I went on,—

"It is not the knowledge of politics in itself of which refined people complain; but its passion and the vindictive feelings which partisanship is sure to foster. The woman who loves her country cannot understand it too well. The unwomanliness lies in the fact that she sometimes plunges into a turmoil of factions, thus becoming passionate and bitter."

"How plainly you draw the distinction between knowledge and prejudice!" she said, with one of her fascinating smiles. "But you must have discussed this subject often—with Mr. Lee, perhaps?"

"Yes, we talk on all subjects here. Nothing is forbidden, because few things that are not noble and true ever present themselves."

"I was sure of it!" exclaimed the lady, starting up with enthusiasm. "I have never been in a house where everything gave such evidence of high-toned intelligence."

She sat down again thoughtfully, dusting her habit with the little whip.

"I have not yet seen my hostess, but that does not arise from increased ill health, I trust. She seemed very feeble when we met on the sea-shore, last season—somewhat consumptive, we all thought."

I did not like the tone of her voice. There was something stealthy and creeping in it which checked the rising confidence in my heart.

"Mrs. Lee is very far from well," I answered, coldly.

"Not essentially worse, I trust."

She was looking at me keenly from the corners of her almond-shaped eyes. It was only a glance, but a gleam of suspicion sprung from my heart and met it half-way.

"It is difficult to tell. In a lingering disease like hers, one can never be sure."

"Mr. Lee must find himself lonesome at times without his lady's society, for she struck us all as a very superior person."

"On the contrary," I replied, with a quick impulse, for she still kept that sidelong glance on my face; "on the contrary, he spends most of his leisure time in her chamber, reads to her when she can bear it, and sits gently silent when she prefers that. A more devoted husband I never knew."

I saw that she was biting her red lips, but as my glance caught hers, the action turned to a smile.

"There is Mr. Lee going to his wife's room now," I remarked, as that gentleman passed the hall-door, with a little basket in his hand filled with delicate wood-moss, in which lay two or three peaches, the first of the season.

The exclamation that broke from Mrs. Dennison at the sight of the fruit arrested his steps, and he turned into the hall, asking if either of us had called.

She went forward at once, sweeping the cloth skirt after her like the train of an empress.

"Oh, what splendid peaches—and the basket! The bijou!" She held out both hands to receive the fruit, quite in a glow of pleasure.

"I am very sorry," said Mr. Lee, drawing back a step, "but this is—is for my wife. She is an invalid, you know."

"You misunderstand," replied the lady, coloring to the temples. "I only wish to admire the arrangement. It is really the prettiest fancy I ever saw."

He hesitated an instant; then held out the basket and placed it between her hands, with some little reluctance, I thought. Her side-face was toward me; but the look, half grieved, half reproachful, which she lifted to his face did not escape me.

"Shall I take the basket to Mrs. Lee?" I said, reaching out my hand. "She must have heard the horses return some time ago, and will expect some one."

"No," said the gentleman, bending his head, and taking the fruit. "I cannot allow you to deprive me of that pleasure."

"And I," rejoined the widow, with animation, "I must take off this cumbersome riding-dress."

I went to my room early that evening. Indeed, I had no heart to enter the parlor. Anxieties that I could not define pressed heavily upon me—so heavily that I longed for solitude. In passing through the hall, I met Mrs. Dennison's mulatto maid, who had, I forgot to say, followed our guest with the luggage. She was going to her mistress's chamber, carrying something carefully in her hand. When she saw me, her little silk apron was slyly lifted, and the burdened hand stole under it, but in the action something was disturbed, and the half of a peach fell at my feet.

I took up the cleft fruit very quietly, told the girl to remove her apron, that I might see what mischief had been done, and discovered a second basket filled with mossrose-buds from which the half peach had fallen.

I laid the fruit in its bed, saw the girl pass with it to her lady's chamber, and then went to my own room sick at heart. The half of a peach, offered among the Arabs, means atonement for some offence. What offence had Mr. Lee given to our guest in carrying a little fruit to his invalid wife?

CHAPTER XII
BREAKFAST WITH OUR GUEST

Mrs. Dennison was late the next morning. Indeed, she generally was late. It was sure to produce a little excitement when she entered, if the family were grouped in expectation, and her system of elegant selfishness rendered any consideration of the convenience of others a matter of slight importance. She was always lavish in apologies, those outgrowths of insincerity; and, in fact, managed to weave a sort of a fascination out of her own faults.

This certainly was the case here. If Mr. Lee was resolute about anything in his household, it was that punctuality at meals should be observed: indeed, I have seldom seen him out of humor on any other subject. But this morning he had been moving about in the upper hall a full hour, glancing impatiently at the papers which always reached us before breakfast, and walking up and down with manifest annoyance. Yet the moment that woman appeared with her coquettish little breakfast-cap just hovering on the back of her head, and robed in one of the freshest and most graceful morning dresses you ever saw, his face cleared up. With a smile that no one could witness without a throb of the heart, he received her apologies and compliments all mingled together on her lips like honey in the heart of a flower, as if they had been favors of which we were all quite undeserving.

We went down to breakfast at last; but just as we were sitting down, our guest took a fancy to run out on the terrace and gather a handful of heliotrope which she laid by her plate, exhaling the odor sensuously between the pauses of the meal. I don't know what the rest thought of all this, but I was disgusted. It is a strong word, I know, but I have no other for the repulsion that seizes upon me even now when I think of that woman. Her very passion for flowers, to me almost a heavenly taste in itself, was so combined with materialism, that the perfume of the heliotrope sickened me.

Jessie did not seem to sympathize in these feelings, nor care that her own choice flower-plot had been rifled of its sweetest blossoms. In fact, the fascination of that woman's manner seemed more powerful with her than it had proved with the proud, strong man who sat opposite me.

Jessie, the darling, either because she did not like the restraint, or, what was more like her, wishing to give me dignity in the household, always insisted that I should preside at the table; Mrs. Lee, from her feeble state of health, being at all times unequal to the task. Three times did that insatiable woman return her coffee-cup: first, for an additional lump of sugar, again for a few drops more cream, and then for the slightest possible dilution of its strength. While I performed these smiling behests, she sat brushing a branch of heliotrope across her lips, exclaiming at the beauty of the scene from an opposite window, and behaving generally like an empress who had honored her subjects with a visit, and was resolved to put them quite at ease in her presence.

But Jessie could not see things in this light. She was evidently as well pleased with her guest as she had been the night before, but, though she smiled and joined in the pleasant conversation, I saw by the heavy shadows under her eyes that some anxiety disturbed her. The fact that she had made an appointment to ride with a suitor whom she must reject accounted sufficiently for this; Jessie had the finest traits of a purely proud nature, and the idea of giving pain was to her in itself a great trial. Still, these observations only applied to the undercurrent that morning; on the surface everything was sparkling and pleasant.

Mr. Lee was more than usually animated, and, before the meal was ended, quite a war of complimentary badinage had commenced and was kept up between him and our guest.

Jessie always went to her mother after breakfast. So, immediately on quitting the table, she stole away to the tower, looking a little serious, but not more so than her peculiar trial of the day accounted for.

I followed her directly, leaving Mrs. Dennison and Mr. Lee on the square balcony, on which the early sunshine lay in golden warmth.

Mrs. Lee had not rested well; her eyes, usually so bright, were heavy from want of sleep; and the pillow, from which she had not yet risen, bore marks of a thousand restless movements, which betrayed unusual excitement.

CHAPTER XIII
JESSIE LEE AND HER MOTHER

Jessie was sitting on one side of the bed holding a Parian cup in her hand; the amber gleam of coffee shone through the transparent vine-leaves that embossed it, and she was stirring the fragrant beverage gently with a spoon.

"Try, dear mother, and drink just a little," she was saying, in her sweet, caressing way. "It makes me very unhappy to see you looking so ill."

"Indeed I am not ill, only a little restless, Jessie," answered the sweet lady, rising languidly from her pillow and reaching forth her hand for the cup. She tasted the coffee and looked gratefully at her daughter. "It is nice; no one understands me like you, my daughter."

Jessie blushed with pleasure, and began to mellow a delicate slice of toast with the silver knife that lay beside it, making a parade of her efforts, which she evidently hoped would entice her mother's appetite: and so it did. I am sure no one besides her could have tempted that frail woman to eat a mouthful. As it was, one of the birds that was picking seeds from the terrace could almost have rivalled her appetite: the presence of her daughter, I fancy, gave her more strength than anything else.

"So you have had a bad night, my mother," said Jessie, tenderly; "once or twice I awoke and felt that you did not sleep."

"Indeed!" said the mother, with an earnest look breaking through the heaviness of her eyes.

"Yes, indeed; but then I never wake in the night without wondering if you sleep well."

"Did you see me?" questioned the mother, anxiously.

"See you, mother?"

Mrs. Lee smiled faintly, and shook her head as if to cast off some strange thought.

"Of course, it was impossible. I must have slept long enough to dream; but it seems to me as if I was in your room last night. Something called me there, a faint, white shadow, that sometimes took the outline of an angel, sometimes floated before me like a cloud."

"Oh, my good mother! it was kind to come, even in your dreams," said Jessie, kissing the little hand that lay in hers.

Mrs. Lee looked troubled, and seemed to be searching her memory for something.

"It took me—the cloud-angel—you know, into the blue room."

"The blue room!" Jessie and I exclaimed together, for that was the apartment in which Mrs. Dennison slept, though the fact had never been mentioned to Mrs. Lee, and another chamber had at first been intended for our guest. "The blue room?"

"Yes, the blue room!" she said; "but like all dreams, nothing was like the reality. Instead of the enamelled furniture, everything was covered with the prettiest blue chintz, with a wild-rose pattern running over it."

Jessie and I looked at each other in consternation, for the furniture which Mrs. Lee described as familiar to the blue room had been removed to the chamber we had first intended for Mrs. Dennison, and that with which we had replaced it being too rich for a sleeping-room, we had covered it with the pretty chintz, without mentioning the fact to Mrs. Lee or any one else.

"There was a toilet instead of the dressing-table, I remember," continued the lady, "with quantities of frost-like lace falling around it and on it; with other things, a little basket, prettier than mine, full of mossrose-buds."

"Was there nothing else in the basket?" I questioned, holding my breath for the reply.

"Nothing else," answered the lady, smiling; "oh! yes, combs and hair-pins, rings and bracelets, the whole toilet was in a glitter."

"But nothing else in the basket?" I persisted.

"No; rose-buds—mossrose-buds, red and white. Nothing more," she answered, languidly.

Mrs. Lee paused a moment with her eyes closed. Then starting as if from sleep, she almost cried out,—

"There was a woman in the room—in the bed—a beautiful woman. The ruffles of her night-gown were open at the throat, the sleeves were broad and loose; you could see her arms almost to the shoulders. She wore no cap, and her hair fell in bright, heavy coils down to her waist. She had something in her hand; don't speak, I shall remember in a minute: the color was rich.

It was, yes, it was half a peach, with the brown stone partly bedded in the centre; the fragrance of it hung about the basket of roses."

"And you saw all this, dear lady?" I exclaimed, startled by the reality of her picture, which, as a whole, I recognized far more closely than Jessie could.

"In my dream, yes; but one fancies such strange things when asleep, you know, dear Miss Hyde."

"Strange, very strange," murmured Jessie; "but for the basket of roses and the fruit, we might have recognized the picture. Don't you think so, Aunt Matty?"

"Did you get a look at the lady's face?" I inquired, suppressing Jessie's question.

"No, no; I think not. The thick hair shaded it, but the arms and neck were white as lilies. She had bitten the peach; I remember seeing marks of her teeth on one side. Strange, isn't it, how real such fancies will seem?"

"It is, indeed, strange," I said, feeling cold chills creeping over me.

"Besides," continued the invalid, while a scarcely perceptible shiver disturbed her, "notwithstanding the freshness and beauty of everything, I felt oppressed in that room—just as flowers may be supposed to grow faint when vipers creep over them; the air seemed close till I got to your chamber, Jessie."

"And there?" said the sweet girl, kissing her mother's hand again.

"There, the angel that had been a cloud took form again. It beckoned me—beckoned me—I cannot tell where; but you were sleeping, I know that."

"It was a strange dream," said Jessie, thoughtfully.

"The impression was very strong," answered the mother, drawing a hand across her eyes,—"so powerful that it tired me. This morning it seemed as if I had been on a journey."

"But you are better now," I said; "this sense of fatigue is wearing off, I hope."

"Oh, yes!" she answered, languidly.

"And you will be well enough to see Mrs. Dennison before dinner, I hope," whispered Jessie.

"Perhaps, child."

"Father will persuade you."

"Where is your father, Jessie?"

"Oh! somewhere about. On the front balcony, I believe, with Mrs. Dennison, who declares that she never will get tired of looking down the valley."

"Yes, it is a lovely view. We used to sit on the balcony for hours—your father and I—but now—" Mrs. Lee turned away her face and shaded her eyes with one pale hand.

I walked to the window and lifted the curtain; but there was a mist over my eyes, and I could not discern a feature of the landscape.

CHAPTER XIV
INTRUSIVE KINDNESS

Some one knocked at the door. I went to open it, and found Cora, Mrs. Dennison's maid, who had been brushing her mistress's riding-habit on the back terrace, and flung it across her arm before coming up-stairs. The girl was a pretty mulatto, with teeth that an empress might have coveted, and eyes like diamonds; but there was something in her face that I did not like—a way of looking at you from under her black eyelashes that was both searching and sinister.

"Mistress told me to run up, and inquire if it wasn't time for Miss Lee to put on her habit," she said, shooting a quick glance into the room; "the horses are ordered round."

I felt the color burning in my face. The impertinence of this intrusion angered me greatly.

"Miss Lee is with her mother," I said, "and cannot be disturbed; when she is ready, I will let your mistress know. Until then the horses must wait."

The girl gave the habit on her arm a shake, and went away, casting one or two glances behind. What possible business could the creature have in that part of the house? Had the mistress really sent her? It was an hour before the time for riding, and it had not been our custom to hurry Jessie away from her mother's room.

While I stood by the window, thinking angrily of this intrusion, another knock called me back to the door. It was the mulatto again, with her mistress's compliments, and, if Mrs. Lee was well enough, she would pay her respects while the horses waited.

I went down myself at this, and meeting Mrs. Dennison on the terrace, informed her, very curtly, I fear, that Mrs. Lee was not out of her bedroom, having spent a restless night, and was quite incapable of seeing strangers.

I put a little malicious emphasis on the word *strangers*, which brought a deeper color into her cheeks; but she answered with elaborate expressions of sympathy, inquired so minutely into the symptoms and causes of Mrs. Lee's prostration, that I felt at a loss how to answer.

"Dear lady!" she went on, "I'm afraid these severe attacks will exhaust the little strength she has left; they must make life a burden."

"On the contrary," I said, "there is not, I am sure, a person living who so keenly enjoys the highest and most lofty principles of existence. With the love of God in her heart, and domestic love all around her, life can never be a burden."

"Indeed!" she answered, with something in her voice that approached a sneer; "I never was sick in my life, that is, perhaps, why it seems so terrible to me. Nothing could reconcile me, I am sure, to a life like Mrs. Lee's. At her age, too, with disease helping time to chase away what beauty one has left, how she must feel it!"

"You quite mistake the case, madam," I answered; "Mrs. Lee never depended on her beauty, which, however, no one can dispute, as a means of winning love; her sincerity, intelligence, and gentle wisdom are enough to outlive the loveliness of a Venus."

"You are enthusiastic, Miss Hyde."

"I love Mrs. Lee, and speak as I feel."

"I am afraid," she said, in her blandest manner, "that my interest in the dear lady has led me into obtrusiveness, or, at least, that you think so. But she is so very superior—so perfect, in fact, that one cannot shake off the interest she inspires. It was this feeling which tempted me to ask for the privilege of paying my respects;—I see now that it was inopportune; but a warm heart is always getting one into scrapes, Miss Hyde. I shall never learn how to tame mine down. It seemed to me that the sweet invalid yonder must feel lonely in her room, and this was why that importunate request was made."

"Mrs. Lee is a woman who would find something of paradise in any position. Her sitting-room, up in the tower yonder, has always been considered the pleasantest apartment in the house."

"No doubt; it was this conviction which made me anxious to be admitted. Still, I must think that a confinement, that only promises to be relieved by death, must be a painful thing."

Why did the woman always return to that point? In my whole life I had never heard the probable result of Mrs. Lee's illness alluded to so often, as it had been hardly mentioned since Mrs. Dennison's arrival. It shocked me, and became the more repulsive from the usual levity of her manner. She seemed to weave the idea of my dear friend's death with every luxury that surrounded her dwelling; to my prejudiced fancy, she even exulted in it. I stood looking her in the face while these thoughts troubled my mind. What my eyes may have spoken I cannot tell, but hers fell beneath them, and, with an uneasy smile, she turned to walk away.

That moment Jessie came out to the terrace, looking a little anxious.

"Where is father?" she said; "mother is up and waiting for him."

I saw a faint smile quiver around the widow's lips, but she busied herself with some branches of ivy that had broken loose from the terrace-wall, and did not seem to heed us. Just then the tramp of horses sounded from the front of the house, and Jessie exclaiming with a little impatience, "Dear me!" walked quickly to the square balcony. I followed her, and saw Mr. Lee standing at the foot of the steps ready to mount. He was giving some orders to the groom, and seemed particularly anxious about the horse which Mrs. Dennison was to ride.

Jessie's face flushed, and a look of proud surprise came across it. Mr. Lee turned his head that way and called out,—

"Why, Jessie, where is your habit? I never found you late before."

Jessie did not answer, but passed me, descending to the terrace and down the flight of steps. She spoke to her father, looking back anxiously. After the first words, he started and seemed taken by surprise. Even from the distance I could see a flood of crimson rush to his forehead. They both ascended the steps together. Mr. Lee went to the tower, and Jessie ran upstairs to put on her riding-dress.

I went up to help her, but walked slowly; everything conspired to depress me that morning. One serpent was enough to destroy the perfect happiness of Eden. Our little paradise seemed changing after the same fashion, and yet no one could tell why.

Jessie was buttoning her habit as I went in. She looked restless and hurt.

"Aunt Matty," she said, "I have a great mind to give up this ride; the thought of meeting that gentleman troubles me. Look how my hands tremble."

Yes, the serpent was doing its work. Even our sweet, honest Jessie was beginning to cover up her true feelings under false issues. It was something nearer home than the dread of an unwelcome offer that made her so nervous. For the first time since her remembrance Mr. Lee had forgotten his wife. But for Jessie's interposition, he would have ridden away without inquiring after her. I recollected how he had blushed when reminded of this.

Of course, I could not speak of the true cause of this discontent, the delicate reticence becoming to a daughter was too sacred for that; but I said quickly,—

"Yes, yes, darling, you must go. It is your duty."

She looked at me earnestly, then dropping her eyes, went on with her preparations.

A second time Mrs. Dennison came to her chamber. Our coldness the day before had left no impression on the materialism of her nature. Sparkling with cheerfulness, and brilliant with smiles, she swept in, bending her flexible whip into a ring, with both hands, and letting it free again with a prolonged snap.

"All ready? That's right, my Lady Jess! The day is heavenly, and our cavaliers are coming up the road!"

"Thank heaven!" I heard Jessie whisper, as she drew on her gantlets.

If she fancied that the coming of Mr. Bosworth and his friend would release Mr. Lee, and leave him at liberty to spend his morning with the invalid, she was disappointed in the result, though not in the fact. Just as the party were mounting, he appeared on the terrace, and, descending the steps, joined them, whip in hand.

I watched all these movements keenly; why, it would have been impossible for me to explain even to my own judgment; but shadows tormented me at this time, and all my senses were on the alert. Mr. Lee rode by his daughter, leaving his guest to the other gentlemen, between whom she rode triumphantly, as Queen Elizabeth may have entered Kenilworth, flirting royally with her handsomest subjects. Jessie and her father seemed to be conversing quietly, as I had seen them a hundred times riding down that road.

CHAPTER XV
THE TRAIL OF THE SERPENT

After the party was out of sight, I went into Mrs. Dennison's room to see that the maid had performed her duty, as was my custom; for I had assumed these light cares in the household, and loved them from the fact that they attached an idea of usefulness to my residence in the house.

Everything seemed in order. Cora, the mulatto girl, was busily arranging the dress her mistress had just taken off. Ear-rings and a brooch of blue lava were lying on the toilet, and the pretty cap, with its streamers of black velvet and azure ribbon, hung upon one of the supports of the dressing-table, as she had left them.

I looked for the basket of mossrose-buds, but it was gone; some buds were opening in one of the toilet-glasses, but that was all. Why had the widow Dennison taken such pains to put the basket out of sight?

"What have you done with the basket?" I inquired very quietly of the girl. "If you wet the moss again, we can fill it with fresh flowers."

"What basket, Miss?" inquired the girl, lifting her black eyes innocently to my face.

"The basket you brought in here last evening."

"Oh, that!" she continued, dropping her eyes; "I've made so many of them things that mistress doesn't seem to care for 'em any more."

"You—you make them?"

"Yes, indeed! Is there any harm, Miss?" she said, lifting her eyes again, with a look of genuine earnestness.

"And you arranged those buds in the moss?"

"Yes, indeed!"

"And placed the half peach among them?"

"Was there any harm, Miss?"

"The half peach—after an Oriental fashion?"

"Dear me! I hope there wasn't any harm in the gardener's letting me have that one. It was the first I had seen this year, so I couldn't give up more than I did; but it was the biggest half that I saved for the mistress."

Nothing could be more natural than her dawning contrition, nothing more satisfactory than the solution she had given to a subject that had kept me awake half the night. What a fool I had been! Was I, in fact, becoming fanciful and old-maidish—ready to find error in shadows, and crimes in everything? Heaven forbid that anything so unwomanly and indelicate as this should come upon me.

Was it possible that I, in the waning freshness of my life, had begun to envy brighter and handsomer women the homage due to their attraction, and had thus become suspicious? The very idea humiliated me; I felt abashed before that mulatto girl, who sat so demurely smoothing the folds of her mistress's breakfast-dress across her lap. It seemed as if she must have some knowledge of the mean suspicion that had brought me there. How artful and indirect my conduct had been! In my heart I had rather plumed myself on the adroit way in which my questions had been put regarding that annoying basket. Now, I was heartily ashamed of it all, and stole out of the room bitterly discomfited.

In shutting the door, I glanced back; the girl was looking up from her work. The demure expression had left her face, the black eyes flashed and danced as they followed me; but the moment my look met hers, all this passed away so completely, that my very senses were confused, and the doubts that I had put aside came crowding back upon me.

I went up to Mrs. Lee's room. She was resting on the lounge, sound asleep; but her face seemed cold as well as pale. There was a strange look about it, as if all the vitality were stricken out; yet she breathed evenly, and though I made some noise in entering, it did not disturb her in the least.

I sat down on a low chair by the side of her couch; for Jessie had desired me to sit by her during all the time I could command. Thus I was placed close to the gentle sleeper. The deathly stillness in which she lay troubled me; it seemed too profound for healthy slumber. One little hand fell over the couch. I took it in my own, and passed my other hand softly over it. Strange enough, she did not move, but began to murmur in her sleep, while a cold, troubled cloud contracted her forehead.

"Ah! now I can see everything—everything; they are cantering by the old mill. I haven't seen it before in years. How beautifully the shadows fall on the water; the waves are tipped with silver; the trees rustle pleasantly! No wonder they draw up to look at the mill; it always was a picturesque object!"

She was following the equestrians in her dreams—those strange dreams that seemed to drink up all the color and warmth from her body.

According to the best calculation I could make, the party would have reached the old mill about this time. It stood under the curve of the precipitous banks, a mile or two up the river, and Mr. Lee had spoken of riding that way at breakfast. Thus it seemed more than probable that the party was exactly as she fancied it. Mr. Lee had doubtless informed her what route he would take, and so her imagination followed him while her frail form slumbered.

She stirred uneasily on her pillow, drew her black eyebrows together, and spoke again:—

"Why does he leave my Jessie? She don't want to be left with that young man;—and he, poor fellow! how frightened he is! What is that he is saying? Wants to marry my Jessie! Alas! how the heart shrinks in her bosom! My poor child! he should not distress you so! Yet it is an honest heart he offers—full of warmth, full of goodness! Can't you understand that, my darling?"

After this speech she lay quiet a few minutes, and then spoke like one who had been examining something that puzzled her.

"Jessie, Jessie! what is this? Why does your heart stand still while he speaks to her? It troubles me, darling. I am your mother, and this thing disturbs me more than you can guess. You have driven one away—he retreats to the rear, heart-broken. That other one comes up. Who is he? what is he? Ask her, for she is watching him, and her loaded heart follows after, though he, my husband, is by her side."

Here she dropped into silence again, only breaking it by faint moans, and a single ejaculation, "Oh, not that! not that!"

Her face grew so painfully wan, and she gave evidence of so much inward anguish, that I was constrained to arouse her. My voice made no impression, and the clasp of my hand only threw her into a more deathly slumber. I began to comprehend her state. I had heard of deep trances, when the soul seems released from the body, or is gifted with something like prophecy. I knew, or believed, that this was an unhealthy state, the result of disease, or the offspring of a badly balanced organization; and this thought horrified me; there was something of the supernatural in it that filled my soul with awe. By the contraction of her pale forehead, I saw that there was some distress in the head; so lifting my hand, I passed it across her brow, hoping to soothe away the pain.

Certainly, the face became calm, a smile stole across the lips, and after a moment her eyes opened, and looked vaguely around, as a child awakes from its sleep.

CHAPTER XVI
AFTER DREAMING

"I have been asleep," said Mrs. Lee, pleasantly; "sound asleep. When did you come in?"

"Only a short time since."

"And you have been sitting here while I slept?"

"Yes; after a restless night, I fancied a quiet sleep would do you no harm."

"Harm? It has given me strength."

"Do you think so?"

She smiled.

"Have you been dreaming again?" I inquired, a little anxiously.

"Dreaming? No, my sleep was profound, perfect rest. But where is Jessie? She sat where you are when I fell off."

"Indeed!"

"Yes, I remember—her left hand held mine, with her right she was soothing the pain from my forehead."

"That was some time ago; she has gone out to ride since, and I am quite sure Mr. Lee came up here after she left you," I said.

"I am glad of it," she answered, gently. "He was rather late this morning, I remember thinking; but Jessie would not own it. So he came up, and I did not hear him. Miss Hyde, this is the first time in my whole life that his lightest footstep failed to awake me,—what can it mean?"

"Yes," broke in Lottie, who had been hanging around the door, unnoticed; for we had all become so used to her presence in that room, that it was no more heeded than that of the canary-bird in its cage on the balcony,—"yes, ma'am, Mr. Lee came up with his spurs on, and his whip all ready, just like a trooper, clang, clang, clang. I thought the noise would make you jump out of the window in that white, loose gown, just like an angel with its wings spread; but law! there you were, ma'am, snoozing away right in his face, and he making up his mind, with the whip in his hand, whether to kiss you good-bye or not."

"And did he?" inquired the lady, with a faint flush of the cheek.

"No, ma'am; I suppose he was afraid of scaring you out of that nice sleep. He only looked at you sort of earnestly, and went off trying to walk on tiptoe; but mercy! didn't them boots creak?"

"I thought not," murmured the lady, with infinite tenderness in her voice; "I must have been dead if that failed to arouse me."

"Lor, Mrs. Lee," continued the maid, spreading her flail-like arms in illustration, "I wish you could have seen that new widder-woman when them two gentlemen helped her on to the horse. Didn't her dress swell out—and didn't she keep Mr. Lawrence a-tinkering away at her stirrups, with one foot in his hand, till it made me sick looking on. Awful 'cute lady that is, Miss Hyde; you ain't no match for her, nohow!"

I really think that witch of a girl was gifted with something almost like second sight. I never had a secret taste or dislike that she did not understand at once, and drag it out in some blundering way before the whole world.

"What makes you think so, Lottie?" I inquired, a little annoyed.

"Because you're straightforward right out, and flat-footed honest; and she—oh my!"

"What makes you say, 'oh my!' Lottie?"

"Nothing, Miss Hyde; only I've got eyes, and can see right through a mill-stone, especially when there's a hole in the middle. Perhaps you can't, then again perhaps you can; I don't dispute anything; only, as I said before, that widder-woman is too 'cute for such a mealy-mouthed lady as you are. My!—wouldn't she ride over you rough-shod and with spurs to her slippers!"

We spoiled that girl. She was neither servant, companion, nor protégée, and yet partook of the position which three such persons might have occupied in the family. She waited upon every one with the faithfulness of a hound and the speed of a lapwing, seemed to be always in the kitchen, constantly flitting through the parlor, yet never beyond the sound of her mistress's voice. She belonged everywhere and nowhere in the household. She had taken her position out of the kitchen entirely, by refusing to sit down at the table there, whatever the temptation was, she invariably carrying off the tray into her own little room, after the mistress was served, taking her meals in solitary grandeur from frosted silver and china so delicate that you could see a shadow through it. Nay, she affected great elegance in this little room, which was a sort of select hospital for all the old finery in the household. Lace curtains, condemned as too much worn for the parlor-windows, after passing through her adroit hands, appeared at the casement of her little room transparent as new; silk hangings, when faded from their first splendor, she managed to revive into almost pristine brightness. She would cut out the freshest medallions from an old carpet, and make it bloom out anew under her own feet. Then she had pretty knick-knacks and keepsakes scattered about, which made her little nook quite a boudoir—indeed, almost the prettiest one in the family.

Mrs. Lee was rather proud of her unique handmaiden's retreat; it gratified her own exquisite sense of the beautiful; and, as the room opened into her own, it was but a continuation of the refinements that surrounded her.

In her dress, too, Lottie was more original than half the old pictures one sees offered for sale. Jessie's cast-off dresses were remodelled by her nimble fingers into a variety of garments really marvellous. Indeed, Lottie was generally the most perfectly costumed person in our household. No one felt disposed to check this exuberant taste in the strange girl: it pleased the invalid, and that was reason enough for anything in our family.

"Yes, I say it again," persisted the strange little creature, folding her arms and setting her head on one side, "widders are monstrous smart, up to a'most anything. I've often wished that I'd been born a widder with both eye-teeth cut, as theirs always is—are, I meant. Lor! Miss Hyde, you ain't a circumstance; just leave this one to me."

"Lottie, Lottie," said Mrs. Lee, shaking her head, "you speak too loud and look bold, it isn't becoming. Besides, the guests in a house must always be honored, never made subjects of criticism: in short, my good child, we are spoiling you."

Lottie withered into penitence with the first words of this reproof. When it was ended, a deep flush settled around her eyes, as if tears were suppressed with difficulty.

"Spoiling me! not with kindness, I should die without that," she said, half sitting down on the ottoman, half kneeling by the couch. "I won't speak another word against that—that lady. There, I've got it out; say you are not angry with me."

"Angry! no, my child. Only be careful not to say harsh things of any one, it is a bad habit."

"I am sorry!"

"Well, well."

"Very sorry!"

"There, there, child, it is not so very terrible."

"I'll never call the lady a widder again. Never!"

Mrs. Lee smiled, and sent her into the next room. She seemed troubled after the girl went out; for certainly tears had glittered in Lottie's eyes, a thing I had never witnessed before.

"Go in, Miss Hyde, and comfort her, poor thing! It was cruel to reprove her so harshly; but my temper is getting ungovernable."

It was almost amusing to hear that gentle creature condemn herself with so little reason; but she would not be convinced that something of the spirit of a Nero had not been manifest in that mild reprimand; so I went into Lottie's room, much better disposed to give her a second lesson than to console her for the first.

Miss Lottie had curled herself up in the window-seat, with both hands clasped around her knees, and her face buried upon them.

CHAPTER XVII
LOTTIE EXPRESSES HER OPINION OF THE WIDOW

"Lottie," I said, going up to the girl, "what are you huddled up in that place for? Is there nothing you can find to do more profitable than pouting?"

"I'm not pouting, Miss Hyde," she said; "only grinding my teeth in peace and comfort. Why can't you let me alone, I should like to know?"

"What folly! Do get down and act like a sensible creature."

"Well," she said, throwing herself off the window-seat with a demi-summersault, which landed her in the middle of the room, "here I am. What's wanted?"

It was rather difficult for me to say just that instant what I did want, having only a charge of consolation on hand.

"Well," she added, "what have I done to you, Miss Hyde, that I can't be allowed to sit still in my own room?"

"Nothing, Lottie; I was only afraid that you might be fretting."

Her eyes instantly filled with tears, which she dashed aside with her hand.

"So I was; what's the use of denying it? She never said a cross word to me before, and wouldn't now but for that Mrs. Babylon. I hate that widder; I want to stomp her down under my feet. It makes me grit my teeth when she comes sailing out into the garden, and looks up to Mrs. Lee's window, just like a dog hankering after a bone."

"Why, how can you feel so bitterly, Lottie, about a person you never spoke to a dozen times in your life?" I said, shocked and surprised by her vehemence.

"Didn't I, though? How 'cute people can be with their eyes shut! Well, I fancy that the widder and I are slightly acquainted—better than she thinks for."

"Why, how can that be possible; you are always in Mrs. Lee's room?"

"Generally, generally—not always. There is hours in the morning, before she gets up; hours in the evening, after she goes to bed; when I break out, and do a little exploring about the premises. This morning I was in Mrs. Babylon's room before any of you were up."

"Indeed! How did that happen?"

"That sneaking mulatto girl came to the chamber-door as I was passing, and beckoned me to come in."

"And you went?"

"Me! Why not? If a girl never sinsatiates around, how is she to find out what's going on? Besides, I wanted to know just how Babylon looked in her own room; so, being invited, I went in."

"But what did she want of you?"

"Don't know. Something besides doing a braid up in eleven strands, I surmise; but that was what she made believe it was about—just as if that mulatto creature didn't understand that much of her business. I did it though, meek as Moses—such hair! a yard long in the shortest part. It was worth while trying a hand at it; but, after all, it seemed like braiding copperheads and rattlesnakes. I hate to touch anybody's hair if I don't like 'em; it makes me crawl all over."

"But why don't you like Mrs. Dennison?"

"Why—because I don't; and because you don't either."

I could not help smiling, and yet was half angry with the girl. She shook her head gravely and went on:

"It wasn't the hair, Miss Hyde; that copper-colored girl knew more than I did about it, often as I've braided for Miss Jessie."

"Then what did she want?"

"I've found out—never you fear."

"Well?"

"Can't tell anything about it. It's like a patch-work quilt in my mind, the pieces all sorted, but not laid together; the colors will get ship-shape by-and-by, and then I'll answer everything. She wants me to come into her room every morning, and I'm going."

"What, when you dislike her so much?"

"Yes, in spite of that, and fifty times as much. I'm going to do up Mrs. Babylon's hair for her."

"Well, well, I am glad you are not heart-broken about Mrs. Lee's mild rebuke."

"Heart-broken! I'd die rather than have a real cross word from her; for I tell you, Miss Hyde, if ever there was an angel with a morning-dress and slippers on as a general thing, that angel is the lady in yonder. Miss Jessie is considerable, and you sometimes come almost up to the mark, but you can't hold a candle to her, neither one of you."

It was of no use reproving or questioning Lottie; she was in reality the most independent person in the house, so I went away rather amused by my efforts at consolation.

Earlier than I expected, the riding party came back. Everybody seemed a little out of sorts. Jessie was pale and looked harassed. Young Bosworth rode by her side, but it was with the appearance of a man returning from a funeral. He lifted Jessie from the saddle. She reached forth her hand before ascending the steps, and seemed to be speaking earnestly. I saw him wring the hand with unusual energy, and spring to his saddle again.

As he was turning his horse, Mrs. Dennison rode up with Lawrence and Mr. Lee. For a voice so musical, hers was rather loud, so I could distinctly hear her call out,—

"Remember, Mr. Bosworth, your engagement for this evening; don't hope to be excused."

Bosworth bowed, and rode slowly away; but Lawrence sprang from his horse, and ran up the steps after Jessie, leaving Mr. Lee to help the other lady from her saddle.

Jessie heard him coming, and fairly ran into the house, a piece of rudeness that seemed to surprise him very much; but unlike as this was to her usual manner, it did not astonish me. The dear girl's face was toward me, and I saw that it was flushed with tears. Bosworth had offered himself, and been refused, poor fellow! I was sure of that.

Mrs. Dennison laughed till her clear voice rang far out among the flowers as she witnessed Lawrence's discomfiture. He colored a little angrily, and would have passed her on the steps, but she took his arm with exquisite coolness, and smilingly forced him into the house.

"Babylon's got two strings to her bow,—smart!"

This strange speech was uttered at my elbow. I looked round and saw Lottie close to me.

"Better go up-stairs," she said, pointing over her shoulder; "she wouldn't let me help her; you must."

Mrs. Dennison entered the upper hall. Her eyes sparkled, her lips curved triumphantly. She had carried away her captive and exulted over him with charming playfulness, which he answered in a low, impressive voice.

I went up-stairs, leaving them together: Jessie stood in the upper passage leaning against the banister. She was pale as death, and her lips quivered like those of a wronged child; but the moment she saw me, the proud air natural to her returned, and she moved toward her room, waving me back.

CHAPTER XVIII
THE UNWELCOME PROPOSAL

It was true, Jessie had received the proposal she so much dreaded, received it exactly as her mother had described the scene. If other and deeper feelings prevailed with her, they were buried far out of sight by the delicate reticence of a nature which shrunk from any revelation of feelings which would, perhaps, never receive a generous response. Though the most single-hearted and frank creature in the world, Jessie would have died rather than confess feelings such as I fear occupied her heart even at this time.

"Well, Aunt Matty, I have obeyed you," she said, with a sorrowful look of the eyes, the moment we were alone together. "It breaks my heart, but I have listened to all he could say, poor fellow! and it is over. What a terrible, terrible thing it must be to love a person who does not care for you. Oh! Aunt Matty, Aunt Matty! it is—" She hesitated, turned crimson, and added, "it must be like death, worse than death; for to crush one's pride is to deprive life of its dignity, and this thing I have done for him."

"And do you begin to regret it?" I said, sitting down, and drawing her head to my shoulder.

"Regret it? The thought oppresses me; I am so sorry for him; my heart aches when I think of the look he gave me. Oh! why is it that love cannot always be mutual?"

"That would destroy half its romance, I fear," said I, smiling in spite of my sympathy in her distress.

She gave a little nervous laugh and said, "she supposed so; but it was very hard to see a good man suffer disappointment and mortification such as she had just witnessed. Some ladies might glory in these things, but, for her part, she hoped never to have another offer in her life. It was hard to give pain, harder by far than to endure it. Poor John Bosworth, how wretched he must be!"

I strove to comfort her, for there was no affectation in all this. She really did suffer all her broken speech implied, but she felt the humiliation she had given too keenly for argument.

"He bowed himself before me as if I were a queen; and to be rejected after all, it was very cruel!" she exclaimed, excitedly; "but what could I do? There was Mrs. Dennison—but no matter about her."

Jessie stopped suddenly, and a flame of crimson spread and glowed in her cheeks.

"You don't like Mrs. Dennison, Aunt Matty?" she said, after a moment's silence.

"No, I never did like her," was my prompt reply.

"She is a strange woman," said Jessie, thoughtfully; "so brilliant, so full of attractions, everybody is charmed with her at first sight. I was."

"And now?" I suggested.

She looked at me a moment, then smiled, a little bitterly, I thought, and said,—

"Who can help like—admiring her?"

Something was wrong in that quarter; I was sure of it. Two natures so opposite as those of our Jessie and Mrs. Dennison could not long harmonize under the same roof.

"Well," I said, smoothing the raven braids of Jessie's hair, "the worst is over now. Mr. Bosworth will think all the better of you for being truthful and honest; we shall have him for a friend still, never fear."

Jessie shook her head quite dejectedly.

"No, that can never be; these rides and invitations have been misunderstood. He really thought I was encouraging him, when you know, dear Aunt Matty, I hadn't the least idea of what it all meant. He talks of going to Europe at once, or—or—"

"Or what?" I inquired, with an inclination to smile; "drown himself by the old mill, perhaps?"

She glanced at me a little roguishly, and said, with a half-sigh, "Yes, aunt, I believe he almost threatened that."

"So much the better," I said, gravely enough; for she was on the alert for any signs of ridicule. "The disappointment that takes that form is not killing."

"Don't!" she said, with a contraction of the forehead, which gave evidence of real pain, "the very remembrance of his face is a reproach to me; and there *they* sat so quietly in the shade of a tree enjoying the scenery. To them, I dare say, the world contained nothing else to think of. Mrs. Dennison even pointed at us with her whip, as if we made up the figures of a picture."

"Well, but she did not know," I suggested.

"Heaven forbid!"

We were interrupted then, and Jessie went to her mother, whose gentle sympathy was always at command, though the cause of grief might be unexplained. The presence of that woman was like a calm autumn day—it saddened while it made you better.

CHAPTER XIX
OUT UPON THE RIDGE

I could not pine why it was, but for some reason Mrs. Dennison appeared ill at ease after her ride that morning. Mr. Lee was about the house all day; but she rather avoided him, and disappeared altogether from the square balcony, where he was in the habit of reading when the shadows crept round to that side of the house.

Late in the day I went out for a walk, and, mounting the hill back of the house, wandered along its upper ridge, where a thick growth of hemlocks and forest-trees shut out a glorious landscape on either hand; for this hill formed a spur of the mountains which partially separated two broad valleys. That on the east I have already described; but the other and broader space of country could only be commanded from one or two prominent points on the ridge. A large rock, fringed with ferns and mountain pinks, marked one of these spots. A footpath led to it through the trees, and, as the rock crowned a precipitous declivity of several hundred feet, it ended there.

I sat down upon the rock weary from my long walk, and gazed dreamily upon the broad plain at my feet. It was in a state of beautiful cultivation: a large county-town lay under the shelter of the near mountains, over which a cloud of smoke floated from the numerous iron foundries in full blast in the environs. The breaks and gossamer floating of this cloud interested me, not the less because its source was in the useful development of the resources of a great commonwealth. I loved to think that with every wreath of that graceful vapor came assurance of bread for the working-man, and profits to the capitalist; for to me such thoughts give dignity to the beautiful. I am not one of those who would object to having the waters of Niagara lowered half an inch, if it would give the poor better and cheaper flour.

Well, as I was saying, the hives of industry which lay in the hazy distance made the landscape one of peculiar interest. The signs of rich cultivation upon the undulating grounds stretching to a range of the Blue Ridge, so far away that the mountain peaks seemed embankments of clouds, took a new aspect every time I saw them.

Like the busy city, every beautiful object conveyed an under-thought of prosperity; even the distant noise of some forges under the mountain sounded harmonious in connection with the broad scene.

As I sat looking upon this glorious picture, reflecting that my beloved country could boast of thousands on thousands equally rich, both in beauty and thrift, a footstep in the grass disturbed me, and, turning my head, I saw Mrs. Dennison walking slowly along the footpath.

The woman was in deep thought, and evidently did not observe me, for I was sitting on a slope of the rock, and a mossy fragment rose up between us. She held a letter in her hand, which seemed to give her anything but pleasure, for as she read, a cloud fell heavily on her forehead, and the beautiful brows contracted. She stopped in the middle of the footpath, and seemed to read the letter over a second time. During all this time she was so near to me, that I could distinguish the heavy sigh with which she folded the paper.

After this she stood a moment gazing upon the landscape at her feet. She seemed to feel the beauties this glorious point of view presented, and her face cleared up.

That moment I spoke to her. She gave a little start, hid the letter away somewhere in the folds of her dress, and sat down upon the rock. That woman, I do think, never took a position which did not at once settle into lines of grace. Just then the scarlet folds of her shawl fell in rich contrast with the green mosses of the rock and cool foliage of the trees, and I could not help observing that, even for my sake, she condescended to be artistic.

"Ah, Miss Hyde, I am glad to find you here; these woods were getting lonesome," she said, pleasantly.

"But it is not lonesome here," I replied; "this moment I was thinking what a cheerful idea of life the whole scene yonder presented."

"Yes," she answered, looking toward the distant city; "after all, civilization has its fine points, even in a picture. I do not wonder you love this spot, if it were only from its contrasts. A moment back, I was almost chilled by the lonely murmur of the pines, and the dull sweep of waters answering them; surely there is some river near, Miss Hyde."

"Yes, at the foot of this hill."

"Oh! true, I can see gleams of water through the gloom. How steep it is!"

"Yes, almost a precipice," I answered. "One would not like to attempt a descent."

"Indeed, I would rather like it. If one had a mania for suicide now, it would be a romance. A single false step, and you could hardly hear the plunge or a cry for help, if the actor were coward enough to give it. The waters are very black and sullen down yonder."

I turned away from them with a shudder; this idea of death and crime which she had advanced chilled me. The waters did, indeed, look black as we saw them weltering on through the piny gloom far below us.

"Do you know," she said, smiling blandly upon me, "I found a pretty bird's-nest under a tuft of fern-leaves up yonder, with four lovely speckled eggs? My red shawl frightened the poor birds, and they made a terrible fluttering; so, in pity to the little creatures, I came away only half satisfied."

"Oh! you have found my nest!" I exclaimed, thanking her kindness from the depths of my heart. "My own little birds; they have built in that spot for three years; I dare say some of the birds hatched under those broken leaves are singing to us now. No one ever molests them here."

"Indeed I did them no harm; only took one little peep at the eggs and ran away; so, don't look so terrified; the birds did not seem half so much frightened."

I smiled and dropped the subject. The truth is, I really am silly about my birds, and always keep their hiding-places secret, if I can, even from Jessie, who does not understand their dainty habits as I do.

Mrs. Dennison busied herself looking about on the landscape.

"Tell me," she said, "whereabouts is that delightful old mill which we stopped at this morning? I do assure you, Miss Hyde, it is the most picturesque bit that I ever saw out of a picture; this river must be the stream on which it stands."

"Yes," I answered; "but the mill is not visible from here."

"We had a delightful five minutes examining it," she resumed, "that is, my good host, Mr. Lawrence, and myself. As for our sweet Jessie and her cavalier-lover, must I say—"

"Jessie Lee has no lovers," I answered, coldly, for there was something in the side-glance of her almond-shaped eyes that I did not like,—a sinister questioning that aroused all the original distrust that her simple manner had, for a time, laid to rest.

"Indeed! What, no lover? and she so beautiful, such a peculiar style! I thought young Bosworth was something more than a neighborly cavalier; a fine young fellow, Miss Hyde, and a catch, isn't he?"

"I don't know exactly what you mean by a catch, madam," I replied, more and more repulsed.

"Oh! I see; not worldly enough for boarding-school vulgarisms; but I, who am naughty enough to remember them now and then, will explain that there is nothing very terrible in a 'good catch.' It only means a handsome, fashionable, and rich man, whom every marriageable young lady is dying for and only one can get."

"Then our young neighbor will not answer to the character, for he is neither fashionable nor more than comfortably rich; nor has he any number of young ladies dying for him."

"Only one, perhaps?"

The same sidelong glance, the same crafty undercurrent in her questioning.

"If you mean Jessie, Mrs. Dennison, I am very sure she has no such feelings as you suspect, toward any one."

"Oh, I dare say not; one always likes to talk nonsense about such things, but it amounts to nothing. Of course, people are always expecting hosts of lovers when an heiress is in question, and Miss Lee has the reputation of immense expectations."

"Yes," I answered, artfully, "I am afraid Jessie will be very rich, indeed. Along that valley she will own land enough for a small principality, if such things were recognized in this country, and many a smoke-wreath that you see curling up from the city yonder comes from the dwellings that will yet be hers, and so will several foundries that are coining money for her out of iron."

Mrs. Dennison's eyes kindled. "Show me," she said, eagerly, and shading her eyes with one hand, "where does the land lie—this principality of which Jessie will be mistress?"

"Yonder to the left, around and far beyond that hill."

"The hill with so many grassy slopes, and crested with groves? That hill, and the lands around it, will it surely be Jessie Lee's inheritance?"

"Every foot of land, every smoke that curls from several blocks of houses in the centre of the city."

"And does Mr. Lee have all this income?"

"Every cent."

Her eyes sparkled. Fresh roses bloomed out on her cheeks. She threw out her arm, and waved it inward, as if gathering the property in one sweeping embrace.

"Ah! what a world of enjoyment you or I could get out of all that if it were ours!" she said, with unaccountable exultation in her voice. "No wonder he lives like a prince."

I answered her with constraint. This enthusiasm disturbed me.

"I am not sure, madam, that either you or I would be happier for possessing so much care as this wealth would bring; for my part, that which I enjoy without responsibility, is enough."

Her beautiful mouth curled with a sneer, the first I ever saw on those lips.

"Ah! it requires taste and habits of power to prepare one for these things; some people are born with them. Some people are born for them, and others—"

"Well?" I said, smiling with satisfaction that she had at last broken loose from her system of crafty adulation.

"And others," she said, adroitly, "are so gentle and unselfish, that they live in the happiness of their friends. It would be a pity to cumber such with all the anxieties of wealth; one would as soon think of weighing the angels down with gold."

I declare, the quickness of that woman frightened me. The sneer left her lips in a glow of smiles before it was formed. Her eyes were bent on my face innocent as a child's. She sat down by me, folding the scarlet shawl lightly around her.

CHAPTER XX
ADROIT CROSS-QUESTIONING

"Now that we are talking of rich people," said Mrs. Dennison, with an air of the most natural confidence, "do tell me about this Mr. Lawrence. Is he very much in love with our Jessie, or not?"

"I never heard or thought that he was in love with her, Mrs. Dennison."

"Nor she with him?"

The question stung me. It gave form to a painful thought that had been growing in my heart, and I felt myself blushing hotly under her glance.

"Mrs. Dennison, are such questions honorable?"

"Not if you cannot answer them without blushes. I beg pardon."

"Are they delicate?" I urged, angrily.

"Not if they touch her friends so keenly. Again I beg pardon."

"Mrs. Dennison," I said, conquering the anger that burned in me like a fire, "excuse me if I seem rude, but if there is anything of excitement in my manner, it is because I am not used to canvassing the feelings of my friends, even with those nearest and dearest to me."

"And me you consider a stranger," she said, deprecatingly.

"Almost," I replied, with blunt truth.

"And one whom you cannot like?"

I bit my lips to keep back the words that pressed against them.

"At my age, Mrs. Dennison, new feelings spring up slowly in the heart."

She made another desperate attempt at my weak side.

"At your age? My dear Miss Hyde, am I to judge what it is by that smooth cheek, or by your words?"

"I am afraid it is best to be judged of by the slow growth of feelings such as we speak of," I replied, gravely.

She looked down sadly, and tears came trembling into her eyes. I really think she felt it. Her habits of fascination were such that she was doubtless wounded that they could fail even with so unimportant a person as I was.

"You are unkind, I would say unjust; only that feeling is seldom a matter of choice. But I, who was prepared to love you as the friend of dear Jessie, who did like you so much at the first sight, it does seem a little cruel that you should meet all this with repulsion."

Her tears made me uncomfortable; one had fallen to her cheek, and hung on its roses like a dew-drop. A man, I think, would have yielded to her then and there; a quiet person of her own sex was not likely to be so impressible. But her grief touched me, and feeling that there had been something of rudeness in my speech, I strove to soften it.

"Not repulsion, Mrs. Dennison, but we country people are a little on the reserve always. Do not think me unkind because I do not care to talk much of those who trust and shelter me."

She laid her hands on mine and smiled sweetly through her tears.

"You are right. It was all rash childishness, not curiosity; how could it be when dear Jessie tells me everything with her own sweet lips?"

I longed to draw my hand from under hers, but conquered the impulse, and seemed to listen with patience at least.

"But we will drop our sweet Jessie," she said, "and talk of some one else—Mr. Lawrence, for instance. Are you sure that he is not really poor?"

"Indeed, I cannot tell. He lives in another State, and may be rich or poor, for aught we know of a certainty; all that I can say is, that his friend Bosworth never represented him as wealthy to us."

"That is a pity," she said, thoughtfully, "a great pity; an heiress stands no chance with such men."

I started, feeling as if it were Jessie she was speaking of.

"And why, pray?" was my sharp response.

"Ah! these splendid men, proud and poor, how can you expect them to face the world as fortune-hunters? After all, wealth has its drawback. I often pity a girl with money, for the most sensitive and the most noble keep aloof. I can imagine a man like this Lawrence now wearing his heart out, or turning it to iron if it brought him to the feet of an heiress. Such men like to grant, not take."

"Isn't that a sort of proud selfishness?" I asked, struck by the force and truth of her worldly knowledge.

"Selfishness? Of course it is. What else do we find in the noblest nature? But you are looking serious, and I have watched that cloud of smoke till it wearies me."

She arose while speaking, and walked away, passing through the trees like some gorgeous bird whose home was beneath the branches.

I watched her with a strange feeling of excitement. What would her object be in cross-questioning me as she did? Was it mere vulgar curiosity, or some deep-seated purpose? Why this anxiety about Jessie's expectations? In short, had the woman come to us bent on mischief of some kind, or was I a suspicious wretch, determined to find evil in everything?

CHAPTER XXI
THE EVENING AFTER BOSWORTH'S PROPOSAL

That evening Messrs. Lawrence and Bosworth came, according to some previous engagement. I was a little surprised at this, but after awhile saw that a generous and noble motive lay at the bottom of it all. Jessie had besought Bosworth to remain her friend; he had promised, and thus generously kept an engagement made before his proposal, and when it must have been a painful sacrifice.

Nothing could be more delicate and lovely than Jessie's manner of receiving him. She neither colored nor looked down, but came toward him with a deprecating stoop of the whole person, while there was a depth of sadness in her eyes that more than begged pardon for the wound she had given.

Bosworth was grave, but very gentle in his reception of this kindness. He moved toward a far end of the room, and they sat down together, talking earnestly to each other.

Mr. Lee was in the room and watched them rather gravely, I thought; but Mrs. Dennison, who was chatting merrily with Lawrence, called him to her side, and after that he seemed to forget everything but her.

Being left to myself, I was crossing the room to go out, when Jessie beckoned me to the sofa, where she was sitting.

"Ah! Miss Hyde," she said, earnestly, "try and persuade Mr. Bosworth to give up his wild plan of going away."

"And have you really formed such an idea?" I asked.

"Yes," he said, striving to smile; "one cannot loiter forever in these pleasant country places. I have been a dreamer too long."

"But not yet," I pleaded, answering the appeal in Jessie's eyes; "you will not go in this unfriendly way."

"Unfriendly?" he repeated, glancing at Jessie. "No, I shall never do that; never feel unfriendly toward any of you, Miss Hyde."

"But we cannot spare you, and I am quite sure Mrs. Dennison will be heart-broken if—" I hesitated, conscious of the impropriety contained in these impulsive words.

"Oh! Mrs. Dennison will never be quite heart-broken at anything, I fancy," he replied, with a faint smile; "but if you really desire it, I will not break up the arrangements of our guests. A few weeks more or less need make little difference in a life-time."

Jessie brightened at this, and looked so gratefully on her rejected lover, that he smiled, but very mournfully, as if reproaching her for being so kindly and yet so firm.

Early in the evening, Mrs. Lee's little maid, Lottie, came into the parlor, and after casting her bright eyes in every corner of the room, went up to her master and whispered something. Mr. Lee arose and went out. I beckoned Lottie, and asked if her mistress was worse?

"No, Miss Hyde, I can't say that she is, or that she isn't; because she hasn't said a word about it. But she isn't asleep, and it seems lonesome up there, within hearing of all the fun, and not know what it is about. For how Mrs. Bab—how that lady's voice rings through the tower when she laughs."

"Yes," said I, "she has a clear, sweet voice."

Lottie gave an almost imperceptible toss of the head.

"Besides," she said, drawing me aside, and speaking in a low voice, "mistress can look right into the window where those people stand; I don't know as she did, but I can."

"Well; could you discover more than we did, who are in the room, Lottie?"

The toss of her head was defiant now, but she made no other reply, except to whisper, "Mrs. Babylon is coming this way, and I'm off."

"Stop," I said; "did Mrs. Lee send for—for any of us?"

"Send? No; but she expected, and being all alone evenings is what she isn't used to."

"I'll go up at once."

"There now, always flying off! It isn't you she wants."

"How do you know that, if she asked for no one in particular?"

"How do I know? Well, that's good! As if I didn't know the difference between her wanting you and him! When she wants you, it's all quiet and don't-care-much-about-it in her looks. When he ought to be there, and isn't, something comes into her eyes that makes your heart ache. I never saw it till lately; but that look is growing on her, and would more, if it wasn't for me."

"Why, how can you prevent it, Lottie?"

"Well, in a good many ways, Miss Hyde. One of 'em is by nice little lies that hurt nobody, but do her lots of good. I know just how he makes bouquets, and when they don't come at the right time, I run down and make up a bunch of flowers myself. I stole some pink and blue ribbons from his room to tie 'em with. Oh! it's worth while to see her eyes sparkle when I bring them in. Then I've studied his way of sending compliments and messages. Don't pretend to be a genius like you that write poetry."

"Lottie!"

"Oh! don't be frightened. I sha'n't bring you to disgrace about it. Made up my mind to that from the first. You needn't get mad and blush so; I ain't a genius, but I can make up stories in my head; and why not tell 'em to her? Why not, I say, when they please her? You should hear the elegant messages I bring from Mr. Lee, at least four times a day. When she gets a nice little dish for dinner, it gives her appetite to think he ordered it; but the cook knows."

"But, Lottie, this is wrong."

"Wrong! Well, I like that, Miss Hyde."

"It isn't the truth, Lottie."

"The truth! Who said it was? As if I didn't know it was lying, and glory in it!"

I could hardly keep my countenance. As for arguing a moral question with Lottie, the thought was too ridiculous. She had her own ideas, and kept to them without the slightest regard to those of other people.

While we were talking, Lottie had gradually edged herself out of the room, and her last speech was delivered on the platform of the terrace. Mrs. Lee's window was up, and I saw her husband enter the room with what seemed to me a reluctant step. He sat down, and opened a book, as if to read aloud. This had been his usual custom, but the last few evenings he had spent in the drawing-room. I would have taken his place, but she rejected my offer with one of those deep sighs that excite so much pity when they come from an invalid.

"You talk against fibs, Miss Hyde; now what do you think of that? She never would 'a' sent for him—died first, like a lamb starving in the cold. Hist! there comes Mrs. Babylon and her private beau."

True enough, Mrs. Dennison and Lawrence had passed through one of the drawing-room windows, and were slowly coming down the terrace platform, which, as I have said, ran around one end and the back of the house. It afforded a fine promenade, and they were enjoying the moonlight that fell upon it. My attention was occupied by them a moment, during which Lottie disappeared. The railing of this platform was lined with a rich shrubbery of hot-house plants, lemon-trees, tall roses, and such creeping vines as bear most choice blossoms. These cast heavy shadows, and I fancy that the girl disappeared among them,—listening, perhaps, being considered as one of the accomplishments which she devoted to the benefit of her mistress.

When I went back to the drawing-room, Jessie was at the piano, and Bosworth sat near, watching her sadly as she played. She did not attempt to sing, and he offered no request of the kind. Altogether, it was a gloomy evening. Really, I think this idea of turning love into friendship is an absurd way of settling things. Throwing ashes on hot embers only keeps the fire in more certain glow. Jessie was young, and had no idea of prudence in such matters. I did not quite understand the undercurrent of her nature, but, in my heart, thought it best that Bosworth should leave the neighborhood.

The next morning I saw Lottie coming out of Mrs. Dennison's room, looking demure as a house-cat.

"I've taught 'em how to do another braid," she said, innocently. "If they tangle it, you know, I ain't to blame."

CHAPTER XXII
SOWING SEED FOR ANOTHER DAY

After our conversation on the ridge, Mrs. Dennison made the best of her advantages, and, having ingratiated herself into the room of our invalid, managed to pass a good deal of her time there. I think Mrs. Lee, without knowing it herself, exercised a little selfishness in this; for it happened—so naturally that I never should have observed it but for Lottie—that Mr. Lee visited his wife more frequently when his guest was there than at any other time. Indeed, it was not many days before the invalid ceased almost entirely to see him alone.

After my attention was drawn to this by one of Lottie's curt sayings, I noticed another thing that troubled me more than Mrs. Dennison's visits. Cora, the mulatto girl, was constantly following her mistress to the room, asking for orders, or reminding Mrs. Dennison of something that she had been desired to remember. She made one or two efforts to fix herself in Lottie's apartment, but that singular female rebuffed the first attempt, by standing square in the door, and asking point-blank if there were anything in that room which Cora wanted. The girl answered, "No," and went away rather crestfallen.

It is very difficult to repress the aggressions of a guest under your own roof, especially one who invariably disarms you with honeyed words and apologies for anything that threatens to offend. It was not for me to regulate a visitor's movements in Mr. Lee's house; and so adroitly were they managed, that no power, however on the alert, could have reached them.

To my surprise, Lottie, all of a sudden, not only seemed to lose her animosity to the widow, but hung about her with assiduity almost equal to that bestowed on her mistress. But one thing was remarkable: none of her bright sayings, or exhibitions of sharp, good sense were manifested in Mrs. Dennison's presence. With her she was dull and quiet, nay, almost stolid. I have heard her ask questions with the most innocent air, which a child of three years old could have answered. It was surprising how anything so near a witch in her real nature could tame herself into that lump of stupidity. She was a great deal in Mrs. Dennison's room; and once I saw them seated together on the hill-side, talking earnestly. Still, for several days nothing happened worthy of remembrance.

Mr. Lee and the widow rode out once or twice without Jessie, who, feeling a little hurt for her mother's sake, decided to remain at home and sit with the gentle invalid. I do not know that she observed it, but there certainly was very little entreaty used to induce her to join them. Indeed, upon the third morning nothing was said on the subject; Jessie was not even invited.

One day, just after Mr. Lee and his guest had ridden from the door, Mr. Lawrence called. He had seen them from a distance, he said, and came to inquire after Miss Lee's health. The flood of crimson that rushed over Jessie's face, when I told her this, made my heart beat heavily. She arose, and went down, avoiding my anxious glance as she passed me.

The doors were all open, but I heard no voices in the drawing-room; they must have been talking very low: what did that portend between two persons perfectly alone? So anxious had I become that it seemed to me as if some harm were intended our Jessie among these strange people. She had never seemed really happy since their advent among us. Indeed, there had been little of comfort for any one.

What passed between Jessie and Lawrence I learned afterward. But only so far as a young girl can force herself to speak of things pertaining to her affections. One thing is certain: when she came up-stairs, after his departure, a look of uncertain joy pervaded her face, and she breathed quickly. I asked no questions, and was not surprised that she said little about the interview. After that day Jessie's manner became more elastic; and from some words that escaped, I am confident that, up to this time, she had fancied Lawrence engaged to Mrs. Dennison; or, at the least, ready at any moment to assume that position. Indeed, the widow had told her as much.

The next day Jessie was invited to join Mr. Lee and his guest in their ride; but she refused it coldly, nay, almost haughtily. Her father, for the first time in his life, seemed really angry with her. He said nothing, however, but rode forth with a flush on his brow.

Again Mr. Lawrence called, or would have called, but that he saw Jessie wandering off toward the pine woods, and followed her. I saw them sitting a long time on a garden-chair stationed on the skirts of the grove, but said nothing to any one, not even to herself when she came down the hill, alone, with a light in her eyes that I had never seen there before.

I think Lawrence must have made five or six of these morning visits before they were suspected by any one in the house. Cora was generally busy in her mistress's room all the forenoon, and Lottie took the occasion of Mrs. Dennison's absence to sit with loving watchfulness by our invalid, only too happy if a low word or patient smile rewarded her devotion. But it came out at last.

One day I went suddenly upon the terrace platform, and found Cora standing close by one of the drawing-room windows, with her shoulder against the framework. The blind swinging open concealed her from any person within; and the position she maintained, while sorting the shades from some skeins of worsted that she held, was that of careless rest. She moved indolently, and sauntered away on seeing me; but it was with a heavy, sullen manner, as if she had been unwarrantably disturbed. I looked into the sitting-room in passing, and, as I expected, Lawrence and Jessie were sitting on a sofa close to that window.

Mrs. Dennison was in splendid spirits when she came back from her ride that day. There was something triumphant in her step which put one in mind of some handsome Amazon returning from battle. She leaned heavily on Mr. Lee, as he lifted her from the saddle; nay, I am certain that she rested against him a moment longer than was necessary.

Jessie was standing near me, but noticed none of these things. Noble girl, she was never on the lookout for evil. Her upright mind tinted everything with its own pure hues.

Mr. Lee stayed a long time, giving orders about the horses. When he came up the steps, I had an opportunity of observing him closely. He was pale, and looked strange. I cannot describe what I wish to be understood, but all the influences that had so long dwelt around that man seemed swept away. The very dignity of his tread was gone. What had occasioned this? I know now, and never doubted then. The woman sweeping through our hall, at the moment, had produced this transformation; yet no words had passed between them that his own daughter might not have heard without reproof.

Mrs. Dennison gave us a triumphant glance, as she passed the balcony where we were standing, and proclaimed that she had never enjoyed a ride so much. It was a heavenly day, and the landscape transcendent.

Jessie smiled softly, and turned a bright glance on my face, which said, more plainly than Mrs. Dennison's words, "I, too, have had a heavenly day, which will go with my dreams into many another day, making an Eden of them all."

CHAPTER XXIII
AN OUTBREAK OF JEALOUSY

In a few moments Mrs. Dennison came out of her chamber, still in her riding-habit. She was pale as death, her eyes gleamed, and her lips quivered. She dashed into the balcony, and laid her hand on Jessie's shoulder with such rude suddenness, that the young girl drew back with an impulse of surprise.

"What is the matter, Mrs. Dennison?"

Mrs. Dennison looked at her a moment, subdued the quivering of her lips with a great effort, and broke into a laugh so hoarse and constrained that Jessie shrunk back.

"What is the matter?" she said. "Why, nothing; only we have but just time to dress for dinner, and here you stand as if the whole world could wait."

I could see that her frame was trembling from head to foot. The color would not come back to her face. With all her powers, she was but a woman, and a jealous woman at the best. From that moment I felt very sure that Cora had performed her mission promptly. Jessie could not understand it, but stood looking at her guest in blank amazement.

"You have ridden too far," she said, coldly, "and the fatigue has shaken your nerves, I fear. Shall I send for a glass of wine? it will be some time before dinner."

"Wine? no; but—but I will take a glass of water, if you please, Miss Hyde."

Jessie seemed anxious to get away, for she started before I could anticipate her to order the water, and I was left alone with Mrs. Dennison. Her self-command was giving way again. She sat down, and, covering her face with both hands, shook from head to foot; but she did not weep. Something too hard and fiery for tears possessed her.

"Yes," she said at last, "Miss Lee is right! These long rides do shake one's nerves terribly!"

Directly Jessie came bringing a glass of water. With her usual delicacy, she would not intrust the duty to a servant, who might witness her friend's discomposure and comment upon it.

Mrs. Dennison held the water a moment, regarding Jessie with gleaming eyes, as if she longed to dash the contents in her face; but the insane fit went off. She drank the water, and arose to leave the balcony.

"I am not usually nervous, but this ride has completely upset me."

With these words she left the balcony and went back to her room.

"She is very ill, I am sure, Aunt Matty," said Jessie, full of gentle sympathy; "pray go and see if nothing more can be done?"

I went to Mrs. Dennison's chamber and knocked; no one came or spoke. But the door stood upon the latch, and the vibration of my hand unclosed it. Mrs. Dennison was standing in the middle of the room, white with rage, and with specks of foam on her lips. She was tearing open her habit with a violence that made the buttons start. The face with which she met my intrusion was that of a beautiful fiend.

I closed the door and went back repulsed. But without giving me time to cross the hall, she came to the door, opened it wide, and called me in with a laugh.

"Come back one moment," she said, "and tell me which of these two dresses is most becoming. That which I had intended for dinner, Cora has been altering, and she has spoiled it entirely. I confess, Miss Hyde, that my temper is not good enough to stand a pet dress in ruins. The fact is, I have frightened poor Cora half to death."

Quick as lightning, while her mistress spoke, Cora laid some dresses on the bed, apologizing, in a low voice, for the mischief she had done. If I had possessed no clue to the scene, it would have deceived me completely; but I comprehended it too well, and absolutely felt myself growing faint with disgust.

"I am no judge in these matters," I said, without any pretence at cordiality; "nor would my opinion be of the least consequence if I were. Your dresses always prove becoming, Mrs. Dennison."

"The first compliment I ever received from you," she answered, impressively; "I shall remember it with gratitude."

I went quietly out of the room, tired of the scene.

A little while after this, Lottie came to me with one of her keen smiles, and, opening her hands, which were folded palm to palm, gave me one glimpse of a little note, primrose-tinted, and sealed with a drop of green wax, in which an antique head was stamped.

"What is it? whom is it for?" I inquired, thinking that it must be intended for Jessie.

"You'll see to-night, or to-morrow morning," she answered. "Mrs. Babylon writes on handsome paper; I won't use white any more. I'll say this for her: when it comes to dress and pretty things, she can't be beat easy. Don't quite come up to Mrs. Lee: who can?—but putting her aside, I don't know Mrs. Babylon's match."

"And is that Mrs. Dennison's note?"

"Ask me no questions, and I'll tell you no lies."

"But how came it in your possession?"

She eyed me a moment sideways, then broke forth as if some grand thought had just seized upon her.

"Now, I'll make a bargain with you, Miss Hyde. If you'll just persuade my mistress, or Miss Jessie, to buy me half a dozen sheets of that straw-colored paper, I'll tell you all about it."

"But what can you want of primrose paper, Lottie,—you that never write letters?"

"No; but I may take to writing poetry; who knows?"

She said this with a twinkle of the eye that provoked me. How on earth had that creature got hold of my secret weakness?

"It isn't at all likely that you'll want paper for that purpose, Miss Lottie."

"Miss Lottie—Miss! Well now, I have always said that if there was a genuine lady, and no nonsense in this house, it was you, ma'am. Even my mistress hasn't got up to that mark—Miss Lottie! Wouldn't that look beautiful on a yellow note like this? Miss Lottie—"

She plumed herself, like a bird, in the ecstasy of my random speech, and both her hands and her heart opened at once.

"Now, I'll tell you all about it! There's no secret, and if there is, I didn't promise not to tell; that is, down in my heart. Cora came to me just now, and says she, 'Lottie, you know all the men about the premises, I suppose?'

"'Well, pretty much,' says I.

"'I thought so,' she said. 'Now, here is a little note that my mistress wants to have sent right off. If you can coax one of the men to take a horse from the stable, and just gallop over to Mr. Bosworth's with it, and bring an answer back, she'll give you that dress you took such a fancy to.'

"'Well,' says I, 'hand over the note; I'll get it done.' She had been holding the note seal up all the time, and says she, 'Lottie'—not Miss Lottie, mind—but, 'Lottie, can you read writing?'

"'Can you?' says I.

"'No,' says she; 'colored people seldom do.'

"'Well, then I don't.'

"'Well, this note is for a lady that is staying at Mr. Bosworth's; she's an old friend of Mrs. Dennison's, and we want to hear from her.'

"'All right,' says I. 'If you hadn't told this, it would be Greek and Latin to me.'

"She handed over the note, and told me to put it in my bosom for fear of its being seen. So I did; and came here, but not till I had read Mr. Lawrence's name on the outside. Now, Miss Hyde, just tell me what to do."

"There is one thing you must not do, Lottie, and that is, tempt any of the men from their duty."

"But then that dress! Light green foulard, with bunches of roses—sweet roses!"

"Wait a moment, Lottie; we must not do anything without Mr. Lee's sanction: that will never answer."

I went up to Mr. Lee, who was sitting in the window recess, apparently reading, and asked if he could spare a horse and man long enough to ride over to Mr. Bosworth's.

"Who wishes to send?" he inquired, indifferently.

"Mrs. Dennison," I answered, not unwilling to give him the information.

He held the paper a little tighter in his hand, repeating:

"Mrs. Dennison! What correspondent has she at Mrs. Bosworth's?"

There was an effort at indifference in his voice, but it did not conceal that he was touched.

I did not feel at liberty to answer his question, and said nothing.

After a moment's silence, he said,—

"Certainly, Miss Hyde. Our guests always command here."

I went back to Lottie, and told her to carry Mr. Lee's orders to the stable, and, if she wished it, claim her reward. She seized my hand in an ecstasy of delight.

"Oh! Miss Hyde, I never will talk about poetry again, never so long as I live; but I'll tell everybody that you don't know a thing about it, no more than I do; and I believe it."

With this outburst she went away. Directly after, I saw one of the grooms riding down the road. Two hours after, he came back, and gave Lottie, who was waiting near the pine woods, with great appearance of secrecy, a note, with which she went at once to Mrs. Dennison, evidently resolved to keep up appearances, and leave her employers in the belief that the whole thing had been managed privately.

I had thrown the subject of the note quite off my thoughts, when the groom, who had been to Mr. Bosworth's, came to me in the garden with distressing news.

Poor young Bosworth was ill—so ill, that he had not been out of his room for some days; and his mother desired very much that I should come over and see him. He had spoken of it several times, and, now that he was growing worse, she could refuse him nothing. It was asking a great deal, but would I come at the earliest time possible?

This was indeed sad news. I liked the young man. He was honorable, generous, and in all respects a person to fix one's affections upon—that is, such affections as a lady just dropping the bloom of her youth may bestow on the man who looks upon her as a sort of relative.

Of course I would go to see Bosworth in his sickness. "God bless and help the young man," I whispered; "if she could only think of him as I do!"

CHAPTER XXIV
THE OLD PENNSYLVANIA MANSION

The Bosworths lived behind the spur of the mountain which shut out a portion of the valley from our house by its crown of forest-trees. I had taken little exercise in the open air of late, for Mrs. Dennison monopolized the horse I had been in the habit of riding, with my usual seat in the carriage. Perhaps I felt a little hurt at this, and would not ask favors that had until now been mine without solicitation. In my love of out-door exercise I am half an English woman. So, mentioning to Mrs. Lee and Jessie that I was going out for a long walk across the fields, I started for Mrs. Bosworth's house.

It was a splendid afternoon. The sunshine, warm and golden, without being oppressive, was softened by transparent clouds that drifted like currents and waves of gauze athwart the sky. The meadows were full of daisies, buttercups, and crimson clover, through which the blue-flies and bumble-bees fluttered and hummed their drowsy music. In the pastures clouds of grasshoppers sprang up, with a whir, from the clusters of white everlasting that sprinkled the slopes like a snow-storm; and little birds bent down the stately mullein-stalks with their weight, and sang cheerily after me from the crooks of the fences.

How I loved these little creatures with their bright eyes and graceful ways! How quietly they opened my heart to those sweet impulses that make one grateful and child-like! My step grew buoyant, and I felt a cool, fresh color mounting to my cheeks. The walk had done me good. I had been too much in the house, indulging in strange fancies that were calculated to make no one happy, and were, perhaps, unjust. How could I have sunk into this state of mind? Was I jealous of Mrs. Dennison? Yes, possibly! But not as another would have understood the feeling. It was rather hard to hear the whole household singing her praises from morning till night; and Jessie, my own Jessie, seemed so bound up in the woman.

Well, after all, these things seemed much more important in the house, where I felt like an involuntary prisoner, than they appeared to me, with the open fields breathing fragrance around me, and the blue skies speaking beautifully of the beneficent God who reigned above them.

I really think the birds in that neighborhood had learned to love me a little, they gave such quaint little looks, and burst into such volumes of song among the hazel-bushes as I passed. Before I knew it, fragments of melodies were on my own lips. I gathered handful after handful of the meadow-flowers, grouping the choicest into bouquets, and scattering the rest along my path. Thus you might have tracked my progress by tufts of grass, and golden lilies, as the little boy in fairy history was traced by the pebble-stones he dropped.

Mrs. Bosworth's house was one of the oldest and finest of those ponderous Dutch mansions that are scattered over Pennsylvania. There were rich lands to back that old-fashioned building, and any amount of invested property, independent of the lands. After all, young Bosworth was no contemptible match for our Jessie, even in a worldly point of view. If his residence lacked something of the elegance and modern appointments for which ours was remarkable, it had an aspect of age and affluence quite as imposing. Indeed, in some respects it possessed advantages which our house could not boast.

Majestic trees that struck their roots in a virgin soil, and shrubbery that had grown almost into trees, surrounded the old house. One great, white lilac-bush lifted itself above the second-story windows, and old-fashioned white roses clambered half over the stone front. Then there was a huge honeysuckle that spread itself like a banner upon one corner, garlanding the eaves, and dropping down in rich festoons from the roof itself.

But all this was nothing compared to that magnificent elm-tree, which overhung a wing of the building with its tent-like branches, through which the wind was eternally whispering, and the sunshine was broken into faint flashes before it reached the roof. I had never been so much impressed with the dignity of old times, as when I approached this dwelling. It possessed all the respectability of a family mansion, growing antique in the prosperity which surrounded it, without any attempt at modern improvements.

The very flowers on the premises were old-fashioned; great snow-ball bushes and rows of fruit-trees predominating. In the square garden, with its pointed picket-fence, that ran along the road, I saw clusters of smallage, and thickets of delicate fennel. On each side the broad threshold-stone stood green boxes running over with live-forever and house-leeks, while all around the lower edges of the stone foundation that exquisite velvet moss, which we oftenest find on old houses, was creeping.

I lifted the heavy brass knocker very cautiously, for it was ponderous enough to have reverberated through the house. Even the light blow I gave frightened me. No wonder people felt constrained to muffle knockers like that in the good old times, when sickness came to the family.

A quiet, middle-aged colored woman came to the door. She knew me at once, though it was the first time I had entered the house in years.

"Come in, Miss Hyde," she said, welcoming me with a genial look. "Mrs. Bosworth said, if you called she would come right straight down and see you; so walk in."

She opened the door of a sitting-room on the right of the hall. It was old-fashioned like the exterior of the building. Windows sunk deep into the wall, ponderous chairs, and a capacious, high-backed sofa with crimson cushions, and embroidered footstools standing before it,—all had an air of comfortable ease. The carpet had been very rich in its time, and harmonized well with the rest of the apartment.

CHAPTER XXV
THE MOTHER AND GRANDMOTHER

I seated myself on the sofa, and waited with some anxiety. Surely, my young friend must be very ill to have abandoned this room for his own! What a comfortable look the place had! How delightfully all the tints were toned down! There stood a queer, old work-table, with any amount of curiously twisted legs, and on it an antique bible, mounted and clasped with silver. Such books are only to be found now in the curiosity shops of the country. Under this table, and somehow lodged among its complication of legs, was the old lady's work-basket, in which I detected a silver-mounted case for knitting-needles, some balls of worsted, and an embroidered needle-book. Ladies are always noticing these little feminine details; they aid us greatly in that quick knowledge of character which men are apt to set down as intuition.

While I was thinking over these speculations, a step in the hall, and the rich, heavy rustle of those old silks that our grandmothers were so proud of, disturbed me. The door opened, and an old lady, very old indeed, came into the room.

I stood up involuntarily, for the person of this old lady was so imposing, that it exacted a degree of homage which I had never felt before. I can imagine a figure like that, wandering through the vast picture-galleries of some fine English castle, and there I should have given her a title at first sight. As it was, her person struck me with amazement. Not that it was out of keeping with the premises, but because this lady was altogether a grander and older person than I had expected to see in that house.

She received my salutation with a slow curtsy, very slight and dignified in its movement, and, advancing to a huge, crimson easy-chair that stood near the work-table, sat down.

"My daughter is in her son's room," she said, in a soft and measured voice, glancing at me with her placid eyes. "He is very ill, and we are frightened about him."

"Is not this sudden?" I inquired.

"Yes, very; we don't know what to make of it. He is always so healthy and so cheerful; something has gone wrong with him, Miss Hyde."

She looked at me earnestly, as if expecting that I would explain the something which was beyond her understanding.

I felt myself blushing. It was not for me to speak of Jessie's affairs to any one, certainly not in a case like this.

The old lady dropped her eyes, and, taking her knitting-case from the basket, laid it in her lap, evidently disposed to give me time. At length she spoke again.

"My grandson has enjoyed himself so much since we came to the country, especially since his friend, Mr. Lawrence, arrived; and now to have him struck down all at once—it is disheartening!"

"Is he so very ill?" I inquired.

"He has been restless and excited, more or less, for a week or more, but during the last three days has fallen seriously ill. Now he is entirely out of his head; my daughter sat up with him all last night; the doctor was here this morning. He pronounces it a brain-fever."

I was really disturbed. She saw it and went on.

"He asked for you three or four times during the night; and—and for another person whom we could not venture to invite here."

"I am glad you sent for me," I replied, anxious to waive all explanation. "At home they consider me a tolerable nurse."

She looked at me seriously a moment, and then said, in a gentle, impressive way,—

"Miss Hyde, be kind to an old woman who has nothing but the good of her child at heart, and tell me if Miss Lee has—has repulsed my grandson?"

"No, not that, madam; but, but—"

"She has rejected him, I see it by your face; I suspected it from his wanderings," she said, sorrowfully.

I was silent; the mournful accents of her voice touched my heart.

"You have no hope to give the old woman?" she said. "Yet to her it seems impossible for any one not to love Bosworth."

"I am sure there is no man living for whom Miss Lee has more respect," I answered.

She smiled a little sadly.

"Respect! That is a cold word to the young heart, Miss Hyde."

That moment the door opened and Bosworth's mother came in. She was altogether unlike the stately old lady with whom I was conversing. Her small figure, wavering black eyes, and restless manner, spoke of an entirely different organism, which was natural enough, as she was only connected with the stately dame by marriage with her son, a union that had been consecrated by an early widowhood.

It was easy to see that the elder lady was mistress of that house, and that the daughter-in-law held her in profound reverence. Poor lady! she was in great distress, and came up to me at once.

"You are kind, very kind," she exclaimed; "he has asked for you so often. Oh! Miss Hyde, it is terrible to see him in this state with no way of helping."

"It is indeed," I answered, pitying her from my heart.

"Will you go up now? He asked for you and some one else only a few minutes ago," she said, walking up and down the room in nervous distress. "It was an out-of-the-way thing to send for you, almost a stranger, for the Ridge has been empty so long that you all seem like new people, but I am sure you will excuse it. Oh! Miss Hyde, we love him so. We two lonely women, and to lose him!"

Here the poor mother burst into a passion of tears; while the old lady sat down by her work-table and looked on with a sorrowful countenance.

A noise from up-stairs arrested the younger Mrs. Bosworth in her walk.

"He is calling," she said. "Oh! Miss Hyde, he cannot bear me out of his sight! Just as it was years ago, when he would plead with me to sit by his bed, after our mother there insisted on the lamp being put out."

The old lady shook her head, and smiled sadly. "You were spoiling the boy, Hester, making a little coward of him; but he soon ceased to be afraid of the dark,—a brave young man, Miss Hyde, and a comfort to his mother; God spare him to us!"

Hester Bosworth began to cry afresh at these encomiums; and, going up to her mother-in-law's chair, bent her head upon the back, sobbing aloud.

The old lady reached up her soft, little hand, and patted the poor mother on the cheek as if she had been a child.

"Don't fret so, Hester. Our boy is young, and his constitution will not give way easily. A little sleep—if we could only induce a few hours' sleep!"

"I have made a hop pillow for him, and done everything," sobbed the mother; "but there he lies, looking, looking, looking, now at the wall, now at the ceiling, and muttering to himself."

"I know—I know," said the grandmother, hastily lifting her hand, as if the description wounded her. "Will nothing give him a little sleep?"

I remembered how often Mrs. Lee, in her nervous paroxysms, had been soothed to rest by the gentle force of my own will. Indeed, I sometimes fancy that some peculiar gift has been granted to me, by which physical suffering grows less in my presence.

"Shall I go up with you, Mrs. Bosworth?" I said, inspired with hope by this new idea. "He may recognize me as an old friend."

"Oh, yes, yes!" she exclaimed, leading the way. "Mother, will you come?"

CHAPTER XXVI
SICK-BED FANCIES

We mounted the staircase, a broad, old-fashioned flight of steps, surmounted with heavy balustrades of black oak. There was a thick carpet running up them; but, lightly as we trod, the keen ear of the invalid detected a strange presence, and I heard his voice, muffled and rough with fever, calling out, "Yes, yes, I knew, I knew, I knew that she would come!" Then he broke into the notes of some opera-song.

There was a cool, artificial twilight in the chamber when we entered it; but through the bars of the outer blinds a gleam of sunshine shot across the room, and broke against the wall opposite the great, high-posted bed on which young Bosworth was lying. The chamber was large, and but for the closed blinds would have been cheerful. As it was, a great easy-chair, draped with white dimity, loomed up like a snow-drift near the bed; which being clothed in like spotless fashion, gave a ghastly appearance to everything around.

Young Bosworth lay upon the bed with his arms feebly uplifted, and his great, wild eyes wandering almost fiercely after the sunbeams which came and went like golden arrows, as the branches of an elm-tree near the window changed their position.

I went up to the bed, and touched the young man's wrist. The pulse that leaped against my fingers was like the blows of a tiny hammer; his eyes turned on my face, and he clutched my hand, laughing pleasantly.

"How cool your hand is!" he said, with a child-like murmur. "You have been among the clover-blossoms; their breath is all around me."

"Yes," I said, dropping into his own monotone without an effort, "I came through the meadows, and brought some of the flowers with me. See how fresh and sweet they are."

He took the flowers eagerly, grasping them with both hands.

"Did she send them?" he whispered, mysteriously. "Did she?"

I smiled, but would not answer. The delusion seemed pleasant, and it would be cruelty to disturb it. He held the blossoms caressingly in his hand;

a smile wandered over his lips, and he whispered over soft fragments of some melody that I remembered as one of Jessie's favorites.

Directly the flowers dropped from his grasp, and he began to search after the sunbeam again, clutching at it feverishly, and looking in his hands with vague wonder when he found them empty.

I do not think the young man recognized me at all; but my presence certainly aroused new associations.

He looked wistfully into my face with that vacant stare of delirium which is so painful, and then his eyes wandered away, as if in search of some object they could not find.

"Jessie," he murmured; "Jessie Lee, are you there? Won't you speak to me once more, Jessie?"

The expression of his countenance changed so entirely—a look of such tender, earnest entreaty settled about his handsome, sensitive mouth—that I felt the tears come into my eyes. When I looked up, I saw the stately old grandmother gazing directly upon me; while little Mrs. Bosworth, in her very efforts to be at the same time perfectly quiet and extremely useful, fluttered about in a feeble way that would have annoyed me beyond endurance had I been the sick person.

But the young man, apparently susceptible neither to outer sights nor sounds, saw nothing and heard nothing but the fanciful shapes and mocking whispers of his fever-visions.

"Put these flowers in your hair, Jessie," he said, somewhat brokenly, "they are wild flowers such as you love, and I love them for your sake—for your sake."

He put out his hands, moving them to and fro over the counterpane, to gather up the blossoms he had scattered there; but his fingers wandered so uncertainly, that even when he succeeded in collecting a few, they would drop from his grasp. I saw he began to grow impatient, and I knew that the least thing would excite his fever and thereby increase the delirium, so I put the flowers softly into his palm. He smiled in a satisfied way.

"Here they are," he said; "take them, Jessie; see what a pretty wreath they make."

Then the smile changed to a look of pain. He let the flowers fall to the counterpane with a low moan.

"She has a wreath on now!" he exclaimed. "Jessie Lee, who gave that? White flowers! Bridal flowers!"

He started up in the bed with such violence, that his mother hurried forward with a cry of dismay, and, getting into mischief, as people in a flurry are sure to do, she upset a bottle of cologne and a goblet, but fortunately the old lady caught them before they reached the floor.

"Oh my!" sobbed little Mrs. Bosworth, in nervous fright, "what have I done? Oh! dear, dear!"

"Sit down, my dear," said her mother-in-law, with a good deal of steadiness; "you only disturb him."

"But he looks so wild. Hadn't I better send for the doctor?"

"No, no. He will be here before long. Leave my grandson to Miss Hyde; she will quiet him."

The old lady looked at me, with confidence in my powers, and the mother joined her in a helpless, despairing manner, mixed with a little maternal jealousy, at seeing me in the place that was hers by right. I felt quite nervous and disturbed by this joint appeal; however, I was not foolish enough to give way to any weakness or nonsense when composure was required, so I drew close to the bed, and laid my hand on Bosworth's arm. He was muttering wildly, and I could catch the words, —

"Are they bridal flowers, Jessie Lee?"

"She has taken off the wreath," I whispered.

"No, no; it is there on her forehead. Who gave it to her?"

"She has thrown it aside," I protested; "she would not wear it a moment after she knew it pained you. It is gone now."

He looked earnestly at the place where he thought Jessie stood, and fell back on his pillows with a sigh of satisfaction.

"Kind Jessie," he said, "kind Jessie!"

But that quiet only lasted for a few moments. He grew more restless than before; and I saw old Mrs. Bosworth looking at me still, as if she had fully made up her mind that I could compose him, and nothing less than that desirable effect would satisfy her. Really, with those old-world eyes fastened upon me, I could not avoid exerting all my powers, although in my heart I fairly wished the fidgety little mother safe in her own room.

CHAPTER XXVII
THE FIRST SOUND SLEEP

I sat down by the young man's bed; I talked to him in a low voice—a great deal of nonsense, I dare say; I was not thinking how it might sound, but was only anxious to soothe him; and while I talked I smoothed his hair and passed my hand slowly across his forehead, after a fashion which I had acquired in my attendance upon Mrs. Lee, during her numerous illnesses.

I cannot pretend to account for it, but from my earliest girlhood I always had a faculty for taking care of sick people, and of soothing them when no other person could.

My art did not fail that time. Bosworth's voice grew lower and lower; his hands crossed themselves upon the counterpane; his eyes closed, and very soon his measured breathing proved that he was quietly asleep. When I looked up, that stately old duchess of a grandmother was regarding me with such a blessing in her eyes, that I felt the dew steal into mine; while the younger lady, subdued out of her fidgetiness, appeared almost tranquil, and was quite silent.

Nobody stirred or spoke. There we sat and watched the sick man as he slept—that quiet sleep which the physician had pronounced so necessary for him, and which his art had failed to procure. It is not often that I feel thoroughly satisfied with Martha Hyde, but I confess that just then I did; not that it proceeded from a sense of self-importance, or anything of that sort, but it is seldom that a quiet person like me has an opportunity of doing good to anybody, and when the occasion does arrive, it is more pleasant than I can at all describe.

Bosworth must have slept nearly an hour; the instant he opened his eyes, I saw that the fever had abated a little. He smiled faintly at his mother and the old lady; then his glance fell upon me. Through the feverish flush still on his face there appeared a glow of thankfulness and pleasure, which was beautiful to behold.

"Is that you, Miss Hyde?" he asked.

"Yes," I said; "I have been sitting here for some time. You have had a nice sleep; to-morrow you will be better."

"Thank you; I hope so."

Little Mrs. Bosworth began to flutter; but the old lady put her down with a strong hand, and the weak female subsided into her chair, meek as a hen-pigeon that has been unexpectedly pecked by her mate.

I saw, by the way Bosworth looked at them, that he wished to speak with me alone; the old duchess saw it too, and said, with the decision which was evidently habitual to her:

"My daughter, if Miss Hyde will sit with our boy a little longer, we will go into the garden for a breath of air."

Bosworth called them to him, kissed his mother's cheek, and the grandmother's hand, and the old lady went out in her stately way, while the small woman followed in her wake, like a little boat tacked to a graceful yacht.

"Miss Hyde," said the young man, the moment the door closed, "you came alone?"

"Yes," I replied; "I hurried off without telling any one where I was going."

"You are very kind," he repeated. "They are all well, I hope, at the house?"

"Very well; they will be sorry to hear that you are sick."

"Miss Hyde!" he exclaimed, hurriedly,—so weak from sickness that he forgot all the reticence and self-command which characterized him in health,—"Miss Hyde, do you think she would come to see me?"

I knew whom he meant—there was no necessity for mentioning any name.

"Would she come, do you believe?" he asked again.

"I am certain that she would," I replied. "You are an old friend to all of us; why should she not?"

"Yes, an old friend," he answered, sadly; "I know, I know! I won't pain her; she shall not be troubled; promise to bring her, Miss Hyde."

"I can promise unhesitatingly," I said; "I have no doubt Mr. Lee will bring her himself, to-morrow."

"To-morrow—oh! how much I thank you!" And he smiled like a tired child. "Will you call my mother now?" he continued; "she will feel troubled if she thinks I can do without her."

I went out into the hall, where the two ladies stood, and beckoned them into the room. We all remained about the bed for a few moments, talking cheerfully; then I bade Bosworth good-bye, answered the entreaty in his eyes with a smile, and went down-stairs.

The grandmother followed me, and, when we reached the outer door, took my hand between both of hers.

"You are very good!" she said. "We have long been strangers to each other, Miss Hyde; but an old woman's blessing cannot hurt you, and I give it to you."

I was so much affected, that it was all I could do to keep from crying like a child; but I did not give way, and, mutually anxious to restrain our feelings, we parted with a certain degree of haste, which an unobservant looker-on might have construed into indifference. But I think that grand old woman understood me, even from that short interview, and I know that, for my part, I went forth from her presence solemnized and calmed as one leaves a church.

CHAPTER XXVIII
THE INTERVIEW IN THE WOODS

I walked slowly homeward, reflecting upon the events of the morning, and waiting, oh, how fervently! that Jessie Lee might learn to know young Bosworth as I did, and be able to shed a ray of light into the darkness wherein he had fallen.

I left the path through the fields, and took my way into the woods, as I knew a short cut that would lead me more quickly into our grounds.

I had passed half through the grove, perhaps, scarcely heeding anything around me, but on reaching a little ascent, I saw, through a break in the trees, two persons standing at a considerable distance from the path. Their backs were toward me, but I recognized them instantly. They were Mrs. Dennison and Mr. Lawrence.

I understood at once the meaning of the note which she had sent to him—it was to ask for that interview.

Every day my dislike of that woman increased; each effort that I made to conquer the feeling only seemed to make it grow more intense, and this last plot that I had unintentionally discovered filled me with something very like abhorrence. Of course, I was not so silly as to conjure anything really wrong out of the request she had made; but I was certain that something more than trivial coquetry was hidden under it.

Instinctively, I began to tremble for Jessie: by what series of ideas I managed to connect her with that meeting, I cannot say; but I did so, and after that first glance I went on, burning with indignation against the artful woman, who seemed to have brought numberless shadows into the sunshine, which, before her coming, had pervaded our pleasant home.

Once, as I hastened on through the dark woods, I looked back at the pair,—they were conversing earnestly. In Lawrence's manner there was a degree of impetuosity and impatience; while from Mrs. Dennison's attitude and gestures I felt certain that she was pleading with him to change some purpose he had formed.

Just as I passed from the woods into the grounds, I saw that ubiquitous Lottie steal out from among the trees, and flit like a lapwing toward the house.

It was not difficult to imagine what new mischief she had been at—spying and listening, no doubt. Lottie did not count it a sin, and I knew very well that she had been coolly out into the woods to overhear Mrs. Dennison's conversation with Lawrence.

Some noise that I made attracted her attention; she dropped down on her knees—like a rabbit trying to hide itself in the grass—and began hunting for four-leaved clovers where clover had never grown since the memory of man.

"What are you doing, Lottie?" I asked, walking toward her.

She looked round with a fine show of innocence, although her eyes twinkled suspiciously.

"Oh! it's you, Miss Hyde," she said, in no wise confused, rising from her knees with great deliberation and majesty.

"Yes, it is I. And what brings you here?" I inquired.

"There's several things I might have been doing," she answered, walking on by my side; "picking flowers, or saying my prayers, or—"

"Well—what else?"

"Oh! anything you please; poetry people ought to be able to guess."

"Lottie! Lottie!"

"There—I won't say a word more! I'm dumb as Miss Jessie's canary in moulting-time."

"Then, perhaps, you will manage to find voice enough to tell me where you have been?"

"Of course, Miss Hyde; I never have any secrets—that's just what I was saying to Cora, this morning."

"Never mind Cora."

"But I do; she's worth minding, and so's her mistress. Mrs. Babylon and I are alike in one thing—we are both fond of fresh air."

"Indeed! You seem well acquainted with the lady's tastes."

"Well, I may say I am; and you needn't take the trouble to contradict! Acquainted with them? Well, if I ain't, I flatter myself there's nobody in our house that is."

I did not answer; the girl's conversation was too quaint and amusing even to sound impertinent, still, I did not wish to encourage her by any sign of approval.

"Miss Hyde," she asked, "did you see any strange birds in the woods?"

"None, Lottie."

"Buy a pair of spectacles, Miss Hyde; don't put it off a day longer! I tell you, out yonder there's two birds well worth watching;—the queerest part is, that it's the female that sings—ain't she a red fellar?"

"I saw Mrs. Dennison and Mr. Lawrence, if you mean them," I replied.

"Hush! don't mention names! You mean Babylon and her prey! Oh my! that Babylon! Well, I declare, sometimes I'm ready to give up beat; that woman goes ahead of anything I ever came across."

Lottie paused, took a long breath, flung up her arms, and performed a variety of singular and dizzy evolutions, by way of expressing her astonishment; then she went on,—

"What do you think she's at now?"

I shook my head.

"It's as good a thing as you can do," said Lottie, approvingly; "but you might shake it till doomsday before you'd get Mrs. Babylon's man[oe]uvres through it, I can tell you that, Miss Hyde."

I wanted to reprove the girl; I felt mean, dishonest; yet I was so anxious about Jessie that I could not prevent myself listening to any revelations the little imp might see fit to make.

"She's put a hornet into Lawrence's hair this time, and no mistake," said Lottie; "and Lord! don't it sting, and make him jump?"

"What do you mean, you ridiculous child?"

"Mean, Miss Hyde? A whole bucketful—a seaful! Why, Babylon's been telling Lawrence that young Mr. Bosworth and our Miss Jessie are engaged."

"Impossible, Lottie! She could not assert so unblushing a falsehood!"

"Oh! couldn't she?" cried Lottie, clapping her arms as if they were wings, and giving vent to a crow to express her enjoyment. "As for blushing, don't she know the rub of mullein-leaves? But she did tell him so. She said she was sure that they had been engaged, and that he, Lawrence, had innocently made trouble between them by flirting with Miss Lee;—now, what is flirting, Miss Hyde?"

"The abominable woman!" I involuntarily exclaimed.

"Oh, no," said Lottie, "she's only Babylon. But I tell you what, that Lawrence isn't much of a snoop. He's a nicer fellow than I took him for. What do you think he did?"

"I can't imagine."

"He just turned on Babylon, like a hawk on a June-bug. 'I cannot believe this,' says he; 'but I will go to Bosworth this very day and explain.'

"Then Babylon began to flutter; she didn't want that to happen, you know.

"'He's sick,' says she; 'not expected to live.'

"'The more reason why I should explain,' says he.

"Then she twisted, and fluttered, and coaxed, and finally got him to promise not to say a word to anybody, to be regulated by her advice, and so on—she would be his friend—oh! how sincere a friend!—and then she took his hand, squeezed out a tear or so, and before long she had him in her clutch. Oh! it was as good as one of Miss Jessie's play-books."

I had not interrupted Lottie; when she paused, I was speechless still.

"What do you think now?" she demanded, triumphantly.

"I do not know," I answered, so troubled and despondent that I had no courage to rebuke the girl.

"We'll fix her yet," said Lottie; "don't you fret, Miss Hyde. I'll pay Babylon off before she's many weeks older, or you may call my head a puff-ball."

"You silly child," I returned, smiling in spite of myself, "what can you do?"

"Come, I like that!" snapped Lottie. "Why, what sort of a state would you all be in if it wasn't for me—tell me that? I've got my dear mistress, and Miss Jessie, and you, and everybody on my hands; but I'll bring you out square, I will, Miss Hyde."

"I wish you would leave things as they are, Lottie, and attend to your own affairs."

"These are my affairs, Miss Hyde, now don't say they ain't! I'm not a bad girl; I love them that have been kind to me, and I'd sooner have my hand burned off than not try to help them when I see they need it."

"Be careful that you get into no mischief."

"I'll take care of myself! Only wait, Miss Hyde. Keep tranquil and cool, Lottie's around!"

She gave another jump, a louder crow, and lighted on her feet, in no way discomposed by her impromptu leap.

By this time we had come in sight of the house. Lottie looked back.

"I see Babylon's red shawl," said she; "off's the word. Good-bye, Miss Hyde."

She darted away before I could speak, and I walked on toward the house, in no mood to encounter the woman at that moment. I saw Jessie and Mr. Lee standing upon the terrace; he turned and went into the house after a few seconds. I paused a moment, collected myself as well as I was able, and walked toward the spot where Jessie stood, determined to tell her at once of my visit to Mr. Bosworth, and urge her to comply with the request which he had made.

CHAPTER XXIX
TROUBLES GATHER ABOUT OUR JESSIE

Jessie did not look up as I approached; she stood absently pulling the flowers from a vine that fell in luxuriant masses over a trellis by her side, and appeared so much engrossed by her own thoughts, that she did not even hear my footsteps.

They were not pleasant reflections which filled her mind. Sunny visions, such as those which, a few weeks since, had made her face so bright and beautiful, were seldom on her features now. I could see by the mournful expression of her mouth, and the despondency of her whole attitude,—so unlike anything I was accustomed to remark in our Jessie, that something was troubling her.

"You naughty girl!" I said, as I ascended the steps; "how can you find the heart to spoil that pretty vine?"

She started, turned quickly round, and a burning blush shot up to her forehead, while she looked at me in a confused way, as if she supposed me able to read her very thoughts.

"Oh! is it you, Aunt Matty?" she exclaimed, trying to laugh and seem more at ease.

"I believe so," was my answer; "I have every reason to suppose that I am that person, and very tired into the bargain."

"You look fatigued," she said, with her usual kindness; "do go up-stairs and lie down before dinner."

"Now, my dear, you know I am never guilty of that weakness."

"I forgot."

"How could you? I am astonished—when you know how much I pride myself on regular habits and a systematic disposal of my time!"

She laughed a little at my nonsense, which was the thing I desired; for it pained me greatly to see her look so weary and disconsolate.

"At all events, you will sit down, I suppose," she said, running into the hall and bringing out a chair. "Your rigid principles do not prevent that!"

"Thank you, my dear. I am happy to say they do not."

I seated myself, really glad of an opportunity to rest; for now that excitement had passed, I was astonished to find myself worn out in body and mind. The mere walk could never have produced that sensation—I was too much accustomed to out-door exercise for any fine lady feebleness of that kind; but my interview with Bosworth and his friends, the sight of Mrs. Dennison and Mr. Lawrence in the wood, together with Lottie's revelations, had so worked upon my mind, that I had no strength left.

"Dear me! Aunt Matty!" exclaimed Jessie; "how tired and pale you look! I never saw you so overcome!"

"It is nothing. I walked faster than I ought, perhaps."

"That is not all," she answered; "I am sure something troubles you."

"So there does!" I said,—"very greatly!"

"Can I help you? You know how gladly I will do it."

She began untying my bonnet-strings, drawing off my shawl, and performing every little office possible to show her solicitude.

Generally, I dislike to have anybody touch me, or assist me in any way; but it was always a pleasure to feel Jessie's fingers smoothing my hair, or arranging my collar; and just then her assiduity quieted me more than anything else could have done.

"Did you take a long walk?" Jessie asked, apparently anxious to turn my thoughts from the painful theme upon which she supposed them to be dwelling.

"Yes, very long, Jessie; I have been over to old Mrs. Bosworth's."

She looked at me in astonishment.

"Why, you hardly know the ladies! How came you to go there, Aunt Matty?"

"The old lady sent for me."

"Sent for you!" interrupted Jessie, in wonder and displeasure, while her great eyes gave me a searching glance.

"Young Bosworth is very sick, and he wished so much to see me that his grandmother put aside all ceremony, and desired me to go as soon as possible."

Jessie turned very pale while I spoke, and leaned heavily against the arm of my chair.

"Was it sudden?" she asked, trembling. "Has he been sick long, Matty?"

"For several days, I believe."

I had not the heart to tell her that he was stricken down the very day after his last visit to her father's house, lest she should accuse herself as the cause.

"What is the matter?"

"He has brain-fever, Jessie."

She uttered a cry.

"Oh! Aunt Matty! Aunt Matty!"

"I hope he is not in great danger," I said, anxious to soothe her. "He was able to talk with me, and he had a comfortable sleep."

She put her hands in mine, with a look so beseeching and helpless, that I answered as if she had spoken.

"He asked for you," I said. "He wants to see you, Jessie."

She shrunk back, and held up her hands like a child pleading for pity.

"Oh! I cannot go! indeed I cannot!"

"That is unlike you, Jessie. I did not think you would have refused a sick friend any request!"

"Don't blame me—please don't! I would do anything for him; but, indeed, I have not the courage to go there."

"Why, what do you fear, my child? I am sure he would not for the world speak a syllable that could pain you."

"I know that, Aunt Matty—I am certain of it."

"Then what is it?"

"Old Mrs. Bosworth has such a stately way; so soft, yet decided. She will look at me so sharply."

"I found her very kind and grateful."

"But she may think that I have done wrong."

"She is too just, too noble, Jessie, to blame any one for that which was not a fault."

"Oh, Aunt Matty! even you speak and look so grave! I cannot bear it—indeed I cannot!"

I was softened at once. How could I speak so coldly to my Jessie, while she stood there trembling, with her great eyes full of tears.

"My own darling!" I said, quickly. "You know I could never feel anything but love for you. Don't shake so, dear! We won't speak of this, if it troubles you."

"No, no! I ought to hear—I must not be so weak."

She struggled against her feelings, brushed away her tears, and stood up so firm and determined, that I felt a new respect for her. It was beautiful to see how the true womanhood that lay at the bottom of her nature roused itself, and asserted its supremacy in that moment of doubt and distress.

"You are a brave girl!" I exclaimed,—"my dear, honest-hearted Jessie!"

"You must not praise me," she said. "I feel so guilty and wicked."

"That is wrong; you should not give way to these morbid feelings."

"Indeed, Aunt Matty, I am not like the same girl I was a few months ago."

I knew whence the change came—I could have given its exact date; but it did not extend back over a period of months—a few weeks had served to bring that unrest and trouble upon the sweet girl. With the coming of Mrs. Dennison all those shadows had crept into the house, gathering silently but surely about every heart, piding those who before had no thought nor wish that was not common to all. I felt, too, that she was preparing the way for deeper and darker troubles, which lingered not far off, only awaiting the command of the arch-magician to approach and wrap us in their folds.

CHAPTER XXX
MRS. DENNISON GATHERS WILD FLOWERS

While I was lost in gloomy thoughts which those words had aroused, Jessie turned from my chair and walked slowly up and down the terrace, after a habit she had inherited from her father in any season of doubt or perplexity. At last she came softly back and leaned over me again.

"Aunt Matty," she whispered, timidly.

"Yes, dear."

"I have made up my mind."

I looked in her face, and its expression told me at once what her decision had been.

"You will go," I said.

"Yes, I will. It is right—it is my duty! If he were never to get well, I should reproach myself bitterly for not having granted his request."

"God bless you, Jessie! I knew you would not refuse."

"I am sure that my parents will have no objection."

"I can answer for that—the most scrupulous person could see no harm. Besides, Bosworth is a favorite both with your father and mother."

"Yes. Dear mamma will be so sorry to hear that he is ill—poor young man!"

"We will go to-morrow, Jessie. I dare say your father will accompany you."

"But I want you also, Aunt Matty; I should have no courage if you were not there."

"I will go, of course. You must speak to Mr. Lee about it—don't forget."

"I am not likely to; I will tell him this evening. But Aunt Matty—"

"Yes. Don't hesitate so. One would think you were afraid of your old friend. Not a cross one, am I?"

That made her laugh again; but the merriment died quickly. Her sensitive heart was so sorely troubled that her usual gayety was quite gone.

"I shall never fear you; but what I meant was that I don't wish Mrs. Dennison to know that I am going."

"She is not likely to learn it from me, Jessie."

"She would laugh at me—and this is no subject nor time for a jest."

"I should think not, indeed. The woman who could make a mockery of such feelings would be a libel on her sex."

"Ah! you must not be harsh."

"Only the old bitterness—don't mind it, Jessie. But we won't tell Mrs. Dennison."

At that moment I detected a rustle in the hall. My hearing was always singularly acute,—Jessie used to say that I was like a wild animal in that respect,—and I felt confident that I heard some one stealing away from behind us.

I started up at once, hurried into the hall, and met Cora, Mrs. Dennison's maid, face to face. She was running off—I could have sworn to that; but the moment she heard my step she turned toward me with her usual composure and pleasant smile.

"What do you want here, Cora?" I asked, more sharply than I often spoke to a dependant; for, of all people in the world, it is my habit to treat servants kindly. "Pray, what brings you into this hall?"

"I was just coming to look for my mistress, ma'am. Excuse me; I didn't know it was wrong."

"I have not said that it was," I answered, still convinced that she had been listening; "but our own domestics are never permitted to pass through this hall unless called."

"I will remember—I beg pardon."

"Mrs. Dennison is not here."

"Oh! excuse me—"

She stopped. I saw her curtsy, turned, and there stood Mr. Lee, looking at me gravely. He had heard my ill-natured tone, and could see the flush of anger on my face.

"What is the matter, Miss Hyde?" he asked, quietly enough; but the tone displeased me, and I replied with a good deal of sharpness,—

"I am not aware of anything, sir; Cora was searching for her mistress."

"That is right enough, I am sure."

"She is not here," I continued, feeling a savage pleasure in the words I spoke; "she is out in the woods with Mr. Lawrence."

Mr. Lee colored slightly, but managed to conceal his discomposure.

Cora hurried away after giving me a spiteful glance, and Jessie, who had heard my words, came into the hall.

"Mrs. Dennison told me that she should be busy all the morning in her room," she said, quickly.

"I can't help what she said, my dear; I only know that I saw her walking with Mr. Lawrence."

"Surely it is her privilege, if she feels disposed, to walk with any person," Mr. Lee said, laughing with a very bad grace, while Jessie looked much disturbed.

"I have no desire to interfere with the lady's movements," I said, my temper still in the ascendant; "but I see no necessity for saying one thing and doing another."

Mr. Lee appeared surprised at my outburst. I dare say it was not lady-like; but I am not made of stone, and my real feelings will peep out occasionally.

"I am afraid Mrs. Dennison would think you spoke harshly to her servant," he said. "I shouldn't like a guest in this house to be annoyed."

For the first time I was angry with Mr. Lee. I was not a dependant; I was not accustomed to anything but affection and respect in that house, and the reproof in his voice, added to my own feeling of self-dissatisfaction, made me quite furious.

"Sir," I said, "you have always requested us not to permit servants to enter this hall; when you wish to change any of your regulations, be good enough to inform me in advance."

I turned away before he could speak, and Jessie went to him, saying something in a low voice.

"Miss Hyde!" he called out, approaching me and extending his hand. "Why, dear friend, you are not angry with me? I would rather cut off this right hand than have that happen."

My anger evaporated at once; like a silly fool as I am, the tears gathered in my eyes. He shook my hand heartily, while Jessie hovered about us like an anxious bird.

"I really meant no harm," he began; but I would not hear a word.

"I am ashamed of myself," I said, "and that is the end of it; I am tired and cross."

"You are not well," he replied, kindly. "Jessie, make her go and lie down."

"She never will, papa."

She put her arm caressingly about my waist, and Mr. Lee stood holding my hand, petting me as if my words had been a matter of the greatest consequence. Suddenly Mrs. Dennison entered from the terrace, and exclaimed, with a gay laugh, —

"What a pretty scene! Are you acting a comedy, Mr. Lee? How well you do it!"

He dropped my hand in some confusion, and turned toward her.

"Better comedy than tragedy," he said.

"Oh, yes, a thousand times! But Miss Hyde's role seems to be a sentimental one—she looks very lugubrious!"

I longed to strike her full in her insolent mouth; but as that was impossible, I determined to pay her off for once in her own coin. A spirit of retaliation was roused within me that I had never before possessed.

"You seem gay enough to make amends," I said. "Did you and Mr. Lawrence have a pleasant walk?"

What a fool I was to think I could send a blow that would have any effect upon that piece of marble!

She laughed outright, and clapped her hands in childish exultation.

"She wants to accuse me of being a flirt!" she exclaimed; "Oh, you naughty Miss Hyde! I did meet Mr. Lawrence, but I had no idea of doing so when I went out. I think now I shall make a merit of my intention!"

"You might always do so, I am sure," said Mr. Lee, gallantly.

She held up a beautiful bouquet of wild flowers.

"I heard Mrs. Lee wish for some blossoms fresh from the woods last night," she said; "so I went to gather them."

Mr. Lee's face grew all sunshine at once; even Jessie was appeased, and, unseen by either, the widow shot me a quick glance of scorn.

"How kind it was of you!" Jessie said. "Mamma will be so much obliged!"

"I wanted to please her, darling Jessie," replied the widow. "But I must make one confession; will you grant me absolution, Mr. Lee?"

"I can safely do that in advance. I am sure you have no very terrible sin to reveal."

"Oh, I told a fib!" And she laughed archly. "I wanted to go all alone, so that dear Mrs. Lee would give me full credit for my thoughtfulness.—You see how vain and selfish I am!—so I told Jessie that I was going to be occupied in my own room."

"I think when selfishness takes a form like this, it is a very valuable quality to possess," returned Mr. Lee.

Mrs. Dennison treated me to another flash from her scornful eyes, then added,—

"And while I was picking flowers, who should pass but Mr. Lawrence; so I made him stop. But I might as well have let him go on."

"Why so?" demanded Mr. Lee.

"Because he was very ungallant; did nothing but talk of Jessie, and never said a pretty thing to me."

Jessie blushed, but the smile on her lips showed that she was far from annoyed.

"So that is all my secret," continued Mrs. Dennison. "Now, we will take this unfortunate bouquet up to Mrs. Lee. Come, Jessie."

"May I go?" asked the gentleman.

"If you will be very good. But mind you do not tease for the flowers—we cannot spare a single one!"

"I promise."

"Then come with us."

CHAPTER XXXI
LOTTIE'S ADVICE

Mrs. Dennison had one arm about Jessie's waist; she kept Mr. Lee close at her side, and so engrossed and fascinated both father and daughter, that they passed on without remembering that I was there.

It was just what the woman intended: she wished to make me feel of how little consequence I was in the house when she chose to exercise her supremacy. That was her way of revenging herself for my rude speech in regard to her ramble.

If it is absolutely necessary for me to tell the entire and exact truth, I must admit that she succeeded perfectly in wounding me. I was greatly pained, but not altogether from jealousy or sensitiveness. Hurt as I was to see how completely my friends were made to forget their solicitude at that woman's bidding, I was still more troubled to perceive how, every day, her influence in that house increased, how artfully she wove the threads of her net about us, and entangled everybody more helplessly in its meshes.

While I stood thinking of those things, I was startled by a sound close at hand—a very singular noise, such as one might expect from an antiquated raven troubled with bronchitis. From behind a screen that stood in the hall bounded Miss Lottie, emitting another of those unearthly croaks, and stationing herself directly in front of me with one of her most impish looks.

"I am astonished at you!" said she, shaking her head, and pursing up her lips until her words came out in a sort of strangled whistle. "I really am more astonished, Miss Hyde, than I should be to see two Christmases come in the same year!"

"What is the matter now?" I asked, laughing in spite of myself.

"To think of your going and trying to circumvent Babylon! Why, she's almost more'n a match for me, and to see you floppin' up at her quite took my breath away!"

"You are impertinent, Lottie!"

"Well, I don't mean to be! But just let me caution you a trifle. Don't try any such game—she'll only fling it back right in your teeth, as she did just now, sail off with her feathers spread, and leave you feeling as flat as a pancake!"

I had an internal conviction that Lottie was correct in her judgment; but not considering it necessary to admit as much, I made an effort to turn the subject.

"What were you doing behind that screen? I hope you haven't taken to listening to the whole house."

"Now, Miss Hyde, I didn't think you'd accuse me in that way. But I don't blame you—Babylon's made you huffy! Cut in agin, Miss Matty, if you want to!"

"But you should not do those things, Lottie!"

"Not quite so fast, if you please. I can tell you what I went behind there for."

"I do not wish to inquire into your proceedings," I said, coldly, and was moving away; but she caught me by the arm.

"Please don't go off mad, Miss Hyde," she pleaded; "I'll tell you the truth. I was in the little room looking out a book Mrs. Lee wanted, when I heard you and Miss Jessie talking on the terrace. I didn't know what you said, and didn't want to; but just then I saw Cora creep through the hall, and stand listening by the door. So I slips out, got behind the screen, and, once there, I had to stay till the folks got off."

"Then she was listening?" I said.

"I should rather guess she was! and a-shaking them big ear-rings. She didn't miss a word, you may be sure!"

"Why does she do those things?"

"Why? Come, now, that's good! 'Cause Babylon tells her to, and 'cause her heart's blacker than her face, and she loves mischief as well as the gray cat does cream."

"You cannot think her mistress would countenance her in such proceedings."

"I don't think nothing about it—I know, Miss Hyde. She's got countenance of her own, though, to help her through a'most anything! But I tell you she's sot on to spy and listen."

"That is a fault you ought to judge leniently, Lottie."

"No, 'tain't, Miss Hyde! I've always been above things of that sort; but since Babylon's come the world's changed, and I have to fix myself according to circumstances. But don't you fall foul o' either of them again—'tain't no use! Why, she walked Mr. Lee and Miss Jessie right off afore your eyes, and you may bet your front teeth that by this time she's made them believe you're cross-grained, and jealous as a lap-dog!"

"I begin to think I am, Lottie."

"No, you ain't—you can't stay cross two minutes! And as for good looks—wal, if you furbelowed yourself off like some folks that shall be nameless, you'd be more than as young-looking as some folks themselves."

I turned again to go, but Lottie had, as usual, a few last words which must be spoken.

"See here, Miss Hyde," said she; "Babylon'll carry Mr. Lee off, I know, and Miss Jessie's got her heart so full that she'll slip away to her own room; so you must go and sit with Mrs. Lee."

"I will go to her room as soon as Mrs. Dennison leaves."

"That won't be long. She ain't going to coop herself up for nobody; trust her!"

"Very well; I shall be ready."

"And, Miss Hyde—"

"Well?"

"Now, don't be mad—I must say it! Just leave Babylon to me—you ain't no shakes where she is concerned; you'll only get yourself into a brile, and muddle matters—leave her to me!"

She gave her head a consequential toss and darted away, singing some dolorous ditty about "Long Ago."

I went up to my chamber, sad and sick at heart. Our little world seemed going very wrong; but how to remedy that which was amiss I could not tell. I was powerless, and could only remain quiet and let things take their course, praying that God would shield those so dear to me from sorrow and harm.

Perhaps an hour after, there was a low tap at my door, and, in obedience to my summons, Lottie danced into the room.

"She's all alone, Miss Hyde. Babylon's trotted Mr. Lee into the garden, and Miss Jessie's in her own chamber. Come right along and sit with Mrs. Lee."

CHAPTER XXXII
MRS. LEE DREAMS OF PASSION-FLOWERS

I rose at once and went to the chamber of our dear invalid. She was lying on a sofa, supported by pillows, and looking with pleasure at the bouquet of wild flowers that had been placed on her table.

"I am glad to see you, Miss Hyde," she said. "Come in and sit here close by me. Look at my pretty flowers."

"They are very lovely!" I replied.

"They make me feel as if I were in the woods."

She sighed, checked the vain regret, and added cheerfully.

"Mrs. Dennison brought them to me. Was it not thoughtful of her? I was wishing for them last night."

"Very thoughtful," I said.

"You look tired," she observed; "sit down and we will have one of our old, quiet hours. Mr. Lee had to go out, and Mrs. Dennison has gone to Jessie's room; so we shall be all alone."

Another falsehood! My blood fairly boiled! Lottie had just seen the pair in the garden. But I could not speak—a word, a look might have destroyed that poor creature's peace forever! No syllable from my lips should send a thought of suspicion to her heart!

I did sit down, and we had a long, pleasant conversation; for with those whom she knew well, Mrs. Lee was an exceedingly agreeable companion, although ill-health had made her nervous in the presence of strangers.

After a time she began to speak of Jessie, and then it occurred to me that it would be a favorable opportunity to tell her of Jessie's desire to visit Mrs. Bosworth.

She was shocked to hear of her young favorite's illness, and when I told her how anxious he was to see Jessie, and how necessary it seemed that he should not be opposed, she agreed with me that her daughter ought to go.

"Certainly, certainly," she said. "Mr. Lee will think so too. You were quite right to promise, Miss Hyde."

"I thought so."

"Poor young man! Do you know, Martha Hyde, I used to think he was very fond of our Jessie? But of late I have so seldom left my room, or seen any one, that I don't know what goes on."

I did not answer, and she changed the subject, with the excitability of all sick people.

"Mrs. Dennison makes the house very gay," she said.

"Very! Her manners are charming!"

"She seems a superior woman. Do you begin to like her, Martha?"

"Oh, I am difficult to please, you know," I replied, trying to laugh. "Girls, old or young, and widows seldom agree; besides, I can only care for people whom I have known a long time."

She did not answer, but pushed her hair back from her forehead, and looked absently at the flowers.

"I have such bad dreams," she said; "I never can recall them distinctly; but they seem full of trouble."

"Of whom do you dream?"

"All of you—principally of Jessie. Sometimes I think I must be awake and standing in her room—the vision is so real."

"Such fancies are very common to an invalid," I said.

"Oh, yes; I don't mind them."

She pulled the flowers toward her, and began playing with them after Jessie's childish fashion. It gave me a strange feeling to see those blossoms in her hand; when I remembered whose gift they had been, I felt as if my friend held Cleopatra's venomous asp in every flower that she touched.

"Will you read to me a while?" she asked, at length. "There is a new poem on the table; take that."

Of course, I complied at once, and read to her for some time; then I saw the flowers drop from her hand—her head sank back among the pillows, and soon her regular breathing proved that she was sleeping quietly.

I laid down the volume, and looked at her with pain and solicitude. She was so helpless! The least shock might terminate that frail existence; and I had grown so nervous that I was always expecting some trouble to force itself into that room, which, until lately, had been securely guarded by a husband's love.

She moved restlessly in her sleep; broken words fell from her lips; very soon they framed themselves into complete sentences. She had sunk into one of those singular somnambulistic slumbers which formed such a strange feature of her illness.

"I am tired," she said; "I have walked so fast! How pretty the summer-house looks! It is so long since I have been here! There is Mr. Lee—"

She paused and breathed rapidly.

"Why, Mrs. Dennison is with him! She said she was going to Jessie's room! How earnestly she talks to him! She lays her hand on his arm!"

She paused again, with a sort of cry.

"Martha Hyde! Martha! my husband is giving her flowers—passion-flowers! She asks him to put them in her hair! What does that mean, say?"

She became so violently agitated that I thought it best to rouse her. I leaned over her and shook her arm slightly. The change of position seemed to alter the dream, and once more she slept quietly.

I went back to the window, and sat looking out behind the curtains. It was sunset, and gorgeously beautiful. But in the distraction of my thoughts I could not heed its loveliness.

While I sat there I saw Mr. Lee and Mrs. Dennison pass along one of the paths. They had been out on the upper terrace, and were approaching the house. The lady had no bonnet on, and wreathed in her hair I saw some superb passion-flowers which the poor wife had described in her dream.

I grew sick and faint with doubt and horror. I must do something; I could not longer sit passive and dumb, and see that woman wreck all our lives. But what to do? which way to turn?

Alas! I was very helpless after all! There was no one to whom I could confide my suspicions—no one to whom I could open my heart, and the only hope I had was in that wild girl, who had understood the real character of our visitor so much more quickly than any of her superiors.

While I was thinking of this thus painfully, the door of the inner room opened, and Lottie stood there, beckoning to me.

I went into her chamber, and she closed the door. She was in great excitement and glee.

"Babylon's been at it," she whispered.

"At what?"

"Talking about you. Oh, my! hain't you woke up a hornet's nest! Cora's mad too; golly, don't she go on. I told you to let things alone."

"I care very little for Mrs. Dennison's anger," I said.

"I don't suppose you do. But she'll pay you off if she can. So look sharp, Miss Hyde; these are times for sleeping with both eyes open. No chance to dream or make verses now."

"Nonsense, child!"

"Nonsense, if you choose; but that don't alter the matter. Babylon's brought Mr. Lee back to the house; she had him out in the garden to make all right about Lawrence."

"Stop, Lottie!"

"I have stopped—sha'n't say no more! Hark! what was that?"

It was a call—an appeal for help. A voice from Mrs. Lee's room cried with energy,—

"Martha Hyde! Martha Hyde!"

I rushed into the chamber, followed by Lottie, and found Mrs. Lee half risen on her sofa, tossing her arms about, and calling still upon my name, although she was yet asleep.

Many moments passed before I could rouse her, and when I did, she sank back on the pillows perfectly exhausted. I administered such restoratives as were at hand, and, with Lottie's assistance, succeeded in bringing her out of the half swoon into which she had fallen; but she was fearfully weak, and much excited.

"I have had such terrible dreams," she moaned, "I am afraid to go to sleep."

"They are over now," I said, soothingly; "you shall sit up and have your tea."

"Yes, please. Don't let me sleep any more, don't, Martha Hyde."

All the while she held fast to my hand and looked wildly in my eyes, repeating,—

"Such dreadful dreams, Martha Hyde—oh! such dreadful dreams!"

CHAPTER XXXIII
COMPANY FROM TOWN

That evening we had a number of visitors from the town, and so much gayety that it quite passed from my mind to speak with Mr. Lee concerning the call upon young Bosworth. Indeed, I was not in the parlors much of the time, for he came to me and asked if I would sit a while with his wife, as he could not leave his guests, and she was so much more nervous than usual, he did not like trusting her entirely with Lottie.

I felt grateful to him for remembering her, and went away at once. As I passed toward the hall, I saw Jessie at the piano surrounded by a group of gentlemen, Lawrence nearest, turning over the music, and talking to her at intervals.

Mrs. Dennison was flitting about like a gorgeous butterfly, making merriment and pleasant conversation wherever she went.

Her quick eyes detected me as I passed the music-room door. She moved along, smelling carelessly at her flowers, the sight of which made me sick; they were roses from the choicest varieties that Mrs. Lee considered peculiarly her own.

"Going to preserve your bloom by an early sleep, Miss Hyde?" she asked, pleasantly.

"I am going to sit with Mrs. Lee," I replied, coldly enough, I dare say. I was not accustomed to dissimulation, and when I disliked and doubted a person as I did her, it was very difficult for me to conceal it.

"You are quite the guardian-angel of the house," she returned, so sweetly that no one except a suspicious creature like me would have perceived the covert insult under her words; "I expect every day to see you unfold your wings and fly off."

"This is my home," I answered, quietly, "so I shall not fly very far from it in all probability."

She laughed in her charming way; but there was an expression in her eyes which would have startled me, had I not felt that she was powerless to do me personal injury.

"And a pleasant home you have," she said, with a sigh; "you can't think, Miss Hyde, how delightful it seems to a tired worldling like me."

I was in no humor to listen to sentiment, and I replied curtly,—

"Not tired, Mrs. Dennison, or, of course, you would forsake the society that wearies you."

She shook her head patronizingly and smiled, oh, such a sweet, sad smile—she must have practised for days to attain such perfection in it.

"How innocent you are!" she said; "I envy you, dear, kind Miss Hyde!"

How I longed to fling back her affectionate epithets with the scorn they deserved; but, of course, that was impossible, so I made a movement to go, trembling all over with repressed indignation.

"You are running away from me as usual," she said, reproachfully; "I never get a moment now of your honest, sensible conversation."

"I trust you do not suffer much from the loss," was all the answer I made.

I know I am not very wise; I do not deny having my share of little vanities; but Mrs. Dennison had not found the road which led to them.

"I do indeed," she replied; "but I see you will not believe me."

"You have not an exalted opinion of my courtesy, Mrs. Dennison."

"Ah, now you are going to be sarcastic—my dear Miss Hyde, that is not in your way."

She added a few more playful words, then I was resolute to go. I left her standing there in one of her graceful attitudes, playing negligently with her roses.

Once in the hall, I glanced back; the widow had changed her position,— she was stationed by a window,—I saw Mr. Lee approach her, and they began an earnest conversation. I turned and went up-stairs, growing sadder and more sick at heart.

Mrs. Lee slept quietly nearly the whole time, so that I had ample opportunity for my sorrowful reflections,—more than I desired, since dwelling upon the things which troubled me only increased my restlessness, without bringing me any nearer a conclusion that could have been of the least value.

After Mrs. Lee had gone to bed, I went into my own room, and saw no one again that night. When it was too late, I remembered that I had not spoken to Mr. Lee, but consoled myself with fancying that Jessie would tell him, or that I should have an opportunity in the morning.

I was disappointed both ways. When I went down to breakfast, I found that Mr. Lee had been obliged to ride over to the iron works. He had gone before any one was stirring, and would not return until late in the afternoon.

While one of the servants was giving me that information, Mrs. Dennison passed through the hall. She hurried on with a smile, but I noticed that the skirt of her dress was wet and soiled; I felt certain that she knew of Mr. Lee's intention, and had gone out to meet him, and hold one of her private conversations.

Before she appeared again, Jessie joined me in the breakfast-room.

"How late we all are!" she said; "it is too bad."

"I quite overslept myself," I replied; then I remembered my thought of the last night. "Oh, my dear! did you ask your father to go with us to Mrs. Bosworth's?"

"I had no opportunity," she answered, blushing crimson. "I am afraid, too, that I half forgot it."

I knew the reason of that; Lawrence had been talking to her all the evening.

"It does not make much difference," I said; "I will go with you."

"I am sure papa would be willing," she observed, looking troubled at the idea of the visit.

"I spoke of it to your mother; she desired you to go."

"Very well then," replied Jessie; "suppose we start after breakfast; we can get back before mamma will want us in her room."

"I shall be ready; we can walk across the fields."

"Yes; then Mrs. Dennison need not know anything about it."

"Hush!" I said; "there she is."

CHAPTER XXXIV
OUR VISIT TO THE OLD MANSION

Mrs. Dennison came in airy and graceful as usual; I noticed that she had changed her dress. She kissed Jessie with as much affection as if she had not seen her for a week, and began discoursing with great volubility.

"I was up before either of you," she said; "I have been out in the garden, ruining my white dress, and racing among the beds, to the great astonishment of the old gardener."

"You look fresh and charming as the roses themselves," Jessie replied.

"Of course. But don't pay compliments; Miss Hyde does not like them."

"If they are sincere, I do," I said.

"Ah! then you must like mine. Indeed, I should be afraid to tell you a story; I am certain those honest eyes of yours would detect it at once."

I disclaimed any such extraordinary powers for my poor eyes, and the widow rattled on about something else. She always went from one subject to another in a rapid, graceful way, like a bird flying about in the trees.

"Why, where is Mr. Lee?" she asked.

"Gone out," said Jessie; "he went early."

"How ungallant," she returned; but she looked so very innocent that I was more than ever convinced she had seen him before his departure.

One thing I could say for Mrs. Dennison, she never troubled her hosts to entertain her. Directly after breakfast, she went, as usual, her own way, and Jessie and I were free to start upon our expedition.

"We had better go at once," I said; "there is no telling when she may dance in upon us again."

"You don't like her, Aunt Matty," replied Jessie; "I am sure you don't, yet she is very charming."

"Never mind; there is no time to discuss my fancies," I said. "Get your bonnet, Jessie."

She hesitated and grew a little pale, but complied at once. We were ready in a few moments, and, passing through the garden, went down the path by the grove, and took our way across the fields to the old house.

Jessie was very silent during our walk, and I was so much occupied with my plans and my fancies that I had little time to break the thread of her thoughts.

When we reached the gate that led into the door-yard, Jessie stopped.

"Oh, I am so frightened," she said.

Poor child! she was very pale, and shook from head to foot with an agitation that reminded me painfully of her mother's nervous excitements. I did my best to soothe her, but, in spite of her efforts, it was some moments before she could go on.

"You will not mind it after the first meeting," I said.

"I am very foolish, I know. There, I am ready now."

As we turned into the avenue, I saw Mr. Lawrence pass along the road on horseback. He gave a sharp, quick look, and rode on. I said nothing to Jessie; it was useless to agitate her further. His passing at that time might have been mere chance.

Jessie clung to me as we went up the two broad steps and entered the hall. I did not speak, contenting myself with a reassuring pressure of the hand; for I knew from experience that in cases of nervous dread one is only made worse by persuasions and cheering speeches.

We were shown into the room where I had before waited for old Mrs. Bosworth, and very soon I heard the rustle of her dress in the hall.

The old lady came in with her stately manner, but I could see that trouble and watching had left their effect upon her, and it seemed to me that I could discover smothered pain in her eyes when she greeted Jessie. But she was exceedingly kind,—so gentle and caressing, that the girl soon recovered from her fright and began to look like herself.

"You will excuse my daughter's absence, I hope," the old lady said; "she is lying down. She is not very strong, and watching has quite worn her out."

"But you think your grandson better?" I asked.

"Much better; yes, much better."

There was thanksgiving in her very voice. Jessie said, tremulously,—

"We were very sorry to hear of his sickness."

"Thank you, Miss Lee; I was sure you would be."

The old lady's fingers worked nervously; I knew, in spite of her pride, what was in her heart. She longed to take Jessie in her arms, to beseech her to speak the one word that would bring her boy back to life and happiness.

"He suffers less with his head, I suppose?" I said, breaking the little pause which would soon have proved awkward.

"It is quite easy this morning; indeed, last night he slept for several hours undisturbed. He is so patient," she continued, "so gentle; but that is natural to him."

I knew she was glad to have that opportunity of praising Bosworth; she felt as if it was indirectly doing something to interest Jessie in his favor.

"It was very kind of you to come, Miss Lee," she said. "I thought you would be willing to humor a sick man's fancies, and he pined so to see all his old friends," she added, quickly, with her old-world tact, for the color began to flicker on Jessie's cheek.

"My father would have come also," said the girl, talking rapidly, "but he was obliged to go out very early; and you know my mother seldom leaves her room."

"It is sad that she should be so great an invalid," said the old duchess—I must call her so. "My daughter and I go out very little. We have often wished to see more of you, but age and infirmity are by force unsocial."

"Mrs. Lee is fond of company," I said. I longed to do all I could to draw the two families together.

"Ah, if that is the case, we shall call frequently upon her. It may do her some good;" she looked at Jessie as she spoke.

"Mamma will be so pleased," she said, quite firmly; "it is very monotonous to live always shut up in her room; she is naturally very social, and to such, solitude is mournful."

"So it is; but I pity the young most! If I could only have taken my poor boy's illness in his stead."

She was checked by the entrance of an old servant, who whispered something in her ear.

"Will you go up-stairs?" she said, turning to me; "my grandson knows you are here."

She took Jessie's hand softly, leading her away, and I followed. Jessie bore up like a little Spartan, but I could see what an effort it was,—I pitied her far more than any one else.

CHAPTER XXXV
YOUNG BOSWORTH'S SICK-ROOM

When we entered the sick-room, it was a shock to Jessie. In spite of all I had said, she was not prepared to find Bosworth so changed. They had put a dressing-gown upon him, but its gay colors only increased the ghastliness of his face, already wasted and worn by fever.

He was so happy to see us—so like a child that fears to give pain by its own pleasure. I think Jessie took heart after the first few moments; and I could see the old lady watching her in secret, as if she thought that, unless she were only a beautiful piece of marble, she must be softened now.

"It was very selfish of me, Miss Jessie," he said, "to call you away from your amusements to visit a poor, sick fellow."

"I was very glad to come," she replied; "my mother is so anxious about you, she could not rest till some of us had been here."

"She is very kind," he said, with the touching smile of illness.

At last we fell to talking quite cheerfully. I did my best to prevent the restraint we were all under becoming perceptible; I dare say it was blunderingly done, but it succeeded tolerably well.

Bosworth made Jessie tell him all about her flowers—he was a great botanist—and I chimed in with the wonderful history of a nest of young birds I had found, and really made him laugh at my nonsense.

But he was weak, and soon grew weary,—I saw it, and made Jessie a sign to go.

"Not yet," he said, as we rose; "stay a while longer, please."

So we sat down again, but I saw by his eyes that his senses began to cloud a little.

"What is that hymn you sing, Miss Jessie?" he asked, suddenly; "it has been running in my head all the morning."

Jessie could not speak; she was trying with all her might to keep back her tears; so I said,—

"You mean that little gem of Mrs. Hemans—'Child Amid the Flowers at Play.'"

"Yes," he replied, "that is it. Won't you sing it for me?"

It really was heroic, the way that poor girl struggled with herself and forced back her composure. She turned her face a little from the light and began to sing; her voice was very low and tremulous, but I never heard it sound so sweet; Bosworth lay back on his pillow and listened with a happy smile.

"Thank you," he said, when she finished; "I can sleep now—you were very kind to come."

He tried to take her hand, said a few more broken words, and then we went away. I saw that Jessie could endure nothing more. Old Mrs. Bosworth detected it too; she must have felt for the girl, and was grateful to her for that visit. She did not accompany us down-stairs, and I was glad to make our farewell as short as possible.

The moment we were out of the house, Jessie gave way completely, and sobbed and wept as I never before saw her.

"Do you think he will die, Aunt Matty?" she asked.

"I do not; he is certainly better."

"But he looks dreadfully; I never saw anybody altered so much."

"You are not accustomed to fevers, my dear. I am, and he will get better. I am glad you have made this visit; it will do him good."

"Then I am glad, too," she replied, wiping away her tears. "Oh! if anything had happened, I never should have forgiven myself."

In reality, there was no blame to be attached to her; she had been guilty of no encouragement or coquetry. I could not bear that she should brood over his illness, until she accused herself as the cause, and really grew horrified at what she might fancy her own wickedness.

"He is in God's hands," I said; "either way it would have been as He willed."

"Then you do not think that any trouble—any—"

"I think he would have been sick," I replied, seeing her unable to go on; "he has not looked well for some time past, and his grandmother told me that he had always been somewhat subject to fevers."

Jessie breathed heavily, and looked relieved.

In our preoccupation we had passed from the grounds into the high-road, instead of taking the footpath.

"We must strike into the clover-field at the turn," I said, when I observed our error; "it would make too long a walk to follow the road."

Jessie did not answer. I heard the tramp of horses' hoofs, and looking up saw Mr. Lawrence riding rapidly toward us. He did not check his horse, but lifted his riding-cap, gave a low, stately bow, a quick glance at Jessie's tear-stained face, and galloped on.

I heard Jessie utter a smothered exclamation, but she did not speak a word.

"Mr. Lawrence seems in great haste," I observed, but she did not answer.

I was confident Mrs. Dennison had been besetting him again, for he was pale and looked fiercely excited.

"Here is the path," said Jessie, suddenly.

We turned into it and walked home, scarcely once breaking that unusual silence.

CHAPTER XXXVI
LOTTIE'S REPORT

When we reached the house, Jessie went directly up to her room. I did not attempt to detain her, knowing that she would be much better alone.

I went to my chamber, likewise, but I was not left long to my bewildering meditations, for Lottie's quick tap sounded at the door, and in she danced in the fantastic manner which always betrayed great excitement.

She closed the door carefully, and stood before me with her hands folded behind her back.

"I told you how it would be!" she exclaimed.

"What do you mean?" I asked.

"Why, you're flying out at Babylon; she's mad, and you'll take the consequences, you will."

"I do not imagine they will be very terrible, Lottie."

"That's as a body may happen to think. There's been a great time since you started."

"What has happened?" I inquired, losing all scruples as to the manner in which Lottie might have obtained her information.

"In the first place, we had Lawrence—"

"Was he here?"

"No, no. Babylon went out to walk for her health—you see Babylon needs exercise. After you stole away, I had my eye on her—"

"Why, you did not see us go."

"Oh, didn't I?" she demanded, ironically, nodding her head with great significance. "I was at my window, Miss Hyde, and I always keep my eyes open. Howsumever, I wasn't watching you; I'm above such tricks, unless I feel it my duty, then I never stop at nothing—anything, I mean, thinking of the grammar."

"Did she see us, too?"

"I don't know; but she knew where you were going."

"Why, how did you find that out?"

"Heard her tell Mr. Lee, to be sure."

I was so angry that I felt myself growing pale. Lottie saw it and tittered.

"You would like to choke her, now, wouldn't you, Miss Hyde? What a pity! it's agin religion and the law. I should just enjoy fixing her myself."

"For shame!" I said, but I am afraid it was only because I thought it a duty to check such expressions, not from any lack of sympathy with them.

Lottie tossed her head; but she was in too great haste to communicate her intelligence for much indignation.

"After you'd gone I watched her; she went about very uneasy for a while, then she put on her shawl and streaked off to the grove. I wanted some wild grass, so I went along, but Babylon didn't see me. She waited in the grove till Mr. Lawrence rode by, when she hailed him.

"'Where are you going?' said she.

"He stammered a little, and said something about it being his custom to ride every morning, and at that she laughed right out in her tantalizing way. Oh, she's awful tantalizing is Babylon.

"'You'd better tell the truth,' says she; 'you didn't believe what I told you last night, and you've been to see with your own eyes. Did you meet them?'

"'Miss Jessie and her friend have just entered Mrs. Bosworth's gate,' he answered, cross as two sticks.

"'Of course,' says Babylon; 'I tell you he is her lover. It was to be expected she'd visit him during the sickness brought on by jealousy. You see a grand flirtation has its inconveniences.'

"He shook uneasily in his saddle, but she hadn't any pity, and went on at an awful rate about all of you. Then she tried the old dodge—she was his friend—he might trust her. She went up to him and reached her hand, but he didn't seem to see it.

"'I must go,' said he.

"She tried to stop him, but he wouldn't hear a word.

"'When will you come again?' she asked.

"'God knows!' was all he said, and rode off like a whirlwind.

"Babylon watched him as long as he was in sight, then she gave way to the awfullest mad fit I ever see. I really thought she'd break a blood-vessel. She danced and wrung her hands, and clenched 'em both into fists, which she shook after him, and she bit her lips to keep from screaming; and then all of a sudden she started for the house on a fierce run. I went after her, and as I got into the garden I saw Mr. Lee ride up. She followed him into the house.

"I went round the corner and stood on the veranda, picking roses and humming 'Katy Darling;' only I chose all the low parts, and heard quite comfortable."

"That was wrong," I said, "very wrong."

"Oh! I didn't listen to him," she replied; "but I had to keep watch of Babylon."

I may as well confess my weakness. I longed to ask Lottie all she heard. However, I did not have to wait long for the communication.

"'Jessie has gone out,' said she. He asked her where, and she put on such an innocent face. 'You must know,' says she; 'your daughter would not have taken such a step without your permission. No, no; I understand Jessie's womanly prudence too well.'

"He just stared at her; then he asked in that voice he has when he's angry, what she meant. She hemmed and hawed, and put him off; said he knew, and wouldn't speak.

"'Mrs. Dennison,' said he, 'what does this mean? Where has Jessie gone?'

"She put on the innocent look again; she really did it beautifully.

"'Don't you know?' she asked; 'don't you actually?'

"She worked him up almost into a fit. Goodness knows what fancy he got into his head.

"'I have seen no one this morning,' he said; 'there were none of the family down when I went away. Where has Jessie gone?'

"Then she pretended to back out; she had been wrong—it was doubtless an innocent little secret of Jessie's—she ought not to have spoken—she was so frank and indiscreet—she would rather bite her tongue off than tell what Jessie wanted kept private, and all that. He grew white as death; you know nothing makes him so mad as to think there's any mystery in the house, or anything going on he don't understand.

"'Mrs. Dennison,' says he, 'if you won't speak, I must go to my wife.'

"'Don't, don't,' she said; 'she is so feeble; don't agitate her.'

"'Then tell me yourself,' says he.

"Then she went all through the old performance, but at last it came out—Jessie had gone to visit Mr. Bosworth in his sick-room. Lord, how mad he was! She told him you was with her, said she didn't blame Jessie, guessed it was all one of your old-maidish romances, and made him furious against you."

"How did it end?" I asked.

"It didn't really have no end; some man called him off on business. Just then you and Miss Jessie came up the steps, and I cut round here to tell you. Babylon—she sat down to the piano, and went to playing a jig; she likes the fun. I tell you she's all right when there's a row. But I'm going to Mrs. Lee; she must want to get up by this time. You're in a hobble, Miss Hyde—a precious hobble—was sure you would be. You playing a game with her—the idea!"

Away she danced, trying to hide her uneasiness; but at the door she stopped and exclaimed,—

"I can't think what ails my head, I'm so dizzy."

She staggered and would have fallen, but I caught her; she was deadly pale. I gave her some water, and she soon grew better.

"Are you ill?" I asked.

"No, I guess not; but lately my head feels so queer every morning. Yesterday, when I went to get out of bed, I fell flat on the floor like a great awkward lobster."

She laughed, but I was very uneasy about her, though she declared she was well again, and hurried away to her duties; for, wild as she was, Lottie was an orderly little thing, and always punctual.

I sat and thought over what she had told me, with some anxiety; but that did no good, so I went down-stairs.

CHAPTER XXXVII
MY FIRST QUARREL WITH MR. LEE

As I entered the lower hall, I met Mr. Lee. He gave me a look such as I never before saw in his face; it so increased my indignation, that, if it had not been for Jessie, I would have walked out of the house that instant.

"Miss Hyde," he said, in the low, measured tone his voice always took when he was angry, "will you step into the library for a moment?"

"Do you wish to speak with me?" I asked, rebelliously.

"If you have leisure."

I swept before him into the room. Every drop of blood in my veins tingled as if on fire. He followed me, and closed the door.

"How does it happen," he began, "that you and Jessie went upon an expedition like that of this morning without consulting me?"

I did my best to answer quietly, although his manner aggravated me almost beyond endurance.

"Simply because you were not here to consult," I replied.

"But you could have told me last night."

Then I flashed up a little, and said,—

"Mr. Lee, I am not a school-girl, to be crowded into a corner and catechized."

"Madam," he returned, "I think I have a right to know everything connected with my daughter; I will permit no mysteries in this house."

"There have been none on my part or Jessie's," I replied.

"Then be good enough to give me an explanation of what, I own, seems to me a singular proceeding in a lady of your acknowledged discretion."

"It is easily done," I answered, still remembering Jessie, and so remaining reasonably calm. "Yesterday, old Mrs. Bosworth sent for me; her grandson is very ill—he has brain-fever. He begged to see us particularly. I came home and told your wife; she said Jessie should go to-day. We expected you to accompany us. Last night there was no opportunity of speaking to you, every moment of your time was occupied. This morning, you were gone; but as I had the mother's permission, I thought it no harm to start. A visit to a sick, almost a dying man, can never injure your daughter, Mr. Lee."

His face flushed at once.

"I was mistaken," he said.

"You must have been cruelly mistaken or misinformed," I replied, coldly, "when you could address me as you have done."

"I beg your pardon, Miss Hyde," he returned.

I granted it with a sullen bend of the head.

"Who told you where we had gone?" I asked, bluntly.

He hesitated, and I followed up my advantage.

"No one knew of it but Mrs. Lee," I said; "you have not seen her to-day. Yesterday you reproved me for sending Cora out of the hall; sir, she was listening while I told Jessie, and repeated it to her mistress. I don't know what you may think of such conduct on the part of a guest; but to me the idea of making trouble in a house where one has been hospitably treated, seems very contemptible."

"Miss Hyde! Miss Hyde!" he exclaimed, "I assure you Mrs. Dennison did it thoughtlessly—she had no idea."

"Excuse me," said I, still burning with indignation, "I am quite capable of forming and holding my own opinions; it is a right I shall not readily relinquish."

I am sorry to say we very nearly had a serious quarrel; but I was so dissatisfied, so indignant that a man of his sense and refinement could be duped in the way he was, that I could not control myself.

We parted civilly enough, however; and when I went up-stairs, Jessie knew all about the affair; Mrs. Dennison had been to her crying and begging for forgiveness. She had thoughtlessly repeated to her father where we had gone, he was angry, and the whole thing was breaking her heart.

"I dare say she meant no harm," added Jessie; "she is so giddy."

"Pray, how did she know?" I asked.

"She fancied it, she said."

"That was a falsehood," I retorted. "Cora told her—I knew she was listening yesterday."

Jessie was as much shocked with me as her father had been. With their exaggerated ideas of hospitality, they considered it little less than a crime to acknowledge that a guest could have any fault.

"Oh, Aunt Matty!" she said, "I never knew you unjust before."

I was forced to go out of the room; my anger was over, and I felt the tears rushing to my eyes. I passed a very uncomfortable day. Jessie and her father came to an understanding; Mrs. Dennison soon had them both under her spell again, and I knew they blamed me exceedingly.

I loved them too well for real indignation; but I was broken-hearted at the idea that this woman could come between Jessie and her love for me.

There was company at dinner. I spent the evening in Mrs. Lee's room— the first comfortable hour I had passed since morning. She did not know that anything had gone wrong, pitied my head, which she was sure ached terribly, and by her sweet and tender kindness made me somewhat more reconciled to life.

I sat in my own room after I left her, but did not retire until very late. I heard the guests go away—heard the different members of the family pass up to their rooms; but still I sat by the window, sad and lonely. At last the clock struck one. I rose, startled into common-sense again, stopped star-gazing, and closing my window, prepared for rest.

Suddenly I heard a noise—very faint, but my nerves were wonderfully acute that night. I opened the door and looked into the hall; as I did so, I saw a figure clad in white glide out of Lottie's chamber, and disappear down the passage.

I fairly thought it something supernatural at first, then I ran out, but there was nothing to be seen. I stole to Lottie's room and looked in; she was sleeping soundly, so I went back to my own apartment. That incident, added to the excitement of the day, kept me awake for hours. I tried to convince myself that it was only one of my ridiculous fancies: but the effort was in vain; I knew that I had seen that white shape steal by—it was no delusion. Who was it? What was it?

I determined to say nothing, feeling certain that everybody would laugh at me. I knew that it was silly, but I could not drive away the terror that chilled my heart. Everything had gone so wrong of late, that quiet house was so changed, that the least thing disturbed me more than events of importance would once have done.

CHAPTER XXXVIII
MR. LAWRENCE MAKES A CALL

Lawrence called upon us the next day: that is, he came to the house and inquired for Mrs. Dennison, without one word regarding the rest of the family. Mr. Lee was sitting in the square balcony when the gentleman rode up, and cast a meaning glance at Jessie, as if he felt certain that the visit was for her. She shrunk from his look with something like affright; and when the servant came up with word that Mr. Lawrence was in the drawing-room, waiting for Mrs. Dennison, she gave me a look of wild reproof, as if I had been the cause of his evident displeasure.

Mr. Lee sat with his eyes upon her; and when Mrs. Dennison came from her chamber, the expression of his face became so like that which pained me in Jessie's, that I could not escape the idea that both suffered from the same cause.

The shock of this thought made me tremble. It had never fastened upon me as a reality before. Why did I turn so faint? Why did my soul rise up in such bitter protest? God help me, I am not wise enough to answer; the tumult of trouble within me was something I had never, till then, experienced. Still the idea was a terrible one. How could a woman of right principles feel otherwise? Thus I explained it away, and soothed myself into a belief that any true-hearted person living in that family as I did must have felt all the miserable sensations that tortured me.

These thoughts made me dizzy. When I could see clearly again, Jessie was gone, and Mr. Lee sat a little more upright in his chair, looking hard at the wall over the top of his book. I was glad those stern eyes were not turned on me.

Mrs. Dennison came sweeping out of her chamber, leaving a scarcely perceptible perfume in the hall as she passed. She did not observe me, for I sat a little out of range from the door, and she evidently was not conscious that Mr. Lee was looking after her. She caught his glance, however, in turning to go down stairs, paused abruptly, and came back as if she were eager to explain something; but again she stopped short on seeing that I occupied a seat which commanded the balcony, and saying hastily, "Oh, I thought Miss Jessie was here," went down the hall again, evidently discomfited.

Mr. Lee resumed his volume, but there were no signs of reading. He simply looked hard at the page without turning it over, and sat gnawing at his under lip with a kind of ferocity I had never witnessed in him before. I was getting sadly nervous, and felt a painful sensation in my throat; what was all this coming to? What did it mean?

I left the balcony and went up to Mrs. Lee's chamber; here everything was pure and quiet. The invalid lay upon her couch, with a book before her; one slender and almost transparent hand rested upon the opposite page to that which she was reading. It started like a frightened bird as I came in, and she turned her head with one of those heavenly smiles I have never seen equalled. But her face clouded over in an instant. Evidently Martha Hyde was not the person that gentle invalid had hoped to see.

I went up to the couch and sat down on the low seat at its head. She handed me the book with a smile, saying that it made her eyes ache. "Would I read a little till Mr. Lee came up?"

She said this languidly, and there was a strange look about her eyes, as if they had been overtaxed. I received the volume, but fell into thought with it in my hand, forgetting that she was observing me.

"What is the matter?" she said, touching me with her shadowy hand. "Has anything gone wrong? No bad news about our young friend, I hope."

"No," I answered, starting; "I have not heard from him this morning."

"Well, what is it then? You look strangely, as if something had frightened you."

"Do I? No, indeed, nothing has frightened me."

"Perhaps," she said, with a little hesitation, "you are getting anxious about me; these heavy feelings that hang about my head in the morning are a little depressing; I don't really know what to make of them."

I looked at her anxiously; there certainly was a singular expression in her eyes which made me thoughtful. She went on in a soft, dreamy way, as if talking to herself.

"Then I used to sleep so lightly. It was a great affliction,—that state of semi-wakefulness which left everything unreal, but was not sleep, wore me out; now I fall into such profound slumber, but it gives me no more rest than the other state; and I awake with the sensation of a person who has been struggling hard through the night."

"But this may arise from opiates."

"Opiates! Indeed, you know that I never take them, Miss Hyde."

I answered with some surprise that I had accounted for the strange feeling which oppressed her by the idea that it must be something of that kind; but omitted to say that Mrs. Dennison had bewailed to me the habit of taking preparations of opium which Mrs. Lee had fallen into.

The invalid seemed a little hurt by this suggestion, and said over and over again in her sweet way,—

"No, no, my dear. It must be terrible pain which can force me to take these things; and thanks to Him and to all the loving care around me, I do not suffer greatly."

"Still you are changed, dear lady," I said. "How, I cannot explain; but in your face I find that look of struggle which you complain of."

"It is oppressive," she said, putting a hand to her forehead, "and I am afraid makes me but dull company. Mr. Lee is not here quite so much as usual: or is that a sick fancy, Miss Hyde?"

I answered with a tremor in my voice, for her earnest look troubled me, that we all thought quiet better for her, even than the pleasant excitement which his company might bring.

She shook her head, and observed with one of her touching smiles, "that it did not help the flowers to keep back the dew when they thirsted for it."

I had no answer; all my petty evasions against her affectionate entreaties were like straw flung on the surface of a brook; I had no heart to attempt more.

She had fallen into silence, and lay shading her eyes with one hand, when Mr. Lee came in with a heavy, ringing step, and a cloud on his face. His wife started up, and her eyes sparkled as she held out her hand.

"Were you asleep? Have I disturbed you?" he said, abruptly.

"Oh! no, that is impossible, I think; but—but you look troubled. What is it?"

"Troubled? Do I? Nothing of the kind. How fanciful you are, my dear! What should any of us have to do with trouble?"

"Not while we are together," she said, touching the seat I had abandoned with her hand, thus delicately inviting him to her side.

But he strode to the window, and looked out with anxiety. Something was evidently on his mind. Just then I heard voices in the garden. It was Mrs. Dennison calling aloud for Jessie.

"Jessie, Jessie, darling, where have you hidden yourself? Here is some one wishes to see you."

The voice came ringing up clear and distinct; Mr. Lee heard it, and the frown grew lighter upon his forehead. Directly a light step came up the stairs. Mr. Lee turned and looked toward the door. Mrs. Dennison entered the chamber without waiting for her knock to be answered.

"Where is Jessie?" she cried, all cheerfulness and animation; "she is wanted, and I am quite out of breath searching for her in the garden, Mr. Lee. Dear Miss Hyde, pray help me to find her."

Mr. Lee came forward at this challenge, almost smiling.

"Have you been to her room?" he said.

She answered him that she had not, but added something in a low, hurried voice. Guarded as it was, I caught the sense.

"There was a little misunderstanding between them," she said; "he wanted me to mediate, and is waiting for her in the garden."

Mr. Lee listened, and one of the rare smiles I have spoken of beamed over his face. He made a movement as if to go out with the widow; but seeing the anxiety in Mrs. Lee's eyes, I went forward at once, saying, as I hurried by the couple,—

"As you are here to sit with Mrs. Lee, sir, I will look for Jessie."

The smile that crept across Mrs. Dennison's lips was like a reptile feeding on a rose.

"You are very kind," she said. "I had no idea of enlisting Mr. Lee; his duties here are too sacred for that."

CHAPTER XXXIX
LOTTIE AS A LETTER-WRITER

I hurried on to escape the sound of Mrs. Dennison's voice, for in any tone it filled me with loathing; but as the door closed after me, that of Lottie's opened, and the imp thrust out her head and emitted a mellow crow, clapping her arms as if they had been wings, thus indicating that for once my conduct had met her full approval.

I could not help laughing; at which she put a finger to her lips, and darted back of the door, closing it softly in the process.

I went up to Jessie's room, but she was not there, nor could she be found in any part of the house. When assured of this, I went into the garden and found Lawrence walking leisurely toward the grove where his horse was tied. He turned as I called him by name, and looked back with an expression of surprise.

"I have been searching for Miss Lee to inform her of your wish to see her," I said; "but she has gone out."

He drew his fine figure up proudly, and said, with a smile that had more of irony than sweetness in it, —

"I beg pardon; but my visit here was to Mrs. Dennison. I was only waiting for her to return with her parasol, as she found the sun rather warm."

I felt myself coloring, but answered the moment I could find voice, —

"Then you did not inquire for Miss Lee?—did not ask Mrs. Dennison to go in search of her?"

"Not that I am aware of," he replied, with the same smile. "I supposed it more than probable that the young lady had gone to visit her sick-lo—friend, over yonder. Heaven forbid that I should disturb an arrangement so full of delicate romance!"

I looked at him steadily. There was more of insult in his tone than these words conveyed. At first I was prompted to explain and defend: but wherefore? If he could distrust a creature like our Jessie, any attempt at exculpation appeared to me like a sacrifice of dignity, so I turned away in silence. He followed me a few paces, as if wishing to continue the conversation; but I hurried on, burning with indignation. Why had those abominable people entered our pleasant homes? Why did they remain there, making us all miserable? Oh! how I wished for authority to send them away together; for in my resentment, I, perhaps unjustly, coupled the gentleman with the lady, and forgot that he was her dupe rather than associate.

When Lawrence was yet almost on a level with me, the widow came out from the tower, looking flurried and anxious. She saw me apparently in conversation with her friend, and turned crimson to the temples; but adroitly dropping the open parasol over her face, she came slowly on, concealing the agitation but too visible a moment before. Without heeding me in the least, she sauntered up to Lawrence, drooping her parasol almost in my face, and said with careless insolence, —

"Now, my good friend, with Miss Hyde's permission, we will go on with the history of that little affair."

So she swept him off, somewhat bewildered, I fancy, and I went into the house, detesting her more than ever.

Before entering Mrs. Lee's room, I opened the door of Lottie's little apartment, intending to inquire if Mr. Lee had gone out. The young girl was seated at a small gilded table, which had been broken in the drawing-room and mended by her deft hands, after which, of course, it became her property; an open letter lay on the table, and she was busy writing. When I opened the door, she started up, snatched at the letter and held it behind her, looking at me with a comical sort of defiance.

"Miss Hyde," said she, "if you'll just tell me what's wanting, I'll come out; but this room isn't large enough for two—no, not if its owner had a twin sister wandering about in want of a bed to sleep in."

"Excuse me, Lottie, but I only want to know if Mrs. Lee is left alone."

"No, Miss Hyde, that thing don't happen while I am on hand. Mr. Lee's in there, and that angel of a woman is talking to him with tears in her throat, if they haven't got up to her eyes yet. I can hear the sound without listening, and I hope it will do him good, that's all!"

I turned to go away, but she followed me to the door, still with one hand behind her, in which I could hear paper rustling.

"Miss Hyde, I can't help but say, if it does puff you up, that are dodge of yours was a crowner; I heard it and all Babylon said: my! isn't she a thing or so? For once you were too smart for her. Didn't her face blaze up when she saw you walking with that chap? I couldn't 'a' done it better myself. Now, mind I say that to encourage you, not to lift you on a high horse; so don't make a bad use of kindness."

"You are very kind, and I try not to be spoiled, Lottie."

"I'm your friend out and out, and the friend of this family, if ever there was one. Never fear about that; but this thing is getting beyond me and destroying my usefulness. I wish you wouldn't give me no more lectures about listening and finding out things. True enough, I don't pay no regard to such ridiculous notions; but then just as a creature gets nestled down under a bush, or fits her ear to a keyhole, comes the thought, 'Now Miss Hyde would call this mean,' and it drags your attention away from what's going on and takes all the relish out of it. I don't like it, Miss Hyde; such peaked notions do well enough for an old maid; but I ain't a going to be that, if there is a man cute enough to match me in all creation."

"Well, Lottie," I said, almost laughing, "as my preaching only annoys you, it is hardly worth while to repeat it."

"That's a good soul!" answered Lottie, with benign condescension. "You hoe your row and I'll hoe mine, we shall come out together at the end of the lot, never fear."

The next morning, when our man brought the letters from town, I noticed Mrs. Dennison examining one which she took from among those left on the hall-table, with the keen look of a person whose suspicion has been aroused. In tearing it open, she examined the adhesive edge a second time, and apparently found it all right, for her face cleared up, and she put the letter in her pocket without reading it. Still she could not have been quite satisfied, for after that no letters of hers were ever left with those of the family to be mailed.

CHAPTER XL
YOUNG BOSWORTH RECEIVES A LETTER

That day I resolved to go and see young Bosworth. I had no lover to get jealous or find fault with this; indeed, it was doubtful if any one cared enough about my movements to observe them when disconnected from the family.

I had no heart to enjoy the walk; it was a cold, raw day, with gloomy clouds floating along the sky, and gloomier shadows sweeping the earth. The dampness of a night succeeded by no sunshine lay upon the meadows; spiders' webs were stretched across my path; and a rain of moisture fell from the hazel-bushes as my garments brushed them in walking. Still, it was not absolutely stormy, and the gray shadows harmonized with my feelings so completely, that I had no wish to change them. Nothing could be more gloomy than my own heart.

When I reached the house, old Mrs. Bosworth came to the door herself. She seemed a good deal disturbed, and I fancied, from the heaviness of her eyes, that she had been crying.

"Come in, Miss Hyde," she said, taking my hand. "He is not so well this morning. Indeed, indeed he is much worse. A letter came here last night, and I was foolish enough to let it go to him. One of your people brought it, and I fancied, perhaps, that it might do him good, for it was a lady's handwriting, and she was so kind that morning."

"You thought it was from our Jessie," I answered, in the first impulse of my surprise.

"Yes, it was a foolish thought, I dare say,—but that was my idea."

"And have you learned whom it did come from?"

"No," answered the noble old lady. "He fainted, and it fell from his hand; but I laid it under his pillow without even looking at it; it might have wounded him, you know."

"And is he so much worse?"

"Oh, Miss Hyde, the fever has come back; he is wild again."

"And had you no way of guessing the cause?"

"I think it was something about Mr. Lawrence, for he called for him till the house rang with his cries, after the first dumb shock went off."

"Did Mr. Lawrence know of this?"

"He was away at the time; and after that your young friend's name was so wildly mingled up with it all, that I could not think it right to bring Mr. Lawrence to the room. It would have seemed like challenging his compassion."

My heart ached, for I saw that her penetration had discovered Jessie's secret, and that she was protecting it with much delicacy.

"Besides, he is our guest," she said, prompted by that old-fashioned feeling of honor which rendered the shelter of a friend's roof a sanctuary, "and he might have construed my grandson's words into a reproach; altogether, we thought it best to keep them apart."

There was a mystery about all this that baffled me. Who could have written that letter brought by one of Mr. Lee's servants? Not Jessie, I was sure of that, for she never could have taken a step of so much importance thus privately. Besides, save for the brief time of Lawrence's visit that day, when, wounded and heart-sick, she left the house, and wandered off into the thickest of the woods, she had not been absent from her mother's room scarcely a moment. Mrs. Dennison had seen her passing through the outskirt of the woods, or she would never have ventured to call for her so loudly.

All this I knew, but it was unnecessary; a thorough understanding of Jessie's character rendered conjectures regarding her part in this matter quite superfluous. But who had written the letter? and what was its import? Of course, my suspicions fell on that woman; but what was her object? Surely she was not anxious to ensnare this young man also—her vanity could not be so insatiable as that.

Perhaps it was Mr. Lee; his handwriting was exquisitely clear and delicate as a woman's; what if his displeasure against our visit had been expressed here? But no, Mr. Lee was not a man to rudely force his anger into a sick-room.

Again my thoughts fell back on the widow; what unprincipled work was she doing here? What benefit could she find in sowing discord upon that poor young man's pillow?

Of course, one thinks rapidly, and all these broken ideas took but little time in flashing through my brain. The old lady stood with one hand on the back of her easy-chair, observing me with a troubled look.

"You think the letter was not from your young friend?" she said, reading my thoughts with that subtle magnetism which is a part of true womanliness.

"I am sure it was not, dear lady!"

"Nor from her father?"

"Not if it gave him pain; Mr. Lee is incapable of that."

The old lady drew a deep breath, as if infinitely relieved, and sat down, spreading out her ample skirts mechanically after her usual dainty habit.

"Miss Hyde," she said, with a little tremor of the voice, and a movement of the hands, which fell into her lap and clasped themselves nervously, "Miss Hyde, I am sure you are my poor boy's friend!"

"I am indeed!" was my earnest response.

"And you know—"

"Yes, dear madam, all that an affectionate heart can learn by its own observation."

"I have thought, perhaps," said the dear old lady, coloring as she spoke, "that Mr. Lee, with his enormous wealth, might have considered the modest property of my grandson insufficient, and for this reason have influenced his daughter."

I had nothing to answer. If Mr. Lee knew of this unhappy attachment, he had given no sign; but I told her that his general character was opposed to anything so mercenary.

"If this were so," answered the old lady, growing more anxious, "I think it would be easily remedied. My grandson, it is true, has little more than a handsome independence; but I, Miss Hyde, am perhaps richer than our neighbors think. In fact," she added, blushing, as if there were something to be ashamed of in the confession, "my income, if I chose to use it, would not compare meanly with that of Mr. Lee. When one spends but little, with tolerably fair possessions, property accumulates rapidly at the end of a long life. I had intended to endow charities, perhaps; but the sight of my boy up yonder has changed all this."

I could only say, "You are very liberal, madam;" for I felt sure that the trouble did not lie where she supposed.

"If you could in any way make this understood, Miss Hyde, without bringing it prominently forward, I should be so grateful. I called you in here for this purpose. You have been so kind, so truly good to us."

"Oh, no, no," I protested.

"So delicate," she persisted; "and now when his life is in such fearful peril, I am forced to take liberties—forced to think if anything can be done to save him, forced to beg for help."

"Oh, if I could help you!" I exclaimed, feeling the tears rush to my eyes.

"You have, you can; already we are greatly indebted to your kindness. I am not eloquent to express thanks, sometimes feeling that silence is most delicate; but I feel all this, Miss Hyde, and so did he, my poor boy!"

Again I expressed the happiness it would give me to help her or him.

"I am an old woman," she continued; "very old, and require so little that property has become burdensome. If—if this thing can be arranged, all that I have, every cent, shall go to him; not after my death, but now, while I can see them enjoy it. They will remember my habits, and my little wants, I am sure; and it will be very pleasant to have young voices around me again. Will you take an opportunity to suggest this to Mr. Lee?—not the young lady—my grandson must owe everything to himself there; but with a parent these are important considerations, sometimes."

I could not see her face, for tears half blinded me. The feeling which could induce this fine old woman to give up all the appliances of her pride, all the power of her life, in order to purchase happiness for her grandson, was one of those noble outgushes of human nature that always make me weep. I could have kissed the hem of her garments, and felt ennobled by the act. It was no little thing to uproot the fixed habits of almost a century. With all that love of property which grows strong in age, from a sentiment of generosity another might have thought of piding, but she was ready to give up all.

I had no heart to discourage her. Warmly and truly as my wishes went with hers, I would not uproot all hope in my own mind. Time, I whispered to myself, has many changes, and so has the human heart. So I took the old lady's hand in mine and kissed it with affectionate reverence. She smiled upon me in her benign way, and called me "her dear young friend, her fair, sweet friend."

Oh! I am getting to be a forlorn creature, or these words would never have swelled my heart with such throbs of gratitude. Have I indeed anything lovable or attractive about me which the old lady's deeper penetration has discovered, or is it only because I have been a little kind to her grandson? I wish it were possible to know about this, for since Mrs. Dennison has been at our house, I have begun to doubt and fear about myself in a way that never possessed me before. Her overpowering elegance has put down all my little quiet claims to notice so completely, that it seems as if I never should lift up my head again. No wonder I cried and kissed that soft hand like a child. People don't think how much we require praise and petting, at all stages of existence, or how much of childhood runs from the cradle to the grave in every human life.

It was very foolish and romantic, but without at all knowing it, I had fallen on my knees by the old lady; and when she saw my eyes so full of tears, she smoothed my hair, and called me a good girl. With this I laid my head on her lap, and begged her to let me love her always, telling her that sometimes I was lonely for the want of a right to love anything. Then I grew ashamed and stood up, blushing through the tears that had betrayed me into such weakness, but her gracious look reassured me.

CHAPTER XLI
OUT IN THE STORM

After this the younger Mrs. Bosworth came into the parlor, her eyes red with weeping, and looking weaker and more in affliction than ever. She had done everything, she said, dropping helplessly into a chair, and nothing would pacify him. There he was, trying to read over a letter that he kept hid away under the pillow, that shook and shook in his hands till the whole room was full of its rustling, and it made her so nervous she was afraid to stay alone with him—muttering, muttering as if he were angry with her, that had been a good mother to him all his days; no one could say to the contrary of that, she was sure.

Another woman of a character so much above the level of that poor mother's, might have become impatient; but the old lady listened to her with great sympathy, excused her futile grief by half implied apologies, and finally succeeded in persuading her to lie down on the sofa, while we went up-stairs and watched by her son.

The young man was indeed very ill, entirely out of his head, and talking angrily to himself. The letter which Mrs. Bosworth had mentioned was crushed in his hand, and he was rolling it into a round ball between his two palms. While I stood looking upon him, thus troubled by some unseen enemy, and flung back upon a sick-bed, it seemed impossible that any one could be cruel enough for such work, unless the heart of a fiend had somewhere taken human form.

I would have stayed in the sick-room longer, for my poor talent for nursing was never more required, but the old lady seemed anxious to send me home. Having done her utmost to relieve the unhappy situation of our patient, she was restless till her object was put in some state of forwardness; so I went away, leaving her rather hopeful, but very desponding myself.

As I went home, the clouds that had been broken and scattered were gathered into vast tent-like masses, and a slow rain began to fall, which gradually wet me through. I did not heed it; nothing could be gloomier than my feelings. It seemed to me as if I were going to a house of strangers, so completely had the machinations of that woman shut me out from my old place in the family. So I let it rain on, without a wish to escape the discomfort.

When I was nearly across the fields, I saw a figure approaching through the gray mists, and would gladly have avoided it by turning into the woods; but a voice called me by name, and I stopped at once. It was Jessie, who had come out into the storm to meet me. Lawrence had called at the house and informed the family of young Bosworth's relapse.

"He is there now, I suppose," she said, excitedly; "but I came away, guessing where you had gone. I cannot breathe in the house when they are together, and he lying so ill and helpless."

I looked up at these words. The storm was beating in her face, but her cheeks were like fire underneath. It might have been all rain that flashed down the burning surface; but I thought not, for there were suppressed sobs in her voice when she spoke.

"Is—is your father at home?" I inquired, hesitating in my speech, I cannot tell wherefore.

"No; he rode over to town before the storm came on. They have the house to themselves."

She spoke bitterly. In truth, I scarcely recognized my own sweet Jessie with those wet garments clinging around her, and that excited face. We walked on in silence, for she turned to retrace her steps. At last she said, abruptly:

"How is he, Aunt Matty? Does he suffer?"

"Greatly, I think, Jessie."

"No wonder he is ill," she said, passionately. "It is enough to break down anything human."

"I am glad you can feel for him, Jessie."

"Feel for him! Who can help it? But who feels for—for—"

She broke off abruptly, turning pale and cold.

I walked on, distressed by this broken confidence, but knew well that Jessie was too proud for anything more definite.

As we came into the field bordered by the carriage sweep, a horseman dashed up to the gate, which had been left open, and was passing at a swift gallop toward the house. It was Mr. Lee returning from town, and riding fast to escape the rain. He saw us dragging our way through the grass, and drew up, regarding our condition with a look so stern that it chilled me.

"He is angry with me for going out, I suppose," said Jessie, drearily. "Well, I could not help it."

After regarding us for a full minute with that hard look, Mr. Lee rode on, his horse tramping heavier than before, and sending back broken flakes of mud, as if casting it purposely against us. He rode directly to the stables. Jessie and I slunk into the house by the back entrance like culprits.

CHAPTER XLII
JESSIE GETS TIRED OF HER GUEST

I kept my chamber that day, striving to make up my mind about what course was best for me to pursue. My life at Mr. Lee's had become so harassing, that it was absolutely burdensome. I did not know friends from enemies in that house, for every being in it seemed changed. I sat down alone and wept in bitter grief. Should I go away and leave the ill-contested field to that woman, who was surely working out some great evil to the whole family? I was not dependent. Considerable property was vested in my favor, but it was in Mr. Lee's hands; and so generously had he provided for every possible want, that even the income remained untouched.

I had ability, and could have earned my bread anywhere, either as a governess or a teacher, had that been necessary. Thus, personal considerations could not have bowed down my spirits to the state of depression that fell upon me. Something deeper lay at my heart. Was it love for Jessie? was it fear that the poor girl would be left without defence, to the machinations of that cruel woman? I cannot tell. If other and more selfish feelings existed in my bosom, I did not know it. Indeed, so absorbed were all my faculties in the difficulties that thickened around us, that I had no time for self-examination. Dear, dear Jessie! how could I help her? That was the burden of my thoughts.

The thorough drenching which I had received made me hoarse and really ill. In my anxiety, I had neglected to change my clothes; but the cold shudders that crept over me aroused my attention to the danger, and, changing my damp garments, I lay down, striving to get warm.

I have a vague recollection that the sun broke out, and came flashing through the leaves into my chamber. Then I heard voices in the garden beneath, which chilled me worse than the cold.

Mr. Lee and Mrs. Dennison were conversing together on the terrace, where camp-stools and garden-chairs were always standing. I could have heard everything; the temptation was great, but I put it away, burying my head in my pillow, and drowning their voices with my sobs.

Toward night Jessie came to my room. She was sad and disheartened; Mr. Lee had not spoken to her since our return; and even her mother was vexed that she should have exposed herself to the storm.

I inquired if Mr. Lawrence was at the house when her father returned. Jessie thought not, but could not say positively; only he seldom was there, except in her father's absence.

She said this abruptly, and turned the conversation; the very name of Lawrence seemed to distress her.

"Aunt Matty," she said, after a dreary silence, "will this widow never leave our house? Shall we remain in this state till it brings ruin on us all? Mother seems fading away, and no one appears to care. You look years older; and as for me—"

"Well, Jessie?"

"No matter about me; but something must be done. So long as it was myself only, I made an effort to bear it; but we are all changed, all unhappy—dear, sweet mamma, and even Lottie. There is poison in the very atmosphere, I think."

"Let us have patience, Jessie; this cannot last much longer; but while Mrs. Dennison remains here, do not forget that she is your mother's guest."

"But how long—how long, I say, will this last? My father is getting more distant and estranged every hour. I feel like an alien under his roof—a stranger to my very self."

She was greatly excited, and wrung her hands with passionate vehemence. The proud reticence of her character was all swept away; she fell upon her knees by the bed on which I lay, and sobbed aloud. I am sure this would not have happened with any one else; but I had become almost a second self to the dear girl, and she was not ashamed to give way to her grief in my presence.

While she was on her knees, Lottie opened my chamber-door and looked in. Seeing Miss Jessie, she drew back, placed a finger on her lips, and performed a series of pantomime that would have been exceedingly ludicrous but for the anxiety that beset me. As it was, I saw that she had something to communicate, but was afraid to ask her in while Jessie was so disturbed.

She saw this, and darting a finger backward over her shoulder and forward at me, as if it had been a weapon, retreated, making up faces that grew more ludicrous with every step.

Jessie had seen nothing of this. She arose, after a little, and went out, sighing heavily.

CHAPTER XLIII
A CONSULTATION WITH LOTTIE

Directly after she was gone, Lottie came back, and, closing the door, bolted it inside and stole up to my bed on tiptoe. She looked pale and frightened, but her eyes shone through the shadows that had suddenly settled around them, and she moved like a hound doubling on its prey.

"Miss Hyde," she said, "just listen while you have time; that red Babylon has gone and done it. I've had my hands full all day scooting about among the wet bushes, and holding my breath behind window-shutters. Now, would you believe it? I've been two hull hours squinched up in that big rosewood book-case with the green silk lining; for them new painted winders in the tower library are the most aggravating things to one as wants to keep her eyes open. Thanks be to goodness! the new books haven't arrived, and I should have had lots of room if human beings had been built flat. As it was, I got along by holding in my breath and bowing the doors a trifle."

"But what did you go into the book-case for, Lottie?" I inquired, anxious to bring her to some point in her communication.

"What did I go into the book-case for? Why, only to hear what was going on in that room, to be sure. Wasn't that Mr. Lawrence and Mrs. Babylon there, sitting on the sofa together two hull hours?"

"And you listened to the conversation?"

"In course I did."

She seemed waiting for me to ask more questions, but I could not force myself thus indirectly to partake in a dishonorable act.

"You won't ask what they said, and yet are a-dying to know, any fool can see that. Well, thanks be to goodness! I ain't a lady, and if I was, for *her* sake I'd do worse things than that; my ears were made to hear with, and I ain't going to fight agin nature."

"But you came to see me for something, Lottie?"

"Certainly I did. But how is one to tell things without talking right out? Well, if you won't ask what I heard in the book-case, I must tell you promiscuous. This she-sarpent has about done up your business for you, as she means to for me and the rest of 'em before long."

"Done my business for me, Lottie! What does that mean? I do not understand."

"Likely enough; but I'll tell you; Babylon is in love with Mr. Lawrence."

"I wish from my heart he'd marry her," I thought.

"But she won't have him," said Lottie, as if answering my thought. "At any rate, not yet."

"Well, well, Lottie, tell me what brings you here? My head aches."

"So does mine," said Lottie, lifting a hand to her head, and pressing her forehead hard with the palm. "Well, Miss Hyde, a little while ago, Mr. Lee and Mrs. Babylon were sitting on the platform under this very window. It was just after the rain, and they happened to meet as he was coming out to enjoy the sunshine. I happened in the same way to be dusting the sofa close by the window, and it took me a good while. Don't put up your hand, Miss Hyde, you'd 'a' listened yourself. She was talking about you."

"About me?"

"Yes. I can't give the words; but she was saying, in her silky way, that Miss Jessie was so much altered since she met her at the sea-shore, so obstinate and demonstrative, vulgarized, as one might say, if anything so very beautiful could be vulgarized. But didn't Mr. Lee think that a companion who followed her pupil into society was rather a drawback, and apt to get a predominating influence over that of the parents? Was he certain of Miss Jessie's friend,—of her prudence and disinterestedness? Of course, she had no right to give an opinion: but when the time came for a young lady to enter society, was there no reason to think that a household companion, like Miss Hyde, might become a dangerous counsellor? Of course, Mr. Lee knew best, his wisdom was never at fault; but would not a companion, perfectly dependent, and who had some experience in society, produce a better result?

"I wish you could 'a' seen Mr. Lee's face, Miss Hyde. He looked up all of a sudden, and his eyes flashed fire; Babylon saw it, and looked down as if butter wouldn't melt in her mouth; and then he took her hand in his,—it wasn't the first time, Miss Hyde, I'd bet my head on that, for it all came too easy—and I've seen what I have seen;—then he said how difficult it was to find such a person,—one who was an ornament to society, and yet willing to live in a place like that which Mrs. Lee's illness made, in some sort, like a prison.

"She left her hand in his, and lifted her eyes to his face sideways—you know how—and said a few words almost in a whisper. I couldn't catch the first word, but he turned red as fire and lifted her hand to his lips, almost; then he dropped it again and begged her pardon."

I had no power to stop Lottie's narrative. The import of this conversation struck me with a sudden pang. It seemed as if sentence of death had been pronounced upon me. What could I do? Where on earth was a home like that to be found? What would Jessie and Mrs. Lee do without me? That woman in my place! The thought was anguish. I almost hated her.

Lottie stood by the bed, looking at me, with trouble in her face.

"I knew that it would be a blow; but this is worse than I expected," she said. "How white you are—how your lips quiver! But don't take on so. Let them try it; let Babylon do her worst—she'll find her match. I've learned a thing or two, since she came, that I didn't know before,—especially how to droop your eyelids and look meek, then open 'em quick and flash out fire. It's taking, I've tried it with—with—"

"With whom, Lottie?"

"With—but no matter; when the birds sing, chickens have a right to peep. Babylon isn't the only person who can turn a feller's head, and good looks is according to one's taste. Then there's a difference in flirting, when the object is a good one; don't you think so, Miss Hyde?"

"I don't know, Lottie," was my dreary answer; "you must ask about these matters of some one who has had more experience."

"Oh! I don't care about asking; it all comes natural enough after the first lesson. But you won't let them drive you away—it would break her heart, I know it would."

Lottie's eyes were full of tears. Poor girl! she had a good heart.

This sympathy touched me deeply. I was so desolate and felt so wronged, that a kind word filled me with gratitude, even from Lottie.

"Oh! ma'am, don't mind it! Babylon sha'n't hurt you while I can help it. Only be firm, and don't go off in a fit of pride. Stand your ground to the last, and when the worst comes to the worst, depend on me."

The girl took my hand and kissed it; then, kneeling down by the bed, laid her face close to mine.

"Miss Hyde—"

"Well, my good girl."

"I have something to say, something that worries me dreadfully; are you listening?"

"Yes, child."

"It is about mistress. Don't you see how dreadfully thin she is getting? You can almost look through her hand."

"Yes, Lottie, it makes my heart ache to think of it. Have you any idea of the cause?"

"*He* don't visit her much now."

"You have noticed it, you—"

"I count the minutes every day."

"This might vex her, but not to the extent that seems so visible."

"No, there is something else. I cannot understand it; but wait awhile, Miss Hyde, I'm on hand."

I hardly heard this. The idea that my presence in that house had become a burden, that I might be at any moment desired to leave my place in the family for that woman to fill, absorbed my faculties, and in the selfishness of my distress, I gave less heed than the subject claimed to what the girl was saying.

She saw this, I suppose; for, with renewed entreaties that I should hold firmly to my position and trust to her for the rest, she crept from the room, almost crying.

CHAPTER XLIV
THE MIDNIGHT DISCOVERY

About an hour after this I arose, bathed my forehead, and went into Mrs. Lee's chamber, for the pain of my solitary thoughts became unendurable. The poor lady was lying on the sofa, with her eyes closed, looking more wan than ever. Something troubled her, I am sure; for tears were swelling under the transparent whiteness of her eyelids, and her hands were clasped over her bosom. This was an attitude habitual to her when disturbed by any grief, and seeing it, I turned to go away; but she heard my footstep and opened her eyes. There was something in her manner that went to my heart—a sort of mournful constraint, as if she shrunk from my presence. Still she held forth her hand.

I sat down in my old place, and she closed her eyes again, as if any effort at speech was beyond her strength. In the broader light which fell upon her face, I saw that she had been crying—an unusual thing with her at any time; for all sources of trouble had been kept so sedulously from that room, that grief amounting to tears seldom found its way there.

After a prolonged silence that chilled me to the heart, she laid her hand on mine, and I saw that her earnest eyes were searching my face.

"Dear Miss Hyde, we have been so happy together—I thought no family was ever united like ours!"

I understood the pathos in her voice, the meaning of her words. Mr. Lee had begun the subject; already they were about to prove how troublesome and useless I had been—how much my place was wanted for another.

"You do not speak," she said, "surely, nothing has been said to wound you?"

"No," I answered, "I only come to see if you were in want of anything."

"Ah! you have always been so attentive, so kind! How shall I get along without you?"

So it was decided. He had spoken, and they had settled my destiny; the gentle invalid yielding without a murmur while her best friend was driven from under her roof. I had no heart to continue the conversation, and she, poor lady! evidently lacked the courage to speak plainer. Thus, with apprehensions and grief, we remained together in silence. Her eyes were closed, but not with sleep, I am sure of that; and I felt a dead heaviness creeping over me, which carried with it a dreary sense of pain.

It was getting dark when I left the chamber. The depression was so heavy upon me that I went down to the kitchen, thinking to ask the cook for a cup of warm tea. Lottie was there busy at the range, and, singular enough, making tea, as if my wants had been pined.

"A handful, cook," she said, holding out the silver teapot for a renewed supply. "I want it good and strong, something that will make one's eyes snap."

When the cook turned to put her canister in its place, Lottie went to the closet and brought out two cups and saucers.

"Miss Hyde," she said, "you have just come in time. I knew it'd be wanted: try a good, strong cup, it will have the ache out of your head in no time."

I thanked her and took the cup she offered. It was strong to bitterness, and I did not like the taste; but when I passed it back, Lottie put in more sugar and cream, but no water. I was too weary for protest, and drank the bitterness without further comment.

Lottie seemed pleased, and insisted earnestly that I should take a second cup, filling her own for the third time, and draining it with what I thought must be heroism instead of desire.

"There," she said, setting her cup down, "that will do, I reckon; it makes my head as light as a cork. How do you feel, Miss Hyde?"

"It is very, very strong, Lottie, and I fear it will keep me awake all night."

"Fear!" cried the girl, "fear! Why, of course it will! To tell you the truth," she added, bending toward me, and whispering, "I begin to think this isn't the house where one can sleep honestly. Now just go up to your room, if you please, and don't let them see you looking so miserable. There's trouble enough without that."

The cook came toward us before I could answer. She was preparing to send up tea for the family, and muttered something about ladies always being in the way in a kitchen. So great was the depression of my spirits, that I allowed this to wound me, and went away in deeper dejection.

No human soul came near me during the evening. I could not sleep— the stimulus urged my brain into swift action. I reviewed all the difficulties of my position over and over again; strange projects came into my mind, ways by which my wrongs—for I had been wronged—should be redressed; speeches more eloquent than ever could reach my lips inspired me, and these were to be addressed to Mr. Lee, in the presence of that woman. A thousand wild fancies seized upon my brain and held it. I had no wish to change my position. Having thrown myself on the bed in my clothes, I remained there, thinking, thinking, thinking till my brain ached, but would not pause for rest—a terrible inspiration was upon me.

I heard a bustle in the house, as if the family were retiring; then the clock struck eleven, twelve, one. The hours did not seem long, but the stillness almost terrified me. All at once, it was after midnight some time, a sound approached my chamber like the rush of a bird through the air. I started up and listened. The door opened softly, and a figure glided in.

"Miss Hyde, are you awake? Get up this minute and come with me; if your shoes are on, take them off. Come."

I sprang up and followed Lottie swiftly and silently as she had reached my chamber. She drew me through the passage into her own little room. As I passed along the hall which led from the main building to the tower, it seemed to me that my dress brushed against some one crouching in a dark corner; but Lottie had not seen it, and I followed her, holding my breath. She glided through her own room into the chamber where Mrs. Lee slept. The carpets were thick as wood-moss, and our feet gave no sound. When she was fairly in the room, Lottie paused, and I heard a slight, scraping noise; then the sudden flash of a match was followed by the blaze of a candle which the girl carried in her hand.

As the light broke up, a faint cry came from the bed; a figure which bent over it rose up suddenly, and I stood face to face with Mrs. Dennison, the whitest woman that ever my eyes dwelt upon. She held a crystal toilet-bottle in one hand, and in the other a wet pocket-handkerchief.

"Stand by the door, Miss Hyde. Don't let her move a foot. I'll be back in a flash."

Lottie darted from the room as she spoke, leaving the candlestick on the carpet.

The woman turned upon me then with the spirit of a tigress. Her eyes flashed fire, the white teeth shone through her curved lips. She attempted to pass me, but I retreated to the door and kept the threshold. She came forward as if to force me away, still holding the bottle and handkerchief in her hands. Never in my life had I seen a face so beautiful and so fiendish. There was desperation in her eyes, violence in her action; but though weaker and smaller than her, I would have died on the threshold of that door rather than have allowed her to cross it.

All at once her face changed. She was looking, not at me, but over my shoulder; a flash of quick intelligence shot from her eyes, and the next moment she had thrown both arms about my neck and pressed my face to her bosom. I knew that some one came close up behind me, and heard the clink of glass; then a rush of feet through Lottie's room, and along the passage. All this could not have lasted a minute. I struggled from the woman's embrace, and pushed her from me with a violence that made her stagger. Her face had changed to its old look of triumph. She laughed, not naturally—that was beyond even her powers of self-command—but in a way that made me shiver.

"Dear Miss Hyde, is it you?" she said, in a voice that quaked in spite of herself. "How terribly frightened I was! Poor Mrs. Lee must have been very ill. I heard her moaning and calling for help in my room, and came at once; she seems quite insensible now."

I looked toward the bed. Mrs. Lee lay upon it, white, and still as a corpse, her eyes closed, and her lips of a bluish white. Was she dead? Had the woman killed her? A strong, pungent smell filled the room—a smell of chloroform. It was almost suffocating.

Mrs. Dennison seemed to think of this suddenly, and, darting toward the window, flung open two of the sashes before I knew what she was about. A gush of fresh air swept through the room; the pungent odor grew fainter and fainter, at which she smiled on me triumphantly.

I looked at her, as she stood in the light; a toilet-bottle was still in her hand, but it was of crimson glass, spotted with gold; that which she held, when I came in, was white and pure as water. How had she managed to change the crystal flask? What had become of the handkerchief?

Still smiling on me, she approached the bed and scattered fragrant drops from the crimson flask over the pillows and the deathly face of my poor friend. How still she lay! The whiteness of her face was terrible, but I dared not approach her; my post was by the door till Lottie came; but it made my blood run cold to see that woman bending over her, smoothing the pillows with her hand, and filling the room with that lying fragrance.

CHAPTER XLV
BAFFLED AND DEFEATED

It seemed an eternity before Lottie came back, yet she had not been absent three minutes. She came alone, and stood by me at the door, regarding Mrs. Dennison's movements with the keen vigilance of a fox. But a glimpse of Mrs. Lee's face made her start forward with a cry of dismay.

"My mistress, she is dead! They have killed her!"

She would have fallen upon her knees by the bed, but Mrs. Dennison put her aside. It was an easy thing, for Lottie had lost all her strength in that terrible fear.

"Foolish child! she has only fainted," said Mrs. Dennison, holding her back; "the air will bring her to."

Lottie's courage returned with these words, and struggling from Mrs. Dennison's hold, she sat down upon the bed, chafing Mrs. Lee's cold hands and kissing them with loving tenderness.

"Is she really and truly alive?" said the poor girl, appealing to me.

I could not resist the wistful anxiety of that look, but came forward, holding my breath, with a dread that her fears might be true.

That moment Mr. Lee entered the room, and directly came Jessie, with a look of terror on her face. She trembled like a leaf at the sight of her mother, and turned to me, looking the question which she could not frame in speech.

"It is not death! I hope and believe that it is not death!" I said.

Jessie fell upon a chair and burst into tears.

"Hush, child!" said her father; "let us learn what has happened. Mrs. Dennison, can you tell me?"

"I hardly know myself," answered the widow, innocently. "I heard moans and a cry for help coming from this room, and, springing up from my sleep, ran to see what it meant. There was no light in the room, but I felt that Mrs. Lee was cold and still as she lies now—alive, but motionless. I had snatched a bottle from my toilet, and was bathing her head with its contents, when Miss Hyde and the servant came in. They were very much terrified, and alarmed the house, I hope unnecessarily. It is a deep fainting fit. I am sure she will come out safely in time."

As the woman said this, Lottie stood looking in her face, dumb with astonishment. She saw the red flask in Mrs. Dennison's hand, felt the changed atmosphere of the room, and, for once, her presence of mind gave way.

"Poor thing! she was half frightened to death," said Mrs. Dennison, casting a patronizing glance at the crestfallen girl, "I never saw anything so wild in my life."

"And I never saw anything so wicked!" Lottie burst forth, clinching her hands and almost shaking them at the woman.

"Wicked! Oh, not so bad as that, my good girl," said the woman, gently. "One can be frightened, you know, without being wicked."

"Yes," said Lottie, with a sob, "and a person can be wicked without being frightened, I know that well enough."

"Lottie!" exclaimed Mr. Lee.

Lottie stood for one instant like a wild animal at bay; but directly her eyes fell upon her mistress, her form relaxed, and, creeping to the bedside, she began to cry.

"Oh, bring her to! bring her to! and I won't say another word," she pleaded, looking piteously at the widow.

"I am not omnipotent, poor child!" was the sweet reply. "But see! I think there is a movement of her eyelids."

Lottie rose from her knees and looked eagerly in that worn face. "Yes, yes, she is alive; she is coming to herself. Oh, my mistress! my mistress! I will never, never leave you again. I'll sleep on the floor at the foot of your bed, like a dog, before anybody reaches you!"

Tears rained down poor Lottie's face, and her voice was so full of grief that no one had the heart to chide her, though it seemed to disturb the invalid, who was slowly recovering consciousness.

Mrs. Lee at last opened her eyes, and looked vaguely around at the people near her bed, without seeming to recognize them; when Lottie caught her vacant gaze, she burst forth, —

"Oh, ma'am, don't you know me? It's Lottie—it's Lottie!"

This pathetic cry gained no response. Those dreamy eyes wandered from face to face, with a helpless, appealing look indescribably touching. Jessie bent over her mother, striving to make herself known; but her sweet voice passed unheeded. Every kind effort failed to draw her from this dull state of half-consciousness, till Mr. Lee passed his arm under her head and drew it to his bosom. Then a thrill seemed to pass through her whole frame, a smile dawned on her pale mouth.

"Have I been ill?" she murmured, resting her head against the bosom to which he gently lifted her,—"very ill, that you all come here in the night?"

"Yes," answered Mr. Lee, very tenderly; for he seemed to forget everything in her danger. "But for our kind guest, I fear it might have gone hard with you."

Lottie, who was crouching at her mistress' feet, with her face buried in the bed-clothes, uttered a sudden, "Oh! oh! I can't bear it!" and, starting up, rushed into her room, looking at Mrs. Dennison over her shoulders like a wild cat.

"Poor Lottie!" muttered Mrs. Lee. "How it troubles her to see any one suffer! And you, my kind guest—"

The gentle lady held out her hand to Mrs. Dennison, smiling wanly, but too feeble for any other expression of gratitude.

"Mamma," said Jessie, quickly, "do not try to speak, but rest. This has been a terrible attack."

"You here, my child, and I not know it!" whispered the invalid; "forgive me."

Mrs. Dennison pressed forward; but Jessie stepped between her and the invalid, not rudely, but with quiet decision which became the daughter of that proud man.

"Aunt Matty," she said, glancing past the widow, "had you not better leave her to papa and me? So many faces excite her."

Jessie was very pale, and I saw that her lips were quivering with agitation. Something had wounded her almost beyond bearing.

"Yes," I answered, promptly, "we will withdraw;" and, looking at Mrs. Dennison steadily, I waited for her to move first.

"This may be of service," she said, sweetly, placing the ruby-tinted bottle in Jessie's hand. "I found it very useful in reviving her."

Jessie took the bottle, but set it down at once. Indeed, her hand shook so violently that it must otherwise have fallen.

"Now, Miss Hyde, I do not see that our presence will be of further use," said the widow, gliding toward the door.

I stepped back to avoid contact even with her garments. My heart was full of bitter loathing. I grew cold as she passed me, and answered her smile with a look that frightened it from her lips. We passed through Lottie's room, but I could not force myself to enter it till even her shadow had disappeared.

CHAPTER XLVI
LOTTIE OWNS HERSELF BEATEN

When the woman was gone, I went in and spoke to Lottie, who had curled herself up in the window-seat, with her knees drawn up, and both hands locked over them.

"Don't speak to me; don't anybody dare to speak to me!" she said, motioning me off with her head. "I ain't worth noticing. I'd give something to any decent person that'd whip me within an inch of my life, or bite me—I don't care which—so long as it hurt."

"Lottie," I whispered, pressing my hand on her shoulder to enforce what I said, "do not speak a word of this till I have seen you. Come up to my room."

"I won't. Nothing on earth shall take me out of her sight again. There'll be murder if I do."

"Hush! Lottie, I do not understand all this."

"But I do; and I give up, she's out-generalled me. I'll never pretend to crow over her again; but it's awful, oh! it's awful!"

She shuddered all over, and crouched closer together, winding both arms tightly around her knees.

"Tell me all about it, Lottie. I must know, in order to judge how to act."

She moved on the window-seat, that I might sit closer to her; then drawing my head down with her arm, whispered,—

"I knew that she was doing something, and that Mrs. Lee was suffering by it; but what? that was the question. I tried to keep awake at nights, but it was of no use; no log ever slept as I did. Last night, you remember, I drank that strong tea. It wasn't because I liked it; but I was determined to keep awake. I wanted you to be on hand as well, and gave you a powerful dose; and wasn't you wide awake as a night-hawk when I came into your room?

"Well, I went to bed just as I always do, and lay down with my eyes shut, waiting. Babylon had gone to her room; but Cora was floating about in the passages a good while; finally she went in, and everything was still. It seemed to me as if I kept growing sharper and wider awake every minute; but I never heard that woman's step till she stood over me, and her shadow fell clear across the bed; I bit my lips to keep from screaming, but lay still and waited.

"She called my name two or three times, whispering louder each time; but I drew my breath even and deep, waiting for her. All at once that strange smell that was in the room when you came almost strangled me; but as I bit my lips harder, down came a wet cloth over my face. It almost smothered me, for she pressed it close with her hand till I felt a strange falling away, as if she had forced me over a rock, and I was myself sinking. One minute more, and I should have been nowhere; but some noise in the entry took her away.

"I snatched the cloth from my face and crept softly out of bed. The whirl and weight made me so dizzy, I could not walk, but crept on my hands and knees through the door which she had left open. Here the fresh air blew over me, and I felt steady enough to run to your room.

"You know how we found her, and how she put us down. I thought we had her, safe and sure; but here we are worse off than ever. I believe she would kill that blessed angel before his face, and no one would believe it."

I sat in silence, wondering what course it was best for me to pursue. That this woman was undermining Mrs. Lee's feeble life, by repeated applications of chloroform, I could not doubt; but how convince the family of this? It was an act so hideous in itself, that the very charge, if unbelieved, would be considered a crime. I was sure that, with the help of her maid, she had changed the bottle which contained the chloroform while struggling with me at the door; but how was I to prove this? Lottie—alas! this woman had so fascinated those who held power in the family, that her story would be of no avail without some indisputable proof to sustain it.

Jessie would believe us, I was sure; but the belief, without power to remedy a state of things so terrible that it made my heart sink, would only produce pain. What could I do? Helplessly I asked the question. Yet a terrible necessity required all my energies.

The dejection of poor Lottie had a numbing effect upon me. She, usually so full of resources, so ardent in her courage, sat on the window-seat, crestfallen and beaten like myself. One thing was certain, Lottie would keep strict guard now. Whatever the woman's motives were, the events of that night would never be repeated, so long as that faithful creature kept her place in the household. But how long would she keep that place? How long should I be left under the same roof with her?

CHAPTER XLVII
MR. LEE SENDS IN THE ACCOUNT
OF HIS GUARDIANSHIP

The pain of my apprehensions hunted me out of all society. I crept away into the woods, the next day, wondering what I should do, how it was my duty to act. I could not bear to see any of the family. No charge had been made, no suspicion cast on Mrs. Dennison; but it seemed to me that every member of the household must read my thoughts and condemn me for them. I felt broken down and driven forth by this woman.

I did not remember or care for the hours of breakfast or dinner; excitement had driven all thoughts of food from my mind. This increased my languor and made me more helpless still. Why had this beautiful woman come to torment me? What had I done to be thus virtually driven into the fields like a wild animal? I wandered off to the ridge, and sat down on the rock where I had once conversed with Mrs. Dennison. I do not know what time of the day it was; for the sun was obscured and the heavens were fleecy with black clouds. My head ached sadly; but that was nothing to the pain at my heart.

A storm came up while I sat there; but I was quite unconscious of it till my clothes were wet through, and I felt all my limbs shivering with the cold. I did not think of the consequences; it seemed so natural that I should be beaten down, that I cowered under the fierce rain like a poor flower that grew by me on the rock. The sunshine might revive that—would it ever come to me?

I remember feeling a mournful companionship with this solitary blossom, and sheltering it with a corner of my wet shawl. It was some distraction to the thoughts that harassed me to fancy the pretty thing as wretched as myself. Still I sat upon the rock, and still the rain beat down upon me. At last I heard Lottie's voice through the drifting storm, calling for me anxiously.

I arose and stood up, trembling from head to foot—the wet had chilled the very heart in my bosom.

"Why, what is this? Where have you been? What's the matter? Ain't you a fool, good and strong? Mercy! how you look—how your teeth do chatter! Now, speak out and let's know if you really are alive!" cried the kind-hearted creature, attempting to shake the wet from my shawl, but, finding that hopeless, wringing it between both hands, like a washerwoman.

"I've been with her all day; haven't left her one minute alone—not even with him. When he came, I planted myself by the bed, and there I stood like a monument. She kept asking for you."

"For me?" I faltered, smitten with compunction. "I did not think of that."

"You've given up thinking of anything, I'm afraid," said Lottie, shivering. "It wasn't just the thing to run off and leave me to bear the brunt of all their looks and questions! Not that I answered them—oh, no! but I wanted to get off and have a good cry as well as you."

"I am very sorry, Lottie."

"But that was nothing till she asked for you over and over again; then I'd 'a' given anything to have jumped up and a' after you. Besides, Miss Jessie was hunting up and down, wondering where you were, and Mr. Lee looked like a thunder-cloud."

"Mr. Lee?"

"Yes, Mr. Lee! But there you stand with your teeth going chatter—chatter—chatter—like a squirrel cracking hickory-nuts. Do come into the house!"

I followed her, meekly enough; she scolding and reviling, and petting me all the way as if I had been a lap-dog out of favor.

When we reached the house, it was late in the afternoon. I had eaten nothing that day, and still loathing the idea of food, felt its want in all my frame.

"Go up to your chamber, quick," said Lottie, hurrying me through the hall. "Babylon is in the drawing-room, and I wouldn't have her see you looking so like a drowned hen for nothing. Wouldn't it tickle her!"

This speech aroused me a little, and I struggled up the stairs and entered my room. Lottie followed me to the door, said something very peremptory about changing my clothes, and went away.

What possessed me, I do not know; I remember flinging off my wet shawl and shuddering, with a sense of extreme coldness, as it fell with a splash on the carpet; I remember, also, feeling how necessary it was that I should exchange my clothes for dry ones. But as I went toward the toilet, a letter lying upon it drew my attention from everything else. I had not the courage to touch it—a reptile coiled there could not have disturbed me more. So I stood looking at it in the dreary wetness of my garments, knowing what it meant, and dreading it. I took the letter up at last. It was thick and heavy; my heart sunk beneath its weight, my limbs trembled so violently, that I was obliged to sit down on the bed.

I broke the envelope. A thick paper covered with figures fell into my lap, a leaf of note-paper on which there was writing, fluttered after it.

I knew what it was. For the first time in my life Mr. Lee had sent me an account of his guardianship. Those figures, dancing in such fantastic rows before my eyes, contained an exact statement of my property, its growth, and aggregate amount. I knew this without the power to read or make an estimate. I knew also what it all meant. I had long been of age; my guardian, in that tedious combination of figures, was giving up his trust. That woman had prevailed; I was no longer welcome under Mr. Lee's roof. The paper fell from my hands. I took up the note, but only read the first few lines. They were very kind, but confirmed my fears. I could not read the note through—the whole room swam around me—a faint sickness crept to my vitals—nothing but darkness; into this I sank helplessly, and lay in its sombre depths for weeks.

CHAPTER XLVIII
COMING OUT OF A DANGEROUS ILLNESS

I asked if it was late—if I had overslept myself. It was Lottie to whom I spoke. She bent her face to mine; she looked into my eyes with a fervor of gladness in hers that made my nerves shrink. She caught up both my hands and kissed them; then burst into tears, and ran into the hall, crying out,—

"Miss Jessie, oh, Miss Jessie!"

My darling came, looking pale and harassed; but for the moment her face lighted up, and she approached me eager and breathless.

"You are better, dear Aunt Matty? Say that you know me."

"Know you, my darling?"

I tried to say this, and felt very helpless when my voice died away in a strange whisper; but a glow was on my face, and I know that my lips smiled, though they could not speak.

"You know me!" she cried, joyously.—"Oh! Lottie, it is true, she knows us—she will get well!"

Had I been ill? Was that the reason I felt so like a little child?

Jessie read this question in my eyes and answered it, kissing my forehead with her cool lips.

"Oh, yes, Aunt Matty, *so* ill! Out of your head, poor soul!"

Out of my head! The thought troubled me. Why? Had I anything to conceal? To question one's soul requires strength, for it is a stern task. I was very weak, and so put the subject aside. The very sight of Jessie's face had wearied me.

She sat down on the bed, and then I saw how sad and thoughtful she had become. Her very lips were pale, and her eyes were shaded by their inky lashes, which threw her whole face into mourning. Had she suffered so much because I was ill, or were other sorrows distressing her?

She held my hand in hers, clasping it tenderly. I strove to return the caress; but my poor fingers only fluttered in hers like the wings of a birdling when it first sees food. She knew that I wanted to return her love, and smiled upon me; but oh! how sad her smile was! Then I fell off into a quiet sleep.

The next day I could ask questions. How long was it? Four weeks—four weeks, in which they had been so anxious! The doctors had given me up, but she and Lottie had always hoped. It seemed as if I could not be taken from her just when she wanted me so much.

"And her mother, was all well?"

Mrs. Lee was better, stronger, and more cheerful than she had been for weeks before I was taken ill. Indeed, she had once crept to my chamber, and cried over me like a child.

"Mrs. Lee better, and more cheerful? Then why was Jessie so sad?"

The dear girl turned away her face and made no answer. Her silence cut me to the heart.

Then I remembered the letter; that sheet of paper, with its red lines, and crowded with figures, came before me with a pang, as if some one had struck me on the heart. The grief that convulsed my face frightened Jessie; she understood it and strove to reassure me.

"It is all well," she said; "never think of it again."

She might as well have asked a wounded man to forget the bullet rankling in his flesh. How much that package had hurt me, no human being could ever tell!

"Father has been very anxious about you," she said; "I never saw him suffer so much."

"What have you done with it?" I inquired.

She knew what I meant, and answered, gently,—

"I gave them back to my father—all except the letter, which I burned."

"Thank you, dear child."

There was silence awhile. I wanted to ask a question, but it made me faint. I think she would have answered that without waiting for words, only that the subject was a pain to her, as it was agony to me.

"Is *she* here yet?"

I knew that a whiteness was creeping over my lips as I uttered the words, and I felt a thrill of disgust pass over Jessie.

"She is here."

The bitter distress in her voice told me all that was in her heart. But it was a subject we could not speak upon.

"I have done everything in my power to send her away; but she will understand no hint, and I have no right to take decisive steps while my parents both like her so much."

"Both?" I questioned.

"Yes; I think so. Mother seemed pleased to have her in the room."

"And is she much there?" I questioned, faintly.

"Yes, very often, and for hours together."

"Alone?" I inquired, starting from my pillow and falling back from weakness.

"Seldom—never, I think. Father is generally with them, and Lottie—what a dear, faithful creature she is!—will never leave the room. If they drive her out, she is sure to retreat into her own little den and will leave the door ajar."

"Faithful, good Lottie!" I murmured.

Jessie kissed me and said, with mournful lovingness, that I must not talk, for I was all the friend she had to stand by her. She hesitated a moment and added, "Except, of course, my parents."

Obedient to her gentle command, I closed my eyes; but the anxieties that had taken flight in temporary insanity crowded back upon me, and my poor brain labored fearfully under them.

Was I right—knowing what I knew, and thinking what I thought—to keep anything back from Jessie? I had been so in the habit of mingling Mrs. Dennison's acts with those of Mr. Lee, that it seemed impossible to separate them, or speak of her without condemning him, at least by implication. I could not do this with his own child; for it was very doubtful if Jessie's entire and now very evident dislike of the woman had not sprung exclusively from the course she had taken with Lawrence. By word or look she had never given a sign of any other thought.

After pondering over these things in my mind, I remembered that, after all, Mr. Lee was not connected with anything I knew, except in my own suspicions; and even then I was not base enough to impute a wrong motive, much less a wrong act to him. Why should I fear, then, to speak openly to Jessie? While chained to that pillow—as I must be for days to come—who could guard Mrs. Lee as well as her own daughter?

While these reflections passed through my brain, Jessie had been sitting motionless on the bed, afraid to move lest she might disturb the sleep into which she fancied me to have fallen. When I opened my eyes, she smiled down upon me.

"You have been a little troubled with dreams, I fear," she said, smoothing the hair back from my temples.

"No, Jessie; I have not been asleep, but thinking. Lie down here on my pillow; I want to tell you something."

She laid her beautiful face close to mine. In a weak voice, and at intervals, I told her everything, but never once mentioning her father, even remotely. Indeed, there was no occasion; for I am certain he knew as little as the innocent girl at my side of that wicked night-work, in which our invalid had sunk so rapidly.

I never saw horror and dismay exhibit itself so forcibly on any countenance as it appeared on that lovely face. It touched mine like marble.

"What can we do?—what must we do?" she said. "Why did you not tell papa at once?"

"I had no proof—he would not have believed me."

"But your word—who ever doubted that?"

"Her word would have prevailed against mine. Oh! Jessie, Jessie, she is a terrible woman!"

"And my mother—my poor, suffering mother! What can her object be? No dove was ever more blameless than poor, dear mamma!" she said, with tender pathos. "Was she not content with what she had done against me? But I will go at once to papa and tell him everything about her."

"No," I said, trying to hold her with my feeble hand; "he will not believe you."

"Not believe me, Aunt Matty?"

"I fear not—Jessie, don't look so wounded! But he would demand your authority, and you would, of course, give me."

"Not without your permission."

"You would have it; but all might end in her triumph over us both. You remember the letter which came to me, that account of his stewardship? Ask yourself if it was the work of Mr. Lee's own heart."

"No, no, I am sure it was not!"

"Yet it came on the very next day."

"And broke your heart, dear Aunt Matty. I could not understand it. The first lines about money fastened themselves upon me I don't know how. I did not think, in my fright, when Lottie told me that you were ill, about its being a private letter; still I only read that and carried the paper back. What was in the letter I did not know; but I burned it to pacify you."

"The rest was only a kind dismissal from the house, Jessie!"

"A dismissal from the house! You—you?"

"Yes. I am only here now on sufferance," I answered, with feeble bitterness, which ended in a flood of more feeble tears.

Jessie was terribly distressed; but she made gentle efforts at soothing me, and at last I sobbed myself into quietness like a child, with my head resting on her shoulder.

"But you shall never go—never while I live," she said, with her old queenliness of manner. "I may stand by and see this woman robbing me of the love that was mine, when pride forbids me to cry out; but you, my oldest, my best friend! She must not attempt that."

Her eyes sparkled, her beautiful face took a positive expression. How I loved her!

"But about my poor mother," she said; "what can we do?"

"Wait and watch," I answered.

She was very thoughtful, and the look of distress upon her face made my heart ache.

"Lottie is honest," she said. "Now I understand why she would never leave the room even to nurse you. Good girl! she has been more faithful to my mother than her own child; but who could have known this?"

"Be dutiful!" I whispered, for this conversation had taken away my last remnant of strength.

"I will,—and watchful. Others may doubt this,—I believe it."

CHAPTER XLIX
LOTTIE SEEMS TREACHEROUS

Lottie came into the room while we were talking, and, after closing the door, Jessie began to question her about the events of that night. To my astonishment, Lottie looked blankly in her face, and protested that she could not understand what we were thinking of. Mrs. Lee had fainted, and Miss Hyde had been called, of course, and that raised a fuss, as such things generally did. This was all she knew about it.

Jessie looked at her steadily a moment and turned away.

I was astonished and grieved. What could the girl mean?

After Jessie went out, the creature came up to my bed, and, doubling up her fist, shook it in my face, thus mocking my indignant weakness.

"You're a pretty Miss Hyde to trust a secret with, you are! What possessed you to tell that? How many cooks do you mean to have in one mess of soup? She can't keep it more than you could; and the next thing will be, you and I'll be swept out of this house like a nest of wasps. Not that I'd go, but there'd be a tussel, such as never was seen here before. Of course, you'd give in, and curl up like a caterpillar on a dry leaf; but I'll never do it while she lives and wants me. But all that don't mean that I'm going to fly in the face of Providence, and give Babylon a chance to turn me out, for it mightn't be convenient for me to get sick—not that I think your sickness isn't the genuine article, mind; I know it is, more shame to 'em, but I'm bound to be on hand with a sharp eye and close tongue. Trust Miss Jessie, indeed! Well, crazy folks will be crazy folks, any way you can fix it."

I was so weary that all this scarcely made an impression on my poor brain. But I had a vague feeling that the girl was right, and that I had acted very rashly. Indeed, I was not sure that Lottie's stout denial of that woman's work might not shake even Jessie's confidence in me. The distress and excitement of these thoughts shook my poor, quivering nerves, till I fell back into the old delirium, and after that no talking was allowed in my room for a long time.

No wonder Mr. Lee started as if he had seen a ghost, when I crept by him in the passage leading to his wife's chamber, the first time that I was permitted to move from my room. The color mounted to his face. He paused, turned back and gave me his hand, striving to smile.

I could not touch his hand, or even attempt to smile. He had wounded me too deeply for that.

"My dear Miss Hyde," he said, dropping the hand which I had no strength to touch, "no one can be more rejoiced than I am at your recovery. Pray forget everything that might make you think otherwise; it was all a misunderstanding."

I did not speak, but tears swelled into my eyes, and I turned away wounded a second time by his confused explanation.

Mrs. Lee was so overjoyed to have me with her again. She looked much better, and seemed more cheerful than I had seen her since Mrs. Dennison's advent in the family.

Mrs. Dennison came into the chamber while I was there. She recognized me with careless politeness, called my attention to the improvement in Mrs. Lee, and, in a thousand adroit ways, triumphed in showing me how completely I was crowded out from my place in the household—even in that sick-chamber, where my chief usefulness lay.

I was feeble and unduly sensitive, or this conduct would not have wounded me so keenly as it did. Spite of myself, the pain of this interview would make itself visible; so I arose and went into Lottie's room, for my strength availed no farther than that.

The young girl sat quietly in her little domicile close by the door, sewing upon some second-hand finery, but with every stitch she cast a vigilant glance into Mrs. Lee's chamber, as if such watchfulness had become a habit, of which she was herself unconscious.

Lottie was always exceedingly repugnant to permitting any one into her room; but when she saw me come toward her, looking so miserably feeble, the frown left her face, and, starting up, she arranged the pillows on her little white bed, and, sweeping back the curtains, motioned me to lie down. I fell helplessly on the pretty couch, and she drew the curtains around it, clouding me in lace.

"Do you feel like sleeping?" she whispered.

"No, Lottie, my heart aches too much for that."

"Then lie still, and keep watch while I go out. It is ten days since I have breathed the fresh air. Can I trust you?"

"Yes, Lottie."

The creature bent down and kissed me with great feeling; she too was affected by the general depression. All her wild animal spirits seemed hushed for the time.

"I didn't mean to be hard with you the other day," she whispered, "so don't mind it. Nobody thinks more of you than this child, you may believe that."

She glided out of the room, leaving the door open. Mrs. Dennison turned her head quickly as she went out, but did not seem to observe that the bed was occupied.

CHAPTER L
CONFIDENTIAL CONVERSATION
BETWEEN THE WIDOW AND MRS. LEE

I was greatly exhausted. The walk from my room to the tower, and that brief interview with Mrs. Lee, had proved more than I could bear. So I lay helplessly on the bed, watching the scene in the inner room like one in a dream. How softly that woman moved about the chamber—how low and sweet were the tones of her voice! No wonder the invalid grew calm and cheerful under such ministration; it soothed even me.

Our invalid had left her sofa, and sat in the easy-chair. The widow arranged her footstool, and settled down upon it, covering those small feet with a cloud of muslin, while her beautiful face was uplifted, and her neck curved back with the fascinating grace of a serpent. Mrs. Lee's dark eyes were bent upon her, so full of affection that the look made my heart ache. In the stillness, I could hear every word that passed between them. I was too much exhausted for thought; but even in another state my position would have been the same, knowing what I knew, and suspecting what I did, no refinement of honor would have driven me from my post.

"Then I am beginning to be a little comfort to you, dear lady," said the haughty woman, looking sweetly in that gentle face, with her eyes full of solicitude, as if the great hope of her life lay in the idea of being useful.

"Oh, a great comfort. If Jessie now were—"

The sensitive heart checked her speech, and she broke off with a sigh.

Mrs. Dennison drooped her eyes in delicate sympathy, and, taking a fold of the muslin dress, which fell like billows of snow over the carpet, began to plait it thoughtfully between her fingers.

"You must not think that Jessie neglects you," she said. "The confinements of a sick-room are so irksome to youth. I am sure she loves you."

"But she used to spend half her time with me. In the morning, she would bring her work or her drawing, and we had such pleasant hours in my chamber."

"Yes, but it was before she came into society; that is sure to distract the attention. Still, the dear girl must be unaware of the higher and purer happiness she sacrifices."

Mrs. Lee's face clouded, and she said, with a sad smile, —

"Well, you have not permitted me to feel this. By-and-by Jessie will get some of your thoughtfulness."

"You must not think of this, my dear friend," said the widow, caressingly. "Only remember how well you are getting. I say nothing of my own poor efforts; but surely Mr. Lee makes up for all deficiencies in our sweet Jessie."

Mrs. Lee's face brightened beautifully. "Oh, yes," she said, "he is with me so much now; you charm him this way, I think."

"Me? Oh! nothing like it. This change in yourself, dear friend, constitutes the charm. You were dropping into such dreary ways, and looked so ill in that eternal white dress; but now that you have consented to brighten it up with ribbons, and pretty French caps, the change is marvellous."

"You think so," was the sweet reply. "I dare say it is true; but Jessie always liked my dress, and she has fine taste."

"But he likes something fresher and more worldly; and one dresses for a husband."

"Yes, yes; and these things do give something bright to the toilet, though Lottie scouts them."

"Well, never mind, so long as *he* is pleased. We need not trouble ourselves about the opinion of a wild, crazy girl like her, or of that prudish thing, Miss Hyde."

Mrs. Lee drew her hand from the widow's caressing clasp, and sat upright in her chair.

"Oh! don't say a word against Miss Hyde," she protested, with unusual resolution. "She is the dearest, best creature."

"I know, I know," persisted the widow, drawing a quick breath. "She is everything that is good, if she only had the power to make her amiability a little more interesting, and, I may add, useful; but when any person comes into a family to attach herself particularly to one member of it, there is a possibility of her gaining too much influence. I know Miss Hyde is very deserving, but has it never struck you that your daughter's heart lies a little too exclusively with her friend?"

"No; I had not thought of that," answered Mrs. Lee.

"It was not my business, and, I dare say, there is impertinence in the observation, but when Miss Hyde was sick, your daughter scarcely left her room. I never witnessed such devoted attention."

The widow sat playing with the knots of lilac ribbon that fastened Mrs. Lee's dress, as she made the observation. I saw the poor lady's face cloud, and her lips began to quiver. She was evidently drawing the contrast between Jessie's devotion to me, and the almost total desertion of her own room. Dear lady! she had no means of knowing that the eternal presence of that woman in her chamber had drawn the most devoted daughter that ever lived from her bedside.

Mrs. Dennison went on with her crafty work, still playing with the knots of ribbon, and pausing now and then to blow them about, till they fluttered like butterflies under her concentrated breath.

"If we only had sweet Jessie entirely to ourselves now to join our pleasant morning readings, wouldn't it be charming? But that is hopeless, so long as she gives herself entirely to one person, you know."

Mrs. Lee lifted her slender hand, passing it with troubled haste repeatedly across her forehead.

"But Miss Hyde has been such a true friend, so faithful, so every way worthy and agreeable, it seems as if Jessie could not love her too much. Then she is such a favorite with Mr. Lee."

"Is she?" was the dry question which followed these remarks.

"Oh, yes! Besides, I never can forget her kindness to myself when Mr. Lee was absent. You know that my husband has a great many duties, and it is only of late that it has been in his power to stay with me so much."

"But his heart—his heart is always with you, dear friend; I noticed that from the first day of my entrance to your house. In conversation, your name is always on his lips, and it is easy to see that you are never for a moment out of his thoughts."

Mrs. Lee leaned back in her chair, and her fine eyes filled with the brightest drops that ever sprung from a loving heart.

"I ought to be more grateful," she murmured, sweetly; "the blessed Lord has been so good to me. Oh! if all this should lead me to think less of Him, and more—sinfully more of my—my family."

"But this will never be; your nature is too well regulated."

"Ah! but Mrs. Dennison, you cannot imagine—you can form no idea how I have worshipped—how I do worship my husband. From the first hour I saw him to this, when we have sunk into mid-life together, it has been one struggle to keep him from overshadowing the love of God in this heart."

A heavenly expression came over that pale face, as the noble woman spoke words that the reticence of her nature had kept back even from me, her tried friend up to that hour; and now they were poured forth to the greedy ear of that woman like an overflow of wine upon the sandvile sand, which a thousand repulsive things had trodden over.

I could scarcely keep from crying out under the pressure of disgust that seized upon me when the creature lifted her eyes to the heaven of that face. In my whole life I had never seen an expression like that—so quick, so unutterably vicious. That instant some evil idea was born in the woman's brain; I saw it clearly, as if the map of her bad heart had been laid out before me. This idea, gendered from the loving goodness of Mrs. Lee's speech, broke into her eyes as the serpent bursts the mother-egg when hot sunshine is upon it.

This expression revelled in her eyes a moment, and then crept away as if a reptile had left her eyes and coiled itself in the depths of her soul. I could detect a tone of exultation in her voice when she spoke again; but it was low still, and vibrated with strange fascination on the ear.

"And you love him so much?"

"I thought in my youth that it was impossible to love him better—that it was wrong to love any human being so much. Night and morning I prayed God to keep me clear of man-worship; but how can one pray against love to a God who is love itself? When I saw how completely my whole being gave itself to my husband, how impossible it was to weaken one throb of the joy which filled me at his approach, I gave up the struggle, and soon rendered double gratitude to the Divine Being for giving him to me. It was all I could do."

"And did he love you so much?"

With what insidious craft the question was put! How quietly the new-born serpent coiled itself in her eyes as the lashes drooped over them!

"So much? That is impossible! No man—no woman ever gave so great worship to a fellow-being! He was not even aware of it, I think; for this love was a treasure that I kept closely locked. It must have been tender questioning, indeed, that could have drawn such feelings into expression."

"But still he loved you?"

"Loved me? Oh, yes; I never doubted it, even then; but after I became so helpless, so dependent on him for my very life—for if he had failed me I must have died—the beautiful affection of his nature manifested itself. He became my support, my very being. Oh! God has been exceedingly good to me!"

"And in all this devotion, this excess of love—for so I must think it—has no distrust ever arisen between you?"

"Distrust? Who could distrust him?"

Mrs. Dennison did not seem to hear—she was musing, with her eyes on the floor. At last she murmured, vaguely,

"But jealousy is the natural growth of inordinate affection. I wonder it never sprung up between you. What if he had loved another person?"

"Loved another person, and I know it? That would have been death!"

Again the woman's eyes gleamed so brightly that I could see the flash through her thick lashes. She arose and walked hurriedly up and down the room.

Mrs. Lee looked at her wonderingly.

"You think it wrong—you condemn me, as I have condemned myself a thousand times," she said, with meek pathos.

The woman returned to her seat, smiling.

"No, no. How can one woman condemn another for a fault so angelic? I only envied you the delicacy that could deem it wrong to give one's whole being up to the first element of a woman's nature—entire love."

Mrs. Lee drew a heavy breath and lay back in her chair, smiling.

"You have seen him," she said, at last. "How grand, how magnanimous he is, never forgetting me, never feeling the solitude of this room irksome, but loving it more and more; giving me hours out of each day till, of late, he almost lives in my apartment and never finds it tiresome!"

A strange smile stole over Mrs. Dennison's lips; but she did not look up, and it passed unnoticed by its object.

As the two ladies sat together, Jessie came into the room. Mrs. Dennison did not move, but, on the contrary, leaned nearer to Mrs. Lee. Jessie paused by the door and seemed about to retire; but Mrs. Lee spoke to her, holding out a hand.

The daughter saw this and came close to her mother's chair, leaning over it; while the widow kept her place, so that every word which passed between the mother and child was subject to her vigilance. Thus the conversation was constrained, and Jessie went away with a sad look, which went to my heart.

Then Mr. Lee came into the chamber, and all was bright as sunshine again. Mrs. Dennison kept her position, and Mr. Lee bent over his wife's chair. It was a beautiful group—I have never seen three more distinguished-looking people in one tableau.

They fell into conversation, in which Mrs. Lee took her gentle part. I listened, with a strange feeling of pain, to the graceful dialogue, and ceased to wonder that the invalid had grown more cheerful under the influence of scenes like this. Perhaps my jealous thoughts invested all they said with unreal attractiveness; for jealousy, like love, creates qualities which do not exist, and I acknowledged now that the feeling which burned at my heart had many a jealous pang in it. How could this be otherwise? For years I had been the closest friend that lady possessed; and, within the hour, had I not heard a woman, who should have been a stranger, decrying me to her as if I had been a servant she wished to see discharged?

In this way I excused the bitterness that filled my heart as the cruel scene passed before me. It was hard to bear when that woman's sweet laugh came ringing through the chamber after some witty saying which brought a thousand animated expressions into the faces of the two persons I prized above all others, but from whom she had separated me.

All the morning they spent in Mrs. Lee's room. Lottie informed me afterward that this had been their habit during my sickness. Why, she could not tell, unless it was that Babylon was hoping to find another chance to finish her work.

I could not sleep that night, and for many a long night after that. The fever had left me very low and nervous; I could not bear to meet the annoyances which were sure to beset me if I went into the family, and seldom left my room. I think Mrs. Lee hardly missed me. Indeed, it is doubtful if my absence was a matter of regret to any one; for Jessie came to my room as a sort of shelter from the scenes that I had witnessed, and thus our family became more and more a pided one.

CHAPTER LI
THE FATHER AND DAUGHTER

I had soon cause to regret my rashness in having opened my heart to Jessie. The dear girl was too frank and high-minded for a secret of that kind to rest safely with her. She believed all that I suspected, and with this conviction came a perfect loathing of the woman, who was now her forced guest. I saw that this subject was preying upon her, and repented keenly having given up the bitter fruit of knowledge before it was an absolute necessity; Lottie was wiser in the rude kindness of her attempt to put me down.

I did not grow strong; the harassing trouble at my heart kept me nervous and irritable. If a person entered my room suddenly, I would start and cry out; if I met any of the family in the grounds, my first impulse was to hide away, or pretend to be occupied till they passed. Lottie scolded me, not in her old way, but with a sort of tearful authority. The humor and drollery of her rare character was changed into quaint sarcasm. The serpent creeping through our house had bitten her most severely of all. To Mrs. Lee the girl was more humble and heedful than ever; to us she was abrupt.

This state of things could not continue without results. With feelings smouldering like the fire which turns wood into charcoal, this general irritation would break forth.

Jessie was the first to give way. For some time she had scarcely spoken to Mrs. Dennison, except in a grave, quiet fashion, which was as far from rudeness as it was from cordial hospitality. Sometimes this checked Mrs. Dennison's great flow of spirits, and she would take on a look of gentle martyrdom that must have had a peculiar fascination to one who did not understand her.

I do not know how it arose, for I had left the table; but one day Jessie came into the library, to which I had retreated, looking greatly excited; her eyes were full of troubled fire, and there was a stern pressure of the beautiful lips that I had never seen before. She did not speak, but walking up to the window, stood looking through it steadily, as if some beautiful landscape lay beyond, which she was examining through the gorgeous coloring, and which admitted of nothing beyond its own richness.

It was a gloomy day outside, and her face looked more sorrowfully sombre from all our surroundings.

I had arisen and was going toward her, when the door opened and Mr. Lee came in. How much the father and child looked alike at the moment! I had never seen either of them so imperial in their anger before.

Mr. Lee did not observe me, I think, but he walked across the library and laid one hand on Jessie's shoulder as she stood with her back toward him. She drew aside and looked up in her father's face.

"Jessie," he said, "what is the meaning of this? What have you been saying to wound Mrs. Dennison so terribly?"

Jessie struggled with herself; I could detect it by the blue veins that rose along her neck and forehead; but her countenance changed in nothing, and she answered his stern question steadily.

"I have done nothing that should wound Mrs. Dennison, father."

"But I left you at the breakfast-table with our guest tranquil as usual. When I came back, you were gone, and I found her in tears."

"I cannot answer for the lady's tears, father. She was shedding none when I came out of the breakfast-room."

"This is an evasion, Jessie. I insist upon knowing what passed between you and our guest after I left the room."

"You have a right to question me, father; but indeed I cannot tell you. Mrs. Dennison said something about what we should do next winter; and I looked at her a moment, in displeasure perhaps, for she has already stayed far beyond the time usual for our guests; and I am not aware that any one has extended a second invitation to her. I certainly have not."

Mr. Lee's face darkened.

"And is this what you have done?—given her one of your haughty looks, and at my table, Jessie Lee?"

"Father!"

"Do not call me father. Do not speak to me again until you have apologized to the lady for this rudeness."

Mr. Lee's voice was stern, almost cruel, as he said this. Jessie grew pale as death.

"Father, I cannot apologize for anything I have done; it is impossible when the lady entered a complaint to you—"

Mr. Lee interrupted her.

"Mrs. Dennison entered no complaint."

"Oh, father! and you were ready to condemn me without a word. When was this so before?"

"When were you rebellious before?"

Jessie's lips began to quiver.

"When did we have trouble like this? When was it that we became a pided family?" she said. "Never till I was unhappy enough to invite this lady here."

"She was your own guest, and you have treated her cruelly," said Mr. Lee, softening a little.

"No, father, not cruelly; coldly, perhaps, but not cruelly!"

"And why coldly?"

"Because I do not like Mrs. Dennison."

"And why, pray?"

"Because she comes between you and your own child—between you and your own wife—because—"

"Jessie," I said, rising from my seat, and for the first time becoming visible to Mr. Lee,—"Jessie—"

"It is well, Martha, that you are here to check her. Another word, and she would have been no longer a daughter of mine."

He was white as marble. Never in my life had I seen him so agitated.

Jessie looked at him sorrowfully. There was something more than anger in his face—a wild, troubled doubt, that made him tremble. Jessie laid her hand on his arm, and her lips quivered into a smile.

"Oh, father! listen to me. Let this lady go; take us back to your heart again; her influence here has been terrible."

He shook off her hand, drew himself up, and spoke with proud calmness,—

"Jessie, be careful, if you would not forfeit my love—at once be careful."

Jessie drew back, and leaned on my shoulder, trembling from head to foot. The idea that her father could ever really turn against her had entered her heart for the first time. She was so white that her very face terrified me.

"Speak to him," she whispered,—"speak to him."

I was about to say something, but Mr. Lee waved his hand, silencing me with a haughty gesture. Jessie stood up, and spoke in a low, sad voice,—

"Father, if I have done wrong, tell me how to atone for it, and I will obey you."

Mr. Lee turned away, walking the room three or four times before he answered. Then he took Jessie's cold hand, with some degree of returning kindness, while she stood, with downcast eyes, waiting for the humiliation his words would convey.

"Be yourself, my child; conquer your unreasonable prejudice against the lady who has been of great service to your mother, and is in every way estimable. I do not ask any unnecessary humiliation of my daughter; but be your own gracious self again, Jessie, and she will understand that you are sorry."

Jessie bent her bowed face a little lower, in token of acquiescence, and, bending his grand head, Mr. Lee kissed her. Then, turning to me, he said, with stern significance,—

"You will remember, Miss Hyde, these scenes are not to be renewed."

When he was gone, Jessie threw herself on the floor, and, folding her arms in the seat of an easy-chair, moaned piteously. She did not cry—the pain at her proud heart seemed too hot for tears. I tried to console her; but she only murmured,—

"You were right; I am not fit to be trusted with such things. They burn me like fire."

CHAPTER LII
THE FATAL LETTER

After this scene, our house was quiet as the grave—not a laugh sounded within its walls, not a brilliant word enlightened the stiff monotony. Jessie kept her promise. Nothing could be sweeter or more gracious than her manner toward Mrs. Dennison; but all this was accompanied by no warmth. It was impossible to find fault with anything she did or said, yet her submission seemed to annoy our guest more than anything. It proved how deep was the gulf which lay between them.

As for me, nothing could render my position more disagreeable than it had already become. A few days after that scene in the library, I was sitting with Mrs. Lee, while Lottie went out for a little recreation. Mr. Lee, Mrs. Dennison, and Jessie, had gone out on horseback, and, with the enemy away, Lottie thought that I might be trusted with her charge; but while Mrs. Dennison was in the mansion, she never would leave her post on any consideration. With all the keen longings of youth for change, this confinement, voluntary though it was, told painfully on the young girl, and when she did get a few moments of freedom, it was seized upon as a bird darts from its cage.

That morning she was gone some time, having taken a run through the grounds with a favorite dog that always followed her footsteps. I saw them rioting up and down among the flower-beds, with a feeling of thankfulness that anything on earth could find enjoyment when my heart was so heavy!

Mrs. Lee was unusually silent that day, and, without asking me to read, amused herself with a book of engravings that Mr. Lee had ordered for her from the town. I felt the change. Every day this lady, who had been my dear friend so long, seemed more and more independent of me. Lottie she still clung to, but I had become a useless waif in the household.

While thinking over these depressing truths, I watched with a vague sensation of regret. All at once I saw her stop, beat the dog back, and shade her eyes with one hand. It was only one of our people, who had been over to the town, and had attracted her observation. I saw the man beckon to her. She darted down the walk, along the sloping lawn, and over the wall, holding out her hands for a package which he held out. There was some talk between them as the man gathered up his bridle, while she examined something in her hands which seemed like a letter. Then, nodding her head repeatedly, she ran toward the house.

I cannot tell why it was, but these movements interested me greatly. A strange apprehension took possession of me, and I began to wonder what the letters could be about—if any of them related to me, and if new trouble was coming.

In the midst of these vague thoughts, Lottie came into the room, with a letter in her hands.

"I left all the rest, papers, books, and trash, on the hall-table," she cried, joyously; "but here's a letter for the dear mistress, and I brought it up. Such a nice letter—white and satiny as the leaves of a water-lily! I know there is something sweet and good in it that will make you smile."

She went up to Mrs. Lee, dropped on one knee at her feet—a common thing with the strange girl—and held up the letter between her hands.

Mrs. Lee took it, with a pink flush of the cheek. During her long illness she had gradually given up writing, and a letter, directly to herself, was an event sufficiently rare to create a little excitement. Lottie's prophecy regarding the letter brought a smile to those usually pale lips. She broke the seal, took the letter from its envelope, and murmured, pleasantly,—

"If it is something very pleasant, you shall have a new dress, Lottie."

This promise kept the girl on her knees, reading the face of her mistress with keen eagerness. She saw it change as if a flash of fire passed from neck to forehead; then a cold, gray tint settled over it so gradually, that no one could tell when it came.

Lottie sprang to her feet with a sharp cry.

Mrs. Lee had fainted—no, not that; no common fainting fit ever took a form so painful—a look of unutterable misery had settled on the face, impressive as the agony which has become immortal in the features of that marble father who strives to rescue his children from the writhing serpents in the Vatican.

Mrs. Lee had fallen sideway in her chair. The movement had been gradual, and accompanied the gray changes of her face with such stillness, that its meaning did not strike Lottie till she sprang up and uttered that cry.

We lifted the lady from her chair and laid her on the bed. She gave no sign of life, but seemed to be growing colder and colder. Lottie attempted to draw the letter from her hand, but her fingers clung to it with a tenacity which could not be forced without wounding the hand; so we left the paper in her grasp.

What we did I cannot tell. Everything that two frightened creatures could devise we attempted, in order to restore her; but it seemed to me an age before any sign of life returned.

At last a shiver passed over her, and, with her disengaged hand, she tore at the muslin over her bosom as if some pain were burning at her heart, and then I saw her poor lips redden for the first time—but it was with blood. Piteously she opened her eyes and looked into ours. She had not recovered then, nor did she remember what event had produced this illness.

I could tell when the first dawn of a recollection came upon her, for she rustled the letter in her hand as if to be sure it was there, and a reality; then the pain all came back to her features, and the blood came in heavier drops up from her broken heart.

They came back from a long ride while she lay thus. We had sent for the doctor, and sat by her in helpless grief, waiting his arrival. I went out to meet Jessie, intending to break the painful intelligence of her mother's attack to her with gentleness. She was coming up the steps with a harassed look. The weight of her skirts seemed to drag at her frail strength. Mrs. Dennison was lower down the steps, looking over her shoulder at Mr. Lee, and talking in a gay, excited manner that did not seem quite natural. Jessie looked upward, with a weary, sad glance as I came down the walk, and I saw that the company of this woman was oppressing her dreadfully.

I was so pale in those days that my countenance did not frighten Jessie as it might have done in happier times; thus I was obliged to tell her in words that something had happened to injure her mother, and that she lay in great danger in the tower-room. I shall never forget the wild agony of those eyes. She did not speak a word, but passed me like a shadow.

Mrs. Dennison's strained laugh followed her with a sound of the most cruel mockery I ever heard. It was altogether unintentional. The woman had not seen me, nor was she aware that Jessie had disappeared; she was only bantering words with her host in her usual fashion, while he was preparing to follow up the steps.

I stood upon the edge of the terrace and watched them as they came up. There was no cheerfulness in the woman. Her cheeks were hot and red, her eyes full of restless fire. She understood my countenance better than Jessie had done; for a look of something like affright swept her face, and the heavy riding-skirt dropped from her hold, entangling her feet till she stumbled and almost fell.

Mr. Lee sprang forward and saved her.

"What is the matter? What has happened?" he questioned.

She laughed nervously.

"Nothing. It was Miss Hyde standing there like a Nemesis that startled me."

Mr. Lee glanced upward, and said something in an under-tone, at which she said, —

"How unkind you are to the poor thing."

I had hesitated to tell Mr. Lee that his wife was on her death-bed—the shock at my own heart was so painful that I pitied him; but now a cruel strength came over me, and I said at once, in a cold, hard way, —

"Your wife is ill, sir, very ill—I fear dying."

He left that woman standing alone in her cowardly sin, and went swiftly, as his daughter had done, toward the tower-room. Mrs. Dennison gave a light scream and followed, demanding of me how it had happened, and who had been near to harm the dear saint.

I gave her no answer. The very sound of her voice made me shudder with fresh loathing. She had been pale for a moment, but now all the fire came into her countenance again, and she passed me haughtily, saying, —

"Stupid as ever—I will inquire for myself."

CHAPTER LIII
DEATH IN THE TOWER-CHAMBER

The woman did inquire, and the very sound of her voice made the poor victim on the bed shake till the counterpane moved like snow disturbed by the wind. Jessie was holding the pale hand, and, feeling it quiver, she clasped it closer, and said to Mrs. Dennison,—

"Madam, your voice troubles my mother; please to leave us alone."

Mr. Lee looked from his daughter to the woman; but it was no time for anger—he only lifted one hand to deprecate further noise, and bent over his wife with such solemn tenderness in his eyes as I had never seen there before.

"My wife, my poor wife!" he said, sheltering the frail form with his arm, as if that could keep death away.

She heard him, and the tension on her delicate nerves relaxed. The letter, which had hitherto been clenched in one hand, fell away and rustled to the floor. Mrs. Dennison picked it up, folded it deliberately, and held it toward Mr. Lee.

"This has just fallen from her hand," she said; "it may have some reference to this strange attack."

Again that shiver ran through Mrs. Lee's form, and her face contracted with the pain, while fresh drops of crimson gathered on her lips.

"Madam, your presence tortures her," said Jessie; "these attacks come and go with your voice."

"My friend, my dear, sweet friend; will you not give me one look before I go?"

Mrs. Dennison bent over the bed as she spoke, and, sure enough, Mrs. Lee opened her eyes wide, and turned them on the woman's face. Never shall I forget that look! Its wounded expression haunts me yet. Those great, mournful eyes dwelt on that face, which grew slowly pallid, for a full half-minute, and then turned away.

Mrs. Dennison was awed; but, feeling our eyes upon her, she took strength, and, with a pathetic "Farewell!" on her lips, pressed them to those of Mrs. Lee.

There was a faint struggle, a gasping cry broke from the bed, and when Mrs. Dennison lifted her face, a drop of fresh blood crimsoned her lips. She did not know it; but with the red blood burning there, retreated into Lottie's room, where she hovered over the scene as if afraid to leave it entirely.

Mr. Lee forgot everything in keen anxiety for his wife. When her eyes turned sorrowfully upon him, he cried out,—

"Oh! speak to me, speak to me, my wife! Give some sign that I have not come too late!"

The most wonderful expression I ever saw stole over that face; it came like moonlight on dark waters,—a gleam of hope breaking through the agonies of death. Her lips moved. He bent down and listened.

"You have loved me?"

There was no noise; but we knew that she was saying this by the movement of her lips.

For an instant, Mr. Lee seemed stunned. The question struck him to the soul; then his noble head was uplifted, and, looking tenderly into those wistful eyes, he said, "I have always loved you, my wife. God is my witness, I have always loved you."

That expression deepened on her face. She lifted her hands feebly, and, understanding the sign, he raised her to his bosom. The muslin drapery of her sleeve got entangled in his dress. I attempted to disengage it while her face lay on his bosom. In doing this I touched her hand; the frail fingers clasped mine with the tenacious feebleness of an infant's; and, laying my palm on Mr. Lee's hand, she pressed them softly together, whispering,—

"Be good to her."

He shook all over, while my poor hand lay quivering on his. I drew it away with hushed breath.

She was dying on his bosom; her eyes were uplifted to his; her breath came in faint gasps; the two frail hands folded themselves; and, as the mists of night settle on a lily, that dear face hardened into the marble of death.

I cannot remember all that passed after this, who came into the room, or who went out. I only know that the stillness of death was in the house, the pain of life in our hearts. Sweet sufferer, gentle lady! How white and still she lay on the pretty French bed, with its volumes of lace brooding over her like the clouds in which we imagine seraphs to be sleeping! There was no noisy grief in the room. Even Mrs. Dennison had fled to her own apartment; the suddenness of our calamity shocked even her.

Lottie knelt by the bed, her face buried in the clothes, dumb and still. Jessie clung to her father, who was striving to comfort her; but struggle against it as he would, the force of a mighty anguish spoke out in his broken words.

Those were mournful days during which she lay in that tower-room. We had the dead to ourselves—that woman never intruded on us. Cora came each day informing us that her mistress was ill from grief. *He* heard the message, but gave no sign beyond a grave inquiry. The sadness in his face deepened every hour; stern thoughts perhaps had stamped the sorrow deeply in his soul. There was something more than natural grief there; gleams of remorse broke through all the rest.

The night before Mrs. Lee was buried, I went into her room; to sleep was impossible, and I longed to be alone with her once more. I am no enthusiast, and have little superstition, but it seems to me impossible to doubt that the dead are often with us on this side the eternal shore. We feel their presence in our heart of hearts without caring to see it with the sense.

How young she looked—how good and quiet! Some white flowers lay on the pillow with rich colors burning in their hearts, that cast a sort of illumination over the frozen stillness of her face. The white draperies gathered above her, the shaded lights stealing like star-gleams through the room, made the stillness of death holy!

I sat down by the bed, in the great easy-chair which she had occupied when Lottie came in with the letter. A faint perfume of violets hung about the cushions, and on the seat lay the delicate handkerchief she had been using. It seemed only a moment since I had seen her resting tranquilly upon the seat that supported me. Could death be so cruelly sudden?

I wept quietly as these thoughts filled my mind, and with them came vague conjectures regarding the letter which had apparently produced a result so fatal. Who had written that letter? What could the subject have been? Where was it now? I remembered that Mr. Lee had taken it mechanically from Mrs. Dennison's hand and put it in his pocket, evidently unconscious of its mysterious importance. Surely the woman could have nothing to fear from that letter; at any rate, she had held no part in its fatal delivery. Then who could have possessed the power to break the frail life which had been quenched? It was all a painful enigma, impossible to solve; but the great, mournful fact lay before me,—my friend—the best friend I had ever known on earth—was dead.

CHAPTER LIV
MRS. LEE'S FUNERAL

As I sat buried in miserable thoughts, a faint stir in the bed draperies made me start and hold my breath. It was Lottie, who had been all the time crouching close to the floor, guarding the remains of her mistress in profound stillness. The light was so dim that I had not been aware of her presence till then. Such companionship did not disturb me; indeed, without the faithful girl that death-chamber would have been desolate indeed.

"Lottie," I said, in a whisper,—"Lottie, is it you?"

She was sitting on the floor, with both arms locked around her knees, on which her forehead rested. The girl looked up, and her heavy eyes met mine.

"Yes, it's me, Miss Hyde; I haven't left her a minute since then," she said, drearily. "Don't ask me to go away—I couldn't do it."

"Ask you to go away, Lottie? Oh! no, my poor girl! We have watched together in this room many a time; but never in this sad way."

"I know it," she said; "you were always good to her, and she felt it. But tell me, Miss Hyde, do you think it was the letter I brought that laid her there?"

"I cannot tell. Still it must have been, she was so well only a moment before it touched her hand. Who could have written it?"

"I have been thinking and thinking, Miss Hyde. The writing was like Miss Jessie's; I thought so at the time."

"Miss Jessie's? Are you sure?"

"So it seemed to me; but I've got the envelope, look for yourself."

I took the crumpled envelope which she took from her bosom and held toward me. It was of creamy-white paper, very thick, and with an inner lining of blue, a color that Jessie affected where it could be delicately introduced among her stationery. The writing was like hers, but with a slight appearance of disguise.

"You see," said Lottie, still in a whisper, "it looks like Miss Jessie's; but what could she write to *her* about?"

"It is strange," I murmured.

"Terribly strange! I can't make it out. All the time, for two whole nights and days, I have thought of it; and the more I think the darker it all grows. Oh, if she could only speak; but that will never be again—"

Her voice broke here, and clasping her knees tighter, she began rocking to and fro, uttering faint, dry moans, that went to my heart. Lottie had not shed a tear since her mistress's death.

"Never again—never again!" she kept whispering.

"Don't Lottie," I said; "it breaks my heart to hear you go on in this way."

She looked at me earnestly; then dropped her face and said, with infinite pathos,—

"Oh! that *my* heart could break!"

I bent over her.

"Be comforted, Lottie. If our friend could speak, this is what she would say—"

"Don't, don't. Who could be comforted, and she lying there like a beautiful lily broken off at the stem? Look at her, Miss Hyde, and see if the smile is there yet."

"Yes, Lottie, there is a heavenly look on her face. See for yourself."

"No, no, I cannot stand it; in the morning I will kiss her hands for the last time. Let her sleep with the angels to-night; I won't come between her and them. They will take care of her now she don't want me."

"Oh, Lottie!"

She shook her head disconsolately, then it sunk on her knees once more, and was not lifted again all night; still I do not think she slept a moment.

Jessie came to her mother's room late that night. Lottie did not move; I arose to go, knowing how sacred were the rights of an only child; but she asked me to stay, saying—oh, how sadly—that her mother's true friend could not be in the way even there.

I told her that Lottie was watching, and had not once left her place by the bed. She went round to where the girl was crouching and kissed that portion of the forehead left exposed by the folded arms. Then, for the first time, I heard low sobs break from the faithful creature, and felt glad to know that she was crying.

"She is happier far than I am," said Jessie, with unutterable sadness. "It seems as if I should never shed tears again."

She came back to where I was sitting, and sinking on the footstool that always stood near the chair, her head fell on my lap, her hands clasped themselves under the pale forehead, and thus she lay, heavy and still, weary with pain, but sleepless, till the day dawned.

That morning Mrs. Lee was to be buried.

With the first gray of dawn, we heard Mr. Lee's step coming up from the library below, where he had passed the night. Jessie and I arose, and, bending over that calm face, left our solemn kisses on the lips and went away, giving her up to the man she had loved so devotedly. Even Lottie was aroused by his approach, and, rising to her feet, went heavily into her own little room, which was soon filled with bitter sobs.

We met Mr. Lee on the stairs. He had not been in bed that night and looked strangely haggard. No words passed among us; but Jessie and her father exchanged a mournful glance that was more eloquent than language.

It rained when we took her away from her home, and a heavy gloom lay upon the beautiful landscape she had loved so well. Across the terrace, and down the flight of steps bordered with flowers that wept heavy drops, she passed away into the valley—away to her eternal rest. On a rise of ground on the verge of the hills, we paused amid a cluster of white stones where sods lay in a heap, and the torn earth contrasted mournfully with the fresh grass.

As we neared the hill, a burst of sunshine broke the clouds asunder and lighted us forward. There were no sobs at the grave; our sorrow was very silent, and solemn as death itself. The very air seemed thrilled with awe as the funeral service rose upon it. Some one, Lottie I suppose, had laid a garland of white flowers on the coffin, knotted together with snowy ribbons. As they lowered the coffin the wind took these ribbons, and they fluttered up from the grave like the wings of an angel striving to rise heavenward; and through the first shovelful of earth rose a faint perfume pressed from the flowers which the gravel had bruised upon her coffin.

It was all over, and we returned to the house. On the steps, Mrs. Dennison stood to receive us clothed in white, with black ribbons knotting up the sleeves and clustering at the bosom of her dress. This was the first time I had seen her since that fatal day.

Nothing could have been more decorous than her demeanor; her beautiful eyes seemed heavy with unshed tears, and Christianity itself is not more gentle than her tone and manner.

"Come," she said, addressing our Jessie, "let us mourn together as friends who have lost one who is dearest to us. If I have ever pained you, dear Jessie, forgive me for her sake."

Mr. Lee heard this, and looked wistfully at his daughter. Poor girl! she was too heart-broken for resentment, and held forth her hand. Mr. Lee stepped forward and laid his hand on those that the beautiful woman had just clasped.

"Jessie," he said, in a voice that thrilled all within its influence, "remember this lady was very dear to your mother."

Jessie did not answer; I think she could not command words, but she bent her head in acquiescence and passed into the house.

It is a strange thing to say, but I believe that the few weeks that followed Mrs. Lee's funeral were the most tranquil of any that had preceded them since Mrs. Dennison came to our house. The great central object of interest in the household was at rest. All the little cares that had occupied us were over; the very altar of our household had been torn away, and for a long time we found it impossible to find new channels of interest, or settle ourselves down to anything. There was no longer an attempt at amusing our guest, and she did not seem to require it; indeed, from all appearances she had become a member of the family. We seldom met now, but kept our own rooms. Jessie became sadder and sadder each day; nothing interested her; she absolutely pined to follow her mother.

CHAPTER LV
OLD MRS. BOSWORTH'S VISIT

Compacts made in a state of excitement are seldom lasting. If Jessie's heart had softened toward Mrs. Dennison in the extremity of her grief, it came back to the old standpoint as that grief took thought. Something more subtile than her own will held her confidence back. But this was no time for excitement of any kind; the depth of grief into which we had fallen kept all worldly passions back. So, as I have said, we were more tranquil than of old.

Poor, poor Lottie! she went about the house like a wounded bird that had seen its nest destroyed. Without asking for leave, she had arranged Mrs. Lee's room, in the tower-chamber, exactly as it had been during her mistress's life, and guarded it from her own pretty den with all the vigilance of old time. If any one entered the chamber and touched an article that had been Mrs. Lee's, Lottie would cry out as if struck by a sudden pang, and fall into a nervous tremor till the intruder had departed. She never allowed any one, not even Jessie, to enter the room without following her like a watch-dog.

No one was surprised at this. The devotion of that girl to her mistress had been something wonderful. That she should feel great attachment to anything belonging to her was beautifully natural. So it happened that she fell into possession of the rooms in the tower, and secluded herself there, taking little interest in anything else.

Some days after things had settled into this state, old Mrs. Bosworth came over in her heavy family carriage. In our sadness, this became an event, and both Jessie and I left our room to meet her, grateful for anything that showed real sympathy for our bereavement.

The sorrows which this good old lady had passed through, placed her in delicate sympathy with us. She met Jessie with such motherly gentleness, that tears came into the young creature's eyes almost for the first time since our loss. The old lady saw this, and, drawing the agitated face to hers, kissed it.

"We have been very sorry for you, Miss Lee. Indeed, ours has been a house of mourning also; for there are cases where the same grief touches many hearts. I have wept for you, my child—prayed for you."

"I know it—I was sure of it," answered Jessie, resting her proud young head on the old lady's shoulder, and weeping those soft, warm tears that relieve the heart so much. "I have thought of you and of him. Tell me that your grandson is no worse."

The old lady kissed her again, and tenderly smoothed the glossy hair upon her temples.

"He is no worse, dear child—a little better, I think, since we have been quite alone—the tranquillity has done him good."

"I should like to see him," said Jessie. "Miss Hyde and I have missed him so much in our loneliness."

The old lady cast a grateful glance at me; then, turning to Jessie, she said,—

"It would make him strong enough to come, if he knew that his sweet friend desired it."

Jessie looked at that dear old face earnestly, and smiled through her tears.

"You are very kind."

While we were sitting together, Mr. Lee came in. He had seen Mrs. Bosworth's carriage at the door, and, knowing how seldom the old lady went out, sought her to pay his respects.

It is seldom that two persons so thoroughly bred, and so singularly intelligent as Mr. Lee and our visitor, ever meet. Notwithstanding the sorrow that oppressed us, the conversation which sprang out of the first greeting brought cheerfulness with it. They did not talk directly of our loss, but every subject touched upon had a tinge of sadness in it, which betrayed the buried feelings and sympathy which lay behind.

I had not believed that such power of pleasing could be carried into extreme old age, as this old lady manifested.

While we were conversing, Mrs. Dennison came in, much to our astonishment; for of late she had rather avoided both Jessie and myself. Mr. Lee presented her to our visitor, who put on her stateliest manner, and, after rising, stood as if ready to go; but her clear eyes were fixed on Mrs. Dennison's face, and she seemed reading her to the soul.

I think that Mrs. Dennison was, for once, awed by the moral force opposed to her; for such it really was. The graceful flippancy of manner, which most people considered so captivating, refused to come into action, and, for the moment, she really was awkward.

"I did not know that you had guests," said the old lady, with a stiff bend of the head. "If I remember, Mr. Lawrence told me that this lady would leave the neighborhood about the time he did."

The color flashed into Mrs. Dennison's face, and she replied, with suppressed anger,—

"Mr. Lawrence presumed, madam, when he ventured to regulate my movements by his own."

Again the old lady gave her a quiet, searching look, and, without replying, moved toward the door.

Jessie and I went down to the terrace with Mrs. Bosworth, while Mr. Lee took her to the carriage.

CHAPTER LVI
LOTTIE'S REVELATIONS

The conduct of old Mrs. Bosworth made a profound impression in our family. Nothing could have been more unfortunate for Mrs. Dennison. Mr. Lee, up to that time, had been so occupied with the genuine grief which sprung out of his wife's death, that he had evidently given little thought to the real condition of his household; but the grave look of disapproval which met Mrs. Dennison's entrance, when the dear old lady made her visit, was too decided for him or any one else to ignore. Jessie's ill-timed remarks had affected him but little, for, alas! he was prejudiced there; but the evident condemnation of this fine old lady had its effect.

Mr. Lee began to understand that a guest in our house just then, not sanctioned by ties of blood, or even of old friendship, must have a strange appearance in the neighborhood. His own fine sense of propriety was disturbed, and this gave his intercourse with the lady, all the rest of that day, an air of constraint which she was not slow to comprehend. She grew more quiet and thoughtful, all her fine spirits vanished, and, more than once, I caught her lifting her beautiful eyes to Mr. Lee's with a sad, misty look of appeal, that would have touched the heart of a savage. It almost reached mine.

This lasted all that day and evening. There was little conversation; but the eloquence of that woman's face was above all language.

At night I went into Jessie's room, as usual; not to talk; everything had become too painful for those little confidential chats that make a home so pleasant; but Jessie was always sad now, and the news about young Bosworth had affected her greatly, in what way it was difficult to determine; so I went to her room, knowing that the presence of an old friend would be some comfort to her.

As we sat together talking on vague household affairs, Lottie knocked at the door and came in.

"I don't want you to be taken by surprise or anything," she said, bluntly, "but Mr. Lawrence will be here to-morrow; and, before twenty-four hours, he will beg Miss Jessie's pardon for slighting her, on his bended knees, and ask her to marry him right out."

Jessie started up, pale as death, her eyes flashed and her lips quivered.

"Lottie!"

The voice was low, but it made the girl hold her breath.

"Don't let her get mad!" cried the strange creature, appealing to me; "I didn't bring him, gracious knows. Mrs. Babylon has done it, that's what you ought to know, and I've told it."

"But how did you find this out, Lottie?" I said, for Jessie had fallen back to her seat, and was shrouding her face with one hand.

"I won't tell you! If I did, some of your queer notions would come in and I should catch it. Just you take care of honor and dignity, and all that. I don't pretend to no such nonsense; I know he's coming, because Babylon sent for him; she's ready to take claws off now that—oh, dear! oh, dear!"

Here the strange girl flung herself down on the floor, and, burying her face, began to cry bitterly.

I knew how she would have finished that sentence but for Jessie's presence, and shrunk from drawing forth another word.

At length Lottie lifted her wet face and shook the hair back from her eyes.

"I'm a queer jewsharp, ain't I?" she said, with a giggle that broke up the sob in her throat; "but it's true as the gospel. Mr. Lawrence is coming, and you mark if he don't go through with that very performance, kneeling and all!"

"Well, well! It was right to tell us, and Miss Jessie thanks you in her heart," I said, raising the girl from her lowly position. "Now go to your room."

She arose, looked wistfully at Jessie an instant; then creeping to her side, knelt down as she had often done at the feet of Mrs. Lee, and, taking the hand which fell listlessly down, kissed it.

Jessie started at the touch, and gently releasing the hand, laid it on the young girl's hair.

"I thank you," she said, looking down to the honest eyes into which great tears were crowding fast; "my mother loved you, and so do I."

"I—I'm a-trying to do my best and be a mother to you myself, now that she is dead and gone," answered Lottie, with a look of honest affection beaming over her face.

Jessie almost smiled; at which Lottie blushed like a child, and, starting to her feet, went away, closing the door softly after her.

"Can you believe this?" said Jessie, after she was gone.

"Yes," I answered. "Whatever her sources of information may be, Lottie is always correct."

"And he will dare—at her request—by her consent, perhaps—he will dare!"

She arose and walked the room, her black dress sweeping the carpet like an imperial robe.

I did not speak; anxiety kept me dumb. Was this a burst of anger that would pass away? When that man, with all his bewildering attractions, should stand before her—humble, imploring—how would it be? The hopes which had begun to dawn in my heart for young Bosworth faltered, notwithstanding this queenly manifestation of pride.

"*She* has sent for him indeed!" burst from those curved lips; "there is nothing humiliating in this, Aunt Matty. She invites gentlemen to my father's house and allows them to approach me. Perhaps she has found out that half this property is mine now, and sent him word."

I started. This might be true. There certainly was something inexplicable in the evident understanding between Lawrence and our guest.

"Well, let him come," said Jessie, drawing a deep breath. "Let him come; I understand myself now."

"You will not accept him then?" I inquired, anxiously.

"Accept him!" she replied, with a calm smile, which told how deep and settled her pride had become, far more clearly than the flashing eye and writhing lip that had startled me a moment before. "You need not fear that, my friend."

"And you do not love him?"

"No, my friend, I do not love him; nor am I sure that he is worthy of any good woman's love."

I clasped my hands in thankfulness. Her words had lifted a painful weight from my bosom.

"Thank God!" I murmured.

She looked at me gratefully, and we parted for the night.

CHAPTER LVII
MRS. DENNISON URGES LAWRENCE TO PROPOSE

The next morning Mrs. Dennison kept up the subdued character of the previous night. Her eyes were heavy and full of troubled mist, her movements had lost their elasticity, and an air of touching depression supplanted the graceful audacity of her usual manner.

Mr. Lee was grave and silent; he once or twice glanced at our guest, with some anxiety in his look, but made no comment on her changed appearance.

After breakfast I went out for a walk. The morning was bright and cool, inviting me to a long ramble. But my health was not altogether restored, and anxiety made me listless; so I walked slowly across the face of the hill, came out at the footpath on the ridge, and wandered on till I came to the rock which terminated it. I had been sitting on it a little while, gazing languidly down at the gleams of water that came up through the green hemlocks, some two hundred feet beneath, when the sound of voices from the grove disturbed me.

I had a nervous dread of being seen by Mrs. Dennison or her friends, and let myself down from the rock to the face of the precipitous descent—a perilous exploit—for a false step might have sent me headlong to the river below. I became sensible of the danger of my position after the first moment, and, clinging to a young ash-tree, pressed myself against the leaning trunk of a hemlock and waited for the persons, whose voices I had heard, to pass.

Directly two persons came winding down the path, and stood upon the rock I had just left. It was Mrs. Dennison and Mr. Lawrence, talking eagerly. The languor that had marked her appearance at breakfast was gone. She was sharp and animated, spoke with earnestness, and seemed now pleading, now explaining. I caught a glimpse of his face. It was flushed with anger, not to say rage.

"It is useless to upbraid me. I loved you; it was death to give you up. At a distance it seemed easy enough; but when I saw you together and marked something too real in your devotion, it drove me mad. I could not marry you myself, poverty-stricken wretches that we are! but you cannot blame me if the trial of giving you to another was beyond human strength."

"But you were false. You told me that she also was false; that she secretly encouraged young Bosworth; that I was treacherously undermining my own friend."

Lawrence spoke in a loud, angry voice. The look which he bent on her was stormy with passion.

"Lawrence, this rage is useless. I did all that lay in my power to break up the work I had helped to do. For a time, poverty, anything seemed better than the possibility of seeing you the husband of that proud girl. Then my own future was uncertain; now it is assured. Between them the father and daughter have unbounded wealth. It is worth a great sacrifice—I make it. This is my first step, my first humiliation. It was false. All that I told you was false. She did not love that young man, she did love you. I fancied—and here the trouble arose—that you were beginning to love her, that it gave you no pain to change. This embittered me. I misrepresented her, told you that she visited Bosworth's sick-chamber from affection, when I knew that it was only the persuasion of that troublesome Miss Hyde which sent her to the house. Now I take it all back. She is heart-whole save in love for you. She never cared for him in the least. It was you she loved."

I caught a second glimpse of his face as he turned it from her; a flash of triumph passed over it, breaking its frowns as lightning cleaves a thunder-cloud. My heart fell. The man loved our Jessie. With his strength and power of character, could she resist a passion that was evidently genuine?

Mrs. Dennison looked at him sharply; but his face was dark enough under her glance, and she went on, perhaps satisfied of his indifference.

"There is no time for hesitation, Lawrence. It will be impossible for me to keep my post here many days longer. The young lady scarcely endures me, Miss Hyde turns to marble when I enter her presence, and there is that imp of a girl crossing my path at every turn. I must leave the house—and that within a few days—unless you forgive me and find means of appeasing the young lady. That accomplished, I shall be more necessary to the household than ever. Everything will be on velvet then."

"Are you so sure of the old gentleman then?" inquired Lawrence, with a half sneer.

She smiled, and gave her head a disdainful movement.

"Am I sure of my life?"

He turned upon her with a look of scornful approbation.

"You are an extraordinary woman, widow."

"You have said as much, in a more complimentary fashion, before this," she answered.

"Perhaps," he answered, carelessly; "but we understand each other too well for fine speeches. Now, let us talk clearly. On your word of honor as a lady, all that you told me regarding Miss Lee before I took that rude departure, was false?"

"Yes; though you might use a softer word."

"And you believe she loves me yet in spite of my ungentlemanly withdrawal?"

"I am certain of it."

"You wish me to beg pardon and propose?"

"Wish!"

The woman locked her hands passionately, and turned her pale face upon him.

"Wish! You know I *cannot* wish it; but it is inevitable."

"In order to smooth your way with this grand old gentleman."

The woman shuddered visibly, and clasped her hands once more till the blood flew back under the almond-shaped nails, leaving them white as pearls.

"How indifferently you speak of a thing which drives me mad!"

"Indifferently? No. You have made your arrangements, and do me the honor to include mine with them."

"You are angry with me—hurt that I can decide on this marriage."

"No, neither angry nor hurt on that point."

She looked at him imploringly.

"Is this said in order to wound me?"

"It is said because I feel it."

"And you do not care that I bind myself for life to this man?"

"Care? Yes; why not?"

"I have thought it all over hundreds of times, when we talked of marriage those lovely nights on the beach. It was a sweet dream, worthy of two young people in their teens. We forgot everything,—the luxurious habits which had become second nature to us both,—the impossibility of making even love wild as ours suffice with everything else wanting. We were neither young enough nor foolish enough to carry that idea out."

"Or, even then, to entertain it seriously for a moment," said Lawrence, coldly breaking in upon her.

"Perhaps not," she said, mournfully. "It was a dream, and as such we discussed it; but the wish—oh! that was strong with us both!"

A cloud of disgustful feelings swept over the man's face, such as fill a refined heart while reviving some passion that has died out in contempt.

"Well, we will not dwell upon these moonlight dreams, but the future."

"Which will, at least, give us the right to see each other, and will secure between us one of the largest fortunes in the United States. If we cannot be all in all to each other, everything else necessary to happiness will be ours."

Again that expression swept over his face, but she was not looking at him; the thoughts in her mind were such as turn the eyes away from any human countenance. I could read all this plainly in their two faces.

"Let us pass over these things," he said, gravely regarding her. "You and I ought to know that human will seldom regulates events; let us try to act rightly and leave them with a higher power."

She looked at him in amazement an instant; then answered, with a self-sustained laugh,—

"Strong spirits make their own circumstances! We are making ours!"

"I know that is your opinion; but no matter, this is no place for discussion. Once again, let me understand. I am not disposed to criticise your motives for this—I will use the softer word—mystification; but now we must take clear ground. You again assure me that, in seeking Miss Lee, I shall not meet with a rebuff either from the lady or her father?"

"I am sure of it."

"Then I will go at once. But how can I explain?"

"Say that you were informed of her visit to Bosworth, and went off in a fit of jealousy."

"And if she asks of my informant?"

"Say that you saw her with your own eyes."

"Don't you think it would be as well to speak the truth for once?" said Lawrence, with a grave smile.

"That *is* the truth; you saw her returning home."

Lawrence sat down upon the rock, and, covering his forehead with one hand, seemed to reflect.

"You find this task an unpleasant one?" said the woman, touching his hand with her own.

He swept the hand across his forehead, scattering rich waves of hair over the temples.

"It is very painful," he said, bitterly; "but, thank heaven! the mischief was not of my own making. No matter; I will go now."

He turned to leave her. She grew pale and troubled.

"Where shall I see you after it is over?"

"Here, if you have the patience to wait."

"Yes," she answered, "I will wait; it will not be long. Oh, heavens! how little time it takes to separate us forever and ever!"

CHAPTER LVIII
AFTER THE PROPOSAL

He did not answer this; but his footsteps were still heard among the leaves that had fallen along the footpath, and she followed his retreating figure with eyes so full of anguish that I could not help pitying her.

When Lawrence could no longer be seen through the trees, she sunk to the rock, folded both her hands over her knees, and fairly moaned with pain. There was no weeping; but dry sobs broke from her lips like gushes of lava from a crater.

I remained still crouching at the foot of the hemlock, and sheltered completely by one of its wing-like branches. I was safe from detection, so steep was the descent that, without stepping to the very verge, there was no chance that any person could discover me. I had no compunction or question of honor to contend against. The contest going on in our household had become too serious for shrinking from anything that was not absolutely criminal in our defence. So bracing my foot against the ash, and sheltering my presence under the dusky hemlock, I too waited, determined not to move till that wretched woman left the ridge.

Mrs. Dennison was very restless, changing her position every moment, and starting up if the least sound reached her from the woods. As time wore on, she seemed to listen till the very breath upon her lips paused. The birds, that, as I have said before, were very tame on the ground, made her restive with their singing. She hated them, I am sure, for the sweet noise that prevented her hearing his footsteps.

I softly took out my watch and counted the time. He had not been absent more than fifteen minutes, when she sprang up, clenching both hands as if about to strike some one, and began to prowl up and down the path like a leopardess searching for her cubs. Now and then her voice broke through the foliage, and I could see her wringing her hands, or stamping her feet upon the dead leaves.

At last a footstep sounded from the woods; it was a man's step coming rapidly through the leaves. It had a hard sound, and I felt sure that the man was desperate. She evidently thought otherwise. Her arms fell helplessly down, and she crept back to the rock, white and still, but with her face turned away as if she would not let him see how anxious she was.

He came up to the rock from the woods, crossed the footpath with a single stride, and stood before her so stern, so bitterly incensed, that she shrunk away from his first glance, yet a flash of irresistible joy shot to the eyes with which she eagerly questioned him.

"Well!"

The lips from which this word came were almost smiling. Nature was strong in the woman, and, spite of her selfishness, she exulted over the ruin of her own plans.

"Well!" was the bitter response; "I have humiliated myself like a hound—proposed and am rejected."

The woman sprang toward him with both hands extended; but he stepped back, and she clasped them in an outgush of joy.

"Then it is over! Oh, heavens, how glad I am! this hour has been such torture! What would a whole life be? I should go mad. Let the property go—sweep the whole thing aside! How many poor people in the world are happy! In poverty or out of it, you and I will be all in all to each other!"

She was "pure womanly" then, notwithstanding her crafty nature and bad heart; there was something in her abandonment that made my blood thrill.

But Lawrence stepped back, and his face clouded.

She looked at him in amazement.

"What is this? Can wounded vanity affect you so much?"

"Wounded vanity, madam? Will you forever misunderstand me? How dare you consider me as an accomplice in your odious designs? If I have passed them by in silence, it was no sign that I approved or shared them."

These words were uttered with the force of terrible indignation. The woman to whom they were addressed stood confounded before the speaker, whom she had evidently, up to that moment, believed to be her lover.

"Lawrence—Lawrence! can this be real?" at last broke from her quivering lips.

While speaking, she laid her hand on his arm, but he pushed it off loathingly, as if a reptile had been creeping over him.

At this repulse, all the queenliness of her air fell away, and she seemed to shrink into a smaller person. The anguish so evident in her face appeared to touch his compassion; his features cleared themselves of stormy rage and hardened like marble. He took one of her hands in a firm grasp, and addressed her from that moment in a low, concentrated voice, that thrilled through one as nothing but true feeling can.

"Mrs. Dennison, this is the last time that you and I shall ever converse together."

The woman uttered a low cry, and seized his arm with her disengaged hand. He paused an instant, glanced calmly down at her hand, which clung trembling to his sleeve, and went on:—

"We met at a watering-place unknown to each other, people of the world, adventurers, if you will, and between us sprang up one of those flirtations which are so far removed from genuine affection that the two never exist together. We called it love—perhaps thought it so—for a brief time; for I confess to a sentiment regarding you which no ordinary person could have inspired."

The woman lifted her eyes at his softened voice, and with an expression that must have gone to his soul; never in my life had I seen so much gratitude in a glance.

"But this was not love!"

The white hand dropped away from his arm; he grasped the other tighter, as if to impress his words more forcibly on her.

"I never did love you, Mrs. Dennison. Such expressions as are admitted in society, without real meaning, I may have used, and you perhaps construed them into deeper significance than they possessed. I—"

Mrs. Dennison lifted her two hands with impatient deprecation.

"Enough, enough!" she said; "more words are useless; I comprehend you."

"And hold me blameless, I trust?"

"Blameless? Oh, yes!" There was bitter whiteness on her lips, and her eyes flashed fiercely.

The sneer relieved him. There had been something of compassion, even of regret, in his voice till then; but the curl of her lips drove all such feeling away.

"At least," he continued, promptly, "any blame that I might myself feel it just to assume, has been a thousand times overbalanced by your conduct, regarding one of the brightest and sweetest creatures that the sun ever shone upon."

The bitter sneer spread all over the woman's face, leaving it cold and white.

"You speak of Miss Lee?"

The voice in which she uttered these words was fearfully concentrated, and her agitation kept her still as a serpent before it springs.

"Yes, madam, I speak of the lady who once, at least, received me kindly; but who, yielding to your machinations, has just sent me from her presence forever, a rejected, desperate man, for I love her better than my own soul!"

A faint sound, sharp as a cry, deep as a grave, broke from the woman. Lawrence did not heed it, but turned away and left her, seemingly forgetful that it was a farewell. She followed him with her great, wild eyes, struggled with herself, and evidently strove to cry out; but her locked features refused to stir. The cold lips took a blue tinge, but gave no sound. She stood like Lot's wife, with all the vitality stricken from her limbs, listening to his footsteps as they died among the leaves. Then she uttered a low cry, sprang forward to follow him, and fell prone across the footpath.

CHAPTER LIX
A HEART-STORM ABATING

I seized the lithe stem of the ash, and lifted myself up the bank, prompted by an irresistible impulse of humanity. The woman lay upon the ground in a position so like death, that it frightened me. Her white face was half hidden by the turf. The folds of an India shawl were entangled around her, like the broken wings of some great tropical bird; one hand was clenched deep in a fleece of wood-moss, where its jewels flashed like rain-drops.

I attempted to raise her face from the turf, but it fell back like lead from my hands; the cheek which rested for a moment on my arm was cold as snow. There was no life perceptible; I looked around for water. A hundred feet below me it was rushing forward in abundance, but that was unattainable. The house was some distance, but there alone could I hope for succor.

I detested that woman in my soul; but some pure womanly feeling impelled me to keep her terrible condition a secret. I could not find it in my heart to expose her humiliation. So entering the hall unseen, I seized a pitcher of water that stood on the marble console and hurried back, carrying it so unsteadily that the ice-drops rained over my hands at every step. When I reached the rock, breathless with haste, the woman was gone, and but for the crushed grass, and a handful of moss torn up by the roots, there remained no proof of the scene I had just witnessed.

Where had she gone? Not to the house. I must have seen her had she taken that direction. Surely she had not followed Lawrence! I stepped to the rock, which gave me a view of the footpath and the precipitous bank. She was not in the woods, nor on the line of the ridge. Had she thrown herself down the bank, and so perished in the river below?

I seized the ash-tree, and, supporting myself by it, leaned over, searching the depths with a trembling dread of what I might find.

Half-way down the descent, I saw the gorgeous colors of a shawl shrouding some object crouched upon a point of rock that jutted out from the bank, and fairly overhung the black waters fifty feet below. In my fright, the ash-tree escaped my hold, and, starting back with a sharp recoil, made a great rustling among the leaves.

The woman sprang up, lifted her white face toward me, and for a moment stood poised over the water, with her garments fluttering in the wind so violently, that their very motion threatened to destroy her balance.

I threw out my arms, pleading with her to come back; but she sprang forward into a heavy covert of pine-boughs that swept the descent, and disappeared.

I waited some minutes, hoping that she would appear again; but everything was still; and after lingering about the rock some time, I returned to the house.

When I entered the hall, Mrs. Dennison was leaning over the balustrade of the square balcony, gazing down upon the scenery of the valley, to all appearance tranquil as a child.

She looked around with a furtive movement of the head as I set the pitcher upon the console, and then I saw that her face was still deathly pale. I said nothing to any one of what I had seen; it could have availed little; my report would only have met with denial and discredence. I felt sure of this and went to my room, there most earnestly praying God to direct me how to act.

Mrs. Dennison did not come down to dinner that afternoon, and Cora reported that she was in her room, suffering greatly. Something was the matter; the dear lady had been crying for hours together as if her heart were broken.

This was said in the presence of Mr. Lee, and I saw that he listened keenly.

"Do you know any reason for this distress?" he inquired of the pretty mulatto.

"No, sir; no reason in the world, without it is the high airs that old lady took with her. I was in the hall, sir, and saw it; since then my lady has been crying half the time."

We were at the table when Cora came down with this account of her mistress. Mr. Lee poured out a glass of champagne and placed it on the silver tray, upon which Jessie was arranging some delicacies from the desert.

"Ask your mistress to try and join us in the drawing-room this evening," he said, kindly; "solitude will only depress her."

Cora bowed and went away, but returned directly with a message from Mrs. Dennison. She had a severe headache, and was afraid that it would be impossible for her to meet the family that evening. To-morrow she trusted to be better.

Poor woman! she was true for once, though even her real illness was afterward turned to account.

After dinner, I found myself alone with Jessie. She had been a little excited after Lawrence left; but as the day wore on, her self-poise returned, and a sweet gravity settled upon her. As I sat by the window, she left the piano, from which a plaintive air had been stealing, and came to my side.

"Aunt Matty," she said, in her sweet, trustful way, "I have something to tell you. Mr. Lawrence has been here."

I did not express any knowledge of the fact, but looked at her, waiting for more. A faint flush rose to her cheek; but her eyes looked clearly into mine.

"You know what he came for?"

"I suppose so, Jessie; and that he went away disappointed."

"I think he loved me, Aunt Matty."

"And you?" I questioned, anxiously.

She shook her head and smiled wistfully.

"You remember the violets we took from the spring down in the meadow yonder? How fresh and hardy they looked! But we tore them up too roughly, and they never would take root again! They were young plants, you said, and hard usage withered them. The violets are all uprooted and dead here."

She pressed one hand to her heart, and, stooping down, kissed me to hide the sadness that crept into her eyes.

"And you do not regret it?" I whispered, drawing her close to me.

"As I regretted the death of our violets, with a little sadness for the perfume that is gone."

"And it is decided?"

"Nothing can change me. His intimacy with that woman gave her influence enough to poison his mind with thoughts that should never enter the heart of a true man. This was reason enough, if love ever reasoned; but his power is gone from me. I could never live with a man who had once been, even partially, controlled by a woman like that."

"Did you give him this reason?"

"As I have given it now."

"And he considers it as final?"

"Undoubtedly. I am glad he came—glad that he has spoken; for it sets me free—heart and soul."

I kissed her fervently, thanking God for this great deliverance.

CHAPTER LX
THE TWO LETTERS

That very evening young Bosworth came to the house, looking almost well, and *so* animated. It was not quite dark, and he saw me walking on the terrace; for I had need of air and solitude. He took my hand with the old cordiality, and would not let it go.

"Lawrence has been at our house," he said. "You know what has happened. She rejected him—she does not love him. This he told me with his own lips. It was generous; but he is a noble fellow. Indeed, I pity him."

I pressed the hand which grasped mine, and, reading the question that spoke from his face, told him to go in, that Jessie was in the drawing-room— and alone.

He listened for a moment to the music which came stealing through the windows, holding his breath in sweet suspense; then he lifted my hand to his lips and went into the house. The roses were bright on Jessie's cheek when I entered the drawing-room an hour after, and, for one night, we had something like a dream of happiness in that gloomy dwelling.

The next day Mrs. Dennison kept her word, and came out from her solitude. She must have suffered terribly; for I have never seen a face so altered. All her bloom was gone in one night; her eyes had grown larger with hidden anguish, which left dusky circles around them. Both Jessie and Mr. Lee were struck visibly by the change.

We were all in the library when she came in, grave, sad, and with that look of deep sorrow in her face. Mr. Lee was greatly disturbed and went forward to meet her, inquiring anxiously about her health.

The woman let her hand rest in his clasp a moment, and drew it away with a sorrowful glance from beneath her drooping lashes. Advancing up the room, she leaned one hand on a table for support, trembling visibly from agitation or weakness.

"Mr. Lee!"

The voice faltered with his name, and once more she lifted those mournful eyes to his.

"Are you ill, or has some trouble come upon you?" inquired Mr. Lee, greatly agitated.

"Yes, I am ill, and in deep trouble," she answered. "Oh! Mr. Lee, let me beseech you to protect my good name from the enemies that have assailed it!"

"Your good name, my dear madam? Who would dare say a word against any one sheltered under my roof?"

"I do not know—the whole thing bewilders me; but some great wrong has been done—some cruel slander said, or I should not be called upon to endure such insults as met me from that proud old lady—should not be outraged by letters like this!"

She took a letter from her pocket and gave it to Mr. Lee, watching him as he read it.

The letter was a brief one; but Mr. Lee was a long time in reading it. His eyes went back upon every line, and the fire burned hotly in them when he came to an end. There was something very startling in the changes of his face as he glanced from the paper to Jessie and from her to me. Never have I seen a look so terribly stern.

"Where did you get this letter?" he inquired, crushing the paper in his hand.

"It came to me by the mail; you will see by the post-mark," was the reply.

He glanced at the post-mark, which was that of the nearest town; then, striding up to his daughter, held the open letter before her eyes.

Jessie read it bewildered; but at last her features settled into a look of astonishment.

"Is this your writing, Miss Lee?"

"No," she answered, but in a hesitating way. "No, no; I never wrote that!"

She had read a portion of the letter, when this emphatic denial broke from her lips.

"Yet a disinterested person would swear that it was your handwriting, Jessie Lee."

The color flashed into Jessie's cheek; but she constrained herself, answering calmly,—

"I did not write it, father."

Mr. Lee searched her through and through with his stern glances; then, coldly taking the letter from her hand, he held it toward me.

"Say, madam, you should be acquainted with that young lady's handwriting; is this hers?"

I took the letter and read it. The handwriting was certainly like Jessie's, but with an attempt to disguise. The contents convinced me that she never wrote it. They ran thus:—

> "Madam: You have wrought mischief enough in the family of an honorable man to be content without bringing disgrace upon your own name. It should be enough that you have broken the life of as good a woman as ever lived; that you have alienated a father from his only child, and separated Mr. Lee from his best friends. If you have still any regard for your own reputation, or for the welfare of those who have never wronged you, leave this house.
>
> "A Friend."

"No," I answered, "Jessie did not write this; the thing is impossible!"

"I make no charges—heaven forbid!" said Mrs. Dennison; "but it is enough that a letter like that could have been written to me while under your roof, sir. Self-respect forbids that I should remain here another day. I have sent to the town for a carriage."

"You cannot intend it!" exclaimed Mr. Lee. "Not till this thing has been thoroughly explained and atoned for, must you leave a house that has been honored by your presence. Jessie Lee, have you nothing to say?"

"Father, what can I say?"

"Nothing, my dear Miss Lee; I ask nothing, and accuse no one further than is necessary to my own exculpation," said Mrs. Dennison, in a grieved voice. "But I have been cruelly assailed. One word more, Mr. Lee, and I am ready to go. Forgive me if I speak on a subject painful to us all; but the death of your wife has been alluded to in that infamous paper—alluded to in connection with myself. When Mrs. Lee was taken ill, she had in her hand a letter, which only left her hold in the last moment. It was open. You may remember I picked it up from the floor, folded it, and gave it into your own hands. Of course, I did not read the letter, and am, to this day, ignorant of its contents; but I did glance at the handwriting, and it was like this."

I felt myself growing cold; the faces before me swam in mist. Had not Lottie said that the envelope was directed in Jessie's handwriting? Had I not myself recognized the fact?

Mrs. Dennison spoke again:—

"Another thing has haunted me since that mournful day. As I bent over the dying angel, she whispered three words in my ear; they were: 'Read the letter.' Sir, there is a connection between this and the letter which your wife held in her grasp when she died. I entreat, nay, I demand, that you tell me what the connection is."

"The letter!" said Mr. Lee, with a start. "She did hold a paper, and you gave it to me, I remember. It is here; I had no heart to read it." Thrusting a hand beneath his vest, he drew forth a small pocket-book, and took from it the paper which I remembered so well. It was crushed and had been hastily folded; but even from the distance I could see that the handwriting was that of the note I had just read.

In Mr. Lee's eyes alone you saw the agony of astonishment that possessed him. At last he turned his gaze from the letter and fixed it on Jessie. She was greatly disturbed—the very sight of the paper in her father's hand was enough for this; but she met his glance with a mournful look. There was neither terror nor surprise in it; simply deep sorrow, such as springs from a renewal of painful memories.

He walked toward her with the paper in his hand, touched it with his finger, and tried to speak, but could not—the anguish that locked his features chained his voice also. Jessie was frightened and sprang up.

"Father, father! what is the matter? What have I done?"

He laid his hand heavily on the paper, and bent his white face toward her.

"Jessie Lee, you have slandered the father that loved you better than his own life. You have killed your mother!"

CHAPTER LXI
THE DEPARTING GUEST

They were gone, and a gloom like that of the grave fell on everything in that room. While Jessie Lee lay cold and insensible on my bosom, smitten to the heart by her father's denunciation, Mrs. Dennison took the letter from Mr. Lee and read it from end to end. After that she uttered some words which I did not understand—for the cold head upon my bosom had frozen up my faculties—and went her way from the room, and oh! thank my God! from our presence, I prayed inly, forever and ever.

I do not know when or how Mr. Lee left the room, but I was alone with Jessie, and she dead, for the moment, as if in her winding-sheet.

I had no strength to lift her, or remove her from the room, but I laid her gently on the carpet, and, taking the crimson pillows from a couch, rested her head upon them. All this had been done with great quietness; no unusually loud word had been spoken during that terrible scene—not a soul in the house, except us four, knew that anything had happened.

Striving to subdue my agitation, I went up-stairs in search of restoratives. The crystal flasks in poor Mrs. Lee's chamber had never been emptied of their contents, so I went there hoping to find something that would bring the stricken girl out of her deathly sleep.

The room was dim, but filled with the breath of flowers, as it had been in its owner's life-time. Every article of furniture was in its old place. The white bed gleamed out from the twilight of the apartment like a snow-bank; the soft lace curtains covered the windows, flowing down beneath the silken over-curtains like ripples of falling sleet. Everything was so natural, so almost holy in its stillness, that even in the terrible anxiety that filled my soul, I felt like falling down by the bed and praying that sainted one to help me save her child.

A wild petition did spring to my lips; but it was a time for action; so, snatching a flask from the dressing-table, I was turning to leave the room, when Lottie arose from a stool, at the foot of Mrs. Lee's easy-chair, and stood before me like a ghost.

"What are you doing here, Miss Hyde?" she said, in a whisper. "She does not like people to come to her room."

I held up the flask and was going on; but she seized it between both hands.

"It is for Miss Jessie—for her child—she is ill."

The girl's hands dropped.

"Take it—take it," she said, and followed me from the room.

When Lottie saw her young mistress lying so still and marble-like on the floor, a cry of anguish broke from her.

"Oh! my poor, poor lady! how much she looks like her—how much she looks like her!"

Jessie came to at last: that is, she breathed again, and her eyes opened; but this was all. She had no strength, and all the rich, young life that made her so beautiful had left her frame.

While she lay thus but half conscious, swift footsteps passed through the hall, a spasm swept over that pale face, and Jessie made a struggle to move and get away from the hateful sound. It was but a faint motion, and she was still again. Then came a low smothered sound of conversation near the door, and all was silent after that.

I had hoped that Mr. Lee would come back and help me save his child from the depths of her trouble; but he did not appear, and I dared not send for him.

"Lottie," I said, at last, "will you help me? Can you and I carry her up to her room, or must I call one of the people?"

"You and I—no one else."

We lifted Jessie from the floor, and carried her up-stairs, meeting no one.

As we came to the passage which led to Mrs. Lee's chamber, Lottie paused and drew a heavy breath; then looking down on that still face, she turned toward the sacred chamber.

I did not protest. That room seemed the most natural place for Mrs. Lee's daughter when driven forth from her father's heart.

Poor Jessie! We laid her down on her mother's bed, and there she rested for many a long day and night—if rest was ever known to a nervous fever like that which fell upon her from the hour of her father's wrath.

While Jessie lay on the bed with her eyes wide open, and shudders of distress passing over her, Lottie drew me to another part of the room, and asked, in a troubled voice, what had made her young lady so ill.

I had no other friend in whom it was possible to confide. Lottie, with all her eccentricities, was true as steel, but I did not myself know the entire cause of all this disturbance, and could not speak of it with anything like certainty, so I only answered her, as quietly as I could, that Mrs. Dennison was going away.

A quick light flashed into Lottie's eyes. She looked from side to side, as if wondering what direction to take. Her sharp intellect almost caught the truth.

"But Miss Jessie isn't fretting so about that. There's something else. Oh, Miss Hyde! do tell me what it is!"

"I cannot tell you, Lottie, what I do not understand myself."

"And you won't listen. High notions will be the death of you yet. Oh, how I hate airs! Now, if it had been me, I'd have known all about it, by hook or by crook, but it's of no use talking. Are you sure Babylon is going; if she is, her last trump has been played, and she thinks she's won High, Low, Game, and a Jack turned up. Oh, if I only had time to make this all out, but it's hop, skip, and a jump; here they jump right into the dark."

"What do you mean, Lottie?"

"Oh, nothing particular. You keep your secrets, and I'll keep mine. That's fair."

As Lottie spoke, the door of our room was open, and this gave us a view of the hall, at the other end of which was Mrs. Dennison's chamber. The door of that room also was wide open, and we saw the widow talking earnestly with her mulatto maid, who had drawn a couple of trunks from the closet, and was now emptying a wardrobe in what seemed to be angry haste. With three or four dresses flung over her arm, she turned fiercely upon her mistress, and seemed to be upbraiding her.

Mrs. Dennison answered with an imperative gesture, at which Cora tossed her head, like a racer under curb, and flung the dresses in a heap upon the bed, stamping angrily on the floor as Mrs. Dennison left the room and turned down the staircase which led to the library.

"By gracious! they are packing up, sure enough!" exclaimed Lottie, "and I standing here like a frightened goose. Take care of Miss Jessie, ma'am. I couldn't help you now—no, not if she were dying. Babylon is playing that last trump this minute."

Lottie left me instantly, and I saw her draw close to Cora, with whom she had become very intimate during the last few weeks.

"Do tell me what all this fuss is about," I heard her say. "Miss Jessie is off in hysterics, and your madam looks like a thunder-gust—quarrelling, I should surmise."

"Quarrelling? I should think so," answered the mulatto. "Here she comes all in a storm, and orders me to get ready in an hour, as if I had a dozen hands—no consideration—no feeling. In an hour, and all her dresses to fold! It's too bad! I believe she thinks I'm her slave yet; but I'll show her—I will! Just look at the pile of dresses on the bed, all to fold and pack in an hour."

"I'll help you," answered Lottie, in her stolid fashion, which I noticed she had always used with Cora, who seemed to hold her in profound contempt. "I can fold dresses first-rate."

"Oh! she would never trust you with them; but I'll tell you what will help just as well; there is her writing-table, with the drawer running over, and the top loaded with books; just pack that heap of things away in the smallest trunk."

"Well, I'll do that, if you'd rather," said Lottie, with apparent reluctance; "but not knowing how to read, you see I might get the wrong things."

"No, everything belongs to her; just empty the drawer, and pack them nicely away."

"But you're not really going?" inquired Lottie.

"In an hour."

I saw Lottie move toward the table, and begin to gather up books and papers with great indifference; but when Cora's back was turned, she grew vigilant as a fox, and seemed to be searching for some particular object with breathless anxiety. I saw her take a book, bound in purple leather, from a back part of the drawer, examine it closely, and thrust it back again as Cora turned toward her, when she became active in tying up other parcels, and packing them away.

All at once Cora seemed to have some doubt regarding the dress she was to leave out for travelling.

"Just like her, not to tell me. Goes off on her own hook in everything without a word, as if I was of no account when she wants to move. Which way did she go?"

"Toward the library," said Lottie; "gone to say good-bye to Mr. Lee, I suppose. You can hear him tramp, tramp, tramp, up and down the floor."

"Tramp or no tramp, I'll know what she wants," said Cora, who was evidently enraged at this sudden movement.

"I'll be back in a minute."

Away Cora darted along the hall, and down the stairs. Just as quickly Lottie seized upon the purple book, flung her apron over it, and ran into her own room, slamming the door in my face. After a moment's absence, she flitted back again, with both hands under her apron, as she had come forth.

"Don't sit there; don't seem to be looking after me. That yellow witch will think something is going on if you do," she said, in a hurried whisper, darting in at the door, and out again.

"But what are you taking away, Lottie?"

"Nothing—not a thing. I'm taking it back again; don't you see?"

Back she went, and directly after I heard her talking with the mulatto girl in the most friendly manner possible.

In half an hour I heard Mrs. Dennison sweep past the door, and knew that she was finding fault with Cora, because everything was not in readiness. The girl answered her sharply, and some angry words passed, such as might have been tolerated in equals, but which sounded strangely out of place between mistress and servant. I knew that this lady was going in anger from our house, but had no desire to see her before she went; for since the scene which had flung poor Jessie almost insensible on that bed, my dislike of the woman had deepened into absolute horror.

In a little more than an hour I heard the sound of heavy trunks being dragged through the hall, and the roll of a carriage along the lower terrace. Then I could distinguish the tread of Mr. Lee, words spoken in a low tone, and a rustle of garments moving down-stairs.

Then all was still for a moment. Lottie stood in the hall, listening intently; I could not breathe, my heart so longed for the sound of that woman's sure departure.

It came at last. I heard the carriage-wheels and the tramp of hoofs bearing her away. I saw Lottie fling up her arms in silent thankfulness. Jessie, too, unlocked her hands, and turned her eyes upon me, drawing a deep, deep breath, as if something had cleared the atmosphere that weighed her down.

CHAPTER LXII
WHOLLY DESERTED

That night I received a message from Mr. Lee, and went to him in the breakfast-room. The passions that had locked his features so fearfully still kept their hold. He was not a man to be reasoned with, or touched by appeal in that state; the ice must melt, and the storm burst, before human sympathies could reach him.

I saw this, and stood silent in his presence—silent, but with a sort of solemn courage. The worst had come, and with that thought strength always lies.

"Miss Hyde," he said, in a voice of ice, "to-morrow morning I leave this house, and in a week this country, possibly forever. I do not stop to ask how far you are to blame for the evil developed in the person who was once my child; but she loves you, and I will not deprive her of any comfort. She will be left in full possession of this place, with everything that a woman can desire. The law gives her this and more. So long as she wishes it, stay with her; for myself, I go alone, wifeless and childless."

I was about to speak, for there was a touch of regretful feeling in his voice; but he motioned me to keep silent and went on:—

"Let there be no explanation to the neighbors or servants. What has passed must rest with the four persons who parted in that library; for this secrecy I trust to you."

I bent my head and tried to speak, but could not. He looked searchingly into my face, and his stern eyes softened a little.

I went up to him, reaching forth my trembling hands; the ache of pain broke away from my heart in a flood of tears. What I said, even a word I cannot recollect; but I have the remembrance of a frail woman standing before that haughty man, with her hands clasped and tears falling down her face like rain. She was eloquent, I know; for the man's face changed gradually, and his eyes grew misty as they looked into hers. But just as an outgush of hope thrilled her heart, a name dropped from her lips—a name that she loathed, and uttered bitterly, no doubt; then all the gentle light left his face, and he was iron again. So the woman went away wounded to the soul, and with limbs that almost refused to support her. She sat up all night watching with the sick girl, while her own heart scarcely beat beneath its load of dull pain.

At daylight, this unhappy creature heard faint noises in the house; but she did not move. Then came the sound of wheels upon the terrace-road; still she sat motionless. You might have shot her through the heart, and she would not have lifted a hand to put back the threatened death.

The sound of those carriage-wheels moving away through the pine grove aroused the beautiful invalid. She started up from her pillow, and throwing out both arms toward the window, cried out,—

"Father, oh, my father!"

No one answered. Her father was gone.

We were alone now—I had no explanations to make. All the family knew that Mrs. Dennison had gone away, and all except Lottie had been informed that Mr. Lee had started on a long tour in Europe. She, good, noble girl, had been so busy caring for Jessie, that the news only reached her after Mr. Lee had been gone some hours. Then she seemed greatly disturbed, and questioned me on the subject in her usual blunt, searching way.

My conversation with Lottie passed in her own room, and I cautioned her against speaking of Mr. Lee in his daughter's presence, telling her truly that no one had an idea how ill her mistress was except ourselves.

There was something more than curiosity on the young girl's mind. I am sure of that, for she was like a wild creature, and seemed frantic to know which way Mr. Lee had gone. But no one could tell her. The coachman saw him take the train for New York, that was all he knew about it; if she wanted to find out, it was not the road Mrs. Dennison had taken. She went the other way—no disputing that. He had taken pains to inquire.

That night, notwithstanding Jessie's illness was becoming more threatening each hour, Lottie, usually so kind-hearted, called me from the room to inquire if she could be spared for a day or two, and if I could lend her ten dollars. It was a great sum, she knew, but she'd pay it back faithfully; yes, if she had to sell the brooch and ear-rings that Miss Jessie gave her out of the dear lady's things.

Shall I own it? This hard-heartedness in Lottie gave me something like hope—the girl was sharp and courageous. She had thoughts which no one could fathom, and which she was evidently hoarding for the good of her benefactors. Still, I was left, in some degree, her guardian. Should I permit her to go off on some wild adventure, only from a forlorn hope that it might benefit her young mistress?

The strange girl did not put me to the test; but judging from my hesitation that I was about to refuse her the money, flew off, saying it was no matter, maybe she should change her mind after all.

The next morning, when I inquired for Lottie, she was gone.

Three days after she came back, looking very much depressed and so cross, except in the sick-room, that all the servants in the house were complaining of her temper.

She gave no explanation of her absence, except that, directly after her return, she gave me a New York paper—one that seldom reached our household—in which Mr. Lee's name was announced among the list of passengers in a steamer that had sailed the day after he left home.

All this time Jessie had been delirious, and knew nothing of the trouble that had swept half our household away. It was a mercy. Had she comprehended everything as I did, that delicate organism, so unused to suffering of any kind, must have given way with more lamentable consequences; as it was, the young life was scarcely kept afire in her bosom.

In her delirium, Jessie was always wandering off into the past, and her pure heart broke forth in a thousand sweet fancies, in which her father and mother were always the moving spirits. Strange enough, she never once mentioned Lawrence or Mrs. Dennison, even in her wildest moments; but once, when Lottie came into the chamber, holding a bottle of perfume such as Mrs. Dennison always used, the dear girl fell back on her pillow and fainted quite away.

The moment news of Jessie's illness got abroad in the neighborhood, old Mrs. Bosworth came to see us—the dear, old motherly lady—how gentle and kind she was! There seemed to be a charm in that plump hand, with the old-fashioned diamond-rings lighting up its whiteness; for when it had rested awhile on Jessie's forehead, the dear girl would drop into a soft slumber, and awake with less tremulous nerves and a clearer brain.

At last the fever burned itself out, and Jessie awoke to a consciousness of actual life. She was too weak for any powerful emotion; and when we were at last forced to admit that her father had gone, and that we had no means of communicating with him, she only heaved a feeble sigh, and, turning her head, lay, weeping softly, on her pillow, till the very exhaustion left her calmed.

Slowly, but with a steady progress, Jessie gained her strength; and, as her mother had rested among the crimson cushions of that couch, sat one day, when Mrs. Bosworth came to spend the morning with us. We had braided her hair for the first time that morning, and prisoned its coils in a crimson net, with drops of gold in the web, and flashes of gold in the tassels. The reflection of its rich Magenta tints gave a faint color to her cheeks; her white morning dress, with its profusion of Valenciennes lace about the sleeves and bosom, lost its chilly look under a rich India shawl that we had folded over it. Indeed, altogether, the dear child looked so like herself, that we were rejoicing over her when the old lady came in.

They had become very good friends during those sick-hours—that dear old duchess and our Jessie. So when the lady came in, rustling across the floor like a rich autumn, our invalid smiled almost for the first time since her illness, and held out her hand.

I was in the habit of leaving Mrs. Bosworth and Jessie to themselves, and was stealing from the room, when the old lady called me back.

"Come, Miss Hyde," she said, "help me to gain a favor of our child. She is looking so well, her hand feels so cool; do you think a little company would harm her?"

Jessie colored faintly and lifted her eyes to the old lady's face.

"He has been here every day—don't start, dear! What was more natural than that an old lady like me should want the care of a man strong enough to help her if her staff gives way? Nothing has been done that could wound you; but he is very anxious—and now that you are so well, and looking so pretty, what if we let him come up? Eh, Miss Hyde?"

Before I could answer, Lottie had left the room; with a chuckle and a leap she cleared the staircase, and, finding young Bosworth in the square balcony, presented Miss Hyde's compliments, and desired him to walk up to the tower-chamber.

I was going down to perform the same ceremony, in a different way, when Lottie met me on the stairs. I stopped on the landing to let the young gentleman pass; Lottie followed, opened the door, closed it softly, and came back.

"What's the use of shuffling about in this way?" she said. "She wants him to go up, and he wants to go. When people want a good slide down hill, what's the use of putting jumpers in the way? I'm getting sick of your notions, Miss Hyde. Wouldn't give a copper for delicacy; and as for honor, see what it's done. Don't talk to me!"

With a sort of Jim-Crow step, Lottie whirled about on the landing, gave a leap down three stairs at a time, and went off somewhat in her former style.

I was glad to see a dash of the old spirit coming back to the strange creature; but a moment after I looked out and saw her crying like a child, behind one of the large garden vases. After all, there was no real cheerfulness about Lottie. Spasmodic flashes of her nature would break out, but at heart she mourned continually.

CHAPTER LXIII
OLD-FASHIONED POLITENESS

When I entered Jessie's room, the old lady was busy arranging some flowers, which they had brought, in a vase near the window. She had put on her gold spectacles, and was examining the tints so carefully, that there was no room for attention anywhere else.

Bosworth was sitting near Jessie, looking so pleased at being permitted to her presence, that I could not help a throb of sympathetic pleasure. He had, I am sure, been holding Jessie's hand; for as I came in, she withdrew it with a hasty movement, and its delicate whiteness was flushed, as if warm lips had touched it. No wonder the young man was happy! Jessie Lee would never have permitted that bearded mouth to approach her hand unless a true heart had beaten quicker to the touch. Lawrence had gained no favor like that in the time of his greatest power.

The old duchess was looking through her spectacles just as I came in; but not exactly at the flowers, or that bland little smile would never have made her mouth look so young, or that demure blush have settled on her soft cheek. Dear old lady! All those years, while they taught her limbs the uses of a staff, had left her heart fresh and modest as a girl's. How transparent was the gentle artifice with which she beguiled me out of the room, to search for some purple heliotrope that might soften the tints of her bouquet!

As Jessie grew better, these visits were repeated. Young Bosworth seldom failed to come with his grandmother; and after a little the old lady would often stay behind, contenting herself with some message, or a present of fruit and flowers. Then no excuse became necessary, except that Jessie required a stronger arm than mine to support her first walks in the garden; and after that the young man seemed more at home in our house than he could have been in the fine old mansion behind the hill.

Spite of the painful circumstances that had left us so lonely, we were beginning to feel the strength of our lives slowly returning. True, there was an undercurrent of deep, deep trouble all the time sweeping through an existence that seemed so bright to others.

The cruel absence of Mr. Lee, his determined silence, always lay heavily upon us; but it was not as if we had deserved the stern displeasure which had driven him away; and if we mourned over this great sorrow, there was some relief in the oppression that Mrs. Dennison's departure had taken away.

Of this woman we heard nothing, and her name was seldom mentioned, even by Lottie. We all shrunk in terror from the reminiscences connected with her. Still our lives were more endurable than they had been for many a month; and but for the aching pain which sprung out of that scene in the library, we might have been tranquil,—sad with the great loss which had fallen upon the house, but hopeful for the future.

But with that gentle woman, lying in her last sleep down in the valley, and the power of our house gone from us, we could only wait and hope that God, in his infinite justice, would yet unfold the truth to Mr. Lee, and give him back to his home.

Sometimes Jessie and I would talk over these matters when quite alone in her room; but the whole chain of events was too inexplicable and full of pain for frequent mention. Jessie hardly yet comprehended the enormity of the charge brought against her. What was in the letter which her dying mother had grasped so tightly to the last moment? Who had written it? Was the handwriting like hers—did I think? Her head had been so dizzy that she could not make out a line of it.

These were the questions she would now and then put to me. I told her what the anonymous letter to Mrs. Dennison contained, but I had no heart to enlighten her with regard to my conjectures about the other. Nor could I for one moment guess what its import might have been, except from Mr. Lee's words, and the terrible effect it had produced upon him. Never for an instant did I doubt Jessie's innocence in the matter, whatever it might prove. She was truth itself.

Sometimes I wondered if Lottie had not written those fatal missives. The girl was bright and sharp as steel. She was not without education; and I remembered, in confirmation of these doubts, that of late I had often found her writing something which she endeavored to conceal. Had she not, in her practice, copied Jessie's handwriting, and taken this method of warning her mistress? Nothing was more natural. The girl might thus unconsciously have cast suspicion on her young lady.

That Lottie was capable of writing the letters, I had no doubt—not with malice, but from an ardent desire to drive the woman who had wounded us so deeply from the house. With her crude ideas, and intense devotion to us all, she might have settled on this method of ridding the house of its torment.

I questioned Lottie on this subject, so far as I could venture, without informing her of what had passed in the library, of which she was entirely ignorant; but she declared that she knew nothing of the letter, which had been given to her mistress, till it was placed in her own hands by the man who brought our mails from the town. As for Mrs. Dennison, she would as soon touch a copperhead as write a word to that she-Babylon.

All this might be true. At any rate, Lottie looked truthful when she said it; but in her sayings and doings, the girl was not altogether as clear as crystal, and, spite of her protestations, I had some doubt left.

No person except Jessie and myself, either in the house or neighborhood, knew the reason of Mr. Lee's sudden departure. It was understood that, broken down by the death of his wife, he had sought distraction from grief in travelling. So the secret, growing more and more bitter every day—for we received no letters—rested between us two. As the time wore on, we became miserably anxious.

Had Mr. Lee utterly abandoned his daughter? Would he never return to his home and prove how true and loving she had always been? His cruel anger had thrown her almost upon a bed of death, yet he could go from his home without a word of inquiry or comfort.

Jessie was a proud girl, as I have said more than once, and as young Lawrence had good reason to know; but all her haughty self-esteem gave way where her father was concerned. She never blamed him, nor ceased to pine for his presence. What it was that had separated them she could not understand; but that her father was unjust or wrong, never entered her mind for an instant.

As for me—but what right had I in the matter? The right of anxiety such as eats all happiness out of a human life—the hungry feeling of a beggar that dares not ask for food.

I think we should have gone insane—Jessie and I—if this terrible anxiety had been without its relief; but, as days and weeks passed, bringing no letter, no message, we sunk gradually into a state of despair, not the less wearying that it was silent.

Thus six months crept by. The duties of life went on—the household routine met with no obstruction. It was wonderful how little change appeared around us. Yet the tower-chamber was empty, and *he* was gone,—we, two lonely women, lived on, to all appearance, the same; but oh! how changed at heart!

CHAPTER LXIV
NEWS FROM ABROAD

We heard of Mr. Lee once or twice through the public journals, now travelling in the Holy Land, again in the heart of Russia, but no letters came. We wrote to him more than once, but directed at random, and our letters probably never reached him.

One day, when Lottie was in the room, I took up a New York journal, and read this paragraph from a Paris correspondent, —

> "A wedding is expected to take place within the month, at the American Legation in Paris. Mr. Lee, a wealthy landholder of Pennsylvania, is to be married to Mrs. Dennison, a beautiful and fashionable widow, who is said to have been the intimate friend of his first wife."

I read this paragraph through. My face must have betrayed the deathly feeling that came over me, for Lottie came behind my chair, read a few words over my shoulder, and snatched the paper from my hand with a suddenness that tore it almost in two.

"What is it," inquired Jessie, started by this action—"any—anything about *him*?"

"About him? I should think so. Sin, iniquity, and pestilence. Read it, Miss Jessie, I can't; it seems as if a snake were crawling over it."

Jessie took the paper, read it, and fainted in her chair.

Lottie did not seem to regard the condition of her young mistress, but ran out of the room, clenching her hand fiercely, as if she longed for bitter contest with some one.

These paroxysms of feeling had been very unusual with her of late; for in the quiet of our mournful lives, she had been left a good deal to her loneliness in the tower, where she still kept guard over Mrs. Lee's chamber.

Sometimes she reverted to the past, and would ask anxiously if I knew where Babylon was spreading her plumes. But I had no means of informing her, being in profound ignorance of that lady's movements from the time she left our house.

This would satisfy Lottie; but I remarked that she had taken a sudden and deep interest in her geographical studies, for I seldom went to her room without finding an atlas open upon the table, and a gazetteer close by, which she seemed to have been diligently studying.

I had thought but little of these things at the time; but they came back to me with force on the very next day, when Lottie came to me in the garden, and inquired anxiously if Miss Jessie wasn't just breaking her heart over that paragraph in the newspaper.

I answered that Miss Lee was very sad and unhappy, certainly.

"I knew it—I was sure of it," cried the girl, with quick tears in her eyes. "It will kill her—she will pine away like her mother. You know she will, Miss Hyde."

"I'm afraid so, Lottie."

"Afraid, and stand by doing nothing but bathe her head with cologne, and cry over her. That isn't the way to cure all this, Miss Hyde."

"But what else can I do, Lottie?"

"You? Nothing."

She went off to a flower-bed, tore some mignonette up by the roots, tossed it from her, and came back again.

"Miss Hyde, I am tired to death of all this. The house isn't fit to live in since my dear, sweet lady was taken from it. There's been nothing but sickness, and quarrelling, and going away since, and I've about made up my mind to go away too. I can't stand it, and I won't, so there!"

"Why, Lottie," I cried, lost in astonishment, "what does this mean?"

"It means that I'm tired of doing nothing—of being slighted, and made of no account. It means that I want to see the world, and know a thing or two about life. You and Miss Jessie just mope about like sick kittens; and as for the servants—well, I don't belong in that crew, anyhow—but they are getting worse and worse. The long and the short of it all is, I have made up my mind to go away right off, and do something worth while. I only wish you would ask Miss Jessie to settle up with me now, right on the nail, for I'm in an awful hurry to get off."

Settle up! I should have been less astonished if the house-dog had made a sudden claim for wages. Lottie had always been considered as a child of the establishment, to be cared for and petted beyond all idea of payment.

She had never seemed to care for money, nor know how to use it. But while enjoying her life in a state of luxurious ease, almost equalling that of her young mistress, she descended upon us with a rough demand for wages—wages from the time she entered the house, a mere child, up to that very day—no inconsiderable sum, according to her own estimate.

This singular outbreak of cupidity astonished me, and half indignantly I expostulated with the girl. But though her cheeks blazed with seeming shame, and her eyes sunk under mine, she persisted in this grave demand. All that she had received, her dear, dear mistress had given out and out—that had nothing to do with wages; there was her bill—four hundred dollars—and she wanted it in gold—hard gold, nothing else.

I went to Jessie with the bill. She did not seem to heed the amount, but was distressed at the idea of parting with her mother's faithful attendant. Hoping that something had gone wrong, and that this was a sudden impulse, she sent for Lottie, in order to expostulate with her; for it seemed like turning a bird, which had become used to its cage, loose upon the world, if we allowed the girl to have her way.

Lottie came in, looking dogged and shy; Jessie held out her hand, with a piteous smile, for she was thinking of her mother.

"Lottie, what have we done that you wish to leave us?"

"Nothing on earth, Miss Jess. I ain't mad at you, nor any one; but yet I want to go down to York and get a place. It's lonesome here."

Jessie's eyes filled with tears. It was indeed very lonesome.

"And will you leave us for that, Lottie?"

The girl was troubled; her color came and went. She was about to burst into tears—but answered still,—

"It's lonesome, and I want to go. Why can't you let me, without all this? I ain't made of cast-iron, nor yet of brass. Please give me my money and let me go."

"But you are so helpless. What will become of you in a great city?" pleaded Jessie.

Lottie came up to her and knelt in her old way.

"Let me go, Miss Jessie, and don't try to stop me, for it'll be of no use, only to make my heart ache worse than it does now. Don't be afraid about me! If God shows the birds their way through the woods, He won't let me get lost."

"Poor Lottie!" said the young mistress, looking kindly on the girl through her tears, "I would rather give up anything than you."

Lottie seized her hand, pressing her lips upon it.

"Don't, don't!" she pleaded. "You would not say a word if you only—"

"Only what, girl?"

"Nothing, nothing. I must go, that is the long and the short of it."

Lottie shook off her tears as a dog scatters the rain from his coat, and, starting up, assumed her rude manner.

"I will not keep you against your will, my poor girl," said Jessie, sadly; "but how can you find the way?"

"Easy enough, Miss. I've been studying geography and the maps, these last three months, besides reading about everything."

"And have you got any idea of a place?"

"Plenty, Miss. I shall be settled the first week. Only give me my wages, and don't try to persuade me again what my mind is made up to."

"Well, Lottie, you shall have the money. I am sure that can never repay all you have done for my mother!"

"Don't, don't, Miss Jessie! I want to make my heart like a grinding mill-stone, and you won't let me. Now don't!"

"Well, I will not distress you," replied Jessie, gently; "but remember, Lottie, when you get tired of this new life, or have spent your money, come back to your old home. No person shall fill your place."

"Oh! Miss Jess, Miss Jess! can't you stop?" cried the wild creature, absolutely flinging up her arms in desperation.

Jessie looked at her thoughtfully a moment; then, unlocking her parlor safe, counted out the gold Lottie had demanded.

"Be careful that the money does not get you into trouble, Lottie," I said, really anxious about the young thing.

Lottie took the gold in her apron, and her tears dropped over it as she turned away. She really seemed heart-broken.

"If anything should happen," said Jessie, regarding her troubles with tenderness,—"if you should lose it, or fall into want, and still not wish to come back, write to me and I will send you more."

"Would you?—would you?" cried Lottie, with quick animation; "then, oh! Miss Jess! make it six hundred now. I never, never shall want money so much again in my life."

"Six hundred, Lottie?"

"Yes, six! I tried and tried to cipher it out that much; but it wouldn't multiply or add up to the mark; but if you would now—"

She paused and looked wistfully at the gold through her tears.

Jessie looked at me for encouragement. Dear girl! she had less idea of the value of money than Lottie herself.

"She was so kind to *her*!" whispered the mistress, drawing close to me.

"Or if you'd just lend it to me," pleaded Lottie. "Now, Miss Hyde, don't go to killing the white dove that I see spreading its wings in her bosom this very minute; I wouldn't turn against you, nor tell anything, you know that."

"I will give her the money—the good child; how could it be in my heart to refuse her?" said Jessie.

Lottie went to the open safe and began to count out the other twenty pieces of gold, which she jingled one by one against their companions in her apron. Her breath came quickly; and when she had done she came toward us eagerly, gathering the apron in her hand, and hugging it with the gold to her bosom.

"Oh! I'm ready to jump out of my skin with joy and thankfulness!" she exclaimed. "Good-bye, young mistress—good-bye, Miss Hyde, I'm so sorry that I ever twitted you about writing poetry, and some other things I won't mention."

Lottie went out of the room in great excitement, and left us astonished and very anxious. We talked the matter over without result. If the girl was determined to go, we had not a shadow of power to prevent it, and we could not yet make up our minds that she was absolutely wrong. There was something in the bottom of her heart that we were unable to fathom.

But we determined that night to make another attempt to detain the strange girl; if that proved impossible, to send a trusty person to protect her on her way to New York and bring back news of her safety. Somewhat consoled by these resolutions, we separated for the night. The next morning, when we sent for Lottie, the servants told us that she had been gone two hours, having ridden to town with the man who brought over the morning papers, before any one but the servants was astir. We sent over to the town immediately, and learned that she had left by a train that passed ten minutes after she reached the depot.

CHAPTER LXV
LOTTIE LEAVES A LETTER AND A BOOK

The departure of Lottie added to our trouble. We had learned to love the girl very much, and this wild work, in a creature so utterly unused to the world, distressed us greatly. Unconsciously even to ourselves, we had begun to rely upon Lottie as a friend, and bright, if not safe counsellor. Her untiring spirit amused us when nothing else could. Indeed, she was like an April day in the house, half storm, half sunshine, but interesting in any phase of her erratic life. It seemed as if half the light had left our house, when the man came back from the railroad and told us that she was absolutely gone. Jessie went off to her own room with tears in her eyes. I would have given the world to know where that strange young creature was going, and half my life could I have followed her.

Sadness is sure to seek shelter in shadowy places. Mine carried me into the chamber of my lost friend. It was dim and orderly, like a church closed after service. The white bed on which she died, gleamed upon me through the dim light like an altar. The blinds were closed, the sashes down; a funereal stillness had settled on everything she once loved to look upon. I sunk down upon my knees by the bed, weeping bitterly. Would that woman ever dare to stand in Mrs. Lee's room, its mistress? Had she ever yet been able to wipe the blood-stain from her own lips gathered from the heart she had broken by a Judas kiss?

Upon my knees in that room, I felt and knew that a murder, so crafty that the criminal herself could torture it into accident to her own conscience, had been perpetrated there. The voice of my dead friend seemed calling on me to avenge her, and save the man she had loved better than her own soul, from a thraldom worse than death. In my anguish I cried out, "What can I do? what can I do?"

Nothing answered me. I was alone, doubly alone, since that girl had left us. Never before had my helplessness been so complete. Perhaps I had indulged in some wild hope connected with Lottie, and that had been cut from under my feet by her desertion. If so, I was unconscious of it; but no lame man ever felt the loss of his staff, as I felt the cruel ingratitude of this girl. Still I had a vague trust in her, a hope changing and fantastic as the wind, but still a hope that she might not prove the thoughtless creature her conduct seemed to bespeak her.

One end of the room was less gloomy than the rest, and a bar of light cutting across it disturbed me. It came through the partially opened door of Lottie's little chamber, in which a blind had been left unclosed. I went into the room, and there, directly beneath the window, saw the girl's writing-desk, on which lay a letter and a blank-book, which I remembered to have given Lottie one day, when she had pressed me earnestly for something of the kind. The letter was placed ostentatiously on its edge, and I saw that it was addressed to me. I opened it with some trepidation and read:—

My Dear, Dear Miss Hyde:—Please do not think me a heathen and a viper of ingratitude, because I have done what I couldn't help, but remember me kindly, and make Miss Jessie do the same. It isn't in me to be really bad, or anything like it, though I sometimes do things out of the common, and make you angry, because you cannot understand why I do them; not knowing everything, how should you? There is one thing on my conscience, and I am going to own up to it. You remember when Babylon went away, I was going in a hurry into my room with something in my hand, when you wanted to know what it was. I bluffed you off and wouldn't tell, thinking to get the article back in good order before she went. But Babylon was in a terrible hurry, and I had no chance to do anything before her trunks were locked; so without meaning it at all, I was what some people might call a—well, I won't use the name, it looks dreadfully on paper, but her journal was left in my hand promiscuously, as one may say. Still I meant to return it to her, and mean to yet, if I ever get a good chance. I only thought at the time to get Mr. Lee to read it, but before I could do that, off he went, circumventing me in all respects, and making us wretched. For my part, with that book on hand—of no use too—I felt like a thief. If he had only waited till I could have seen him; but he didn't, and that has made me so unhappy that I cannot stay at home. I have copied off that she-Babylon's book, almost the whole of it, and I leave the copy for you— read it, and then say if Judas Iscariot wasn't a gentleman and philosopher, compared to this woman. I have got her book in my trunk. You wondered what I was writing so much about. Well, it was that. When she went out to ride days,

Cora was sure to be down-stairs, and I knew where she kept her keys, so after awhile I had only to copy what Babylon wrote over-night, having got the rest copied by hard work. Well, at last everything was huddled up of a sudden, and I was behind-hand three or four days—so I made a dash for the book and hadn't time to put it back. I wonder if she's missed it? Mercy on us! what a time there will be when she does. I wouldn't be in that yellow girl's skin for something; but never mind, it will do her good—the black snake!

Read the book, and then you will find out what a rattlesnake we have had curled up in the bosom of our family.

Good-bye, Miss Hyde; don't think I'm crying because there is a drop just here. It's something else, I don't just know what, but crying is out of my—my—Oh, Miss Hyde! Miss Hyde! I do think my heart is breaking. I can't stand it. Don't expect me to say good-bye. Don't think hard of me for going. What else can I say. Oh, do, do think well of me; I am not a bad girl, nor ungrateful, believe that, and believe me your true   Lottie till death.

I read the letter through more than once. Then I sat down and deliberated with my eyes on the book. Had I a right to read it, after all I had seen and heard of this woman; was I justified in searching out her secrets in that way?

But for the suspicions that still haunted me regarding Mrs. Lee's death, I should have decided against it, but I had learned too much for continued hesitation. Still, my very soul recoiled from the task of searching the life of this woman. When I reached forth my hand for the book, it seemed as if my fingers were poisoned with the touch. I would not take the volume to my own room, but sat down by the window and read it through before I arose from my seat. The pages frenzied me.

Lottie wrote a bold, plain hand, copying anything before her clearly enough. In places the writing gave evidence of hurry and nervousness, but it was in no part really difficult to read. The journal began at the marriage of Miss Wells with old Mr. Dennison, and seemed to have been detached from the other portion of her life about that time. If anything preceded it, Lottie had failed to take a copy.

CHAPTER LXVI
MRS. DENNISON'S JOURNAL

How many years will this last? I did not expect that this dull stagnation of life would oppress me so. I knew that he was seventy years of age, and thought it would be no great hardship to be petted as an old man's darling, for the few years that might follow. Indeed, he is a gentleman, and loves me, I am sure, more devotedly than ever a young man loved his bride. At first I really thought myself almost happy. It was so pleasant to get away from my old home, after it had been torn to pieces by hungry creditors, and all the old servants driven into new places, that protection and kindness made everything seem like a blessed new life. Mr. Dennison told me that he has loved me ever since I was a little girl, and always intended to make me his wife. He has been a firm, firm friend to my father, I know that well enough, and never would have permitted the old home to be torn up had poor papa lived. As it is, he let all the rest go, and rescuing Cora and myself from the wreck, made me his wife and gave her the liberty she would not take.

"He was kind in showing us something of the world, before he brought us here for good, yet I am not sure that it was wise to throw me suddenly into the society from which I was to be withdrawn so soon. I learned one thing there which sometimes stirs the wish in my heart that I had waited. This thing I have become assured of: I am beautiful, and beauty is a great power. No matter, it has done something for me in winning this fine old gentleman; but when I think what it might have accomplished, I feel defrauded out of half my life. No, no, I do not often feel this. My life was pleasant enough at first, when our wedding brought so many gay and clever people around us. But now that we have retreated to the plantation, everything is dull as the grave. Cotton-fields here, blossoming all over, as with snow by the handful, corn there, tall and thrifty, great live-oaks bearded with moss, and half strangled under the everlasting clasp of mistletoe, make the landscape beautiful, and these things interested me greatly for a time. But I am getting weary of them, and of the grand old house, with its endless verandas and clinging roses, its delicate India matting, and the snowy whiteness of its draperies. I long for change—pine for society, while he seems to think that his presence alone should make this place a heaven. What is it to me, that even in mid-winter I can stoop from my window and gather oranges from the green boughs that bend across it? The novelty has worn away, and this profusion of roses satiates me. You find them everywhere, hiding the fences in ridges and slopes of glossy foliage, studded thickly with great stars of whiteness, that would be exquisite but for the commonness, the negroes bringing them to me by the basketful, until I sicken with the fragrance,— yellow, white, crimson, and damask, all heaped together in gorgeous masses that delight you at first, and then become tiresome, are every day brought to me from the grounds.

"Yesterday one of the negroes came in with a whole armful of magnolias in full bloom. The marvellous white blossoms, with their great chalices running over with fragrance, filled the air with such richness as I have never dreamed of before. I sat down upon a low stool on the front veranda, and with the quivering shadows from a great catalpa-tree falling around me, had these noble blossoms heaped at my feet, yielding myself to the exquisite perfume, till the atmosphere made me faint with delight. It was a delicious, sensuous enjoyment which I shall never forget, but one cannot repeat such things, and 'not even love can live on flowers.' Where love is not and never can be, such things sicken one.

"While I sat there, with the great white blossoms breathing at my feet, and a mocking-bird up in the catalpa-tree thrilling the air with music, a horseman came riding up the avenue, now in the sunshine, now in the shadow of the great live-oaks, leisurely, as if he found pleasure in lingering on a road so beautiful and tranquil. He was a young man, tall and well-formed, who rode his horse with an easy military air full of command. Even at the distance I could see that his bearing was noble and his face a grand one.

"The sight of this man aroused me from the dreamy languor which had been so delightful, and I watched his approach with interest. Directly I was sensible that he had discovered me sitting there in the shadows; for his horse quickened its pace, and in a moment he drew up, and, leaning from his saddle, addressed me,—

"'Excuse me, madam; but I have been unable to discover any servant on the ground, and may have intruded. Does this place belong to Mr. Dennison?'

"I answered that it did, and arising from my seat, desired him to dismount. Mr. Dennison, I said, would be at home in a short time, and would doubtless be happy to see him.

"The stranger sprang from his horse, and flung the bridle to one of the men who came lazily from the house to receive it. I made a movement toward the door, but he gave a glance around at the beautiful view—the flowery thickets and rich slopes of grass—as if reluctant to leave them. Then his eyes fell upon me, and I saw them light up with sudden admiration. I did not intend it, but at the moment I must have taken some attitude of grace to bring such light into a stranger's countenance. He stood for a whole minute gazing on me as if I had been a picture. I felt myself blushing, and drew the flowing muslin of my sleeve over the arm on which his glance fell as it left my face. Then he turned away, and as I sunk to my seat again, placed himself in a garden-chair, drawing a deep breath.

"'Ah, forgive me,' he said, 'what awkwardness. I have trodden upon one of your beautiful flowers.'

"'But there still remain more than enough to make the air oppressive,' I answered.

"'For my part,' he said, smiling pleasantly, 'I could breathe it forever. Indeed, lady, you have a paradise here.'

"Was it indeed so lovely? A moment before my soul had wearied of its very beauties; now a feeling of pride that they were mine stole into my thoughts. It certainly was something to be mistress of a place like that. While our visitor seemed to give himself up to enjoyment of the scene, I saw that his eyes were constantly returning to me. I had been sitting in the open air a long time, and felt that my hair and dress must be in some disorder. This idea made me anxious. I arose, and asking him to excuse me, ran up to my room to make sure that I was not altogether hideous. One glance in the great swinging mirror reassured me. No cloud was ever more pure than the muslin of my white dress; a cluster of red and white roses held back the thick ringlets of my hair, and a single half-open bud fastened the white folds on my bosom. My maid Cora had followed me out on the veranda that morning, and thus arranged the finest flowers she could gather. Had I studied at my glass an hour, nothing more becoming could have been invented. That girl is a treasure; she loves and serves me as no other creature ever did or ever will. She was my dower, my inheritance. The only possession I had in the world was this one girl, when Mr. Dennison married me. I sometimes wonder if he knows why I love and prize her so much. I heard her voice through the window. The stranger was asking her some question which she answered modestly, and was going away. I wonder if he thinks her beautiful. To me the pure olive of her complexion, which just admits of a tinge of carnation in the cheek, is wonderfully effective. She is a brunette intensified, but oh, how the poor thing hates the blood that separates her from us by that one dark shade. No wonder! no wonder!

"Why should I think of this, while looking in the glass to assure myself that I was presentable? I cannot tell, except that this unhappy girl is an object of such profound compassion with me at all times. The education which she has received, I sometimes think, renders her life more bitter than it might have been; but my father would have it so, and perhaps he was right.

"I went down to the veranda again, and found the stranger talking to Cora, who stood with her back against one of the pillars, answering his questions with downcast eyes. She moved away as I appeared, and went into the house. I saw the stranger follow her lithe movements with his eyes, and felt myself coloring with anger. Was he searching her features from admiration or curiosity? I wish it were possible to discover.

"I had been reading, and left a book on one of the little marble tables that stood in the veranda. Some richly colored embroidery lay in my work-basket close by it, and in taking it up, the volume fell.

"The stranger stooped to replace it on the table, but his eye caught the title; a flash of crimson shot across his forehead, and he cast a quick glance at me, as if the question in my eyes disturbed him.

"'A new book, I see; have you read it?'

"He was turning over the leaves, as he asked the question.

"'Yes,' I replied, 'I have read it more than once.'

"'More than once?'

"'Yes, it is a book that requires some thought. Full of ideas and original suggestions. The story itself is a painful one. Indeed, I have my doubts—'

"'Well, you have your doubts?'

"His face flushed, his eyes searched mine with a look almost of defiance in them.

"'Yes,' I continued, coloring painfully, for I am young and afraid to express adverse opinions, 'I sometimes doubt if it is not a little wicked.'

"He laughed, 'Oh, you are young, and a woman.'

"'Well,' I answered, 'this is what I mean, when I finished reading that book, it made me restless, unhappy—discontented with everything around me.'

"'That is, perhaps, because you did not understand it.'

"'But goodness is so simple, I can understand that always.'

"'I grant you, but human life is not all perfection; unfortunately, good and evil are pretty nearly balanced on this earth, and there is nothing picturesque enough in a dead-level of goodness to interest the reader through an entire story. To attempt that, would be like painting a picture without shadows. Your real author understands the force of contrasts.'

"'But a book which has so little of the virtuous and pure in it, yields up this power of contrast, by letting no sunshine into its pages,' I said. 'The fault of this work is, that it dwells too entirely on the dark passions.'

"'Then you condemn it?'

"'No, indeed, the pictures are too grand, the passions too strongly portrayed for that. The author, whoever he is, must be a man of powerful genius. I only wish he had softened his pictures and let in a few of the gentler sentiments.'

"'And so do I.'

"He spoke with emphasis, closing the book. Then I noticed that a flush was on his face, and he cast the volume from him with a gesture of dislike.

"'You know the author of that book?' I said on the impulse.

"'Yes, lady, I know him well—some day he shall be made the wiser, by learning your opinion.'

"'Oh, I hope not. It was rash, perhaps altogether wrong. I am no critic, and only spoke as the book impressed me.'

"'That is criticism,' he answered, 'and I dare say correct, but the volume is hardly worthy of so much consideration. The author is too much honored, that you have read it at all.'

"I was about to answer, when Mr. Dennison rode up in his carriage, and seeing my companion, waved his hand with that cordial welcome so universal in the South. The moment he appeared, I felt chilled, and took up my embroidery, knowing well that no more conversation that I could join in, would be offered that day.

"Certainly, Mr. Dennison is a handsome old gentleman. As a father, one might be very proud of him, but now a strange feeling comes over me at his approach. I turn from his elaborate elegance of speech and manner with a wish for something fresher. Cora is not more my slave than I could make him, but the task of perpetual fondness is too much. Oh, if he had only adopted me!"

CHAPTER LXVII
OUR FIRST VISITOR

"Mr. Dennison descended from his carriage and came forward with more haste and animation than was usual to him. He was evidently delighted to see his guest.

"'Why, Lawrence, is it you; when and how did you reach us?' he said, extending his hand.

"'Half an hour ago, by rail and steamer,' answered the gentleman, meeting Mr. Dennison half-way, and shaking hands with him.

"'Made the acquaintance of my wife, I see?'

"As he spoke, Mr. Dennison glanced smilingly toward me.

"'Oh, yes, I think so; if this young lady is your wife.'

"The gentleman hesitated in some confusion. I think he had taken me for Mr. Dennison's daughter.

"The old gentleman turned suddenly red, and laughed a little unnaturally.

"'My wife, yes, almost a bride yet, but we are making her blush. My love, this is Mr. Lawrence, of New York, one of the best friends I have. You must take him into especial favor for your husband's sake.'

"I am sure there was color enough in my face then. Why will Mr. Dennison constantly drag that odious word, husband, into everything he says? Does he think I can ever forget it?

"We sat down in company, enjoying the cool shadows of the veranda. All my pleasure was at an end; the conversation turned upon stocks, railroads, and mining. I gathered from it that Mr. Lawrence was a stock-broker or something of that kind, and that Mr. Dennison was connected with him in an enterprise for which money was to be supplied. Once or twice I caught the stranger looking at me while my husband conversed, but I was occupied with my embroidery, and did not seem to notice him; perhaps he was admiring the contrast between the pure white of my dress and the gorgeous richness of the worsteds in my lap.

"While they were talking, Mr. Dennison insisted that I should sit closer to him, and more than once he placed his hand on my work and prevented me going on with it, as if I had been a child. This annoyed me. After all, one does not care to be so obviously exhibited as 'the old man's darling.' It is embarrassing when the fine eyes of a man like that are upon you.

"After dinner that day, Mr. Dennison stole off to a low pan in the library for his half-hour of sleep. I usually occupied my own room at this hour, but as I went that way, our guest came in from the veranda, where he had been smoking a cigar, and laughingly entreated that I should not leave him alone.

"I ran up-stairs, threw a black lace shawl over my head, Spanish mantilla fashion, and joined him. It was sunset, and all the beautiful landscape lay wrapped in a veil of purplish mist, through which trembled a soft golden glow that brightened all the west, and shimmered through the tree-tops like flashes of fire.

"We walked on through the delicious atmosphere, to which the perfume of innumerable flowers gave forth their sweetness, as they brightened under the soft dews that had just began to fall.

"Unconsciously, we turned out of the oak-avenue and walked toward a pretty pond, or miniature lake, which lay to our right, sheltered by one live-oak and a cluster of magnolia-trees, from which the blossoms brought to me that morning had been cut. A shrub-like species of the magnolia grew around the pond, hedging it in with great white blossoms, and the sedgy borders were aglow with wild flowers. It was not yet time for the water-lilies to be in blossom, but in some places their large green pads covered the lake with patches of glossy greenness, while a light wind rippled through them, stirring the waters like ridges of diamonds between the trembling leaves.

"How beautiful it was! The birds were no longer musical, but we watched them fluttering through the leaves and settling down in safe places among the rushes, while the sweet stillness of the closing day fell upon them.

"My hand rested on the arm of our guest; he was talking earnestly, and his eloquence thrilled me with sensations unlike anything I had felt before. There was unmeasured poetry in every word he uttered. We had, I do not know how, got on to the subject of that book again, and he was defending it in language warm, fervid, and startling, as the story itself. My hand shook on his arm; a new idea had seized upon me, and against my own will I spoke.

"'You wrote the book,' I said, 'I know it by your language. I can read the fact in this defence.'

"'And you will like me no longer. You will condemn me as you have that poor volume,' he answered, turning suddenly, and looking into my eyes with the glance of an eagle.

"'Condemn you!' I said. 'What, I?'

"'But you condemn my book?'

"'No, I did not. To question a thing, is not to condemn it.'

"'But the doubt wounds me. You might have found sympathy for much that the book contains. It should appeal to a heart like yours.'

"He held my hand firmly in his clasp. How it got there, I do not know. I struggled a little to free it, but his fingers closed around mine like a vice.

"'Say that you will read my book again.'

"'I will. Nothing could prevent me now.'

"'And you will read it with a new inspiration?'

"'After this conversation, yes.'

"'That is, for one day you will think my thoughts, and give them fresh beauties as they pass through your own vivid imagination.'

"'I will read them, and remember all that you have said.'

"'Sweet woman, I thank you. If my poor words can touch a heart like yours, it is enough.'

"He bent and kissed my hand, thus releasing it from his clasp. It seemed as if some of my strength went out as he did this. The intense eloquence of this man had inspired me for the time, now I was weak and silent.

"'Tell me,' he said, 'what particular passages you disliked in my poor volume.'

"I could not answer; the book itself had gone out of my mind. I had only power to think of the man who stood before me, with that earnest protest burning on his lip, and those eyes, dark and luminous, bent upon me. I think that he did not observe my trepidation. He was carried away by a wish to protect the offspring of his brain from misconception or censure. I had read the volume hastily, and found it too brilliantly intense for the idle lassitude of my humor. It had startled me into more thought than I cared to exercise. The quiet of my home seemed like dulness after reading it. Now this man, its author, had come and completed the discontent his book had engendered. I had never seen a man of his class before, and to me the charm of novelty and romance surrounded him with a sort of glory.

"'Tell me,' he repeated, 'in what a thought of mine could have offended a creature so lovely and so rich in talent.'

"Was he mocking me because of my absurd criticism? I looked up suddenly, and met the full glance of those eyes. The blood rushed to my face, and my eyelids drooped.

"'You will not help me to amend a fault,' he said, in a tone of reproach.

"'Because I cannot. It was no particular thought—no description in itself that disturbed me; but, if I may so express it, the entire atmosphere of the book. It made me unhappy.'

"I was driven to desperate frankness by his persistency, and spoke out almost with tears in my eyes.

"'Then some thought in the volume, or the narrative itself, struck upon your heart, or disturbed your conscience?' he answered, in a low voice.

"I started. Was this true?

"'Perhaps some points of the story were not unlike your own experience?' he continued.

"I felt the tears starting to my eyes. Yes, he was right. It was a sense of the barrenness of my own future that had made me so restless. If the volume had produced this effect, how much greater was the disturbance when its author stood by my side, with looks and voice more eloquent than his writings. He waited in silence for my answer; it only came in low sobs.

"'Forgive me; I have wounded you unthinkingly.'

"His voice was like that of a penitent man in prayer; his face grew earnest and sad.

"'Look on me, and say that I am forgiven.'

"I did look at him, and met the tender penitence in his eyes with a thrill of pain. How had the man won the power of arousing such feelings in a few brief hours? Was it because I had been familiar with his thoughts so long? I could not answer; but the very presence of this stranger disturbed me. Sensations never dreamed of in my previous existence rose and swelled in my bosom. The impulse to flee from his presence seized upon me. I did turn to go, but he walked quietly forward at the same time.

"The sunset was now fading into soft violet and pale gray tints. Dew was falling thickly in the grass, and fire-flies began to sparkle all around us. In the stillness and beauty of coming night, we walked on together almost in silence. I had no words for conversation, and our guest seemed to have fallen into deep thought. As we drew near the house, Mr. Dennison came out to meet us. He had been smoking a cigar in the veranda, and flung it away as he drew near us. How heavily he walked. How dull his eyes seemed as he bent them upon me, after the passion and feeling I had read so clearly in those of our guest.

"Mr. Dennison took my hand and placed it on his arm, laughing pleasantly, as he asked Lawrence how far we had been walking. Lawrence did not answer. He was regarding us with an earnest questioning look, from which I turned away half in anger. Was he reading me and my position so closely as that?

"Why should I think of this man so much? Has the isolation in which we have been living made the advent of a stranger of so great importance that his presence must fill all my being? The first thing this morning I looked out of my window, wondering if he would be visible anywhere in the grounds. Yes, there he was standing by Mr. Dennison, admiring a blood-horse that a colored groom had brought from the stable. It was a beautiful animal, coal-black, wonderfully symmetrical and full of graceful action. Mr. Dennison had bought him only the week before, and this groom had been ordered to break him for my use as a saddle-horse. The gentlemen seemed to be examining him critically, as the groom led him to and fro upon the lawn. For the first time I took an interest in the beautiful animal. Being up to that time a timid and inexperienced rider, my husband's purchase had afforded me little pleasure. He had long since given up horseback exercise, and a solitary ride, followed perhaps by a groom, did not hold forth much promise of happiness for me, so I had allowed his new purchase to stand in the stable unnoticed. But now I looked upon the creature with interest, as he stood restlessly, with the sun shining upon his glossy coat, and shimmering like quicksilver down his arched neck.

"All at once, I saw Lawrence spring upon the horse and dash off across the lawn, sitting bravely as if he and the beautiful animal were one creation. The horse was restive at first and plunged furiously, for they had put a sharp curb in his mouth, and Lawrence was bringing him to subjection with a heavy hand. I shrieked aloud at the first plunge, but there was little need of fear. The next moment horse and rider were in full career over the lawn. That day week I rode my new purchase for the first time.

CHAPTER LXVIII
THE WATERFALL

"I did not know that the world was so beautiful. This spot is indeed like paradise to me now. There is joy in the very breath of the mornings. When I open my window and let in the gushing song of the mocking-birds, and the sweet breath of the flowers, sighs of exquisite delight break to my lips. Things that wearied me two weeks ago are taking new beauty in my eyes. It seems to me that I love everything in the world except this one old man.

"We have been riding every day miles and miles over the country. There is not a broad prospect or a pleasant nook within a ten-hours' ride, that we have not visited in company. Mr. Dennison encouraged these excursions. He is anxious that I should learn to ride freely, and seems grateful that Lawrence is willing to teach me. The weather has been more than pleasant, and these two weeks have gone by like a dream. How brief the time has been, yet how long it seems, one lives so much in a few hours.

"My heart is full, so full that I cannot write anything that it feels. In fact, there is nothing tangible enough for words. Dreams, dreams all, but such delirious dreams. Last night I lay awake till a rosy flash broke through the curtains telling me that it was morning. All night long I lay with the curtains brooding over me like a cloud, and the silver moonlight shimmering through the windows half illuminating the room and the bed upon which I rested, which was all whiteness like a snow-drift. There I lay hour after hour, with both hands folded on my breast, whispering over the words that he had said to me. They were nothing when separated from his looks, or disentangled from the exquisite tenderness of his voice, but oh, how much, when so richly combined, for never in one human being, I am sure, were looks and voice so eloquent.

"I could hear the deep breathing of my husband in the next room, and this made me restless. But for him those words, meaningless in themselves perhaps, would have taken life and force. Ah, why is youth and ambition so rash. Had I only waited before these golden fetters were riveted upon me!

"A vase of moss-roses stood upon the little table near my bed. He had gathered them for me just as the sun was setting, while the first dew bathed them. I took some of these flowers together in my hands, and kissed away their perfume, with a delightful consciousness that he had given it to me. Out of all the wilderness of flowers, now fresh from the dew, these were the gems, for he had brought them to me.

"When daylight came, I arose and went down to the veranda, not weary from sleeplessness, but with a gentle languor upon me which was better than rest. For the first time since Lawrence had been with us, I opened the book he had written, and read passages from it at random. How beautiful they were! and I not discover this before. The truth is, their very excellence carried with it exaltation.

"I read them with a new sense and a keener relish. Their very intensity had, at the first reading, disturbed me almost painfully, now each sentence brought thrills of appreciation. In all respects it was a new book to me.

"I felt that this second reading was dangerous, but the thoughts fascinated me, and I read on, while orioles and mocking-birds held a carnival of music in the thickets around me, and a bright sun drove all the rose-tints from the sky. All at once I looked up, a shadow had fallen across the page I was reading; I closed the book at once, blushing like a guilty creature.

"'Confess,' said Lawrence, with a gleam of laughing triumph in his eyes, 'that you have in some degree changed your opinion.'

"'I have no opinion to change,' was my answer; 'for until now I never really understood your book.'

"'And you understand it now?'

"'Yes.'

"'And feel it?'

"'Too much.'

"I felt the blood rush into my face with very shame at this hasty admission. When I ventured to look up, a faint wave of color was dying out from his face, leaving it grave and pale. Was he condemning me already? That moment Mr. Dennison came through the front door, looking cool and tranquil in his dress of pure linen, which was scarcely whiter than his hair.

"'Come,' he said, in jovial good humor, 'throw by your books, and let us have breakfast.'

"I was glad to see him,—grateful that he had released me from the thraldom of those eyes.

"We rode out that day. A waterfall some eight miles off was almost the only point of interest that I had not visited, and there our ride terminated.

A colored groom always rode after us, but his presence was no check upon conversation, and sometimes he loitered behind so far that we lost sight of him altogether. In fact, our whole excursion was one long *tête-à-tête*.

"Lawrence had been grave and preoccupied all the way, but when we quitted our horses and went down to the fall, his spirits rose, and he looked around upon the scene with animation. The cataract, for it was little more, leaped through a chasm between two precipices, formed by a vast rock, which some convulsion of nature had split asunder. Down this chasm the crystal waters plunged nearly a hundred feet, like a stream of shooting diamonds, covering the sides of each precipice with fleeces of emerald-green moss. From these mosses sprung ferns that waved like ten thousand plumes in the current of air that blew coolly down the ravine, keeping every thing in graceful motion. Young trees added their luxuriance to the scene, crowning the summit of the rocks like a diadem, and a host of clustering vines fell over the edge of the precipice, streaming downwards like banners on a battlement, and sometimes sweeping out with the current.

"We entered the ravine first, and stood within the very spray of the cataract; for the stream widened out directly after it left the chasm, and went rioting off among boulders and broken rocks, across which a plank bridge had been flung, which commanded a full view of the fall. We stood a while enjoying the view, and then moved up a footpath that ran along the right-hand precipice, from which we could look down the ravine, and attain an entirely different view from the one we had left. The path was broken and abrupt, but this was scarcely an objection to us. There was something exhilarating in the exercise, and I rather liked the vigorous climbing after so long a ride on horseback; even with the obstruction of a long skirt flung over one arm, it was scarcely fatiguing. We had nearly reached the top of the precipice, I had taken Mr. Lawrence's arm, for he insisted that I must be out of breath, and I was protesting against his assertion, when a large dog rushed out of the undergrowth, which grew thickly on that side of the path, as if frightened at something, and made a plunge directly against me.

"My arm was torn from its support, I staggered—reeled on the verge of the precipice, flung out my arms, and plunged down—down—down into chaos. I had neither struck the earth nor water, something hard and firm girded my body. My face was smothered in green, damp leaves, and my hair already dripped with falling spray.

"I heard the roar and rush of waters all around me, and through it a fierce cry as of some one in agony. I attempted to move, but the branches that supported me swayed downward, and with a desperate spring I caught at the stem of a wild vine, which clung to and spread over the face of the precipice, twisting itself in with the young tree, which but for that would have broken under my weight. Looking upward through the blinding mist, I saw a white face bending over the precipice, and heard a voice hoarse with terror calling upon me to hold firmly and keep still.

"I did hold firmly, but the trembling of my frame shook the tree and clinging shrubs with a dangerous vibration, and it seemed to me that their roots were slowly tearing out from the soil which held them in the cleft of the rock. This shook me with an awful terror; I tried to close my eyes and be still, but that was impossible. I saw the blue sky bending so calm and quiet above me. I saw the quivering greenness that clothed the rocky face of the precipice, and ten thousand tiny white flowers trembling through it so close that my face almost touched them. The fall, like a sheet of melted glass, rolled and plunged so near, that it seemed ready to leap upon me. My appalled eyes turned shuddering from a vast whirlpool of foam that rioted thirty feet beneath me, shooting forward, curving over, and plunging down great watery hollows, then leaping suddenly upward, as if maddened that their prey had not fallen at once into the white caldron of their wrath.

"In vain my eyes closed upon all this threatening horror. Then all was darkness, and the roar of the fall became terrific. The spray swept over me like a storm of shooting diamonds, wetting my habit through and through till it dragged me downward with heavier weight and fresh peril. I could feel the drops falling like rain from my hair, and my poor hands grew cold as they clung to the vine. A cry broke from my lips. Surely the tree was uprooting beneath me. I could feel it giving way inch by inch. A handful of loose earth broke away and rolled over me, rattling down to the white gulf below. Shriek after shriek—oh, my God! they were smothered and lost in that roar of waters, and could warn no one of this new peril. I seized upon the wild vine higher up, and strove to press less heavily on that breaking tree; my foot found a crevice in the rock, and, forcing itself through the wet moss, in some degree sufficed to lessen the weight that was dragging me down to death. But still my support was slowly giving way, I could hear the small roots snap, and feel the earth break from around them. My hands were numb and cold, my brain began to reel, and ten thousand broken rainbows seemed shooting up from the falls, and tangling themselves around me, dragging me down—down—down.

"A human voice brought me back; a wild, cheerful shout forbade me to give way, and broke the delirium, which in a moment more would have loosened my hold, and sent me whirling through that white gulf of waters into eternity. 'Hold fast one moment! For God's sake, be firm!' It was his voice. A thrill of hope drove back the delirium that had seized upon me. I pressed my foot more firmly into the crevice, and forced myself against the rock, clinging with both hands to the vine. A trail of blackness fell over the face of the precipice, and I heard the clank of iron striking against the rock. Directly the air above was darkened, and, with a thrill of horror, I saw Lawrence fling himself over the face of the precipice, and glide slowly down to my side. He crowded his foot close to mine, thus attaining a foothold, but otherwise supported himself by the line of leathern straps that had aided his descent. With one hand clinging firmly to this support, he placed the stirrups from my saddle under my feet, told me how to seize upon the straps to which they were attached when he should call out, and seizing the double straps above my head, swung himself upward, and left me alone, shaken with double terror. Then I knew that a life dearer than mine was in peril, and my soul went up with him, uttering a cry of thankfulness when his voice reached me, calling out, cheerfully, from the edge of the precipice, —

"'Stand firm; do not move till you feel the straps tighten around you!'

"I obeyed, holding desperately to the vine with one hand, while the other was ready for action. I felt the stirrups tighten under my feet, — the leather straps were taut and motionless, — I grasped one with my left hand, but still clung to the vine, afraid to swing out over that awful abyss. It was a moment of sickening horror.

"'Be bold—fear nothing—trust yourself to me!'

"Instantly my hand left its hold on the vine, my feet were lifted from their frail support, and with the stirrups beneath them, swung out from the rock. Oh, how fearfully those lines strained and quivered! how those white waters leaped and roared under me! I drew no breath; my heart stood still; a shock of awful terror seized upon me; the minute in which I swung out into mid-air seems to me even now as a long, long day. Oh, it was terrible!

"The faces of the angels, when they meet you after death, must give such promise of new life, as his gave to me when my frightened eyes first saw him bending over that precipice. The trust of the angels must be like mine when I felt his arms around me, and knew that he had lifted me out of chaos. Never, on this side of heaven, shall I have another sensation like that.

"How long I remained in those arms it is impossible for me to say. When I came to life, he was sitting upon the turf, where they had laid me, with my head resting on his knee. Some brandy from a flask, which the groom always carried with him, had been forced through my lips, where I felt the taste still burning. That had checked the shudders of cold which were creeping over me, and for a while I lay speechless, feeble as a child, but oh, how happy! He had saved me. It was his strength which had rescued me from that whirlpool of waters, from the horrible death, for which I was so unprepared.

"These were the first thoughts that came to my brain, as I lay there so deathly and motionless. The light fell rosily on my eyelids, but I had no strength or wish to unclose them; nay, I checked the very breath as it rose to my lips, fearing that it would betray the life rekindling in my bosom, and thus break the dream which was so like Elysium.

"He bent his face to mine and called me by name. His voice shook with apprehension; I could feel that he trembled.

"I could not help it: a smile crept to my lips and warmed them into redness. He held my hand, and was chafing it between his smooth white palms.

"'She is recovering,' he exclaimed, joyfully.

"'So she am, marser,' answered Tom, the groom; 'beginning to look mighty natral. Lor' knows dis darky thought she was done gone sure 'nuff.'

"I moved then. Tom's voice had broken up my dream.

"'Are you better? Speak, dear lady, and tell me that you are not seriously hurt.'

"Opening my eyes wide, I looked into his, and closed them again, feeling the warm, fresh life rushing to my face with a glow.

"'Ah, your looks tell me that no serious evil will come from this,' he said. 'Let us thank God.'

"'I do thank God, but you most of all,' I whispered; 'without that, life would—'

"What was I about to say. My voice was weak, I do not think he heard me. I listened for some response, but none came, and when my eyes turned upon him, the look with which he met them was grave and thoughtful.

"Tom was busy about the saddles at some distance. With that prompt action which is in itself success, Lawrence had taken the girths and stirrups from the saddles, the martingales and bridles, all of which he had buckled and knotted together into the cable that saved my life. While Tom was repairing all damages, I grew strong enough to sit up, but my habit was so wet and heavy that it seemed impossible for me to walk. A slight lunch had been prepared for us which Tom had brought with him. Lawrence found a bottle of champagne in the basket, and poured out a brimming cup which he entreated me to drink while the sparkles were rising. I drank eagerly, again and again, till the slight chills that had begun to creep over me were broken up, and a glow of strength enabled me to rise.

"'Now,' said Lawrence, 'that you have some color in those cheeks, and the deathly look is gone, let us mount and away. It will be a miracle if you are not ill from this shock.'

"I arose and prepared to go, but faltered, and found the weight of my skirt oppressive. Lawrence threw one arm around my waist, and almost carried me to the horse. For one moment he folded me close in his arms before lifting me to the saddle, and whispered, —

"'Forgive me, that I led you into this danger.'

"I could not answer. The man who had saved my life, at a terrible risk to his own, asked me to forgive him. Did he guess that it was worship, not forgiveness, that I felt.

"We rode home at a gallop. Exercise drove the chills from my frame, and a strange excitement took possession of me. When I reached home, my cheeks were on fire. It was not fever, but a sensation stranger and wilder than I had ever felt before. Instead of returning home, I would have given the world to turn my horse and flee to the uttermost parts of the earth, where no one but the man who had saved me could ever know of my existence.

"Still, the horse was bearing me forward at the top of his speed, and no one attempted to check him or turn him aside. In the madness of my folly, I almost hoped to see Lawrence seize the bridle, and swerve his course away from the home I was beginning to hate."

CHAPTER LXIX
THE THREATENED DEPARTURE

"We reached home. The groom had ridden on in advance, to have dry clothes prepared for me; but it was of little use, for my habit had gradually lost its dampness, and I was feverish rather than chilly. Mr. Dennison came forth to meet us, his face full of alarm, his walk unsteady as if fright had shaken him. The old man lifted me from my saddle, and held me fondly in his arms, kissing my lips and forehead with passionate thankfulness before he set me down. Drops like rain fell upon my face, and I knew that the stout old man was weeping, though I had never seen tears in his eyes before.

"'My darling—my own beautiful wife,' he said, in the abandonment of his gratitude, 'what should I have done without you?'

"Mr. Dennison spoke so earnestly, that Lawrence must have heard him; but he was busy about the horses, and seemed quite unconscious of the tenderness which disturbed me so.

"'Thank God! you have not suffered as I feared,' continued my husband, encircling me with his arm, and almost carrying me into the house. 'Your cheeks are flushed, your eyes bright. Oh! my poor darling, I expected to see you white and drooping.'

"I leaned on him heavily, for my limbs were stiff, and I could hardly walk, besides a dead heaviness had seized upon my heart. When I shrank from the open caresses of my husband, this man did not seem to observe them. Was it that he did not care? This question drove all the unnatural excitement from me. I was white and cold enough then.

"No, I would not be forced into a dreary bed, and left to my thoughts. Exhausted as I was, anything seemed better than that. After Cora had taken off my soiled and torn habit, smoothed my hair and bathed my head with cologne, I girded a wrapper of soft white cashmere around me, with a scarf of scarlet silk which lay upon the sofa, and went down, spite of the girl's remonstrance.

"They were sitting together, those two men, conversing earnestly. I think Lawrence was giving an account of the terrible danger I had escaped, for Mr. Dennison was saying as I came up, treading so softly, that he had no idea of my presence:

"'My friend, it would be a little thing compared to this, that you had saved my life, for no human being will ever guess how much dearer this sweet creature is to me than that.'

"'She is indeed a most lovely woman,' answered Lawrence; 'any man might hold his existence light, in comparison with hers.'

"He spoke quietly, but I observed that his eyes did not seek those of my husband, and a cold whiteness lay upon his face. Was it the shock of that scene at the falls harassing him yet, or were unrevealed thoughts struggling with him?

"My husband started up joyfully when I appeared. He drew an easy-chair to the window, placed me in it, brought a stool for my feet, and sat down upon it, lifting his glad eager eyes to my face, with the devotion of a spaniel, while he patted and caressed the feet his movement had displaced.

"I felt myself growing angry. Why would the old man thus expose his folly before our guest, who seemed hewn from marble, so little did he regard the fondness that filled me with repulsion and shame.

"'Ah, my friend, see how she blushes at her husband's great joy and thankfulness. My poor child, Lawrence has been telling me all, how brave and steady you were, held almost by a thread over that fearful whirlpool without a shriek, and obeying orders like a veteran. He would not tell me all, but Tom did, so far as the fright would let him. Now say, my angel, what reward can we give our brave friend? He will not take my gratitude.'

"'But he must take mine,' I cried, reaching out both hands, with sudden appeal. 'He must not sit there cold and calm as if he had no interest in my safety. I cannot bear it.'

"Lawrence started up, and the quick fire leaped to his eyes. He took both my hands in his, with a firm, almost painful grasp.

"'Not gratitude. I will not have that, because—because it is all so undeserved. I did nothing that Tom himself would not have thought of. It was her own sublime courage, sir, that saved us from a terrible calamity.'

"Mr. Dennison gave me a look that seemed almost like adoration.

"'I am sure she would behave like an angel anywhere,' he said, 'but that does not lessen the value of your own brave action, my friend, and for that we are both bound to you forever.'

"'Well, let it rest so,' answered Lawrence, with an uneasy laugh. 'Just now I feel more like thanking God for a great mercy given, and terrible peril escaped, than anything else. Upon my word, Dennison, I can almost feel those white waters boiling around me now.'

"'They would have made an awful winding-sheet,' I said, with a shudder. 'But you saved me, oh, yes, you saved me.'

"'And your husband also, dear one,' said Mr. Dennison; 'for what would my life have been without you. Why, Lawrence, I have worshipped her ever since she was a little girl; even then, her proud saucy ways had their enchantment. She did not know it; how could she? but the old man's heart was set upon her while she was playing with her doll and bowling her hoop. Her own father never watched her growth with more interest than I felt, and when she learned to love me, why then, Lawrence, I knew for the first time what heaven was.'

"Lawrence looked at me steadily while the old man was speaking, so steadily, that I felt the hot blood rush to my face. Mr. Dennison observed this, and went on triumphing in the love he so truly believed to be his.

"'You see, my friend, how the very remembrance of that sweet confession bathes her face with blushes. She had taken a fancy to the old fellow long before a younger rival could think of entering the field against him, and married him for true love only, not because he was considered the richest planter in this district. She was innocent as a lamb, and as disinterested.'

"'Oh, Mr. Dennison,' I broke forth, 'do not talk about these things, they only weary Mr. Lawrence.'

"'Certainly not. I am deeply interested in everything that makes the happiness or misery of my friend,' said Lawrence, coldly.

"'Ah, she is too modest, I have always told her so, and far too careless about her own interests. Why, would you believe it, Lawrence, I could not get her to look into the state of my property, and learn how much or how little might hereafter come to her. She did not marry my property, but my own dear self; these were her very words, and for such words you cannot blame me if I adore her.'

"I felt myself glowing with shame. If I had ever used such words, it was when this old man seemed the only refuge left to me in my utter desolation. Perhaps I said them and felt them just then, for quiet home, protection, and a shelter were all I asked or hoped for in life; but now, with that man drinking in every word, I felt such protestations as a bitter humiliation.

"I arose to go. The conversation had become unbearable. I felt my lips quiver, and tears of intense mortification gathering to my eyes.

"Lawrence came toward me a step or two, and then retreated, for Mr. Dennison had given me his arm, and I left the room, bowed down with humiliation, and burning with shame. Why would the old man talk of me as he did? Even if I had loved him, it would have been embarrassing; as it was, all pride of my nature rose up in revolt against him. At the foot of the stairs I dropped his arm, and insisted on going up alone. He seemed astonished and a little hurt. How would it have been had I dared to express all the rage that was struggling in my bosom?

"Cora was waiting for me. Poor girl! she had been sadly shocked by the abrupt account of my danger, which Tom had repeated to every one he met. She is a wayward creature, and at times, I really believe, hates herself with bitter detestation for the black tinge which taints every drop of blood in her veins. Never in my whole life have I seen a human being so sensitive. No matter to her that she is beautiful, and that even the blacks look upon her as apart from themselves, this bitter truth is always uppermost in her mind. She has black blood in her veins, and she was born a slave. I remember how this beautiful girl hated her mother, because it was through her that the taint and the bonds came. One would have thought this wretched woman was the slave of her own child, for one was made to feel all the degradation of her lot, and the other was, to a certain extent, lifted out of it, from the day she was given to me—a child myself—as my especial maid. How it used to amuse my father when this colored child would domineer over and scorn her own mother.

"Sometimes I think Cora is seized with a venomous dislike of myself. I do not wonder at it. In her way, she is quite as beautiful as I ever was, and as for talent, the girl surpasses me in everything. Her industry is untiring, her perceptions quick as lightning. In some other country she might marry well, and take rank in social life scarcely second to my own. Sometimes I think her ambition turns that way, for she is constantly teasing me to take her to Europe. I only wish it were in my power, for I love the poor girl dearly, and should rejoice to see her lifted out of the pitiful condition that all of her race must occupy here, bond or free, for at least a century to come.

"I have been writing about this girl Cora, because she is so connected with my own life that nothing can separate us. We played together on equal terms as children, and when she gradually dropped into the habits of a servant, it made no change in my affection for her. In my chamber we have always been friends, more than that—more than that!

"Cora saw that I was disturbed, and sitting down at my feet, besought me to tell her the cause.

"For the first time in my life I had a secret to keep from this girl. I could not own to her that a few garrulous words from an old man, who had been so kind to us both, had filled my heart with indignant shame, for she would have asked why such fond words had the power to offend me, and there was no answer ready to my lips.

"Perhaps Cora guessed this, for she was quick as the flash of a star in her intelligence; at any rate, she asked me no questions, but contented herself with braiding my hair, smoothing it with her soft palms, and stooping to kiss my forehead when she saw a shadow of discontent pass over it.

"'Do not fret,' she said, softly, whispering back the thoughts I was striving to drive from my brain; 'seventy years is longer than most men live. Only have patience and wait.'

"I was angry with her for understanding that, which I wished buried from the whole world. Dashing her hands away, I swept the hair she was braiding in a coil around my head, and turned upon her with such sharp rebuke, that she retreated from me frightened.

"'Ah! has it gone so far?' she muttered, shaking her head. 'Well, after this there will be neither patience nor peace for any of us.'

"I ordered her to be silent, and directly after heard her sobbing in the next room as if her heart were broken.

"Why did Cora's words haunt me all that night? are evil thoughts the only ones which cling tenaciously to the brain? I tried to cast them off, heaven knows I did! but that was impossible, nor could I sleep. The shock upon my nerves had been far too severe for that.

"Why would the old man haunt my room and sit by the pillow on which I could find no rest? His presence tortured me. I could not keep my aching eyes from his white hair and the wrinkles on his forehead, which seemed to deepen and grow prominent in the moonlight of my shaded lamp. How could I forget his seventy years, with such things before me in my wakefulness? But he would not leave me; anxiety kept him watchful. It seemed to me that those bright, earnest eyes read all the dark thoughts that haunted my brain. I turned my face to the wall and pretended to sleep. He sat motionless, holding his very breath, for he knew how much rest must be needed after the awful shock I had received, and would not frighten it away by a single motion. After a while, when everything was still, I felt him bending over me; directly his quivering old lips touched my forehead, and what appeared to me like a heavy rain-drop fell upon my closed eyelid.

"'Thank God,' he murmured; 'she is asleep at last!'

"This child-like gratitude touched me more than the protest of a thousand clergymen could have done. How purely and dearly the old man loved me, and how unworthy I was! Great heavens, why did I ever marry him, and thus make deception almost a duty? There is one excuse for me—I did not then know what love meant.

"Toward morning, Mr. Dennison went into his own room; then I breathed again; true, he was very near, and by changing my position I could see his white head and grand old face upon the pillow, where he had fallen asleep with a smile of thankfulness upon his lips. After all, he is generous, good, and rich in intelligence. Why is it that love will not go with the reason?

"They would have kept me in bed the next day, but I resisted. The minutes were too precious for such waste. I went down-stairs, feeling like a criminal and looking like one, Cora said, but the two gentlemen regarded my sadness and my pallor as a proof of illness, and would scarcely allow me to speak, such was their anxiety for my welfare. So I sat in my easy-chair languid and still, listening to them as they conversed, and yet gathering but few of their words into my mind. All at once a blow seemed to have struck me. It was only a word, but that one word took away my breath. Mr. Dennison had been asking some question, and Lawrence answered,—

"'To-morrow.'

"'Not so soon as that. Indeed, my friend, we cannot spare you,' said Mr. Dennison.

"I held my breath. It seemed as if my heart would never beat again. A slow faintness crept over me while Lawrence answered,—

"'But I must: the business which brings me South is too important for delay. Already I have spent nearly a month that may cost me dear.'

"His eyes turned full upon mine. They were dark and heavy with sadness. God forgive me if mine expressed too much!

"'But my wife will never consent to this. Speak, dear, and give him one of your pretty commands. It must be important business indeed, which can win him to disobey you.'

"I opened my lips to speak, but no words followed the effort. A choking sensation came into my throat, and the very light went out from before my eyes. They thought me insensible, but my faculties were locked up; I knew everything.

"Mr. Dennison ran into the house, crying out for Cora. That instant Lawrence took me in his arms; I felt his breath upon my face when he drew back with a faint exclamation. Cora stood close by him.

"'She is faint, she is insensible,' he said, hurriedly. His voice was confused, and I could feel that the arm which held me was seized with sudden trembling. 'It was imprudent to let her come down.'

"Cora put him aside, and took my hand from his, just as Mr. Dennison came back to the veranda.

"'Ah,' he cried, joyfully; 'she is better, the color is coming back to her mouth! poor child, poor child! we have let you come out too soon.'

"He stooped down and kissed me tenderly, but I shrunk from him with sudden recoil, and leaning upon Cora, entered the house, so weary and sick at heart that I almost prayed to die.

"There was no rest for me that day. One thought occupied my whole mind: he was going in the morning—going I knew not whither, and the history of the last two weeks would be henceforth all of life that I should care to remember. I wandered from room to room, wondering what course I could take, and how it would be possible to appease the aching pain at my heart. Sometimes I could hear his voice rising up from the veranda. It was low and grave, sometimes I thought constrained, as if the words he uttered came from a preoccupied heart.

"No criminal ever listened for the steps that were to bring him a reprieve with more interest, than I felt in gathering up the broken sentences of that conversation. He was going away, first to New Orleans, then back to New York, where business must suffer until his return. I heard this clearly. It was no rash speech, but a settled determination; yet up to that morning he had never spoken of it."

CHAPTER LXX
THE MIDNIGHT WALK

"I could not sleep, though I had seemed tranquil all the evening. Mr. Dennison, having been broken in his rest the night before, slumbered heavily, and this made my wakeful solitude unendurable. The moon shone brightly, and the cool air came through the window with enticing sweetness. All day long I had been cramped and restless in the house, which was growing hateful to me. Oh how I longed for that grand solitude which lies in space! A wild desire to escape from the deep breathing of my husband seized upon my mind. I dressed myself in noiseless haste, and gliding down-stairs, opened a French window, and fled through it breathlessly. I had no object in view, and all places were alike to me, so long as I could breathe freely, and cry aloud without fear of being overheard. But a footpath lay before me, and I followed it on and on till I came to the pond, or lake, which I had visited with Lawrence on the first day of his coming. It was perfectly beautiful that night. Here and there a ripple, as of ten thousand diamond chains tossed on the waters, followed some current, and died off in the shadows. The dusky green of the magnolia-tree was kindled up with gleams and touches of silver, while its sleeping flowers filled their great chalices of snow with moonlight, and bathed themselves in its dewy radiance. If my heart had not been sad before, the exquisite stillness of this scene would have rendered it so; the very ripple of the waters among the lily pads affected me like music, and the dark trailing of the mistletoe-boughs, which were strangling the great live-oak with ten thousand leafy caresses, made me almost afraid, they were so ghostly.

"I went into the black shadow of this grand old tree, sat down with my back against its trunk, and fell into a passion of bitter weeping. Why had I become all at once so unhappy? What sorrow, or cause of sorrow, had fallen upon me? I would not even attempt to answer this question, but asked it over and over again, as if the solution were not in my own heart reproaching me.

"All at once I heard a noise in the grass—the steady fall of a man's foot. I hushed my tears, and drew my shawl over the white dress that threatened to betray me, even buried as I was in deep shadows. A tall figure directly after appeared in the moonlight, standing by the lake. I knew it at once. He also had come out into the beautiful night, unhappy, perhaps, and restless as myself. He stood awhile motionless, then I saw him move away, and walk quickly up and down the shore, as if the beauty of the night filled him with irrepressible inquietude. Then I asked myself why he could not rest, and what feelings had driven him forth. My heart gave a reply which turned its sadness into excitement. Still I neither moved nor spoke, but watched his abrupt movements to and fro with breathless interest. Ah, he was wretched as myself—the thought of parting had driven him forth. I was sure of that, and the certainty was like a triumph.

"All at once Lawrence turned from the moonlight, and plunged into the black shadows of the oak, where he walked up and down like a disturbed spirit. I could hear broken words fall from his lips, as if he found it a relief to speak aloud in the solitude. There was passion and pathos in his voice, but I gathered no other meaning from the sounds that reached me.

"Perhaps I stirred, and by a movement of my shawl revealed the whiteness of my dress, for he came toward me, exclaiming,—

"'Great heavens! what is this?'

"I shrunk back against the body of the oak, and huddled the shawl around my person, hoping thus to escape his observations; but he came close to me, and said very quietly, though his voice trembled a little,—

"'Do not hide yourself, but come out into the moonlight. I felt that you would be here.'

"I arose, obedient as a little child, and walked by his side toward the magnolia-tree, where the moonlight fell in white radiance.

"'Why did you come out at this late hour?' he said, looking down upon me with gentle compassion in his eyes.

"'I could not sleep. I was so unhappy that the close air of the house stifled me.'

"'I understand,' he replied, almost mournfully. 'It is the old story. I too—but what matters that—the air of the house was oppressive. No matter, I shall quit it to-morrow.'

"'To-morrow,—and you will go?'

"'Yes; Dennison is an old friend—a dear old friend. I shall go to-morrow.'

"'To-morrow, and forever!' I cried, in a burst of passionate despair, which frightened me the moment it left my lips.

"He did not answer in words, but took my two hands between his, and bent his eyes upon me with a glance so searching, that I shrunk away from him, for the moonlight gave supernatural intensity to his face.

"'To-morrow, and I think forever; believe me, it is better so.'

"'Better? Forever! forever! Oh, these are terrible words!' I cried, scarcely caring to conceal the anguish which wrung such expressions from me.

"'They seem terrible to youth, I know,' he answered, sadly; 'but after a while you will learn that time softens even our ideas of eternity. Life is, and must be, one continued scene of parting.'

"'But parting is such pain,' I pleaded.

"'Pain does not last forever.'

"'Oh, it will; it must!' I cried out, in a passionate protest.

"The man smiled, and shook his head, sadly enough.

"'It seems so now; but you will know more of the world some day, and learn to cast deep feeling from you. It is a sad drawback in life.'

"'And you have learned this lesson?' I asked, half in tears, half angrily.

"He paused a moment, made a gesture as if he were casting some great restraint upon himself, and then answered:

"'Yes, I have learned the lesson. So must you.'

"'But I can not. God made me as I am. It is my nature to feel and suffer keenly.'

"'I think so. Yet in a little time how all this may change!'

"'Never!'

"'Ah, yes; and when that change comes—when you are brilliant, careless, a beautiful coquette, perhaps we can meet again, and play with the foam of life pleasantly, as it is tossed to our feet by the waves of society; but deep waters are treacherous; we must not trust to them.'

"'You talk strangely,' I said, feeling an angry fire kindling against him in my bosom.

"'I talk honestly, as you will admit some day.'

"I turned from him, angry with the tone of protection and superiority which he had assumed. Surely I was no school-girl to be thus adroitly put upon my good behavior.

"'You are angry with me?'

"'Yes; I have cause. You seem to speak from premises which I do not understand. What have I done that you should lecture me so?'

"My anger seemed to amuse him. His eyes flashed, and he laughed a low, sweet laugh, that the rippling wind carried off in its murmurs.

"'What have you done, child? Why, wandered off here, at the peril of your health, when you should have been quietly sleeping!'

"'But you have done the same thing!'

"'Yes; but nothing harms me. Being a man, I know how to take care of myself.'

"'Is it a part of manhood to be without feeling?'

"'And you charge me with that?'

"'Yes, I do, or you would never speak of me with an idea that I could become a brilliant coquette.'

"'Indeed! Why, are you not a woman?'

"I turned to move away. There was something bitter in his utterance of the last word that irritated me.

"He followed me.

"'You did not hear me out,' he said;—'and a beautiful woman—can such rare beings escape admiration?'

"Still I walked on, leaving the live-oak and magnolia-tree behind. His last speech seemed hollow and conventional. Did he think to appease me by commonplace flattery like that?

"He walked by my side in silence some minutes, looking earnestly in my face when it turned to the moonlight. All at once he broke out earnestly, passionately, throwing off all the constraint that had made him seem so artificial.

"'Let us be frank with each other,' he said. 'You are my friend's wife. I go from his house to-morrow, because I am afraid of loving you more than an honorable man should. Is this honest? Are you angry with me?'

"My face was lifted to his; my hands unconsciously clasped themselves. I trembled in every limb; but it was neither with anger nor pain.

"'Am I not right?' he demanded, turning his face away.

"I did not answer, for I knew well that, right or wrong, his going would leave me miserable.

"'I thought myself stronger and wiser,' he continued, without seeming to heed my silence; 'but that day when you were in such peril I learned how deep was the impression your beauty and loveliness had made upon me. Since then I have been resolved to go—my honor and my happiness demand it.'

"Still I was silent, partly from a wild sense of triumph, partly from terror lest he should guess at the feeling.

"'You will not answer me; my frankness offends you.'

"He seemed touched and hurt by the silence, which I could not force myself to break. All at once I was sobbing. He took my hand gently in his, and led me back along the path we had been walking. I cannot repeat all that he said to me. It was himself on whom all blame rested. This was the spirit of his conversation. Not for one moment did he hint that I could have been interested in anything he did, save as the hospitable lady of a mansion in which he was a guest. Was he deceived? I cannot tell; but this I do know, every word he uttered was full of loyal respect for my husband. He did not seem to understand or notice the tears I was shedding, but quietly led me toward the house. At last he stopped, took my hand, pressed it to his lips, and left me standing alone within sight of my dwelling.

"Lawrence left the next morning at daylight. I had been dreaming on my sleepless pillow that scene by the lake over and over again. Every word that man had uttered passed through my brain, and made a sweet lodgment in my heart. How careful he had been to save my pride while confessing his own weakness. If he had been masterful, and treated me like a child, no word of his had conveyed a suspicion that I too was in danger. His delicacy enthralled me more by far than persuasion could have done. He spoke only of his own struggles and his own danger, never hinting that I might share in one or the other. How magnanimous, how self-sacrificing he was—and this man loved me!

"All at once I heard a noise of wheels in front of the house. A sharp apprehension broke up my dreams. I sprang out of bed, lifted the lace curtain, and saw my husband's light buggy drawn up on the carriage-drive. While Tom was packing a valice under the seat, Mr. Lawrence stood near drawing on his gloves.

"He was going without one word of farewell. The thought made me wild. I flung up the window with a violence that tore the valenciennes from the sleeve of my night-dress, and called out,—

"'Not yet, not yet!'

"He did not hear me, or perhaps would not. That instant he sprang into the buggy, snatched the reins from Tom, and drove off. As he passed a curve in the road, he drew up and looked back at the house, as if unable to leave it without a farewell-glance. I was still at the window, half shrouded by the curtains, but leaning out, with wild unconsciousness of my position. He waved one hand, drew his horse up with the other so sharply that the buggy was half wheeled across the road; the next instant the horse made a plunge forward, seemingly unmanageable, and in an instant bore him out of sight.

"I knelt by the window a long time, looking upon the spot where he had disappeared in blank despair. In one minute my life seemed to have become a barren waste. Points in the landscape that had been so beautiful over-night, struck me with a dreary appearance of change. My eyes grew hot and ached with the pain of my sudden desolation. I could neither weep nor cry out, but knelt there with a dull sense of sorrow and utter loneliness creeping over me. Burdened with these wretched feelings, I crept back to my couch, and burying my face in the pillows, suffered silently."

CHAPTER LXXI
AWAY FROM HOME

"This house is not the same now; its stillness oppresses me, its magnificence palls on my senses. Wherever I turn, some memory starts up to pain me. Why have I filled every beautiful spot with associations that sting me so?

"I think that my husband is watching me with more interest than formerly. If he sees a cloud on my face, some gentle act of attention seeks to drive it away. Sometimes he asks, in a troubled voice, what makes me so sad and thoughtful, as if he guessed at the truth, and the suspicion wounded him. Then I fly from the stillness of my sorrow, and force a wild sort of spirits, that make him still more depressed. This old man has seen a great deal of the world in his life, and perhaps reads me better than I think. Is deception ever a duty? At any rate, it is the refuge of cowards, and sometimes of kindness. Now, I should not really be afraid to lay the whole truth before this old man, so far as its effect on myself is concerned; but when I think of him and all the pain it would certainly give, my heart recoils from its expression. If he would only be a little unkind, I should not care so much. But, after all, what is there to explain? No word of *his*, or act of mine, could be censured justly. True, I met him at night, unknown to the family, in a beautiful and solitary spot, where some conversation passed which made me both sad and happy, but no wrong was done to any one, and the whole scene, if thoroughly explained, should bring no blame with it. I left the house without one thought of meeting any human being. If he saw and followed me, it was for a most honorable purpose—honorably, but, oh, most cruelly carried out.

"How miserably slow the weeks and months roll on. I can endure this irksome sameness of life no longer; the very fragrance of the air sickens me. I long for change—for excitement. Youth has no need of rest; its aspirations are always pressing onward. *He* said that I was beautiful. My husband has told me this a hundred times, but it made little impression, for what is the worth of beauty in a great dull house like this? I long to go out into the world again, for there is a chance that I may—no, no, I will not think of that. He did not even tell me where he was going. But change I must and will have; it is the want of excitement that makes me a slave to these fits of depression. While surrounded by the homage of other men, I shall learn to forget that this one refused it to me.

"This evening I ventured upon the subject which has been haunting me for weeks. Mr. Dennison remarked that I was getting pale, and had lost all the brilliant glow of spirits which made my first coming home like an opening of paradise to him. Was I ill, or had he failed in anything that could have made me happy?

"I did not complain, but smiled upon him in a way that brought light into his eyes, and said pleasantly enough, that I was not quite myself in splendid solitude, that female friends were necessary to me, and I had parted with them perhaps a little too suddenly. Sometimes, I confessed, a feeling of discontent would creep over me, and but for him and all his generous attentions, I should grow weary of our grand lonely life.

"Mr. Dennison became anxious at once. 'Would I have guests invited? It was the easiest thing in life to have the great house filled with the most agreeable company to be found in the State.'

"'Guests? Oh, nothing of the kind! The duties of a hostess were beyond me just then,—but a little journey somewhere—how would he like that?— say to New Orleans?—the approaching autumnal weather would render a trip to the city pleasant, and we could come back any day.'

"Mr. Dennison accepted this proposal at once. He had seemed a little anxious at first when I spoke of leaving home, as if some doubt rested in his mind; but when I mentioned New Orleans, the cloud left his face, and he fell in with the suggestion.

"My suspicions were right. Mr. Dennison was not altogether at rest about Lawrence. At first he suspected that I was anxious to be thrown in his way again. I could see it in his face, and dared not speak of Saratoga, Newport, or any Northern watering-place, which it had been my first intention to suggest. So I mentioned New Orleans, and he was satisfied, while I fairly bit my lips white with the vexation of my failure. But New

Orleans was better than nothing. There, at least, we should find society, amusement and distraction. Besides, our names would be announced in the public journals, and *he* might learn of our presence there. Yes, yes, New Orleans was preferable to home, especially as the autumn was near, and the gay season northward already breaking up.

"Cora was in ecstasies when I told her that we were going away. Poor girl, she had found my domestic life very dull and depressing; I could see that by the alacrity with which she went to work. Once more she became bright and animated as a bird. My wardrobe was speedily put in order, and we left the plantation, much happier to go away than we had been to enter it."

CHAPTER LXXII
OUT IN THE WORLD AGAIN

"Lawrence was right. Beauty is a great power, and I am beautiful. I know it in a thousand ways, but best of all by the homage of men and the envy of women. Both are sweet to me. I love to see these envious creatures turn pale and whisper their venom to each other, as I am besieged by the attentions of their favorites. At first I was a little timid about asserting the power that I felt myself to possess. Mr. Dennison, I thought, might be displeased, were his wife to accept the position offered her as a belle and leader in the best social circles of the South. I think he was at first annoyed by the great popularity which followed my advent into society, but I soon forgot to notice these indications, and resolved to live my life whether he was pleased or not. After all, there is a great deal in this world worth living for besides love as a grand passion. The adoration which others are forced to give you has its charms; besides, there arise episodes of love in one's life, which come and go like the rosy dawn and golden sunset of a summer-day, which for the time charm one's heart out of its one deep passion. In society here I forget how deeply I loved that one man, and better still, I forget to think of my husband. For his sake my heart was thrown back upon itself, and he had become the cause of my humiliation; but for that, Lawrence might have been my slave, as other men have been, and will be, so long as I allow them to kneel at the altar of my vanity. Had I remained at the plantation, this conviction would, I do believe, have deepened into hatred of my husband; but I was too pleasantly occupied, brain and sense, for any deep feeling to reach me in that whirl of society; just then it would have been as impossible for me to hate, as to love my husband. I simply cared nothing about him, save as he was the source from whence I obtained gold in which to frame my beauty. Without that, half my power would have disappeared.

"Lawrence was right. The time has come when I am a careless, brilliant, beautiful coquette, and this he has made me. 'Then,' he said, 'we can meet in safety and play with the foam of life pleasantly, as it is tossed to our feet by the waves of society.'

"I understand all this now. When I am heartless, and altogether given up to vanity, he will not be afraid of loving me, because, to a man like him, love for a woman so transformed would be impossible. But am I transformed? Is not the old nature still alive in my bosom? I have no time for a serious answer. The foam he speaks of is mounting too whitely around my feet.

"'What is this? Mr. Dennison ill? Falling away? Forgetting to smile? Looking the very ghost of himself?' These were the very words I overheard this morning, as I stood unnoticed behind two ladies conversing in the great drawing-room of the St. Charles. Was this true? I had not noticed. The old man never complained, and I saw nothing. If he had fallen away in his appetite, no one was less likely to be aware of it than myself, for it was very seldom that we breakfasted at the same hour, and at dinner I was always too pleasantly occupied for any thought of his appetite. But one thing was true, he did look thin and terribly depressed. His white linen coat was hanging loosely around his person. The silvery hair, which everybody admired so much, seemed to have grown thinner. Never in my life have I looked on so sad a face.

"I crossed the room at once, and sat down by Mr. Dennison. His face brightened, he swept the white hair back from his forehead, and smiled upon me.

"'Are you ill?' I said, laying my hand on his.

"'No, not ill; only a little lonesome.'

"'Lonesome among all these people?' I answered, still pressing his hand.

"He looked down at my hand, which was blazing with great diamonds that he had given me.

"'There is room for one more,' he said, with a sigh. 'I bought it for you weeks ago, but have found no time in which you could receive it.'

"He took a star of diamonds from his pocket, and placed it on the only one of my fingers that was not already ornamented. His old white hands trembled a little as he put the ring on my finger, and I could see tears trembling up to his eyes.

"'How kind, but how childish you are,' I said, kissing the ring, for it was well worth that small sign of gratitude. 'Now tell me what makes you look so pale and so—'

"'Old, you hesitate to say; but I know it. You are not the only one, child, who has discovered that you are married to an old, old man.'

"'I have not thought of it. Indeed, indeed the idea never enters my mind,' I answered, honestly enough, for he had very seldom been in my memory at all; 'but what makes you look so miserable? Not that idea, I am sure. Is it because I have been so extravagant, and spent such loads of money? Sometimes I do get frightened about that.'

"'But I scarcely regard it—perhaps I ought; but money seems so trivial compared to other things.'

"'Your health, for instance; for you are ill,' I answered, brushing the white hair back from his temple with my hand, while the ladies opposite were watching me in a flutter of curiosity.

"'You are kind to think of that,' he said, gently; 'but I am not ill, only reproaching myself.'

"'Why?'

"'For the bondage which you are beginning to feel so heavily.'

"I looked at him earnestly a moment, and in that glance gathered a knowledge of all he had suffered. My heart smote me, for that moment I was ready to make any sacrifice that would do him good. In truth, the life I had been leading had already become wearisome. After all, empty homage satisfies no real want of the heart.

"'Shall we go home?' I said, with a sudden impulse of kindness.

"He grasped my hand so tightly that the diamonds hurt me.

"'If you would—if you only would!'

"'Let us go to-morrow, then,' I answered. 'No, that cannot be, I have engagements; but next week. We shall get home in full time for the orange-blossoms.'

"'And you *will* go?'

"'Certainly. All this is getting very tiresome. Even the spite of the women has lost its charm.'

"That morning we went into the breakfast-room together, and then I remarked how completely Mr. Dennison's appetite had failed. This made me very thoughtful. What if he should die?'

"'Cora,' I said that night, as the girl was undressing me, 'have you observed how ill Mr. Dennison looks?'

"'Yes, I have, young mistress, and it has frightened me dreadfully.'

"'Frightened you, Cora? Is he so far gone as that? I did not dream of your caring so much for him.'

"'Neither do I. It is you that I care for.'

"'And you think that I would grieve?'

"'Yes, I do.'

"'It should be so. Indeed, Cora, he is a good man, and has been kind to us.'

"'But that won't last forever, young mistress. The old master is keen as he is kind. If he was to make his will now, have you much idea that his property would go to the wife, who scarcely speaks to him once in twenty-four hours?'

"I started, and turned upon the girl.

"'Why, Cora, you frighten me!'

"'Not so much as you have frightened me. Poor white widows aren't to my taste. We have tried that once, and I didn't like it.'

"'Cora, we will go back to the plantation.'

"'That is the best thing you can do,' answered the girl, quietly. 'Home is the place for a man to die in.'

"'Why, girl!' I cried out, in nervous dread, 'you speak as if he were really in danger.'

"'And so he is; people seldom get over the disease that has been creeping on him ever since we came here.'

"'What disease? What are you speaking of, Cora? What disease do you think Mr. Dennison has?'

"'A broken heart.'

"'Cora!'

"'None of your sudden fits—people get over them; but slow and sure: I have been watching it from the first.'

"'And you think I have done this?'

"'Of course. Who else?'

"'Cora, we will go home next week.'"

CHAPTER LXXIII
FIRST WIDOWHOOD

"I am a widow. The name fills me with awe, as if I had never heard it before. It has a new meaning now—a terrible meaning of death, which is full of reproach and horror. He lies yonder, cold and still, the smile which he had almost forgotten of late frozen on his white lips, the lines of age graven deeply in his face,—with something more terrible still, which makes me shiver and shrink as I gaze upon it.

"Have I done this? Is that look of sorrow but the shadow of a charge which the recording angel is now writing down in the eternal book against me? Am I the murderer of this good old man? How he loved me! how kind, how generous, how delicate he was! And I—no, no! it must have been old age. Men of seventy do not sink down and perish in silence because they are not loved with the intensity given to youth. Oh, how I wish it were all over! While he lies in the house, so frozen and cold, I shall not draw a free breath. It seems to me as if he could rise up any moment out of that marble sleep with the power to search every thought that has been in my heart during the last year. His knowledge is perfect now; he reads my soul as I dare not read it myself. *Have* I wished his death? Have I ever thought of what might happen after that? God forgive me, for I seem terrible to myself.

"Death in the house; this great lonely dwelling, with all its luxurious appliances, is but a tomb. The air chills me; its solitude is terrible. Cora comes to me once in a while with her silky flatteries, and attempts to convince me that I have never been blamable as a wife. I know that she does not believe this, and almost hate her for thinking that her sophistry can reconcile me with myself. Yet what have I done? Amused myself—gathered crowds of admirers around me—neglected the only true love that ever lightened my life. Shall I ever be worshipped again as that old man worshipped me?...

"They have carried him out from his home forever, and now the old house seems more vast and lonely than before. I still hear the tramping of his bearers' feet, and shudder as the pall seems to rustle and sweep by me. Ah! the first feelings of widowhood must be mournful indeed to a devoted wife; to me they are terrible. The very air seems to reproach me. I start at each sound as if it were a denunciation. The very air I breathe seems heavy with funereal shadows....

"The first great horror has left me, but a feeling of blank desolation still remains. I have not yet thought of the future, or asked myself what may be in store for the woman whom so many are loading with praises and commiseration which she knows in her heart are undeserved.

"This morning I was aroused from the heavy apathy which has made my life a blank, by the arrival of my husband's solicitor. Mr. Dennison has left a will making me the inheritor of everything he had on earth. The lawyer told me this, and, for the first time since my widowhood, I felt the heart in my bosom stir like a living thing. Was I indeed so wealthy, and free, too!

"I observed in a dreamy way that the lawyer looked anxious and oppressed, as if something yet remained to be told.

"'Is this all,' I said; 'has he mentioned no other person in the will?'

"'No other person,' was the reply; 'but I have something to explain which may change the aspect of my news. It seems that within the past few months a heavy mortgage has been laid upon the plantation, and it must be sold.'

"'A mortgage!' I said; 'that is something which prevents a man holding or selling his own land, is it not?'

"'It is a debt for which the estate is pledged,' answered the lawyer; 'but I wonder you do not understand it better, for your own signature is attached.'

"Then I remembered that, during the stay of Mr. Lawrence at our house, Mr. Dennison had called me to the table in his library and asked me to sign a paper. He explained to me clearly enough, no doubt, that the paper might deprive me of some claim for dower; but I did not heed it at the time, and now it was to fall upon me with all its force. The plantation must be sold, the lawyer said, for he was one of the executors to the will. The mortgage once cleared off and the debts paid, there would still be a handsome property left.

"All at once I was seized with intense love for the old place. Where should I ever find a home so rich in comforts, so beautifully surrounded?

"'Is it not possible to keep the place?' I demanded, with growing interest.

"'No; the mortgage was given, I imagine, in order to raise funds for some dazzling speculation in which Mr. Lawrence was concerned. At any rate, there is no money to pay it with, and the estate must go to the hammer.'

"'This is cruel, it is unjust,' I said, angrily.

"'It was wrong and foolish to involve the estate as Mr. Dennison has,' answered the executor, 'and the loss is a heavy one. Let us be thankful that our good friend has left enough without that.'

"'But his losses were brought on by Mr. Lawrence?' I questioned, speaking the name with a thrill of pain.

"'No! they were fellow-sufferers. It is understood that Lawrence has lost heavily, and will perhaps be ruined.'

"Instantly my heart swelled with sympathy for the man who had helped to impoverish me.

"'Oh! if he had but left the estate unburdened, I should not care.'

"Heaven knows I was thinking of the man who had, perhaps, wronged me, but the executor misunderstood my words and looked at me wonderingly. I saw this, but could not explain that the great wish of my heart was that there might be enough to redeem the losses that had fallen upon Lawrence. I could not endure to think of him as a poor man. A poor man—that is a terrible word to the ears of a Southern lady.

"The executor tried to explain everything clearly, and I made an effort to understand. He was anxious about the property, and thought the times unpropitious. The North and South were that hour verging closer and closer toward a civil war, in which the value of property would become uncertain, and I might be a sufferer.

"I knew all this before; rumors of political strife had reached even our secluded home. I knew that the bitter animosity which had been long growing between the North and South had even then broken into open hostilities. Southern statesmen had retreated in a body from the United States Senate, and resigned their seats in the House. I had taken a blind interest in this matter, and, in a loose way, hated everything that opposed the dominant power of my own section; but it was as a child takes sides. I did not, and do not, really understand the questions which give rise to all this turmoil. Of course, the whole affair will be settled somehow; people never do fight when they threaten so much. Besides, the South is so reasonable; she only asks to set up for herself, and be let alone. What objection can there be to this? I dare say the Northern people will acquiesce; but if not, it will only take a month or so to gain our independence. I think the executor is right to put off the sale till then; for of course property will rise enormously, and this may compensate me for that great drawback, the mortgage. But until the estate is settled, I must remain a slave here. Perhaps that is best; it would not be proper for a widow to seek society under a year; but oh! how dreary that year will be!

"I wonder if Mr. Lawrence has heard of his friend's death? Months have gone by and not a word from him, not even the usual letter of condolence. Perhaps he is coming. Surely the share he has taken in the ruin of this property ought to bring some explanation. There is no reason now why he should keep aloof.

"At last I have heard from him. A letter came to the executor, enclosing one for me. It is in my bosom. I have covered the senseless paper with kisses. Yet there is nothing in it but gentle condolence for sorrow. The reason he has not written before is that the news of Mr. Dennison's death reached him in Europe, where he will remain until the end of this year. His letter to the executor was long and thoroughly explanatory of all the business which lay between him and Mr. Dennison. This mortgage, it seems, was only the accumulation of many others that had from year to year been a burden on the estate. Through the influence of Mr. Lawrence, a New York capitalist had paid up these mortgages, and concentrated them into one which, after all, does not cover half the value of the estate. It was this act of friendship which brought Mr. Lawrence to our house. There was neither risk nor speculation in the whole business. Even with this encumbrance, Mr. Dennison's will would have left me wealthy, but for the terrible civil war which has broken over us. As it is, there are three hundred slaves, which the mortgage does not touch, and they are a handsome property in themselves.

"The estate is sold, and the result scarcely covers the mortgage. Still the slaves are left, and my jewels are of great value. Sometimes, when my hand rests upon my black dress, the diamonds with which my husband loaded it flame up and burn into my conscience. How could I be so negligent and cold to him?

"Some months longer I shall remain on the estate. The new owner wishes to hire most of my slaves; that arrangement will supply me with an ample income, and permit me to go anywhere; that is, if I can get away, when the whole country is swarming with armed men. Thank heaven! my home has escaped all these military disturbances; but they build a wall of bayonets between me and *him*. I cannot even get letters....

"I am going: an opportunity offers. This very day I start for the North. My pass is ready, my escort waiting. How my heart swells! how my courage rises! The dangers of war have no terrors for me. I am going to the North, and *he* is there....

"How long it is since I have written a line in my journal, or even seen it! In our rough journey there was little time or opportunity for writing, but here I have rest and am entirely out of danger.

"Lawrence is in the Federal army, commanding one of the city regiments which have gone down to the war for special duty. How vast and lonely this hotel seems! I am lost in this great wilderness of people. The streets are full of military men; regiments are constantly passing through on their way to the war. Great heavens! did our people hope to wrest away any portion of this great country from men like these? For the first time I understand the madness of the rebellion. It is no light thing to rend a great nation asunder. I begin to feel this, and tremble for the people of the South. In the insanity of their ambition they have sacrificed everything....

"He is coming. His regiment is ordered home. I am here at the Fifth Avenue Hotel—his home when he is in the city. Lawrence must not find me here. His fastidious delicacy might take the alarm! Besides, I have made acquaintances, and am almost acting over the *rôle* that made me so popular at New Orleans; else the suspense of this long waiting would have been intolerable. Yes, it is far better that I should be away when he comes. If he hears of me, it will only be from admirers. Even with the women, I think that I have left no enemies. It is early for the season, but this very day my rooms at Long Branch shall be taken. Will he follow me there? The question drives the breath back from my lips....

"I have been at the Branch three weeks. His regiment has returned to New York, but I have not seen him: this suspense is terrible. Yesterday I sent Cora to the city, ostensibly to get some articles that I left at the hotel, but in fact to bring me intelligence of him, for which my soul was thirsting.

"She came back radiant, for the poor girl understands how anxious I am. She saw him—talked with him. He has been very busy with his regiment, and attending to neglected business on Wall Street; but next week—next week—oh, how long the days will seem till then!...

"He is here. I have seen him; we have walked together, free as birds upon the shore, where the sea rolls in with bewildering harmonies for the happy, and solemn anthems for those who suffer. To-day the very air was jubilant; the waves came rolling in crested with foam, and dashing the sand with shimmering silver. How the sunshine danced and broke and laughed over the broad expanse of water! The sea-gulls, as they swooped down and dipped their wings in the curling foam, were like doves to us. Indeed, this flat, treeless shore on which the ocean is eternally beating, is just now the brightest paradise I ever knew.

"Weeks roll on, and our companionship is perfect; but he says nothing of the future. We talk of books, of friendship—love even—but in a vague, dreamy way, that confirms nothing. I wonder at this, and it disturbs me. Is it that he is no longer a rich man? I have heard this, but am not sure, for the rumor is often met with contradiction. If this should prove true, it will account for his conduct. I know him well enough to be sure that his sensitive honor would take alarm at the thought of marrying a woman whose property would more than match his own; and mine, notwithstanding all losses, is of no ordinary value.

"These thoughts trouble me. Nothing can be more impressive than his devotion; my society seems all in all to him, but our relationship remains the same.

"A rather singular family has just arrived—some rich iron-man from the interior of Pennsylvania. His wife is a confirmed invalid, but one of the most refined and lovable women I ever saw. She must have been very beautiful in her youth, for her features are singularly like those of her daughter, who is considered the most lovely girl at the Branch this season. The rooms which Mr. Lee occupies open on to the same veranda with mine, and as the lady spends a great deal of her time in looking out upon the ocean from her luxurious easy-chair, I managed to open an acquaintance with her and a lady who is her constant companion, and either an elder sister of the beautiful girl I have spoken of, or some near friend of the family. My first advances to this lady were rather coldly received. She has evidently been out of society a long time, and appears shy and reserved. The younger lady seemed to be reading my face with more scrutiny than pleased me. She is not really handsome, but has lovely hair and an abundance of it, with deep gray eyes that are almost always shaded by long curling lashes, which gives them intense expression when she lifts them suddenly and meets your gaze. Her complexion is pure and bright, but the mouth is a little too large for harmony with the other features. Still, her smile is peculiarly expressive when she does smile, which is not often.

"I can hardly tell why this person impressed me so forcibly, but a strange sensation came over me when those eyes were first lifted to my face. She is not imposing in her presence, but very modest and very unobtrusive. Her attentions to Mrs. Lee were more than affectionate; and with the young lady she has the air and manner of a sister who feels her superiority in age, and nothing more.

"This morning I met Mr. Lee on the shore, walking alone. He is a princely man in appearance, taller than Mr. Lawrence, and of more noble proportions. Still, his finely-cut features lack the keen intelligence which is only seen where great genius exists. The years he has already numbered scarcely count to his disadvantage. Not very long ago I should have considered this man as far the handsomest of the two; but now the splendor of genius alone can satisfy me....

"I have had terrible news. President Lincoln has issued a proclamation which emancipates all slaves in the rebellious States. If this act is lawful, and can be enforced, I am almost a beggar. All the property to which I have a right lies in the strong arms of nearly three hundred negro slaves. A single word, the mere writing of a man's name, has swept all my wealth away. With the exception of my jewels, I have nothing. This is a terrible blow, for I have endured poverty, and shrink from it with absolute dread. To me a luxurious ease and elegance are a fixed habit, and so necessary that I could not live without them.

"One consolation comes out of all this ruin. I am sure that Lawrence has hesitated to say all that is in his heart on account of my wealth, which, if rumor speaks truly, was far greater than anything he can command. When I think of this and glory in his sensitive delicacy, the loss of all my slaves seems a less crushing calamity. This very day I will tell him how suddenly the Act of Emancipation has placed me on his level.

"I have told him of the sweeping misfortune which has left me on the verge of poverty. He looked at me in alarm. His face clouded over, his eyes turned away from mine. It was moments before he spoke.

"'It is a misfortune,' he said, at last, and there was bitterness in his voice, as if some wrong had been done himself. 'Poverty is a terrible thing; from my heart I pity you.'

"'But it is not everything,' I faltered; 'surely happiness can exist without wealth: you must not frighten me with the thought that my future is all broken up.'

"He shook his head, moved away from me abruptly, and stood for a moment looking out upon the ocean in gloomy silence. At last he came back and took my hand, which was growing cold.

"'It is a misfortune,' he said, 'but you will hardly feel it. Something is left, if properly managed. You are young and splendidly beautiful. A few smiles—a little condescension—and fortunes will be laid at your feet, compared to which that which you have lost will be nothing. As for me— but I will not talk of myself. It is only another dream broken up.' He turned abruptly, dropped my cold hand from his clasp, and walked away, leaving me stranded, as it were, like a wreck upon the shore.

"What does this mean? 'It is only another dream broken up.' These were his words. Merciful heavens! has this ruin fallen on my whole life. Will poverty frighten back the heart that was mine?

"'Another dream broken up.' These words signify everything that is humiliating and painful. If they have any meaning at all, he is ready to give me up rather than face the difficulties of my position. And I thought him so disinterested, so proud!

"Alas! I thought myself unhappy before, but this is perfect desolation. 'Another dream broken up' for him—a life broken up for me.

"I do not believe it. I mistook the meaning of his words. He loved me; I know he did. Was it not a consciousness of too passionate tenderness that drove him away from me when I was a married woman? Has he not sought me since, and told me in a thousand ways how dear I was to him? Has he not so mingled our future lives in his conversation that there could be no mistaking the drift of his thoughts? I am foolish to think that this will make any lasting difference. Besides, Lincoln must be master of the South before my slaves can be reached by any act of his.

"It is true: Lawrence, during the last week, has been gradually withdrawing himself from my society. I have seen him less frequently of late; he seldom joins me unless I am surrounded by others. Our walks on the beach are entirely broken up, and he no longer seeks me when I purposely sit apart on the veranda of the hotel.

"I have been so annoyed and felt so wronged by his conduct, that a spirit of bitter retaliation is aroused in my bosom. The most aristocratic and splendid man here is Mr. Lee. I have noticed once or twice that Lawrence has seemed a little disturbed by the slight interest this gentleman has taken in me. He shall feel this more keenly before the week is over. By that time a prouder and more fastidious man than he is shall be my slave. That idea of the power a brilliant coquette may wield, which he first planted in my mind, shall bring forth bitter fruit for his eating before I have done with him.

"This man shall be at my feet again—I do not know whether in love or hate; but no living creature shall ever cast me off in this slow, heartless fashion. I am young, beautiful, the fashion—but these things count for but little in a contest with men like Lawrence. He it was who first told me that I possess something far more powerful than all these—intellect, talent, powers of combination, and that subtle magnetism which no man has ever yet had power to resist: compared with this, beauty, youth, and fashion are trivial possessions. But I have them all, and it shall go hard if this proud man is not made to feel their influence. He thinks I accept the position, and do not feel. Let him. I have not mingled in society and practised his lessons for nothing. The 'brilliant coquette' with whom he could associate with safety has at least learned how to conceal her anguish. He shall yet find how fatal and poisonous is the hatred growing up like a upas-tree in the desert he has made. My acquaintance with Mr. Lee thrives. I have become the intimate friend of his daughter, a tender nurse to his invalid wife. They are a singularly refined and intelligent family, so loving and true that I almost envy the simplicity which springs from so much goodness. In my friendship for his wife and daughter I find the surest means of interesting Mr. Lee.

"What do I purpose by this? Why, to triumph over that ingrate Lawrence by a conquest of the only man within reach who is admitted to be his superior. He has humiliated my pride, wounded my vanity, and, oh heavens! thrown back the most passionate love that woman ever bestowed on man, as too worthless for his acceptance without money. Were Mr. Lee an unmarried man, this Lawrence should be invited to act as his groomsman within the month. As it is, he is distinguished and unapproachable to the common herd. As to the rest, wait and see—wait and see!

"Even here that man seems determined to thwart and wound me. Once, when I was talking with Mr. Lee in a low voice, watching the effect of this intimacy on Lawrence, who stood near, from under my half-closed eyelashes, he came up quietly, and desired to be introduced to my companion, who that moment moved away unconscious of the request.

"Lawrence has become acquainted with the young lady. I do not know how he managed it, but this morning when I looked out upon the sea, thinking only of him, they were standing together on the shore, conversing like old friends. My heart stood still; I felt my very lips turn white. The girl is rich, beautiful, and of good family. Almost her entire life has been spent in France, and she has undoubtedly brought all the arts and graces learned in foreign society in order to insure her conquests here. How did she manage to attract Lawrence? No woman has been able to do that since he came here. Until now my influence has been supreme, my society sufficient to his happiness;—*now* he is standing by her—yes, looking down into the eyes of that girl with the air of a man entranced. What can it mean? what can it mean?...

"I have not slept all night. My brain whirls, my heart aches; all the pride in my nature rises up in rebellion. I hate that man. He loves her. I can see it in his eyes; I can hear it in his speech. There is homage in the very bend of his person when he salutes her. Never, even in the first days of our acquaintance, has he addressed me with such tender admiration. Oh, how I hate her! The blood burns hotly in my veins when she approaches me. I long to strike her down. But be quiet, proud heart! the time will come—the time will come!

"A gentleman has just arrived at the Branch from the neighborhood of Mr. Lee's residence in Pennsylvania. He is a bright, chivalrous, noble-hearted young fellow, evidently in love with Jessie Lee, who looks upon him only as a generous young man whom she has known all her life, and cannot be particularly interested in. I discovered all this at the first interview. Besides the disadvantage of a long intimacy, she does not care for him because of the fascinations this other man has thrown around her. Poor fellow! how sad and bewildered he looks when she turns from him with such unconscious indifference to listen for the footsteps of his rival. How her cheek burns and her eyelids droop when the one man approaches her! Ah! I know the feeling, and could almost give pity for the disappointment in store for her; for she shall be disappointed. His 'brilliant coquette' is on the watch, softly, stealthily, but vigilant as a fox. Where two men are in love with the same woman, opportunities for complications are always arising. I shall neither overlook or throw them aside.

"Days and weeks have worn away,—that is the word,—worn away with such dull joylessness that they seem to me like the heavy dreams of a sick man. It is true this man would have married me out of lukewarm love and a thirst for money; but it is all over now. Both inclinations have kindled up into fiery passion for this Jessie Lee, and she is in love with him—a first love, deep and shy, but positive. He sees this and exults in it, utterly careless that I see and suffer.

"My friends reproach me for my reckless gayety. They complain that I am too greedy of pleasure, and give myself no rest. Greedy of pleasure! I am only fleeing from pain; I cannot pause to think without loathing the past and dreading the future. I rush onward like a wounded animal, afraid to pause lest I should be tempted to lie down and bleed to death.

"Lawrence has become close friends with young Bosworth. They have known each other before, it seems, and the acquaintance has been warmly renewed. There is craft and calculation in this. Let me watch and wait. I knew it. Lawrence seldom attempts to attract man or woman in vain. This morning the blinds of my window were closed, and I sat thoughtfully in the twilight of my room, listening to the murmurs of the ocean, that seemed to grow softer and more slumberous as the sun poured its silvery radiance upon them. I was very sad. No one would have complained of my spirits could they have seen me then.

"All at once, voices startled me. Lawrence and young Bosworth had paused near the closed blinds of my room. Just before this, some invitation had evidently been extended to Lawrence, and he accepted it with evident satisfaction.

"'Of course I will come, my good fellow. Fine shooting, a good horse, and such neighbors as the Lees, would draw a man out of paradise. You may count on me for a month.'

"'Then it is settled,' answered Bosworth, with a little reserve; perhaps he was not altogether pleased that the Lees were considered as an inducement for the visit. 'Then it is settled. We will do our best to make your visit to the old house pleasant.'

"They passed on after this, and left me trembling with indignation. Lawrence had made arrangements to follow Jessie Lee in a way that would commit him to nothing. Here, my presence has been some restraint upon him. In the country, his opportunities to see her will be far greater, and he will become thoroughly acquainted with all the advantages of her position.

"Lawrence is going to visit his rival, Mr. Bosworth. I will visit my rival, Miss Jessie Lee, at the same time. Before the night closes in, I will have an invitation from both the young lady and her invalid mother. As for Miss Hyde, it would be a thousand years before I got one from her. She does not like me, but I will become an inmate of her friends' house nevertheless. I can almost smile when I think of the confusion this arrangement will make.

"The night has not darkened yet, and I am invited to The Ridge. This is the name of Mrs. Lee's place in the country. How easily these gentle and truthful women are managed. They had not the least idea of inviting me when I entered their parlor, but in ten minutes after it was all arranged. I did not promise to go, however, but left the acceptance for a future day. This uncertainty will prevent them mentioning the visit to Lawrence....

"I am here at The Ridge, an honored guest, welcome to every one except Miss Hyde, who never has even pretended to like me. She has great influence in the family; but how long will it last? My enemies usually get into trouble in some unexpected way before I have been with them long.

"Lawrence is here, but I have managed that he shall not know of my presence until we meet face to face. We have a delicate game to play, and I shall enjoy the first move.

"I have seen him. We went out on horseback this afternoon, and he joined us. I was in my saddle when he rode up, and smiled upon him as if we had met only yesterday. His face flushed scarlet when he saw me. I made no effort to have him near me, but rode on with Mr. Lee, who is really one of the most charming men I ever saw. I watched Lawrence closely, to detect some annoyance at this intimacy; but his face was inscrutable. One thing was positive: my presence annoyed him.

"I think there was an effort made by Miss Hyde to keep me from Mrs. Lee's sick-room, but all her petty obstacles were swept away like a handful of rushes. Let this dainty little person take care, or she may not long remain the friend *par excellence* of the family. Mrs. Lee is very delicate, and may at any hour drop out of life. They are enormously rich, and most of the money comes from her real estate. I suppose Lawrence knows all this, or he would not have been in the neighborhood; but he shall never marry this girl—never—never!

"I am gaining something of my old ascendency over this man; and as I gain, she loses—no matter how—but she does. There are things which we never write, or care to see on record even in our own hearts. I think the devoted attentions of my host wound his vanity a little; and it is for this reason I encourage them—with another, so vague and remote that it scarcely takes shape as yet. But this is certain: I will not be made bankrupt in everything. If love fails me, I will have power and wealth. If he attains this girl, I will sweep everything else out of his reach. The pale woman up yonder in her tower-chamber cannot live forever.

"There is a little imp of Satan in this house, who is constantly with Mrs. Lee, vigilant as a fox, but, to all appearance, stolid enough in everything where her mistress is not concerned. She is completely uneducated, and seems to observe or know nothing beyond her duties in the sick-room; but she is forever there, and, I am sure, listens sometimes to our conversation, though it makes no visible impression upon her. I have told Cora to gain some influence over this strange creature. Since then she has been in my room frequently, and yesterday proposed to dress my head, which was beautifully done. She is very quiet, and takes no interest in anything around her, but talks to Cora when I am away, and the two are becoming very intimate. I shall find her useful. In her simplicity she will tell Cora everything.

"Young Bosworth has proposed to Jessie and been rejected; I am sure of this, though she is honorably reticent, and Miss Hyde refuses to speak. My relations with Lawrence are getting more and more confidential and friendly. Yesterday he even hinted at his attachment for Jessie. I listened in dead stillness, holding my breath, for it seemed as if some cruel hand were clutching at my heart. Does he think that I have no feeling, no pride? Sometimes I hate the man. How would he open this subject? How was I endowed with power to listen without shrieking forth the agony it inflicted?

"He asked me, with an effort at carelessness, if I thought there was anything serious in young Bosworth's attentions to Miss Lee. His voice faltered a little, and I knew that he was anxious. So I answered with gentle deliberation that I knew very little of the matter. Cora had gathered from the servants that they were mutually attached, but Mr. Lee opposed the marriage, as young Bosworth's fortune was in no reasonable proportion to that Miss Lee would inherit. Lawrence winced at this, unless I am greatly mistaken. Bosworth is a millionaire compared to him. If he has property of any amount, I have been unable to learn the fact. Indeed, he speaks of himself always as a poor man; but that may be from calculation. Thinking that Bosworth might know and have spoken of his friend's affairs, I have brought up the subject once or twice when conversing with Miss Hyde, but she evidently knew little or nothing about it. Oh, why is he not a rich man! The temptation of Miss Lee's fortune would be nothing to him then, and that girl and I would stand on equal ground. With the odds so completely against me, I have sworn to myself that he shall never, never marry her.

"She loves him, and I think he loves her; still he turns to me for sympathy and counsel, believing that I forget and forgive.

"Yes, she has rejected young Bosworth, and he is ill, very ill. That fine old lady, his grandmother, has sent for Miss Hyde, who will take Jessie Lee to visit her sick lover. Lawrence shall know this. He shall watch for her, going and coming. What, but intense love, can account for a step so singular—taken, too, without the knowledge of her father, for I will see that no communication of the fact shall reach him.

"It is exactly as I wished. He saw her on the road; he knows how angry her father was. His mortification is complete. He suffers enough to make my soul rise up in arms against him. To-day he betrayed one fact. The hope of gaining her property was a powerful incentive, however much he may love her. The man is worse than poor—heavily in debt—and feels himself compelled to marry riches. Perhaps this is the sole motive that brings him to the feet of this beautiful heiress. If I thought so, he might marry her; and I would wait a little till that frail woman—no, that is a terrible thought; let it sleep—let it sleep. Still, what would I do, even if Lawrence loved me? With extravagant tastes like ours, and high social positions to maintain without means, and he in debt, a marriage would be madness. If I were only sure that he sought her for her money alone—but I will not think of it.

"Lawrence has gone. I could not endure to see his disappointment, and let him depart supposing her engaged.

"I cannot live without him. This beautiful place is a desert, with all its blossoming flowers and rich appliances. When I feel that he has gone, a gloom falls upon everything around me. I am more lonely and miserable than his devotion to this young heiress could make me. Without his society, life would be a heavy burden. But how is that to be attained?

"These few days have been important ones to me. I have conjectured and thought till my brain aches and my heart is sore. To-day I stood upon the top of the Ridge, looking out upon the town and the vast landed estate owned by this man. Miss Hyde was with me, and something she said led me into a new train of thought. It seems that Jessie Lee is an heiress in spite of her father. At her mother's death, she will come in possession of half the estate. Of course, she will always live near the homestead, and the man she marries must necessarily be almost an inmate there. I have thought of this a great deal. New combinations are arranging themselves in my mind. If this rich man were free—but I dare not think of it.

"This lady is very lovely, but life must be a burden to any invalid. I should think death a mercy compared to the dull monotony of a sick-room. He is very tender and kind to her; but full health and continued illness cannot long remain in sympathy. He has learned this within the last two months, or I am greatly mistaken. Jessie Lee is getting distrustful of me. Miss Hyde has disliked me from the first, but in the sick-room I am all-potent, and this proud man does not himself dream of the power I have attained over him....

"I will do it; what choice have I? Poverty on one side, loneliness, desolation. On the other, wealth, position, his society. Oh, if I could only be sure that he does not love her!

"Having made up my mind, I am not one to falter. Yesterday I was talking with her about opiates. She is very nervous and wakeful at night, but refused to take laudanum. Very well; I have persuaded her that chloroform will bring rest, and she has some in her room. If she should take an overdose, who can be astonished?

"Last night I had a fearful struggle in her room. That girl seems endowed with wonderful resistance. I cannot put her so deeply into insensibility that she does not come out with a suddenness that frightens me. Perhaps I am nervous; everything startles me, and I feel panic-stricken at the least sound.

"After several failures I at last got the imp into perfect unconsciousness. *She* was lying on her white bed, more like a ghost than a human being. I stood over her; the dim outline of her person was just visible, but my hand crept slowly through the darkness, grasping the bottle, which was already uncorked. I was resolute. There was no tremor of heart or hand to hold me back. Slowly and steadily she inhaled the drug. Her breath stopped—her hand, which I grasped in mine, was growing cold, when I heard a scraping noise behind me. In an instant the room was illuminated with pale blue light. I turned in horror, and saw the girl Lottie and Miss Hyde, both pale as death, gazing upon me. I escaped them almost by a miracle. Cora came to my aid, and, quick as a flash of lightning, changed the bottle in my hand for another, while Miss Hyde was absolutely holding me in her arms. The whole family were aroused, but I received them calmly: the moment of peril had passed, and, instead of sinking, my energies rose to the conflict. But after I reached my room, the reaction was terrible. I fell from one fainting fit to another until morning.

"That girl Lottie suspects me. No fox waiting for prey was ever more vigilant. I dare not venture to that room again.

"An idea struck me this afternoon. A few words, spoken sadly and secretly by the sick woman, revealed means of reaching the end I wish, which are entirely free from danger, and may lead to other results. Let me think; let me plan. Why did this idea never present itself before?

"'To think that he did not love me, would be death,' she said. I felt the blood leap from my heart. This sentence revealed a terrible power which might safely be used. A power so subtle and deep-working that no human being would ever guess at its fatal effects.

"I have written this woman a letter, so completely imitating Jessie Lee's handwriting that no human being can detect the difference. In that letter I have accused myself of attempting to entrap Mr. Lee, and of usurping the affections that should belong to his wife. I have pointed out proof after proof that he has ceased to regard her, and is becoming weary of the life her illness forces upon him. I have warned her that his love is already given to another, and that her very life is becoming burdensome to him.

"The letter is adroitly written, but has no signature. Who could suppose any woman capable of maligning herself? I have sent it to the mail. It will reach her to-morrow. I cannot sleep to-night. Work like this requires a heart of brass and nerves of steel.

"It is done. She got the letter while we were out riding. When we came back, her heart was broken—poor thing, poor woman! I almost wish it had not been done. The feeling of terror that seized upon me when I saw their white faces, was awful. A faint sickness crept over me, but I must go on and face the work I had done.

"I kissed her while she was dying. Did Judas feel so when he betrayed the Saviour? No wonder he went out and killed himself. A drop of her life-blood clung to my lips. I washed it off again and again, but it burns there yet—it burns there yet....

"Weeks have passed, mostly in solitude, for we keep apart from each other, and meet gloomily when forced into domestic companionship. I am sure this man loves me, though as yet he has given no sign. I am equally sure that the other inmates of the house hate me.

"I have written to Lawrence, explaining away many things that drove him from the neighborhood. I have told him that Jessie Lee is not engaged — that she has loved him from the first. This will bring him back. Let him marry her; his presence is my life. That much at least will be secured.

"He has been here, she has refused him utterly, and he is furious. Oh, such words as he used, such cruel, hard truths as he told me! They pierce my heart like arrows poison-tipped. He does not love me — never did. This thought makes me hard as iron, resolute as a tigress.

"I am about to leave the Ridge. I have separated him from his household. It was the necessity of my position. Had these two women regained their influence over Mr. Lee, I should have lost him too. As it is, they will be left alone. I shall not be absent from his house twenty-four hours before he will depart also.

"He intends to leave home at once and travel in Europe. About the end of this year he will be in Paris. He asked no questions about my movements, but there was anxiety and deep distress in his eyes that I understood.

"I shall go at once to New York, sell my jewels, and hold myself in readiness for anything that comes. But one thing is certain — this man and I meet again."

Mrs. Dennison's journal closed here. I read it through, word by word, until my very heart grew cold with horror and dread. It is a terrible thing to be made the custodian of a great crime. It haunted me night and day, until the very burden of it threatened to undermine my health.

I hid the book away, and locked it close from all knowledge but my own. For the universe I would not have told Jessie one word of the awful crime it revealed. I think it would have killed her. But all this time my soul grew faint with apprehension. The year was wellnigh at its close. Would this woman carry out her project and meet Mr. Lee in Paris? The thought drove me wild. I resolved to leave home and cross the ocean rather than allow a noble and good man to be wiled on to a union with that terrible woman. But this was difficult. How could I leave Jessie to such perfect loneliness? These thoughts filled my mind day and night, haunting me almost into insanity.

Sometimes I thought of Lottie with a gleam of hope: possibly she had undertaken the daring enterprise which I contemplated with so much terror. I resolved to wait a while, hoping that she might send us some intelligence.

Weeks went by and we heard nothing of her. She had not promised to write—still we anxiously expected to hear of her welfare; but nothing came. Like Mr. Lee, Lottie seemed to have been swept out of our lives.

All this was very sad; but we received a little sunshine in the constant visits of young Bosworth, who was so happy now in his but half acknowledged engagement to our Jessie that all our troubles were chased away in his presence. As for the old lady—but it is impossible to explain what a protection and comfort her society proved to us at this time.

A month—six weeks went by, and still nothing of Mr. Lee or of Lottie; both had deserted us, and we were indeed alone. Jessie had some consolation in the dawning tenderness of her second love; but I—oh! those were dreary, dreary days to me!

CHAPTER LXXIV
LOTTIE'S LETTER

One morning I found a letter on the hall-table, which sent all the blood from my heart. The handwriting I did not know, but it had a foreign post-mark, and that set my hand to trembling as I touched it. The address was to myself.

Jessie was still in the room; so, like a thief, I snatched the precious messenger, and went off to my old place on the Ridge, where I could be sure of solitude. I was breathless on reaching the rock, and sat down with a hand pressed hard against my heart, which throbbed with suffocating violence.

I sat down and tore open the envelope. It was a long, heavy letter, closely written. I recognized the handwriting with a thrill of dread. With a sinking heart I turned over the pages, and saw "Lottie" written on the extreme corner of the last sheet.

"Lottie!" and the letter dated in Paris! What could it mean? It was some moments before I composed myself sufficiently to make out the first few lines, though they were characteristic enough.

"My very dear Miss Hyde," the letter began, "I a'n't much used to writing letters, and it seems to me as if this would be long and hard work; but things must be told, and if I don't write them, who will?

"You thought hard of me, I dare say, for leaving you just as I did; but I thought just the other way about it, and haven't changed my mind yet. It was tough work, though, to get away from home and bid you both good-bye, as I did. I hope to goodness you will never have to go through with anything like it. I could not tell you then what it was that set me off; but I will now.

"That very morning, before I came down on you for the money, the man from town brought over some things done up in a newspaper more than six weeks old, and in it I read that Mrs. Bab—I beg pardon—Madam Dennison had set sail in a steamboat for a place called Havre, across the Atlantic Ocean; I know more of places and things than you might believe. I was sure that Havre was in Europe, and knew well enough that Mr. Lee was there—a rich widower—with no one in the wide world to keep him from getting into scrapes. Of course, anybody that could see through a mill-stone might have known what that she-Bab—no, I mean that lady and servant—went to Havre for.

"Well, I thought it all over, and made up my mind what to do. First, I concluded to keep a close mouth in regard to Miss Jessie, for I was sure that she would wilt right down; and as for you—well, no matter: that little secret lies between you and me. Silent was the word then; but I had made up my mind to travel, and was bound to do it. But people can't sail across oceans, and gulfs, and inlets, and such kind of waterworks, without money, and I hadn't but two half-dollars in the world. You know how I came down on you and the dear young lady like a roaring lion, and got that six hundred dollars; I'd rather have danced on red-hot coals an hour than do what I did. It was just highway burglary, and nothing less. I hate myself for it yet.

"Well, after I got the money I made quick work of it, sat up all night, did a little packing, a little praying, and a great deal of crying till daylight came; then I put for the railroad and flashed down to New York. A newspaper that I bought of a little boy in the cars told me that a steamer sailed for Havre that very day. The minute we stopped in New York I got lost in a crowd of carriage-drivers and long whips, that seemed terribly glad to see me; and one of them took me on one side as kind as could be, asking where I wanted to go, promising to take me right there—that is, to the steamer—trunk and all, in no time.

"The man kept his word. I got into his carriage, and we drove through long streets, and cross-streets, down among acres of ships that looked like blasted trees, and at last we got to a steamer with stairs down its black sides, and smoke puffing out from its chimneys in a frightful way.

"The man climbed up the stairs with my trunk on his shoulder; I followed. He set it down, and I sat down on it. Then the man wanted two dollars, and I gave him one, at which he grumbled a little; but I told him that I had travelled, and knew what was what. Then he went away and left me alone in the crowd; so I had a good cry all to myself, thinking of you folks at home, and wondering what would become of me in the end.

"While I was sitting there *so* heavy-hearted, the bells started out a-ringing, the steamer began to heave and groan, half the people went helter-skelter down the side of the vessel, and the other half crowded toward one end. Then we began to move, and I felt the blood creep up and down my limbs as shivery as ice. I remember seeing, through the tears that almost blinded me, handkerchiefs waving and people crying on the deck and down on the wharf; but there was nobody to cry about me, nor shake away their sorrow from a white handkerchief; so I just huddled down on the trunk and gave right up.

"Oh! how my heart sunk as the steamer swung round and dashed out into the great river; and, to scare me worse, a gun went off, bang! sending a stream of smoke behind us. I covered my face in my hands and cried—oh! how I did cry!

"When I looked up again, New York was a great way off; the ships looked like a forest of dead pine-trees, and everything else lay in a blue fog. I looked the other way, where the sun was going down in the deep, deep water. There everything was lonesome as the grave, and I almost wished that I was dead. But the steamer kept on prowling along the water, like a great wild beast, worrying us all into the next world. It seemed as if I was going off, far, far away from where my mistress had gone.

"I had been lonesome before in my life; but this was worse than that. I wanted to creep into some corner and die. Then I remembered that I had promised *her*, when she lay dead in the tower-chamber, to be a mother to you and Miss Jessie, and made a little prayer to God that He would help me in the thing that I was going about. It was all I could do.

"When the steamer was out in the deep waters, and the dark came on, a man stood by my trunk and asked why it was that I stayed out of my room. Then I told him my trunk was room enough for me just then; so he went away and brought another man, who asked if I had a state-room and a ticket.

"I told him the truth—that I didn't know what a state-room was; but that something I had eaten must have made me sick, and I wanted to lie down dreadfully.

"The man told me that a state-room would cost more than a hundred dollars; so I told him I'd rather stay on deck, for there was no certainty how much money I might want to spend before I got back.

"Then they began talking about second cabins, and asked how much money I could pay; but, somehow, I was too sick to care much, and let 'em pay themselves; so they took me down into a room with beds made like shelves along the sides, and I fell into one. Oh, mercy! I can't think of it now without being dizzy.

"Day and night—day and night—rock, rock—plunge, plunge—till at last there was an end of the eternal waters, and we landed at Havre,—an old fussy place that seemed as unsteady as the ship.

"Europe is a large place, Miss Hyde, and I didn't know whereabouts in it Mr. Lee or that woman was to be found; but I had money, and the mistress always taught me to trust in God when I couldn't do anything on my own hook. So I watched everything that went on among the passengers, and kept a prayer for help stirring in the bottom of my heart.

"At first I was about to ask some of the passengers which way I'd better turn, but concluded to wait. So I followed the crowd when it left the steamer, and it took me into a hotel as old as the hills, where women were running round in their nightcaps and chattering like tame crows.

"I went into a room with the rest, and sat down with my satchel on my lap, keeping a keen eye on everything. We had to wait a good while; for the men at the wharf wanted to see if everything was put up nicely in my trunk; but they promised to give it back, and a passenger said he would send it with his to the hotel, as I was alone. I had to wait.

"As I sat there watching, some gentlemen came in that seemed to know some of our passengers. They had just run down from Paris, I heard them say, to meet their friends on landing. They were nice, genteel men, and I listened to their talk, having nothing else to busy myself with. After a good deal of shaking hands and questioning about the voyage, they began to talk about Paris, especially about its hotels, and what Americans were at them.

"I held my breath and listened. The Hotel de Louvre, or Loofer, or something like that, they said, was the hotel where Americans went most. There was a great number of distinguished persons there now, and they went over a list of names. When they came to that of Mr. Lee, I caught my breath, and sprang up, dropping my satchel, with the gold in it, with a clank to the floor. No one minded me; so I sat down again, trembling all over, and listened. Then Mrs. Dennison's name was huddled in among the rest, and I knew that the persons I was in search of were in the same town together, and very near too; for the men who had run down from Paris didn't seem out of breath or the least tired. So I made up my mind to go there at once, and come back in an hour or two after my trunk.

"'Please, sir,' said I to one of the gentlemen, 'can you tell me just how far Paris is from this hotel, and which way I must turn?'

"He looked at me a minute, and smiled with his eyes.

"'It is about six hours, I think,' he answered; 'any coachman will take you to the depot.'

"I was rather discouraged. If it took him six hours to run the distance, I should find it a long walk. So I concluded to hire a carriage and take my trunk along.

"After awhile my trunk came up with a heap of other baggage, and, as everybody else was starting off in carriages, I hired one too; and when the man asked where I wanted to go, I told him to the Louvre Hotel in Paris. He drove away at once, and after a few minutes stopped at a railroad depot, and opened the door for me to get out.

"'This is the right train,' he said, in the queerest English I ever heard. 'I will get you a ticket.'

"I felt myself blushing, but said nothing. He didn't know that I had thought of walking. In less than ten minutes I was whizzing along like anything over the most beautiful country, and through the queerest old towns, and by the strangest houses with points and caps and corners like great table-casters cut in stone. Then the dark came on, and I fell sound asleep, till a great crash and jar awoke me in a depot right in the midst of a city larger than New York, all blazing with lights and crowded with folks.

"I had learned a thing or two by this time, and when a driver put himself in my way, told him that I wanted to go to Mr. Louvre's Hotel, and that he'd better get my trunk. He didn't seem to understand a word except the name of Mr. Louvre; but he caught that at once and nodded his head.

"'We, we!'

"'Yes,' I said, 'both of us. You couldn't very well drive me without going too, I should think.'

"So up he came with a little one-horse concern, and in I got. Oh! what streets, and lanes, and roads of lamps I went through! What crowds of people—what tall, tall houses! They made me more dizzy than I had been, and that was bad enough."

CHAPTER LXXV
LOTTIE IN PARIS

"At last we reached the hotel—a great, grand house, that frightens one by its size; it must cover acres and acres; you could not count the number of lights, and crowds of people going up and down the stairs.

"They took me into a room half-way up to the sky, and there I sat down with my head aching and clear tired out. You didn't know, I suppose, that I have learned a good many French words from the mistress: such as *du pain*, which means bread; and *le the*, for tea; and *sucre*, which a'n't much different from our sugar, only you mumble it up in your mouth before speaking, and let it all out at once.

"Well, I was dying with thirst, and my head throbbed terribly. The man called me *madmoiselle*, and looked polite and sorry; so I said:

"'*Donna moia* a cup of *the*, if you please, *mousheu.*'

"He looked bewildered a minute, and then brightened up so pleasant:

"'*Ah! le the! We, we!*'

"'No,' said I, thinking how improper it would be for that strange man to sit down to tea with a young girl in her room that time of night; 'only for myself; one cup will do. Excuse me.'

"He did not stop to hear, but went off and came back with a china cup and saucer on a little silver tray, as if I had been a born lady. I stirred up the tea and tasted it.

"'*Donna moia un petite* more *sucre*, if *vous* please,' said I.

"'*We, madmoiselle, toot sweet,*' says he.

"The fellow pronounced 'too' as if it had a *t* in it; but then, how could he understand good English?

"'No, no—not too sweet' said I; 'the contrary way. I want more *la sucre*, sugar, you know.'

"The fellow really did not understand his own language, but stood there looking wild as a fish-hawk. All at once he brightened up and ran out of the room. Directly he came back with another man. The moment I saw his face I jumped up, ready to scream with joy, and—and—yes, Miss Hyde, don't blush! but I sprang right into his arms and gave him a kiss.

"Who was it? Why, James, Mr. Lee's own man—a person—well, Miss Hyde, we all have secrets; but if ever a girl had a right to kiss a friend in a strange place, I had—that's all.

"'Oh! James, James Grant! It's Providence that sent you here!'

"'No,' he said, holding me tight and stopping my mouth while choke-full of words, 'I rather think it was your bad French, Lottie.'

"I would have struck him; only he held me so near and so tight it was impossible.

"The waiter went out softly. What sensible people these Frenchmen are! Then I forgot my headache and everything but the business in hand. James is a good scholar, you know, and understands French like a book. If ever Providence sent a friend at the right time, He did it that night. First I began asking questions.

"Mr. Lee had been away down East in Jerusalem, Palestine, across deserts, and over pyramids, for almost the whole time since he left home. Sorrowful as a man could be, but always going ahead, as if comfort lay in sharp work. Then he had come back into Italy, and so into France, which is Paris, you know.

"Mrs. Dennison was in the hotel when Mr. Lee got there; James thinks, unexpectedly to his master, but is not certain. He knows that she wrote letters to him, any way.

"'She is here, then—she has been setting her traps,' I said. 'Tell me everything, James, if you ever loved the sweet lady who is dead, or her child, who is pining herself to death at our own dear home. Tell me everything!'

"'Yes,' he said, 'it's no use going over the tracks; but she's got him, and to-morrow they will be married at the American Embassy.'

"'To-morrow! Married, to-morrow!' I almost screamed.

"'Yes,' he answered; 'nothing can stop it. I passed a woman who brought home the wedding-dress as I came up-stairs.'

"I caught hold of James and held his arms down tight.

"'Nothing can stop it, James? Yes, sir, you and I can stop it; you and I *will* stop it! I never promised right out before, James; but if you'll help me to expose this woman, I'll—I'll—yes, you and I'll take their place, and be married at the American Embassy right off ourselves.'

"He—well, Miss Hyde, I won't worry you by telling what he said or did just then; but my face burned like fire half an hour after.

"Now comes the hardest part of my story. Don't clasp your hands and pray for me, as the worst sinner that ever was; for I a'n't quite that! Still, you think so much of a little fib, and listening, and breaking open seals, that I'd rather not write it if a great deep ocean of water wasn't rolling between you and me. Miss Hyde, I own it, lies a'n't my delight; but I can tell 'em. Peeping through keyholes and windows isn't my nature; but, anyhow, I did it. More than that: I never let one of Mrs. Dennison's letters leave our house without reading it. One or two letters I kept back altogether, because they were written in French, and I couldn't read that. They are with me here. It was to give them into Mr. Lee's hand that I came across the wide ocean. She suspected me—or her girl Cora did—and hired one of the men to mail them safely; but I knew a better way of bribing him to give them up. True, it made James jealous to see how thick I was with the man; but I couldn't help that.

"Babylon was cute, though; she wrote carefully. It was to some old friend—who was as bad as herself—to whom the letters were sent. I have some of her answers, too, as well as the journal; these were the papers that I laid before James Grant that night.

"I could only make out a word here and there in the French letters. If you hadn't been so crank about honor and all that, I would have brought them to you; I couldn't make up my mind to take the preaching. But I watched. You know, Miss Hyde, no dog ever kept watch as I did over that angel!

"She died. The worst came while I was wondering what to do. There was no use in telling what I had done. She was dead; and I thought then that the woman would go away and leave us to our mourning. If she came back again, I meant to give the journal up and have you read the French letters. You know how she left, and why it was Mr. Lee went off in that strange way; I could only guess. You wouldn't trust me; so I wouldn't trust you. But when I found that Babylon had gone chasing after Mr. Lee, just as his year of mourning was over, I followed her.

"I gave the journal and letters to James, and we read them over together. James reads French, and can turn it into English as easy as talking. So he gave me the English, which was a good deal like her journal, full of sin and iniquity."

CHAPTER LXXVI
THE CASKET OF DIAMONDS

"When we had read the letters and the journal, I tied them together, and sat down to talk the matter over with James, who is as good as a lawyer any day.

"'Where is our master now?' I said. 'What time is it?'

"'It is nine. I think he may soon be in Mrs. Dennison's parlor; for Cora told me that her lady wished to try on the wedding-dress, and hoped Mr. Lee would come in when it was complete. I took the message, and he answered, 'Very well.'

"'James,' I said, 'we have no time to lose. Is there no way by which I can get into Mrs. Dennison's rooms before the master comes in?'

"James thought a little, and said, 'Yes, it will be easy. When Mrs. Dennison is dressed they will go into her parlor. It opens from her bedroom by an arched doorway hung with silk curtains. When they leave the bedroom, I will let you in.'

"He went out to see what was going on, and came back all in a hurry, opened the door, and whispered, 'Come, quick!'

"I went, and in two minutes was in a large bedroom, warmed up like sunset with the light that came pouring through the broad red curtains which hung between it and the next room.

"'Step softly, and hide somewhere if they come in,' whispered James.

"'I will,' says I.

"Then I crept up to the curtain, pushed the red folds back a trifle, and looked in.

"It was a large room, lighted, like our drawing-room, with a great chandelier, and furnished beautifully. *She* and Cora were standing under the blaze of lights, all in a flutter of pride. It's no use, Miss Hyde: I've wanted to think that woman wasn't good-looking, but it's fighting against one's own eyes. There she stood, with that wedding-dress of white moire antique a-sweeping down her tall figure, and lying behind her like ridges of snow on the carpet. All down the front and around the neck, which was smooth as a japonica leaf, lace was fluttering, till the whole dress looked soft as snow. On her head she wore a sort of crown made of pearls like the mistress's necklace that she thought so much of, and from under that fell a lace veil that looked like frostwork on a window, and covered her from head to foot.

"Cora was spreading down the veil as I looked in. Then she stepped back and had a good survey.

"'Will it do?' said Mrs. Dennison, drawing herself up proud as a peacock.

"'It's superb!' answered Cora.

"'We will make it a little more perfect before he comes in,' says Babylon; and, going to a desk, she took out a long morocco case, and opened it under the light, when a flame of fire flashed out of it.

"Cora took the box out of Babylon's hand.

"'From him?' says she.

"'Yes,' answers Babylon, curving her neck.

"'How much did they cost?'

"'Of course he did not tell me that, Cora. Ten or fifteen thousand dollars, I suppose; but they are nothing to what I'll yet have.'

"'You will not wear them to-morrow?'

"'Well, no. It would be a little too much, I fear; but we will put them on now, just to try the effect.'

"'No,' says Cora, looking very stubborn; 'I want these. It's no more than fair.'

"'Cora!' cried Babylon, with fire in her eyes.

"'Why not?' says Cora. 'You have promised over and over again to provide for me when you had the means. Here is something sure.'

"'Cora, this is too impudent!'

"'Why? Is it wrong for sisters to share each other's good fortune, especially when one has done as much to earn it as the other?'

"Babylon doubled up her white fist, and looked a whole thunder-gust from under her bent eyebrows.

"'Sisters! How dare you?'

"'Because I am your sister.'

"'You! whose mother was a black slave!'

"'And my father your father! What can you say against him?'

"Babylon seemed to struggle against her temper, and got the better of it.

"'Give me those diamonds, Cora. Of course I do not dispute what you say, and always meant to make you independent; but not after this fashion. Wait till this ceremony is over and I have control of sufficient means. You must see that it would be ruin to part with these.'

"'I cannot help that. What security have I that you will keep your word when you are married? It never has been kept. The truth is, I mean to stay in this country, where my color is not sneered at, and I must have the means.'

"'But have I not promised?'

"'Yes, a good many times; and I mean that you shall perform too! This ceremony shall never take place till I am sure of that!'

"Babylon grew pale as a ghost; something seemed to swell in her throat.

"'Give back the diamonds,' she said, speaking as if she had a cold; and you shall have a written promise for twice their amount three months after I am married.'

"'When?'

"'Now. I will write out the paper at once.'

"'Well, but remember it is made out to Cora, *your half-sister*, or I will not take it.'

"Mrs. Dennison came to a little table that stood close by the arch, and, kneeling down on one knee, began to write. She seemed to hold her breath, and was pale as the pearls on her head. I could have touched her with my hand, but I stood still as a mouse until the paper was written. Cora came and looked over her shoulders as she signed her name. Just as it was done, there came a knock at the door, and both the women started away from the table, leaving the paper on it. I reached my hand softly through the curtain, and got it safe just as Mr. Lee came in.

"Babylon was white as a sheet, and shook so that the dress rustled around her.

"'Is she not beautiful, sir?' says Cora, looking as innocent as a lamb.

"Mr. Lee smiled. Oh! Miss Hyde, isn't he grand? But in a minute his face changed, and, coming up to Mrs. Dennison, he took her hand and kissed it.

"'How pale you are! Does the thought of to-morrow terrify you so much?'

"She gave him one of her looks, and drew closer to him, like a lamb wanting shelter. He bent toward her, and, as Cora slid out of the room, put his arm around her waist, whispering something that I was too mad to hear.

"I couldn't stand it. My poor mistress seemed to whisper, 'Now, Lottie, I trust to you!' I pushed the curtains aside, and, walking right straight in, stood before them.

"'Mrs. Dennison,' says I, 'let go of my dead lady's husband. Mr. Lee, an angel has just come down from heaven to save you from a wicked, wicked fiend. I, a poor girl, am doing her work. Step back, Mrs. Dennison, till my master reads these letters, and this journal, with its purple cover and heaps of sin inside. If you want to know all about the bad heart of this woman, read it,' says I to Mr. Lee again; 'then ask her to look into your eyes if she dares.'

"The woman turned on me with her great scared eyes—saw the journal in my hand—gave a wild look at the table—staggered toward the curtains—flung them back with an outward dash of her arms, and fell upon the floor of the other room. As the red curtains closed over her, I reached out the papers to Mr. Lee, and whispered, with tears in my eyes:

"'Oh, master! read them for her sake, who loved you so dearly.'

"Mr. Lee put me back so fiercely that I almost fell. He went right up to the woman where she lay shivering and shaking till her white dress heaved and fluttered like a snow-heap in the wind. He was pale as a sheet, and his eyes looked mad as fire when he turned them toward me; but I stood my ground like a marble image planted on a rock. I hadn't come sailing over the raging ocean, like a pelican in the wilderness, to be looked down by him or fainted down by her—not I, if I know myself, which I think I do.

"'My darling,' says he, bending over her, 'why should the sight of this wild girl agitate you so? She can have no influence on me.'

"Babylon seemed to get strength from this. She lifted up her head, flung the veil back from her face, and looked me through and through with her wild eyes.

"'She is put up to this. They hate me. It is another effort to prejudice you against me. You remember the last. Now they will no doubt resort to forgery. People who write anonymous letters will not hesitate to go further. Oh! they will separate us—they will separate us!'

"'Is this book a forgery?' says I, holding up the purple journal. 'Is this writing yours?'

"Her face seemed to cramp up; her lips turned blue-white.

"That moment Cora made a leap upon me, and snatched at the book like a hungry wolf; but I wrenched it away from her, and pressed myself back against the wall, holding it behind me.

"That moment James came in and stood by me like a hero, as he is.

"'No you don't,' said I; 'no person touches this book till Mr. Lee has read it.'

"Mrs. Dennison turned her eyes upon me—such beautiful begging eyes—that, if it hadn't been for my dead lady, I might have given up the book; but I thought of her, and was firm as a rock. 'Leave this room,' said Mr. Lee, turning upon me like a lion. 'How dare you come here!'

"'My dead lady, your wife, commanded me to come,' I answered, feeling myself grow tall and strong. 'She was murdered by that woman, and you are bound to know it. Read this—it is in her own handwriting.'

"'It belongs to my lady. The imp of Satan stole it!' cried Cora, fierce as a wild-cat. 'No one has a right to read it.'

"Mr. Lee had helped Babylon to her feet, and stood, with one arm around her waist, looking from her to me.

"'It is mine,' she whispered; 'make her give it up.'

"'But I have read every word of it. I have left a copy at home, which Miss Hyde has now. A minute ago you said it was a forgery; now, you both own up—you and your yellow sister there.'

"At this, Mr. Lee seemed to be turning into stone, all but his eyes, that shot fire at me.

"'What does she mean?' asked Babylon. The words dropped from her like lead. It seemed as if she hadn't the strength to speak.

"'She's crazy!' says Cora. 'My mistress never had either brother or sister.'

"'Hadn't she?' says I. 'Just look at this paper, Mr. Lee, and then ask her how she came to write there that this yellow girl is her father's child. I heard the impudent creature threaten her, if she didn't give up the diamonds you sent here this morning, or write this promise just so.'

"'The diamonds!' said Mr. Lee, loosening his arm from Babylon's waist and looking in her face. 'How could this girl know about them?'

"Babylon shivered, and her eyes seemed to shrink back under her eyelids when she looked at the table and saw that the paper was gone. Cora crept softly up to where I was standing, and whispered: 'Half the money if you hold your tongue. If you don't, I'll kill you!'

"I gave the creature one of my looks, handed the journal over to James, and held the paper open between my two hands, before Mr. Lee's eyes. He could not help but read it. Babylon lifted her hand as if to strike it down, but it dropped by her side when she saw that he was reading, and she leaned against the door-frame, clenching at the red curtains in a spasm. Oh! she looked awful splendid with her white dress pressed against the red curtains, that shook around her like flaming fire. The diamonds on her head seemed to burn through and through her veil, but her white face was cramped worse than ever, and I almost thought she would drop down dead at Mr. Lee's feet.

"He took the paper from my hands and read it through. Then he looked once or twice from Mrs. Dennison to Cora, who was turning whitish-gray, and looked awfully.

"'Is there any explanation of this strange paper?' he said; and his voice seemed to come out of a heap of ice, it had changed so.

"Babylon opened her lips, but they would not give out the lie that was ready, I haven't the least doubt. But Cora came forward bold as brass.

"'It is a forgery!' she said; 'the lady never promised me anything after she was married. I am no more her sister than that imp of Satan is.

"'But if this paper was a forgery, how did you know what it contained?' said Mr. Lee, in the same cold way. And, with this, he walked out of the room without saying another word.

"Babylon made a spring toward the door when he went out of it, with her hands clenched together, and her veil streaming out behind; but when she saw that he never turned or looked back, her knees gave way, and she fell in a white heap on the carpet.

"I began to feel sorry for the poor creature then, and tried to help her up, but Cora pushed me away; and would have sent me whirling through the door, but James caught me in his arms, and so seemed to lead me out. When we were safe in the passage, I told James to take the journal right to his master's room and strike while the iron was hot, or those two sea-serpents would get around him again.

"He went—like a good fellow as he is—and I shut myself up in my room, knowing well enough that I had done right, but feeling sorry in my heart for poor Babylon all the same. So I sat down by the window and had a good cry all to myself.

"In half an hour James called me to his master's room. He was white as marble, and tears stood in his eyes. He took my two hands in his, pressed them hard, then, leaning one elbow on the table, covered his face with his hand. I saw great tears drop through his fingers; they broke my heart. The first thing I knew, down I had fallen on my two knees, and was kissing his other hand as if he had been my dear mistress who is dead and gone. That night I told him everything about Miss Jessie, and all your goodness. Oh! how he thanked me! Miss Hyde, don't ever want to see a man cry; it's enough to break one's heart!

"The next morning Mrs. Dennison and her servant had left the hotel. In three days I shall be on my way home. Do be glad to see Lottie; for she feels like a bird far away from its nest, and has been, ever since she left the Ridge.

"Your old friend till death, Lottie."

CHAPTER LXXVII
ALL TOGETHER AGAIN

After reading this letter, I told Jessie everything. She had no heart to read the journal in my possession, and its worst points—those which related to her mother's death—I kept from her in common mercy. Of course, all that she did learn was a relief to her. She knew that her father would soon be at home again, and that no cause of estrangement now existed between them. This removed the only shadow now falling upon her young life. That very day she began preparations for her father's return; and when young Bosworth came, there was a joyous consultation between them about the best way of receiving him. I saw them looking toward me and whispering mysteriously. Were they consulting about the propriety of my residence in the house after they left it? The thought fell upon me with a shock of such pain as I pray God may never be repeated. Let what will come, my fate seems to be one of utter loneliness. But I am glad to see these young people so happy: never, I do think, was love more complete than that which exists between them now.

It scarcely seemed possible for a letter to reach us from Europe, when Lottie herself rushed in upon us with an exquisite French bonnet on her head, and a dress that trailed sumptuously behind her little figure. In she came, darting through the room like an arrow, and was in my arms, bathing my face with tears and smothering me with kisses, before I was quite aware of her presence. When Jessie came in with Mr. Bosworth, who had been walking with her in the garden, Lottie sprang upon her like a pet spaniel, clung to her neck, her waist, and at last fell to the floor in an outburst of gladness, and embraced her knees, crying, laughing, and murmuring words of tender endearment, in which some rather curious French was mingled.

After this Lottie resumed her self-poise. She shook hands with young Bosworth in a patronizing way, and gave the servants an audience in the basement sitting-room, informing them all that she had just returned from a pleasure-trip to Europe, where she had seen the Emperor, and should, doubtless, have been invited to court, only the Empress did not happen to be very well while she was in Paris.

In this way that strange, heroic girl came back to her old home, which was brighter and more cheerful after she resumed her place, not as a servant, but as a tried friend of the family, which she retained till her marriage with James.

A fortnight after Lottie's return, Mr. Lee came home. He sent us a letter from New York, saying that he had landed there, and desiring that the cause and events connected with his absence might never be mentioned among us after his return. Everything was understood and explained; all that he asked now was a perfect reunion.

One night about dusk, Mr. Lee came home very quietly and quite unannounced. He was calm, cheerful, and his own noble self again, and his absence seemed almost like a dream to us.

That night, before he retired, I saw him going toward the library with his arm around Jessie's waist. When they came out again, I could see that Jessie had been crying; but she looked happy notwithstanding these traces of tears, and when she bade her father good-night, he left a blessing upon her forehead.

In the solitude of that half-hour, the proud man had asked forgiveness of his own child, and she came forth with a heart almost broken with tenderness for him.

After this his love for Jessie became a part of his life; he fairly worshipped her. But his manner to me changed. He was kind, gentle, generous; but all this was accompanied with a sort of reserve almost amounting to shyness. Had I indeed offended him beyond forgiveness? How often I asked myself this question, and each time my heart sunk into deeper depression; for who could answer it? Let who would be happy, it seemed that I was always to suffer. Indeed, it required some little magnanimity not to feel the difference between the lonely, unloved existence reserved for me, and Jessie's brilliant lot.

A few months after Mr. Lee's return, wedding preparations were making cheerful progress in our house. Jessie would leave us on a bridal tour, and then come back to the old mansion behind the hill, which the two Mrs. Bosworths had vacated for a pretty cottage on the grounds, and refurnished sumptuously for the young people. Everybody was pleased — everybody was happy, except myself. What could become of me? When Jessie was gone, my home would be broken up again. I must be cast forth a waif upon the world. How could I help being sad?

Just a week before Jessie's wedding, I sat alone in the deep window of the drawing-room, thinking of my desolated future, and weeping those still tears that one learns to shed after much sorrow. It was sunset. Young Bosworth and Jessie were in the garden, and I could hear their happy voices coming up from among the flowers.

As I sat there, so dreary and loveless, some person entered the room. I knew by the tread that it was Mr. Lee, and tried to conceal myself; but he came directly to the window and stood at my side, looking out upon the glorious view. In those times I was timid, and almost afraid of his presence; so, rising quietly, I attempted to leave the window. But he begged me to remain. There was something that he wished to say.

I sat down, trembling with dread. Was he about to tell me, what I knew already, that Jessie's marriage would render my stay at the Ridge impossible? I would not wait for that, but said at once,—

"Oh, Mr. Lee, it is quite unnecessary. I know what propriety demands. The very day she leaves home, I shall go back to the old farm-house. It will not be an unhappy life."

"But I have come to prevent this," he said, in a low, strange voice. I looked up in sudden surprise, a smile was trembling on his lips. "Never, if I can help it, shall you leave a home which owes half its sunshine to your presence. Without you, the old place would be lonely indeed. You must not all forsake me at once."

"But it is impossible!" I faltered. "Even kind old Mrs. Bosworth would set her face against it. I might, perhaps, stay with Jessie," I added, with a piteous attempt to smile; "but she has not invited me."

"Because she knew from the first that I could not give you up. She guessed how dearly I loved you, almost before I was sure of it myself."

I felt myself turning white. This great happiness was beyond all realization. I looked timidly in his face, and read in his eyes what I had never dreamed of before. He sat down by me very quietly, and, with a little gentle violence, drew my head upon his bosom. I could hear the strong, irregular beating of his heart, and his words, so persuasive, so manly, charmed away the shock and tremor of his first sudden avowal.

"I have not spoken till now," he said, "because circumstances, that we will never speak of, have made me for a time doubtful if they ever would be forgiven by a proud, good woman like yourself. But I love you, dear girl, with my whole heart and soul; first for your own sake, and next because the angel who blessed our home so long, owed everything to your care. She loved you dearly, and said it with her last breath."

I was sobbing upon his bosom. The memories so sad and touching which sprung out of his words flooded my heart with tender grief. Yes, she loved me; and that, perhaps, was the golden link which had drawn his soul to mine.

"Do not weep," he pleaded; "but look up and bless me with one smile, one word. Do you love me a little in return for all I feel? Can you love me entirely some day?"

I looked up and my eyes met his. "You know; you are sure. Why ask that?" I whispered. "There has never been a time since I was a little girl that I have not loved you; first as my kind, kind guardian, then as the being *she* loved better than anything on earth, and now—"

"Now as your own husband!" he exclaimed, folding me close to his bosom, and pressing kisses upon my lips. "Oh, my darling, you have made me completely happy."

In twenty different ways he told me of his happiness, his love, and the sweet necessity there was for my presence in his life. At first it seemed impossible for me to believe him; but after a while my heart received the full conviction of his love, and settled down into that fulness of content which makes some one hour of every human life a heaven.

As we sat together, with the twilight gathering around us, the curtains falling over the recess of the window rustled apart, and Jessie came through them. Her father did not move, but looked up smiling. I felt a flood of crimson burn across my face. She looked at him a moment, then at me, but obtained only a timid glance in return: it was enough. She bent down and kissed me with affectionate warmth; then disappeared quietly as she had come, leaving me the happiest mortal that God ever blessed.

One week from that day two weddings were solemnized in that house; but only one couple went away. That home was too dear for any thoughts of fashionable travel with us.

The last year of the war we took a trip to the White Mountains, and made some stay at New York on our return home. Having nothing special to occupy us, one evening we joined a party from the hotel, and went to hear a reading from the poets, to be given at a public hall in Broadway. It so happened that no one mentioned the name of the reader, and we had not thought enough about the matter to inquire.

The hall was full of what seemed to be persons from the upper classes, and some little excitement prevailed, as if there was a peculiar interest taken either in the subject or reader. This aroused our curiosity a little, and we waited with more than usual impatience for the lady to appear.

She came at last from the side platform, a radiantly beautiful woman, with the air of an empress. Her black lace dress, richly flounced, swept the floor; her white neck was exposed, and her superb arms uncovered to the shoulder. A cluster of scarlet flowers glowed in her hair and on her bosom. My heart gave one bound, and settled back with a sickening recoil.

It was Mrs. Dennison.

She approached the reading-desk, rested her hand upon the volume that lay upon it, and looked around upon the audience. Her eyes fell upon us. She recoiled a step; a flash of red shot across her face. But instantly she resumed her former position, looked steadily in our faces, and then quietly allowed her eyes to pass over the crowd.

While her hand rested on the book, a cry broke over us from the street. Some newsboy, shouting as he sped along, sent his voice ringing through the open doors:

"Further particulars of the battle of the Wilderness! Death of Colonel Lawrence!"

The woman heard this cry. Her hand fell heavily away from the book—her face grew livid under the gas-lights—she staggered, and fell to the floor.